"SIR, PLEASE RELINQUISH MY PARROT TO ME," THEODOSIA ASKED.

"Lady, I've got a good mind to put this damned bird to rest for all of eternity!"

Theodosia peered up into eyes so blue, they defied description. One moment they appeared turquoise; in the next they rivaled the clear true blue of cornflowers

The intensity of his gaze caused a fluttering sensation inside her. It warmed her, tickled a bit, and quickened her breath and heartbeat. Disturbed by the unfamiliar feelings, she bowed her head for a moment to seek composure and found herself staring at the lower part of his anatomy.

"What are you gawking at?" he demanded.

She continued to stare, completely unable to stop herself. "I am astonished by the size of your vastus lateralis, vastus intermedius, and vastus medialis. Why, even your sartorius is clearly defined and equally amazing."

He had no idea what she was talking about, but he saw that she'd directed her total attention to the area below his belt.

HEARTSTRINGS

REBECCA PAISLEY

A DELL BOOK

Published by
Dell Publishing
a division of
Bantam Doubleday Dell Publishing Group, Inc.
1540 Broadway
New York, New York 10036

ISBN: 0-440-21650-8

Printed in the United States of America

Published simultaneously in Canada

September 1994

10 9 8 7 6 5 4 3 2 1

OPM

Prologue

Lillian's baby died.

The terrible words echoed endlessly through Theodosia's mind as she stared from the threshold of her sister's room toward the canopied bed where Lillian lay sleeping.

Another cross will be planted in the family cemetery alongside the three others. No grave; only a tiny cross commemorating the passing of a tiny life.

Theodosia's fingers curled around the envelope in her hand; the paper crackled, and the sound grated. She'd arrived home only moments ago with such happy news to share—news for which they'd all been waiting for weeks.

News that suddenly didn't seem important at all.

"Come in, my dear," Upton called softly.

Theodosia stepped into the room and caught the scent of lemon verbena, Lillian's favorite perfume. She stopped before nearing the bed. "Lillian. The baby." Her own words sounded ragged to her, as if someone had ripped them out of her.

Her brother-in-law rose from his chair beside the bed and joined Theodosia in the middle of the large elegant room. Embracing her tenderly, he smoothed her bright gold hair, then drew away and gazed into her huge brown eyes. "She lost the baby soon after you left this morning, Theodosia. It happened very quickly this time. There was little discomfort, and the doctor said she would be up and about in a week. I would have sent for you, but I didn't know where you were."

Slowly, Theodosia looked up at him, her eyes caressing every line of the face of the man she'd loved like a father for as long as she could remember. "I —I was walking. In the Common. Reading. The letter. I was reading the letter, and . . ."

She couldn't finish; too many thoughts crowded her mind. Lifting her hand to her temple, she glanced back at Lillian and felt guilt stab through her sorrow. Her sister should have begun her family long ago. Lillian and Upton had waited too long, and now, not only did Lillian experience great difficulties conceiving, but she'd lost four babies, each in her second month of pregnancy. The physicians had made it clear that the only chance Lillian had to deliver a full-term baby now was to carry it into the third month. But so far she hadn't succeeded.

Everyone, including Upton, had suggested adopting an infant, but Lillian wouldn't hear of it. She desperately wanted a son or daughter of her own flesh and blood, a child who would resemble her and Upton, and her desire was planted so deeply within her heart that there was no uprooting it.

It's all my fault they have no children, Theodosia thought miserably. She closed her eyes; memories whisked her back to the day when she'd come from New York to Boston.

She'd been a frightened, lonely, and devastated child of five whose parents were killed when lightning struck a tree beneath which they'd been picnicking. She'd watched them die, and the unmitigated horror of it had nearly destroyed her.

Lillian and Upton's unwavering love had saved her. They'd been newlyweds at the time, ready to start the Peabody family. But because they believed Theodosia needed their undivided attention, they'd chosen to postpone having children. And no doubt, it had taken most of their savings to provide for her.

Lillian, guided by maternal instincts, had taught Theodosia the feminine arts that a mother shares with her daughter. And Upton, a distinguished Harvard professor, had seen to her academic education. The man was a true genius, and thanks to him, she was every bit as brilliant as he. Indeed, her intelligence surpassed that of many of his Harvard colleagues and had gained her much recognition throughout the academic world.

Patiently, willingly, Upton and Lillian provided her with their love, knowledge, home—everything they had to give, sharing nothing at all with the children they'd yet to have.

And now those children would never be born.

"Theodosia?" Upton took her chin in his hand. "What letter are you talking about?"

She blinked, then looked up at him. "Letter?"

"You said you'd been reading a letter while strolling in the Common."

"Oh." She showed him the envelope. "Dr. Wallaby's letter."

Upton brightened visibly. "Finally. I knew Eugene would answer you. He wants to interview you, of course."

His heartfelt confidence in her future intensified

her guilt. "It's the very best of news, Upton," she murmured.

"Theodosia?" Lillian rubbed sleep from her eyes and lifted her head from the mound of pillows. "Come here, darling."

Upton whispered a few words of caution into Theodosia's ear. "You know full well how she will endeavor to conceal her grief from you. Spare her from having to discuss her loss right now. Instead, share your glad tidings with her. I've no doubt she will be overjoyed to hear them."

Theodosia crossed the room to the bed and smiled into her sister's big brown eyes. Like a shimmering fan of gold, Lillian's hair lay spread over the mound of white satin pillows; Theodosia fingered one bright curl, feeling as though she were peering at her own reflection in a mirror. But for their sixteen-year age difference, she and Lillian might have been twins.

She leaned down, and while she pressed a tender kiss to her sister's smooth forehead, the fragrance of lemon verbena floated around her. "I've something wonderful to tell you, Lillian," she said, struggling to maintain a calm demeanor. "Dr. Wallaby has agreed to interview me for the position as his research assistant in Brazil."

True happiness lifted the sorrow from Lillian's eyes. "South America," she murmured through her smile. "Your dreams are all coming true for you now. You must write to me every day. Upton, my love, how long will it take for our Theodosia's letters to arrive from Brazil?"

"I'll be writing from Texas first, Lillian," Theodosia clarified. "That is where Dr. Wallaby will conduct the interview. He has exhausted his research funds, has left Brazil, and is in Templeton, Texas, waiting for further financial backing. Once he receives the grant, he will return to Brazil. And if he accepts me as his assistant, I will go with him."

Upton put his arm around Theodosia's shoulder. "You've worked very hard for the opportunity. I have no doubt that once Eugene interviews you, he will hire you on the spot. Why, I'd venture to hypothesize that the interview is a mere formality, Theodosia! After all, the two of you have been corresponding for almost two years, and he most certainly understands the extent of your interest and intelligence."

"That he does," Lillian agreed, reaching for the envelope in Theodosia's hand. "May I, darling?" When her sister relinquished it, Lillian opened the envelope. As she unfolded the letter, a stiff oval-shaped paper fell to the bed. "Why, he included a miniature painting of himself," Lillian exclaimed. "Probably so you will know what to expect when you first see him. How thoughtful."

"A miniature?" Theodosia asked. "I must have overlooked it." She glanced at the small painting, then leaned forward for a better view. "My goodness, he looks like you, Upton! Same thin angular face, long straight nose, bright blue eyes, and gray hair. He's obviously older than you, but the resemblance is nothing short of amazing."

"He's nine years my senior, which would make him fifty-three," Upton said. "He'd already graduated when I entered Harvard, but he continued to avail himself of the library, and that is where I met him. The two of us soon became a familiar sight on campus, and many people believed he was my older brother. He was a fine friend, Theodosia. A

pity he never married and raised children, for I am
sure his offspring would have inherited his passion
for scientific research. The world might have bene-
fited from their studies. For personal reasons, however, he chose to remain unwed. But he is a good
man. Of course, I haven't seen him in many years,
but his reputation remains untarnished. You will be
in excellent hands, my dear."

Nodding her agreement, Lillian scanned the letter. "Upton, Dr. Wallaby writes that Theodosia is to
travel to Oates' Junction, Texas. From there, she
will ride to Templeton, in the company of an escort
he will send to meet her."

"You must leave at the first opportunity, Theodosia," Upton declared.

"Don't be silly, Upton," Lillian admonished him.
"Our Theodosia will need no less than a month and
a half to prepare for her trip. She might need as
much as two. One cannot pack a simple overnight
bag for such a journey, and there are many things
we must purchase for her."

"Very well," Upton conceded, smiling indulgently. "You will leave when Lillian deems you are
ready, and you will take John the Baptist with you.
The parrot will keep you company during your
travels."

"You will also take the gold that Father left to
us," Lillian added. "I've kept it for you all these
years. You know very well that Dr. Wallaby will be
unable to pay you a salary in Brazil. He will need
every cent he has to continue with his research. The
gold will see to your needs for a long while, and
when it is gone, we will sell Father's business. It
continues to thrive, and I am sure we can sell it for
a substantial amount of—"

"We will not sell Father's business, Lillian," Theodosia argued. "It means as much to you and me as it did to Father, and you know it. And as for the gold, I will take my share of it. You must save your half for—"

"For what? I've no one else to spend it on. I— what I mean to say, is that I—"

It took only a moment for Theodosia to understand what Lillian was thinking. There were no Peabody children to spend the gold on, so she wanted Theodosia to have it. "Lillian—"

"You will take the gold. I have no need of it." Lillian glanced around the opulent bedroom. "I have everything a woman could want. A beautiful home. A loving sister. A wonderful husband. Everything . . ."

Her voice trailed away as she lost the battle with her sorrow. Tears blinded her to everything except her all-consuming grief. "I have everything except what no one can give me."

Quickly, Theodosia stepped aside as Upton moved to take Lillian into his arms. Watching the couple cling to each other, she felt a wave of helplessness course through her.

If only there were something she could do to repay them for saving her very life. Something that would make them as happy as they had made her. If only . . .

Her desperate thoughts ebbed away when the miniature of Dr. Wallaby fluttered to the floor and landed by her foot. For one fleeting moment, she thought it was Upton, not Dr. Wallaby, looking up at her from the dark green carpet.

Same thin angular face, long straight nose, bright blue eyes, and gray hair.

Same brilliant minds.

An idea struck so suddenly that she staggered backward, forced to grab the bedpost for support. Her distress vanished as swiftly as a shadow confronted by light.

She would give her sister what no one else on earth could give her.

A child of Lillian's own bloodline, one who would inherit many of Lillian and Upton's personal traits.

And the man who could assist in the creation of that very special child was in Templeton, Texas.

Chapter 1

"Dr. Wallaby, would you be willing to impregnate me?" Oblivious to the appalled stares of the nearby passengers aboard the train, Theodosia hugged her parrot's cage to her breasts, settled back into her seat, and contemplated the sound of her query. Ever since leaving Boston five days ago, she'd been pondering the all-important question. Now she felt the need to hear it with her own ears.

Nibbling at her bottom lip, she glanced out the window and saw a mass of huge pecan trees. Primrose and thistle painted the edge of the grove with bright hues of pink and purple, and yellow butterflies floated above the flowers like bubbles turned gold by the kiss of the sun.

But the beauty of the landscape began to fade, finally escaping her altogether. She could not concentrate on anything but the estimable Dr. Wallaby. Indeed, she imagined she could see the renowned scientist's face within the sun-filled windowpane.

"Dr. Wallaby," she began rehearsing again, "it is imperative that I conceive a child. You meet all the qualifications regarding the paternity of the child, and it would please me enormously if you

would consent to be his or her sire. The act
required for the conception is, of course, a mere
scientific procedure, and I don't believe I am mistaken in believing that it can be accomplished in a
totally objective manner and, no doubt, in a relatively short amount of time."

Gasps and loud whispering filled the compart-
ment. Theodosia focused her attention on her fellow passengers, noting their mouths were agape. "I
apologize for disturbing you. I was conversing with
myself."

"I was conversing with myself," John the Baptist
echoed. "Awk!" he screamed, then splashed a
beakful of water onto Theodosia's dark blue skirt.

Cooing to her bird, Theodosia met each person's
stare directly. "Allow me to elaborate. I'm of the
inclination that the ear must hear thoughts before
the mind is able to grasp their full significance and
keep them in separate and precise order. And if
one's thought pertains to a specific conundrum,
said problem is quite likely to be solved if one simply voices it rather than merely contemplates it.
That is the reason why I converse with myself."

John the Baptist stuck his beak through his cage
bars. "That is the reason why I converse with myself," he mimicked.

Theodosia sprinkled a few sunflower seeds into
her parrot's cage, then turned back to the window.
Fondling her small heart-shaped ruby brooch and
the delicate gold chains that hung down from it,
she realized the train was slowing in preparation
for the arrival at Oates' Junction. She dug into her
reticule and withdrew the slip of paper upon which
was written the name of the man Dr. Wallaby had
arranged to escort her to Templeton. "Roman Mon-

tana," she read quietly. "Tall. Long black hair. Blue eyes."

She wanted to believe Mr. Montana would be at the station waiting for her, but she prepared herself for the possibility that he was not. Upton had explained that in the South people were slower, their way of life unhurried. She wasn't certain of the reasons behind such leisure but decided that in all likelihood Roman Montana would be late.

The tinge of irritation she felt impelled her to take a moment to analyze her mood. The train hadn't even come to a complete stop yet, and here she was already impatient with Roman Montana.

"Theodosia," she scolded herself out loud, "impatience is an emotion that is rarely advantageous and often leads to true anger. If indeed Roman Montana is unpunctual, you will accept the situation in a self-possessed fashion and keep in mind the fact that not everyone enjoys being as prompt as you do."

As the declaration left her lips, the train came to a hissing halt. Theodosia pulled her gloves onto her hands and her escort out of her mind.

After all, she reminded herself, she had not journeyed all the way from Boston for the company of some long-haired, lackadaisical Texan named Roman Montana.

Theodosia gave a great huff, choking as the blistering heat filled her chest. "One would think there was invisible fire in Texas air," she mumbled. One at a time, she lifted her overly warm feet off the sunbaked platform at the depot, hard pressed to keep from being knocked to the ground by the other passengers hurrying toward the shelter of the train station.

Where was Roman Montana?

"There now, Theodosia dear," John the Baptist squawked from within his cage. "Here's a nice cup of hot tea."

At her parrot's words, Theodosia felt another heat wave shimmer through her. John the Baptist had repeated what he heard Lillian say every afternoon at precisely three o'clock. While Theodosia realized her bird didn't understand what he was saying, his suggestion was unbearable at this moment.

"One sugar today, Theodosia, or two?" the parrot continued with his tea talk.

Theodosia frowned. "That's quite enough out of you, John the Bap—"

"Impatience is an emotion that is rarely advantageous," the bird stated. "Would you like cream in your tea as well, Theodosia, dear?"

Ignoring the loquacious parrot as best she could, Theodosia patted her moist brow with her lacy handkerchief and studied her surroundings.

Wagons crowded the dusty street that separated the depot platform and the train station. A drunken man wove among the vehicles. With each faulty step, he spilled whiskey from the bottle he clutched in his hand. As he neared Theodosia, he stopped and scratched his crotch.

"Sir," she said, pinning him with a sharp look, "it must be close to one hundred degrees out here. Did you know that drinking alcohol raises the body temperature? You are out in this hot sun and drinking whiskey as well. Is it your intention to kill yourself?"

The man blinked several times, then raised his bottle. "Y'on't some?"

She drew away. "No."

Shrugging, he staggered back through the wagons, still digging at his crotch.

Dismissing the vulgar man from her mind, Theodosia scanned the area once more. A dog with a scarred ear barked at her. Nearby horses stomped their hooves, then sneezed as dust floated into their nostrils. Bags and trunks slammed onto the platform as a station employee flung them from the train. A street hawker selling flasks of an elixir for fatigue called out his prices to her. Someone shouted, "Go to hell, you damned son of a bitch!"

Theodosia shook her head. "Ah, these must be the sweet sounds of Texas." Lips pursed in distaste, she stepped off the platform and made her way across the street. Mr. Roman Montana could look for her all week; she'd had enough of waiting outside in the torrid heat.

The interior of the train station wasn't much cooler, but at least its roof kept the sun from beating down on her. Trash, cockroaches, and sleeping cowboys littered the hardwood floor, and the walls were covered with flies, train schedules, outdated Wanted posters, and lopsided paintings. One painting was of a seminude woman; someone had sketched a beard on her face and a bolt of lightning across her bare breast. In the far corner two old men played checkers. One was smoking a cigar and dropping ashes all over the playing board; his opponent kept blowing them off.

Theodosia's distinguished life in Boston suddenly seemed a million miles away.

After a moment she spotted a refreshment bar

and hurried toward it. "I'd like a cold lemonade, please," she said, setting the bird cage on the counter.

The barkeep stared at her thoughtfully, his long black moustache twitching as he chewed his wad of tobacco. "Well now, little lady, I reckon you *would* like a cold lemonade, but I ain't got nary a lemon left." He paused a moment to dig at some dried food encrusted within the pair of initials someone had carved into the wooden bar. " 'Spect I won't be gittin' no more fer at least another week. They come from Mexico, y'know. Lemon trees don't grow good here."

Theodosia winced at his atrocious grammar. "They don't grow *well* here."

"Yeah, I know. Wonder why?"

"It's not a suitable climate, but that's not what I was trying to . . . You see, sir, you said lemons don't grow *good* here. You should have said they don't grow *well*. And while *ain't* was once an acceptable word, it isn't any longer. Oh, and you've a fondness for using double negatives."

"That so?" He moved his chaw of tobacco to the hollow of his other cheek. "You from England?"

"England, sir?"

"You talk like them London folk. You a teacher over there? Can you speak in them furrin tongues?"

"I am not from England, sir, but from Boston. Nor am I a teacher. My brother-in-law, Upton Peabody, however, is a professor at Harvard. I have been under his tutelage since I was five years old, and yes, he has given me extensive instruction in many languages."

"Harvard, y'say?" Rubbing his grizzled chin, the barkeep nodded slowly. "That's somewhere in

Floridy, ain't it?" He paused to glower at a man demanding service a short distance away. "Shet your trap, mister! I'll git to ya when I'm damn well ready to git to ya!"

Theodosia's eyes widened. "The man is probably as thirsty as I am. I'll have a glass of cold tea and leave you to attend to the rest of your customers."

The barkeep retrieved a glass from a shelf beneath the bar and began wiping it with his apron. "I had me a teacher when I was a young'un, but she packed up and moved on when me and Gubb Siler filled her desk drawer with a mess o' jest-hatched rattlers. I ain't had much schoolin', but I ain't dumb. No, siree, I'm smarter'n most folks figger. I once readed a whole book from back to front. Won't never do it again, on account o' all that readin' give me a headache that liked to never go away. Ain't got no tea, ma'am. Bugs got in it. I usually jest pick them bugs out and serve the tea right up, but this time there was jest too many."

Theodosia glanced at her watch and realized it had taken him almost three whole minutes to address the subject of the tea. Interested in such oral meandering and knowing that Upton's interest would equal hers, she withdrew her writing materials from her reticule and jotted down a reminder to contemplate the possible reasons behind the man's digressive discourse.

"Whatcha writin', ma'am?"

She slipped the paper and pencil back into her handbag. "A note. Sir, plain water will do, thank you."

He poured her a glass of water. "Ain't cold. I had to give my ice to Doc Uggs on account o' ole Sam Tiller's got him a fever that won't git brung down fer nothin'. Doc Ugg's got Sam packed in ice. I don't reckon Sam's got much of a chance, though. If the fever don't kill him, he'll freeze to death. Purty bird ya got there, ma'am. What with his gray body and bloodred tail, he looks like a piece o' fire embers. Howdy, bird."

"Ole Sam Tiller's got him a fever," the parrot declared. "Howdy, bird."

The barkeep's mouth dropped open; his wad of tobacco fell out and hit the floor with a loud splat. "He—he *talks!* And I'll be damned if he don't know ole Sam Tiller!"

Warming to the friendly man, Theodosia smiled. "He doesn't know Mr. Tiller. He merely repeated what he heard you say about the man. His talent is extraordinary, even for a bird of his species. Most of them must hear a word or statement many times before they are able to repeat it. Of course, I've worked with mine for incalculable hours."

The barkeep gave a slow nod. "What kind o' bird is he?"

"A *Psittacus erithacus.*"

"Piss what?"

"A *Psittacus erithacus*, which is the scientific name for an African gray. Of all the species of parrots, African grays are quite the most impressive mimics."

"Uh, yeah," the barkeep mumbled. "I think I readed that somewhere." He stuck his finger into the parrot's cage.

"Be careful," Theodosia warned. "The sharp angle of his jaw muscles on the bones that close his bill combine to create one of nature's most powerful crushing mechanisms."

"What?"

"He can bite your finger off," she translated, collecting her belongings. "Good day to you, sir, and thank you ever so much for the highly interesting conversation and the water. I feel totally refocillated now. That is, I am completely refreshed," she added upon seeing his frown of confusion. "Say good-bye, John the Baptist."

The parrot flapped a wing. "I'm smarter'n most folks figger. Say good-bye, John the Baptist."

Theodosia left the astonished barkeep and crossed to the ticket window, determined to begin an intense search for Roman Montana. "Sir," she said to the ticket clerk, "I am to meet a man by the name of Roman Montana. He's tall and has long black hair and blue eyes. Have you seen anyone fitting that description? Perhaps he has inquired about my whereabouts? My name is Theodosia Worth."

The clerk pushed his spectacles back to the bridge of his nose. "Welcome to Oates' Junction, Miz Worth. Name's Tark. You from England?"

"Boston. Mr. Tark—"

"I thought England. Y'talk kind o' funny, like them London furriners. It's fancy talk, though. Meant that as a compliment. Tark's my first name, Miz Worth. Damn flies." He reached for a stack of papers, rolled them into a tube, and began swatting flies. Only after he'd killed about a dozen did he speak again.

"Last name's Krat. Tark, ya see, is Krat spelled back'ards. Mama figgered that out when I was two days old and thought it was right cute. Ain't that funny? So y'say you're lookin' fer Roman Montana, huh?"

Theodosia felt more eager than ever to discover

the reasons behind this circumlocutory conversation.

"The man's name sounds a mite familiar," the clerk informed her, swiping at another fly. "He's pro'bly done some work 'round here, or somethin'. Nobody's asked about ya, though. Is Roman Montana a drinkin' man, ma'am?"

"A drinking man?" She gave him a thoughtful look. "What do his drinking habits have to do with my searching for him?"

Her question gave him pause. "Well, ma'am, if he likes his whiskey, y'might find him over at the saloon, don'tcha think? Head on out that side door over yonder and stay stuck to the windin' path. You'll pass a horse paddock, a mound o' salt licks, and then a purty little patch o' bluebonnets. After y'pass the purty little patch o' bluebonnets, the main street'll be dead ahead o' you."

He pushed his spectacles back up again. "The main street's lined with buildin's. Saloon's the third one on the left. But if ya don't find your Roman Montana there, don't go to frettin', hear? He'll be along sooner or later."

Theodosia hoped it would be sooner. But hoping was like wishing, and wishing was a useless pastime. "And may I leave my baggage here, sir?"

"Oh, shore, shore. Bags don't git stole from here but about once a month, and one was jest stole yesterday, so I reckon another month'll pass afore one gits stole again."

Trying to take comfort in his disturbing reassurance, Theodosia exited the station. Once outside, she removed John the Baptist from his cage and slipped a glittering collar around his neck.

Leashed, the bird waddled alongside his mistress as she proceeded into town.

Within moments, Theodosia stood in front of a building with a sign that said SHIT'S SALOON. She realized someone had tampered with one of the sign's letters and that the name of the saloon was SMIT'S SALOON. Patting the side of her bonnet, she approached the swinging doors.

A round of gunfire exploded from within the establishment, and two brawny men came flying out. They slammed onto the boardwalk, then rolled into the dirt street, where they continued the brawl they'd begun inside the saloon.

Frightened by the loud ruckus, John the Baptist let out a high-pitched, long-winded squawk. Before Theodosia could reach for him, he had pulled his head out of the collar and scrambled down the boardwalk, his escape accelerated by his intermittent bouts of flying.

Frantic, Theodosia chased him, but the bird took a zigzag course that included dodging beneath low-lying fence posts and shrubbery. In no time, John the Baptist had scooted out of town, leaving a puff of dust in his wake.

Still giving chase, Theodosia saw her parrot head straight for a horse and rider who were just arriving in town. "Stop!" she screamed at the man on the silver steed. "Stop immediately! You're going to injure my parrot! Please—"

Her shout died away when John the Baptist left the ground and flew directly into the huge gray horse's chest. The skittish stallion reared suddenly, pitching his rider into an enormous pile of discarded stable flooring that lay on the side of the road.

Knowing the man's landing into the soft odorous heap couldn't have hurt him, Theodosia raced past him, still intent on catching John the Baptist.

The fallen rider started to rise but fell back again when a flurry of blue skirts swiped him full across his face. Disbelieving, he watched the young woman weave along the dusty road in an effort to overtake the hysterical bird.

Anger curled through him, as well as a hint of embarrassment. He couldn't remember the last time he'd been flung off a horse, and he'd certainly never been thrown into a smelly mountain of horse manure.

He rose to his feet. While he brushed off his clothes, the squawking bird scurried toward him.

Theodosia gasped in astonishment as the man scooped up her parrot with one smooth motion. "Oh, thank you!" she gushed, holding up her arms to receive her bird.

The man did not relinquish the parrot. Lifting it higher, he stared up at it.

John the Baptist stared back. "Would you be willing to impregnate me?"

The man's forehead furrowed into a deep scowl. "What the hell—"

"Sir, please relinquish my bird to me," Theodosia asked. "He's unaccustomed to strenuous movement in such sultry heat."

He decided she was from one of those northeastern cities, where people dressed real fancy just to sit on little satin sofas and drink hot tea. People from there talked as she did, with a clipped accent sharp enough to slice leather if put to the test.

"Sir," Theodosia continued, "I must take prompt measures to provide my parrot with a cool place in which to reconcile himself to this change of environment."

He frowned in bewilderment. "What?"

"He must rest."

"Lady, I've got a good mind to put this damned bird to rest for all of eternity!"

Theodosia peered up into eyes so blue, they defied description. One moment they appeared turquoise; in the next they rivaled the clear true blue of cornflowers.

The intensity of his gaze caused a fluttering sensation inside her. It warmed her, tickled a bit, and quickened her breath and heartbeat. Disturbed by the unfamiliar feelings, she bowed her head for a moment to seek composure and found herself staring at the lower part of his anatomy.

"What are you gawking at?" he demanded.

She continued to stare, completely unable to stop herself. "I am astonished by the size of your vastus lateralis, vastus intermedius, and vastus medialis. Why, even your sartorius is clearly defined and equally amazing."

He had no idea what she was talking about, but he saw that she'd directed her total attention to the area below his belt.

He felt a profound urge to drop his hands to his groin.

But he didn't. He still held her bird and wasn't about to take the risk of being turned into a eunuch by a pecking parrot. "Here, take your stupid bird."

His command snapped Theodosia out of her deep state of contemplation. Quickly, she slid John the Baptist out of the man's hands. "Your irritation toward my parrot is totally unjustified. He can in no way be held accountable for the fall you took.

Apparently, you don't ride well. Riding requires superb equilibrium, something you obviously do not possess. Moreover, I refuse to believe you are injured. Your little tumble was cushioned by that mass of—"

"My little *tumble* never would have happened if that feathered maniac hadn't scared the hell out of my—"

"Feathered maniac?" Theodosia clicked her tongue and shook her head. "Sir, that is a very poor choice of words. You may not refer to a bird as a maniac."

He gaped at her. "I may not?"

"No. The word *maniac* is used for humans only. And I will have you know that my bird is an African gray, a species of parrot that is very much admired throughout the civilized world."

"Oh, of all the—I don't care if that feathered maniac's a *Japanese purple,* my word choices are none of your blasted business! And you've got some damned nerve telling me I can't ride, lady." He swiped his hat from the stone-peppered road. "I can't remember a single day of my life when I haven't mounted a horse!"

"My goodness, sir, you are becoming crazed."

"*I'm* crazy? All *I* was doing was riding into town! *You're* the one who was running all over the place chasing a pampered parrot and correcting people's word choices!"

Theodosia walked into the shade beneath a towering oak.

Through narrowed eyes the man watched her. Her gently rounded hips swayed, and her dark blue traveling suit hugged her tiny waist and rustled around what he guessed were long, slender legs.

He could see nothing of her breasts; her damned bird snuggled against her chest. And since he'd been too angry to notice her bosom before, he couldn't remember if it was small, or the big and full kind he liked.

Liked? He didn't like this woman at all. Even if she did have big full breasts, he wasn't going to like her.

Still, he mused, he didn't have to like her to appreciate her looks. Indeed, in his opinion big full breasts had a lot to do with the one and only thing women were good for.

"Your quick temper is interesting, sir," Theodosia announced abruptly, her skirts brushing across thick patches of bluebonnets and orange-red Indian paintbrush. "Oh, I realize that falling into a hill of reeking fertilizer is far from a pleasant experience, but you became instantly livid. So much so that I wondered if some form of cicuration would be necessary."

So intently was he watching her, he barely heard her. But after a moment of thought, he realized what she'd said. His eyes widened to such an extent, his eyelids ached. "Good God, do *all* northern women go around threatening men with castration?"

She cocked her head slightly. "Whatever are you talking about, sir? I said nothing at all about castration."

"You said—"

"*Cicuration.* To cicurate is to calm. To tame. Your ferocity made me wonder if I would have to somehow coax you out of your frenzied state."

He frowned, no more able to comprehend what she had said than he could understand why he was still here listening to her. "Lady, I get the feeling you must be some sort of genius, but I'll be damned if you aren't a lunatic too."

He stalked over to his horse.

"My brother-in-law, Upton, and I studied the emotion of anger at great length a few years ago," Theodosia elaborated, watching him mount and settle his large frame into the saddle. "We became interested in psychology, and it was most fascinating. Our research taught us that many people who possess quick tempers underwent various and extended forms of strain and or grief during their childhoods. But of course, there are also people who possess violent characters because they were extremely spoiled as children. Which is it in your case, sir?"

Surprise, like an unseen fist, hit him hard.

Strain and grief.

How had this woman guessed?

He slid his hat on. Without another word to her, he urged his stallion into an easy canter toward town.

Once he arrived at the train station, Roman Montana dismounted, tied his horse to a post, and dug into his saddlebag for the sign he was to use to find the woman Dr. Wallaby had sent him to meet. Upon withdrawing the sign, he looked at the name on it.

Theodosia Worth.

"Theodosia," he muttered. Peculiar name. He wondered if she was as odd as her name. Maybe.

But no one could be as strange as the woman he'd just left outside town.

Thank God for that.

"Nice horse," a deep voice said from behind him.

"Nimble, yet rugged. Unusual combination. Is he fast?"

Accustomed to such curiosity, Roman turned and waited for the man's next words. He knew full well what they would be. Almost every man who saw his stallion, Secret, wanted to buy him.

The man examined the stallion again. "I've got a ranch about seventy-five miles west of here. Wouldn't be willing to sell him, would you? I'd pay good money for him."

Roman smiled. The man was mistaken if he thought to use Secret as a stud horse, for the stallion was but the *result* of some unusual and mischievous crossbreeding that Roman had indulged in ten years ago. He'd never told a soul about his youthful transgression or the particulars of its unexpected yet extraordinary outcome, nor would he.

His future depended on his keeping the secret.

"Sorry," he said. "He's not for sale."

"Damned shame. Well, good luck to you."

"Thanks." Roman swiped at his soiled clothing again and entered the station. Holding the sign above his head, he walked through the milling crowd. Many people hastened to step out of his way. He understood why they gave him a wide berth. He certainly didn't smell of sandalwood soap or rosewater. He smelled of . . .

What had that demented woman called it? *Reeking fertilizer.* Shaking his head, he made another journey around the stuffy room. By the time he'd completed his third trip, he saw her.

That crazy genius. She stood by the side door of the station; her feathered maniac sat perched on her shoulder, pecking at a bit of ribbon on her bonnet.

He started to turn away from her, but before he could give her his back, he saw her move toward him.

In only a moment he found himself staring into the most beautiful eyes he'd ever seen. Almost perfect circles, they were the color of fine whiskey and every bit as intoxicating.

He lowered his gaze and saw that one long lock of her bright gold hair lay over her breasts, which were, indeed, the big and full kind.

Not that he gave a solitary damn.

He spun on his heel and strode away from her.

"Roman Montana?"

At the sound of his name, Roman stopped in his tracks. Oh, God. She knew who he was.

That could only mean one thing. Dread coiling through him, he felt as though he'd swallowed a poisonous snake.

"Roman Montana?" Theodosia said to the back of his head. "I didn't recognize you while we conversed outside of town." She tapped him on the upper back; the tips of her fingers touched his long hair.

She drew her hand away immediately, unnerved by the strange emotion that the feel of his hair evoked.

It was sun-warmed. The same color as the two shiny black guns he wore at his hips, it spilled over his broad shoulders and down his back in thick waves.

She'd never seen such hair on a man and knew an almost uncontrollable urge to touch it again.

Baffled by her odd reaction to it, she took a step away and forced herself to concentrate on the situation at hand. "I am Theodosia Worth, the woman you are to escort to Templeton," she said, still speaking to his back. "You have a sign with my name on it, and you are exactly one hour, twenty-two minutes, and forty-nine seconds late."

He clenched his fists around the sign. The woman actually counted seconds!

When he still didn't answer her or turn around to face her, Theodosia contemplated the remote possibility that she'd made a mistake. "My goodness, sir, you *are* Roman Montana, are you not?"

John the Baptist squawked shrilly. "It is imperative that I conceive a child," he called out. "My goodness, sir, you *are* Roman Montana, are you not?"

His dread deepening, Roman wished to God his name were anything *but* Roman Montana.

Chapter 2

Soused. Liquored up. Under the sauce. Stewed to the gills.

Drunk.

Roman could think of no other state of being that would enable him to get through the three-day journey to Templeton with Theodosia Worth. "For all I care," he mumbled to the bartender, "she can fly to Templeton on her parrot's back."

"Whatever y'say," the bartender answered, refilling his customer's glass.

Wrapping his hand around the glass, Roman looked into the mirror on the wall behind the bar. Its reflection showed him a cloud of blue-gray smoke, with weak rays of sunshine filtering through it. Beneath the haze a half dozen men sat at tables, playing cards and stealing a feel or two from the voluptuous barmaids. Others stood at the bar, nursing their drinks in solitude. Most were drifters like himself, he knew. They wandered here and there, earning money when they needed it and handling their days the way a child builds with blocks—one by one, with no specific scheme in mind.

That was where the similarities ended, Roman thought. *He* had a definite plan, and it wasn't some sort of castle in the air, as his stepmother had so coldly put it.

It was a dream so big that only twenty-five thousand acres of the richest grassland that the Rio Grande Plains had to offer could support it. He'd raise a remarkable breed of horses on that beautiful land and then make a fortune off the cattle ranchers who would undoubtedly pay any price he named to buy his stock.

To *make* that fortune, however, he had to *spend* a fortune. True, he was only five hundred dollars short of being able to purchase the land. And the herd of sturdy Spanish mares wouldn't be expensive.

But the English Thoroughbred stallions would not come cheap. The best in the country, bred and raised on various farms in the east, cost nearly their weight in gold. He would get them somehow, though, for he wanted the finest money could buy.

Nothing—*no one* in the entire world was going to keep him from realizing his dream. As he had done for ten long years, he would accept any and every job that came his way until he possessed the funds he needed.

He would just have to find the patience to put up with Theodosia Worth during the trip to Templeton. He couldn't afford to pass up the money Dr. Wallaby would pay him for completing the job.

"Reward money, that's what it is," he muttered, raking his fingers through his hair. "Like the kind a man gets for bringing in some sort of menace to society."

"A real menace," the barkeep agreed automati-

cally. "Hey, don't I know you? Ain't I seed you.
. . . Yeah, you're the same feller who come
through a few months ago. Roman Montana, that's
who ya are. Folks ain't quit talkin' about that horse
o' yours. Still ain't sellin'?"

Roman shook his head and sipped his whiskey.

"Y'know, Will Simpson said his horses ain't
never been shod they way y'shod 'em when ya was
here last. Said your blacksmithin' weren't nothin'
short of amazin' and that he'd like to know how
y'got them shoes to stick s'good."

"Tell him to drive the nails home with one blow.
More than one strike gives the nail a chance to
loosen before it's even in."

"Really? Hmm. Didn't never know that. Well,
what about ole Herman Gooch? Jest the other day
he said he was hopin' you'd come back and bigger
his wife's parlor. She really liked how you biggered
her kitchen. Y'on't me to fetch him over here?"

Roman drained his glass. "Another time, maybe.
I've got another job to do right now. A real headache of a job by the name of Theodosia Worth. And
her damned parrot's every bit as much of a pain in
the—"

"Parrot? A big gray bird with red tail feathers?
Oh, I seed that woman. She stopped in front o' the
saloon fer a second. Purty little thing. Skin so
white, it looked like it come from a milk bottle.
Whatcha gotta do fer her?"

Roman sloshed more whiskey into his glass.
"Take her to Templeton. She's over at Claff's livery
now, trying to pick out a horse and wagon. I had a
mind to stay and help her, but when she asked Claff
about a certain *Equus caballus*, I couldn't leave fast
enough."

"Equus caballus?" The barkeep scratched his head. "What the hell's that?"

Roman swallowed his fifth shot of liquor and wiped his mouth with the back of his hand. "Best as I can figure, that's genius talk for *horse.*"

"Mr. Montana!"

Roman swiveled on the stool and saw Claff's son standing between the saloon doors.

"Paw asked me to come git ya! Said fer ya to hurry up. That Miz Worth woman y'brung to the livery ain't speakin' no kind o' English we ever heared, and Paw's beside hissef tryin' to make out what she wants."

Roman folded his arms across his chest. "Claff's upset? Don't tell me—that Miss Worth woman is now trying to cicurate him."

"Cicurate?" The boy shook his head. "Naw, she ain't hurtin' him none, but she's sure got him riled. Will y'come?"

With a fair amount of whiskey flowing through his veins, Roman felt more inclined to deal with the obnoxious Miss Worth. He paid for the liquor and headed out of the saloon.

As he stepped into the street, he spotted her in front of the livery. Her hands clasped behind her back, she was slowly circling a bay Thoroughbred.

Several buildings away, in front of the feed store, three burly, well-armed men stood watching her. Even from where he stood, Roman could tell they were up to no good. And whatever evil thing was on their minds, it involved Theodosia.

His steps long and purposeful, he strode across the street, careful to keep his instincts trained on the three outlaws.

"Oh, hello, Mr. Montana," Theodosia greeted him and smiled.

The sparkling prettiness of her smile captured his attention. He was halfway tempted to smile back.

But only halfway. He frowned instead. "You aren't buying that horse, Miss Worth."

She ran her hand down the horse's sleek flank. "Yes, I do believe I shall, Mr. Montana. This gelding is a Thoroughbred. He is not the finest I have seen, but I find his spirit highly desirable. I'm quite familiar with this breed because my father—"

"That horse is *too* fine," Roman flared. "Claff, show her a few sturdier—"

"I have already seen the others," Theodosia announced, smoothing the back of her hand across her moist forehead. "I cared for none of them. And I would sincerely appreciate it if you did not become roinous over the matter, Mr. Montana."

The warm, whiskey-induced mellowness that Roman had hoped would see him through a few hours in Theodosia's company quickly turned into cold anger. "I'll be as *roinous* as I damned well want!" He had no inkling what the word meant but wasn't about to cow before the might of her vocabulary. "Now, pick another horse, because you are *not* taking the Thoroughbred."

John the Baptist screeched from within his cage, which Theodosia had placed on top of several bales of hay. "I'll be as roinous as I damned well want," he called out.

Theodosia bristled. "Now look what you have done, Mr. Montana. My bird has never—not once—spoken a profanity. Five minutes in your company, and he—"

"The word *damned* ain't s'bad, Miz Worth," Claff

ventured. "There's a helluva lot worser words he might could learn to say. Why, I know some that near 'bout turn my mouth inside out when I say 'em."

"Please don't tell me what they are," she entreated, then turned back to Roman. "I am anxious to get to Templeton, Mr. Montana. That is why I was not inclined to accept your suggestion that we stay here tonight and begin our journey in the morning. It is also why I prefer this Thoroughbred. Thoroughbreds are well known for their speed. I happen to know a great deal about them because my father—"

"Yeah, I'm beginning to realize that you know a lot about a lot, but you don't know much about much. Take that Thoroughbred, and by tomorrow night I'll be forced to shoot him to put him out of his misery. Templeton is almost a three-day ride away and over rough terrain. The Thoroughbred is famous for its speed but not for its ruggedness."

"That chestnut over there's a strong 'un," Claff offered. He ambled forward, a long piece of straw hanging from his mouth. "Trained to pull a wagon too."

Playing with the fragile gold chains that dangled from the bottom of her ruby brooch, Theodosia glanced at the small scraggly animal Claff had indicated. "That is a mere pony. And a sick one at that."

"It's a healthy mustang," Roman corrected her. "No horse in the world has as much stamina. It might not be pretty, but that horse'll get you wherever you want to go." He nodded at Claff, then turned his attention to the group of vehicles. "And she'll take that buckboard."

"That rickety wagon?" Theodosia exclaimed.

"It's small and lightweight, and the wheels are made of seasoned orangewood."

"And what, may I ask, is so special about orangewood, Mr. Montana?"

"Seasoned orangewood won't shrink much, Miss Worth."

"Really?" She looked at the wheels. "How interesting. But be that as it may, I have already chosen my conveyance." She pointed to a dainty buggy whose black lacquered body gleamed in the late afternoon sunshine.

Roman flicked a bothersome fly off his arm. "May as well sail through a hurricane in a paper boat. The bolts on the running gear aren't riveted. They'll come off, and I'll be damned if I'm going to stop every ten miles to—"

"But—"

"Get the wagon, or walk. The choice is yours. How's that for being *roinous*?"

Theodosia swallowed further argument and reminded herself that in only a few days she would be parting company with the arrogant man and his insufferable obstinacy. "Very well, sir," she said to Claff. "Do as the roinous Mr. Montana says."

When Claff finished hitching the horse to the buckboard, Theodosia dipped her hand inside the bulging velvet pouch that swung from her elbow.

Sunlight dazzled off the fistful of gold coins she withdrew.

The blinding glitter nearly stopped Roman's heartbeat. Never having seen so much money at one time, his mind reeled with disbelief even as his body tensed with apprehension.

Sliding his gaze to the right, he saw the three

men. They continued to watch Theodosia and had no doubt seen her gold.

Damn.

He grabbed her hand and dragged her inside the stable. "Have you lost your mind, woman? What the hell are you doing, flashing all your gold around like that?"

"All my gold?" She attempted to pull her hand away from him but succeeded only in wrenching her arm. "Mr. Montana, the gold I carry in this bag is but pocket money. The rest is in my blue trunk."

Roman swiveled in the hay and saw her blue trunk lying beside her other belongings. Surely it wasn't filled with gold, he tried to convince himself. No one in their right mind would travel with such a fortune.

But then, Theodosia didn't seem to possess the sort of mind normal people did.

"As for what I was doing with the gold I withdrew from my bag, Mr. Montana," Theodosia continued, "I was merely trying to pay for the horse and wagon. In order to successfully accomplish the task, it was necessary for me to remove the money from my bag and hand it to—"

"You should have counted out the money where no one could see you do it!"

"And how, pray tell, might I have managed such a procedure when the price of the horse and wagon was unknown to me?"

"*What?*" He jammed his fingers through his hair. "For God's sake, all you had to do was ask Claff! Any simpleton could figure that out! Use some common sense, if you have any. Look, you aren't at some peaceful, elegant garden party, surrounded by your top-hatted, lily-white-handed gentlemen admirers. You're in Texas, where a lot of men are leashed and led by pure greed. They can sniff out women like you the way sharks smell blood from miles away."

"Mr. Mon—"

"Dr. Wallaby is paying me to escort you to Templeton, and I'm sure as hell going to get you there in one piece. If I don't, I won't get a measly cent of the money he'll owe me for doing the job. When you get to Templeton, you can glue your gold to your face for every thief in the world to see, for all I care. But for now, give me that damned bag before someone slits your pretty little throat for it." He yanked the pouch off her arm.

"Mr. Montana! You—" She broke off; through her mind drifted words of wisdom that had served her well in the past. *"Aequam servare mentem,"* she murmured. "Yes. *Aequam servare mentem."*

Roman saw fire. Here he was doing his damnedest to see to her welfare, and she was spitting foreign curses at him!

He decided they were French profanities; they sounded a bit like the love words a French saloon girl had once whispered to him. "I might not speak fluent French, Miss Worth, but I know an insult when I hear one," he spat smugly. Giving her his back, he took a few coins from the bag, stalked out of the barn, and handed the money to Claff. "Thirty dollars, Claff. The horse and rig aren't worth more than twenty-five, but I'm giving you a tip for having put up with Miss Worth."

Theodosia emerged from the stable as Roman began to load her belongings into the bed of the buckboard. Through the thin fabric of his beige shirt, she saw the muscles in his arms, shoulders, and back. They bulged, then coiled, then stretched in rhythm, as if he worked to the sound of some graceful melody.

Only when he reached for her blue trunk did she lose her concentration. "Mr. Montana, that trunk is frightfully heavy. It took two men to deliver it from the train station. If you lift it alone, you might injure yourself."

Her concern caused him to spin in the dirt and face her. An unfamiliar warmth settled over him, a gentle heat far more comforting than the sunshine.

Why should she care if he got hurt? he tried to understand. But maybe she really didn't. He'd probably only imagined her worry. After all, he was nothing but an escort to her.

God, he must have downed more whiskey than he realized. It wasn't like him to fantasize over a woman's feelings.

"Perhaps your friend Mr. Claff will assist you," Theodosia added.

Friend? Roman thought, glancing at Claff. Oh, Claff was a good man, but Roman had never considered him a friend.

Truth was, he'd never had a real friend; had never had the chance or time to make any.

"Mr. Montana, did you hear what I said?" Theodosia asked. "Mr. Claff could—"

The remainder of her suggestion faded into nothingness as she watched him lift the trunk from the ground. It might as well have been filled with feathers.

"Did you buy all the supplies I told you to?" Roman asked after setting the trunk in the buckboard.

Lifting her skirts, she walked to the wagon and climbed in. Never having taken to wearing the mul-

titude of underwear most women wore, she had little trouble adjusting herself to the wooden seat. She
picked up the reins, then pointed to a small pile of
merchandise. "The supplies are there, Mr. Montana."

Roman loaded up the provisions. *"Vamanos."* He
smiled inwardly. She might know French, but he
knew Spanish.

"Sí," she answered. *"Ahora que estamos listos
comencemos nuestro viaje."*

"What'd she say, Roman?" Claff asked.

"I said, Mr. Claff," Theodosia replied, "that now
that we are ready, let's begin our journey. Oh, and
Mr. Montana? *Aequam servare mentem* is Latin and
means 'to keep an unruffled mind.' It is my intention to ponder the quote while you and I travel. I
advise you to do the same."

Roman folded his arms across his chest. "Yeah?
Well, let me tell you what you can do with your
advice, Miss Worth."

"No, I don't believe I shall." Her fingers whit-
ened around the reins as her poise began to waver.
"Mr. Montana, I have always endeavored to maintain self-control in any given situation. However,
after only a few hours in your company, I find myself not only exasperated but at a loss as to how to
regain my composure."

"The little genius mind's getting a little ruffled,
huh?"

She stared into his snapping blue eyes for a long
while. "How utterly convenient it is that you already understand that the definition of *roinous* is
nasty and contemptible. I suspect I shall be using
the word frequently during the next three days, and

your knowledge of it will save me the task of having to explain it to you."

Her intellectual sarcasm snapped the last shred of patience Roman possessed. To hell with the money he'd receive from Dr. Wallaby for taking the woman to Templeton! There was money to be made right here in Oates' Junction making parlors bigger! "And your going to Templeton alone, Miss Worth, will save me the bother of having to take you." He tossed her bag of gold into her lap and a sardonic grin into her eyes.

"But I don't know where—"

"No? I thought you knew everything. Well, you can always ask a Comanche for directions. You'll probably meet up with a few along the way. Or maybe the Blanco y Negro Gang can help. I hear they've broken out of jail and are back at their usual work of robbing, murdering, and ravishing anything wearing a skirt. You'll recognize them right away, Miss Worth. They all ride white horses, and they all wear black."

Theodosia refused to show the rogue one more hint of her shock. Surely she could find Templeton on her own. "Fine. When I arrive in Templeton, shall I inform Dr. Wallaby that you are no longer working for him?"

"You don't think he *shall* figure that out by himself, when I don't show up?"

"Good-bye, Mr. Montana. And the very best of luck with—with whatever it is you do." Theodosia slipped the strings of her velvet bag around her wrist and set the horse into a brisk trot, leaving Roman and Claff in a cloud of dust.

"She's headin' north," Claff drawled, still chewing on the piece of straw.

Roman grinned. "I know."

"Templeton's nigh on a hunnerd miles south o' here."

"I know."

"She's got right much book learnin', but she sure don't got much sense."

"I know." Still grinning, Roman turned and started to head for the saloon. But one glance at the feed store erased his grin and brought him to an abrupt halt. He'd forgotten about the three outlaws.

They'd vanished.

And every instinct Roman possessed told him they'd left to follow the scent of gold.

He found her buckboard fifteen minutes out of town, stopped beside a persimmon thicket. Her trunk of gold was still in it.

But Theodosia wasn't.

"Here I am again, Secret," he muttered to his stallion. "Right back where I started, taking care of women. Which means I'm as stupid now as I was then. Damn that asinine Worth woman to hell and back!"

But even as he spat the curse, his apprehension rose.

He dismounted swiftly and secured Secret to the back of the wagon. Both Colts drawn, he followed the trail of footprints that led into the grove of trees and soon came upon a scrap of lace-edged white silk on the ground. Crumpled beside a rotting log, it was spotted with what could only be blood.

He stuffed it into the waistband of his breeches and proceeded deeper into the woods. The sun-dappled persimmons gave way to dense patches of willow and cottonwood, which grew near slushy areas of stagnant water. The musty smell of plant rot filled his nostrils, somehow intensifying his anxiety. He quickened his pace, soon exiting the thicket and coming to a leaf-strewn slope.

At the bottom lay Theodosia, face down.

In his haste to get to her, he slipped in the thick layers of leaves and made the downward trip on his belly. When he finally stopped, he found himself nose to nose with a wide-eyed Theodosia.

She'd taken off her bonnet. Her golden hair poured over her shoulders like streams of melted butter and looked just as soft. He almost reached up to touch it, but the impulse passed when he remembered why he'd come after her. She was supposed to be hurt or dead, but the confounded woman didn't have a scratch on her. On the contrary, she was looking at him with bright, curious eyes that held not a tinge of discomfort.

"What the hell," he rasped, as if he had gravel in his throat, "are you doing?"

With the exception of Upton, she'd never been so physically close to any man. Roman's thick black hair pooled over her hands, causing tingles to glide up her arms. His breath whispered across her cheeks, and the heat of his body filtered toward her, warming her as surely as the sunshine pouring down from the endless Texas sky.

"Miss Worth," Roman ground out.

"Yes?" Blinking, she touched her fingers to her forehead and tried to remember what he'd asked her. "I—my goodness, my mind has gone blank. Such a thing has never happened to me before."

She sat up and saw she held a fistful of bright red phlox. "Oh, yes. I was gathering these—"

"I thought you were dead!" Roman knifed to his feet and stuffed his Colts back into his belt.

His shouting served to bring back her presence of mind. "Dead, Mr. Montana? But what might have killed me?"

He noticed her velvet bag hanging from the crook of her elbow. It was safe, her trunk was safe, she was safe. He decided not to tell her about the three men. If he did, she'd probably cry with fear, and he'd dealt with enough female tears to last him several lifetimes.

He yanked out the blood-splattered scrap of silk. "What else was I supposed to think when I found this? Then I find you sprawled facedown at the bottom of this—"

"That is a piece of my petticoat. I cut my wrist on a nail that protrudes from the seat of the wagon, and I stemmed the bleeding by using a bit of my petticoat to apply pressure to the wound. I'm sure the lesion will heal quite nicely, and—"

"I don't give a damn about some stupid scratch on your wrist! What the hell are you doing out here?"

She picked a few more phlox and smiled. "I was and still am collecting these fine samples of *Phlox drummondii*. It is cultivated in Boston gardens, but I have never had the opportunity to see it growing wild. Lying on the ground better enabled me to examine it. It is not only the visible elements of plants that interest me but the root system as well. Would you care to hear an amusing story about the Polemoniaceae family, Mr. Montana?"

"Why would I want to hear a story about a family I don't even know, Miss Worth? And what the hell does that have to do with those flowers?"

She smiled gently and raised her crimson blossoms. "Phlox belong to the Polemoniaceae family. It is not a human family but a plant family."

"A plant family?" He looked at her flowers, then touched three of them. "Don't tell me. This is Papa Flower, this is Mama Flower, and this is Baby—"

"Excuse me if I interrupt your witty flow. You see, Mr. Montana, plants and animals are classified—"

"Never mind all that scientific hogwash! Now get back to the wag—"

"But I was going to relate the amusing story. In 1833, a Scot by the name of Thomas Drummond visited this area to collect a wide variety of specimens. He harvested more than seven hundred species of flora. These," she said, holding up her flowers, "he liked especially. So he sent seeds to Edinburgh. From Edinburgh, the plants were marketed all over Europe. Finally, they reached Boston and New York, where they became highly prized. The New Englanders, you see, were under the misconception that this plant was a rare and fine European import. Several years passed before they came to realize that it was actually a lowly native of the Republic of Texas. Now, isn't that one of the most amusing anecdotes you have ever heard?"

"Hilarious. Now, get back to the wag—"

"Thomas Drummond died of cholera."

"Sad. Now, get back to the wag—"

"I was under the impression that you were not going to accompany me on my journey, Mr. Montana." She rose from the ground, careful not to crush her phlox. "I haven't had the slightest difficulty with my travels as of yet."

"No? I thought you wanted to get to Templeton."

"That is precisely where I am—"

"Templeton's near the coast." He retrieved his hat from the blanket of phlox and slid it on his head. "Keep traveling north, and in about nine or ten days, you'll cross into the Oklahoma Territory." He waited for her reaction to his revelation. Surely someone as smart as she was would be embarrassed by having made such a dumb mistake.

"How do you know I'm traveling north? Are you carrying a compass?"

"No, I just know."

"But how—"

"For God's sake, I've lived in Texas all my life! I know what it looks like, smells like, sounds like, and feels like. Hell, I can even *taste* it! I know what is where, and where is what. Rivers, animals, rocks —everything has a way of telling me where I am. Now, get back to the wag—"

"But what if you were lost outside of Texas? How would you—"

"I'd study the trees and wind!" Totally irritated, he started toward the embankment.

"The trees and wind, Mr. Montana?" She hurried to join him, her insatiable curiosity not to be denied. "But what would it be about the trees and wind that would aid you?"

He spun to face her, instinct telling him that she wasn't going to give up until he answered her question. "The tops of tall trees lean toward the strongest sunlight, which comes from the east. Trees felled by strong winds—and not by rot, lightning, or human hands—fall toward the south because it's usually a norther that's felled them. And last, the direction of wind doesn't normally change during the day. If a southern wind is at my back in the

morning, it's probably a southern wind at my back
in the afternoon. All right? Satisfied?"

She deliberated upon his explanation, finding it
quite sound. "How interesting. And what—"

"Can we start for Templeton now, Miss Worth?"
Roman demanded. "Or would you rather keep be-
heading this flower family and then continue on
toward the Oklahoma Territory?"

Lifting her skirts, she started up the hill. "I assure you, Mr. Montana, that by nightfall I would
have realized my error in direction. I would have
understood immediately that I was following the
North Star, which, of course, would have alerted
me to the fact that I was traveling north. To find the
North Star, I would simply have had to locate
the constellation Ursa Major. Across from said constellation is another, Cassiopeia. Cassiopeia is
composed of five stars. The North Star is located
between the middle star of Cassiopeia and the star
at the end of Ursa Major's bowl. So you see? I
would not have even come close to the Oklahoma
Territory." She reached the top of the slope and
continued into the dim thicket.

Following her, Roman decided that the three
would-be gold thieves presented no danger to her.
She was perfectly equipped to defend herself by at-
tacking them with her intellect.

They'd die of sheer boredom.

And he had no doubt that he would meet the
same fate before reaching Templeton.

Chapter 3

Tugging at the neckline of her thick flannel night-gown, Theodosia emerged from the private spot she'd found in the woods.

Roman decided her nightwear was about as sexy as a burlap sack. Irritating though she was, she did have a few nice curves he'd hoped to get a peek at.

"I've never bathed in a moonlit stream before, Mr. Montana. Nor have I ever eaten rabbit cooked over an open fire."

How like a woman, he thought. No matter what a man did, they were never satisfied. "The nearest hot-water-filled tubs and restaurants are in Wild Winds, a town about five miles northwest of Templeton. A cool stream and charred rabbit are the best I can provide. If you don't like it—"

"My goodness, Mr. Montana, I voiced no complaint. What reason do you have to become so defensive?"

Reason? he repeated silently. He had thirteen years worth of reasons, and every time he thought of them he cursed himself for a fool.

Never—not for as long as he lived—would he be stupid enough to bow to a woman's bidding again.

"Mr. Montana?"

"What?"

Theodosia shrank back. He'd growled the word. Indeed, if he had had fangs, she felt sure he would have bitten her. He was quite the most fascinating study of hostility she had ever encountered.

"Are you going to stand there staring at me all night, Miss Worth?"

She sat upon her sleeping pallet, hugged her bent knees to her chest, and watched the dying flames of the campfire. Overhead, branches of post oak and blackjack rustled in harmony with the warm and gentle night breeze. She was going to enjoy her first night under the stars. It would prepare her for the nights in Brazil, where she would most likely sleep in the jungle. "What was it that changed your decision not to accompany me to Templeton, Mr. Montana?"

"The money," Roman lied from his spot on the other side of the fire. He tossed his empty plate aside. Taking a long swallow of water from his canteen, he appeared relaxed.

But every fiber in his body tensed with readiness. No sound escaped his attention. He'd checked the campsite thoroughly and had discovered no sign of the outlaws. It occurred to him that he might have been wrong in thinking they were after Theodosia's gold. Maybe they'd given up the hunt.

Ha! The sooner he got Theodosia to Templeton, the safer she and her dizzying amount of gold would be. "We'll be traveling hard tomorrow. Get some sleep."

John the Baptist spoke before Theodosia could. *"Przez caly dzien wczoraj wozil buraki z pola."*

Theodosia laughed.

Roman had the distinct impression that woman and bird were making fun of him. "What are the two of you talking about?"

"*Przez caly dzien wczoraj wozil buraki z pola* is Polish and means, 'All day yesterday he was carting beetroot from the field.' "

"Beetroot? Why the hell is he talking about beetroot?"

"He doesn't know what he's saying, Mr. Montana. He's merely repeating what he has heard. Several months ago, Upton entertained a Polish doctor, and the beetroot statement was one the man told us we could practice in order to get a better feel for the language. John the Baptist remembered it."

"John the Baptist," Roman mused aloud, shaking his head. "Why'd you name him that?"

The parrot stretched out his neck. "Any simpleton could figure that out!"

Theodosia smiled. "For as long as I've had him, he's had the terribly rude habit of throwing water at people. After the first few times I saw him do it, I decided to name him John the Baptist. He's an extraordinary pet. He can mimic not only human speech but animal sounds and other common noises, such as the rattle of carriage wheels upon streets. It doesn't matter what sort of sound he hears, he can imitate it. But he often speaks when he should not, and he possesses the annoying aptitude for saying things at the most inappropriate times."

John the Baptist nibbled at a piece of the apple Theodosia had given him, then spread his wings and opened his beak.

The sound of gunfire rent the air.

Both pistols drawn, Roman bolted to his feet, ready to shoot at the first thing that moved.

Theodosia smiled inwardly. "Mr. Montana?"

"Quiet," he whispered, staring into the dark shadows of the woods.

"But Mr. Montana, it was only John the Baptist. He was mimicking the sound of gunfire. You see, he and I were near the saloon this afternoon when someone shot a gun from within the establishment. John the Baptist is merely repeating the sound he heard. I'm sorry he disturbed you. I just don't know what to do with him."

"Wring his neck!"

John the Baptist turned his black eyes to Roman. *"State zitto."*

"Italian," Theodosia explained calmly. *"State zitto* means to hold your tongue. A polite way of saying 'shut up.' Of course, as I said earlier, he doesn't know what he's saying."

Roman pitched the bird a glare. Replacing his Colts in his belt, he crossed to where his saddle lay.

Theodosia watched him retrieve his bedroll and return to the fire. Though she saw him walking, she heard no evidence of his footsteps. He moved with the sleek grace of a cat. A black panther, she decided, watching his long ebony hair slide across his broad chest and thick arms.

Unable to resist, she studied him more intently. His face, bronzed by endless days in the sun or perhaps by Latin lineage, appeared sculpted. Ruggedly so, for he had high sharp cheekbones with deep hollows beneath them and an exceedingly square jaw that tapered slyly into a strong clefted chin.

His eyes blazed. Not with fireshine, nor with an-

ger. With something deeper, something she'd never
sensed in any man she knew in Boston.

Something primitive, untamed.

Silently, it sought, found, and beckoned to some
unknown part inside her.

"Something wrong, Miss Worth?" Giving her his
back while he spread out his bedroll, Roman
smiled. She might as well have reached for him
with her hands; he felt the caress of her eyes as
though they touched him with delicate fingers.

"I don't believe anything is *wrong*, but I am unaccustomed to the odd feelings that come to me when
I watch you. It happened this afternoon when I first
met you and again while you loaded my belongings
into the wagon. It is happening a third time now.
My breath quickens. Warmth flashes through me. I
realize this is nonsensical, but if there were such a
thing as a heated tickle, that would describe the
feeling."

Bent over his bed, Roman straightened slowly.
His first reaction was shock. He'd never met a
woman who talked so freely about desire.

But as he pondered what she'd said, he realized
she didn't *know* she was talking about desire. All
she knew was that a hot tickle flashed through her.

Well, well, well, he mused. He'd finally discovered a subject the little genius knew absolutely
nothing about. One *he* knew as well as he knew his
own hand.

He wondered if she'd like a little schooling. He
certainly didn't have to be overly fond of her to tu-
tor her. Stifling a rakish grin, he decided to play
with her for a while. "Does this uh—*hot tickle* hurt,
Miss Worth?"

She wrapped a long lock of hair around her

thumb, contemplating her emotions. "It isn't painful. It—well, perhaps it is painful in a certain sense. It's much like a pang of want or need. Like hunger."

"Sounds serious." His lips twitched with restrained mirth as he stretched out on his bedroll and propped himself up on his elbow. "I might be able to help you figure out what it is, but to do that I have to ask you a personal question. Can I?"

"*May* I," she corrected him. "Yes, you may."

He ignored her grammar lesson. "How many men do you know in Boston?"

She didn't see anything at all personal about his question. "Fifteen or twenty, perhaps. Why do you ask?"

"What sort of relationships do you have with them?" He picked up a twig and began drawing swirls in the dirt while wondering just how bold Bostonian men were.

"I study with them."

"Study? That's all? Don't they ever take you anywhere? To a party? Out for a walk?" *Have any of them ever stolen a kiss on some moonlit balcony?*

"Mr. Montana, the men I know in Boston have little time for socializing. I have never acquired a passion for it, either. And what's more, I fail to see what my relationships with my male acquaintances have to do with—"

"I'm getting to that." He held back yet another grin as he imagined the men she knew in Boston. Scholars, all of them, just like her. If indeed they ever got the itch to kiss her, it would probably be a half-second peck on the tip of her nose. Then, after that highly erotic interlude, they'd get back to their books. "These feelings, Miss Worth—you said they're sort of like hunger pangs. What is it you think you're hungry for?"

Theodosia lay down upon her own bedroll and watched the stars glimmer between the swaying branches of the trees. "If I knew what it was I wanted, I would find the means with which to obtain it, Mr. Montana."

He could no longer keep himself from smiling. God, the woman was too innocent to believe!

He decided to put her out of her misery. "You want *me*, Miss Worth."

When she turned her head to look at him, she saw him smiling. His grin was lopsided—only the left side of his mouth turned upwards. It reminded her of the way a little boy smiled when he was up to mischief.

Only Roman Montana wasn't a boy. He was a full-grown man with a smile so charming that it caused those warm flutters to race through her again. "I want you?"

Roman tossed the twig into the nearby shadows. "Me. You have ever since first laying eyes on me. After I caught your bird this afternoon, didn't you compliment me on the size of my vast meatus? Now, if you weren't interested, why would you study the size of my—"

"Vastus medialis, vastus intermedius, vastus lateralis, and sartorius. Those are the names of various muscles in the human thigh."

Her explanation surprised him into a long moment of silence. *Thigh muscles?* "I knew that."

"What are you trying to tell me, Mr. Montana?"

Renewed smugness replaced his chagrin. "You want me the way a woman wants a man, Miss

Worth." At her look of puzzlement, he elaborated. "The hot tickle you're talking about is desire."

"Representative toward what specific thing?"

"What?"

"What sort of desire are you saying I have?"

"How many kinds of desire are there?"

"Desire is an impulse toward something that will gain enjoyment and or satisfaction. One desires water when one is thirsty. Upon drinking the water, one's thirst is satisfied. Therefore, desire, in itself, does not indicate one specific—"

"All right, dammit! What you feel is *sexual* desire. Got that? *Sexual* desire, Miss Worth!"

Theodosia deliberated. "And just how is it that you are so certain of that? You are a man and cannot know about the feelings a woman—"

"I know."

The authority in his deep voice convinced her that he did indeed know. "And do you feel the same desire toward me, Mr. Montana?"

Her boldness intrigued him. He raked his gaze over her, aggravated again that her flannel nightgown prevented him from seeing anything. Still, he remembered her lush breasts, tiny waist, and rounded hips. A man didn't forget a body like the one she had. "Yes."

His affirmation stunned her. Could it really be possible that Roman desired her in a sexual way? Unfamiliar with the prospect, it took her a moment to grasp her surging emotions and tuck them away. "If what you say is true, we must endeavor to maintain firm control over our feelings. A sexual union between us might very well lead to conception, and you are not at all the sort of man who could be considered a candidate to father the child."

"Candidate? What—"

"Speaking of the child . . ." She turned to her side to face him. "What can you tell me about Dr. Wallaby? I know of him through his letters and reputation, but I am extraordinarily interested in the aspect of his basic character. Is he given to laughter? What does he talk about when not discussing his research?"

Roman watched her lips move but paid little attention to what she was saying. What was this child and candidate stuff the woman was talking about?

"Mr. Montana?"

"What? Oh, Dr. Wallaby." He struggled to remember the questions she'd asked. "I've never seen him laugh. Never even seen him smile. He hardly talks. He's either got his nose in a book or his eye stuck to his microscope."

"How did you come to meet him, and what exactly is it you do for him?"

Roman watched a few moths flutter around the crackling fire flames. "I had business in Templeton and saw an ad in the newspaper about a house that needed repairs. I took the job, and at about the time I'd finished, Dr. Wallaby arrived and rented the house from the man who owns it. He asked me to stay on and chop his firewood, make sure he had fresh meat on his table, and build a few bookcases for him. Now, what is this about a candidate to father a—"

"You sound as though you're leaving Dr. Wallaby. Are you?"

Apparently she wasn't going to tell him anything more about the child and possible father, he realized. "The salary he paid was steady, but it wasn't a lot. It's time for me to move on to better jobs, better money."

"What sort of work do you do?"

Accustomed to keeping to himself from a very early age, he felt ill at ease with her rapid-fire queries. "Why all the questions, Miss Worth?"

She arched her brow at him. "Why the hesitation to answer them?"

"Are you doing that psychology thing on me again?"

She laughed.

Her laughter danced through the woods, Roman thought. As if someone were playing it on a musical instrument.

He relented. "I've built homes and barns and even a church up near Yost Creek. I've cleared forest for farmland, then plowed and planted. I've dug wells and driven cattle. And there's nothing I can't do with a horse. I work with my hands, Miss Worth," he explained, his gaze penetrating hers. "With muscle and sweat, and sometimes, if the situation is a dangerous one, with blood."

His description of the work he did conjured up vivid images in her mind. She pictured him chopping down a large tree. Plowing fields. Building, and training horses. He labored beneath the hot sun and wore nothing but his pants and boots. Sweat glistened on his well-muscled back, shoulders, and chest, and his long black hair swayed sensuously with each of his movements.

She imagined him with his guns, too, those heavy revolvers he wore as casually as he wore his hat. His long dark fingers were wrapped around the butts. He held them steady; they looked so right in his hands.

He'd said blood was sometimes a part of his work, which meant he knew how to use those lethal weapons. She envisioned him facing danger, but it didn't bother him because he was more dangerous than the peril he confronted.

No other man she knew had ever created and held fast the fascination she felt now. Only a man like Roman could. A man who worked with his hands, sweat, muscle, and guns.

Her heart beat so forcefully, she could hear it hammering in her ears. "It's happening again, Mr. Montana."

One look at her flushed cheeks told him what she meant. He grinned. "The hot tickle strikes again, huh? Do you think we should do something about it?"

His question deepened her desire. "Ignore it," she whispered.

His grin broadened. "It might not go away."

"It will if I think of something else," she decided aloud. "What are your plans for the future?" She watched as her query turned his amused expression into one of deep contemplation. "Mr. Montana?"

He never talked about his dreams. His stepmother had been only the first person to scoff. He'd learned long ago that the only person in the world who had faith in him was himself.

Theodosia saw his hesitation. "Is there something wrong with your plans for the future?"

He slid his gaze over her face. "There's nothing wrong with them."

"I see. Well, I'm sorry you aren't happy about them. That you aren't proud of them."

How dare she think that! he fumed. "I'm pretty

damned thrilled with them, woman! You would be too if you'd worked for them as hard and long as I have!"

She feigned a hurt look. "Mr. Montana, are you saying I don't understand how it feels to work for something I desire to have?"

He sat up, brought his knees to his chest, and laid his arms across them. "What have you ever had to work for? Some good grades on your schoolwork, maybe? How would you like to work for twenty-five thousand acres of prime grassland? Do you even know the price of that much land? It's costing me over two thousand dollars, Miss Worth, and I'm only five hundred dollars away from owning it. I've been working for ten years to earn that much money, and if I have to, I'll work ten more to get the rest!"

"Is it your intention to grow corn?" She knew full well he would not be growing corn. He was too impatient to tend to plants, but she suspected her question would lead him to reveal more of what she knew he was trying to conceal. "You could grow quite a lot of corn on twenty-five thousand acres."

"*Corn?*" he shouted. "The only use for corn I'll have is for feed! I don't plan on being some squatting farmer, for God's sake! I'm going to raise horses!"

Theodosia's eyes widened with pleasure. "Horses! Why, my father happened to—"

"Yes, horses, Miss Worth. Got that? *Horses.* On the finest prairie you've ever set eyes on. The grass grows waist-high there. When the wind blows across it, it looks like a green sea. And the spring-fed streams and creeks flow with the clearest, sweetest water you've ever tasted."

She watched his horse paw the ground nearby. Moonlight coated the stallion's gray coat with shining silver, and Theodosia thought him a beautiful sight to behold. "You've a magnificent mount, Mr. Montana. How do you call him?"

"His name's Secret."

"He is your pride and your joy, isn't he?"

So she wouldn't realize just how precious Secret was to him, Roman gave his horse a disinterested glance. "He's just a horse."

Theodosia disagreed. The stallion was not just a horse. There was something unusual about him, something very special, but she couldn't understand what it was.

She looked at Roman again. "Why must you buy the land, Mr. Montana? I've heard that many men simply work land that is vacant. They make quite a good living without having to purchase the land."

He sneered. "And what's going to happen to those men if the owners decide to use the land, Miss Worth? They'll be run off, that's what. I've made sure every blade of grass on the land I want will really belong to me. It took me a while, but I found Señor Alvaro Madrigal, the man who holds the original Spanish land grant. He lives in Templeton, and when I asked him about the land, he was more than willing to sell it. He has no family to leave it to, and no plans to return to it. Every so often, when I have a fair amount of money, I go give it to him. That's what I was doing in Templeton when I met Dr. Wallaby. Once Señor Madrigal signs the warranty over to me, no one is ever going to take the land away from me."

She knew by the way he spoke that his horse

ranch was his passion, as going to Brazil was hers. "Do you plan to raise a family as well as horses?"

"No," came his swift and adamant reply. God, the very idea brought back the desperation and frustration he'd been dealing with for thirteen long years. There was no way in hell he'd go through it again.

He'd been a fool to go through it the first time.

"You don't want a family," Theodosia deliberated out loud. "Why?"

"Weren't we talking about Dr. Wallaby?" he flared.

Evasion, she mused. A sure sign that something about family was highly disturbing to him. "I'm sorry if talking about your future upsets you."

"My future doesn't upset me at all, Miss Worth. *You* do. Can we just have a normal conversation without you picking apart every damned word I say?"

"Very well. Dr. Wallaby is not a wealthy man, and that is why he is unable to give you a higher salary. Indeed, his financial straits are the reason for his being in Texas. He is awaiting funds from his benefactors in New England. Once he receives them, he will return to Brazil. And if he finds me suitable to be his assistant, I shall be traveling there with him. Are you familiar with Coleoptera?"

He found it hard to keep up with her and took a moment to ponder all the things she'd just told him. "Cleopatra? Some ancient queen, that one who killed herself by letting a snake bite her. Hell of a way to go."

Theodosia stared at him for a moment. "I didn't say Cleopatra, Mr. Montana. I said Coleoptera. That is an order of insects having four wings, of which the outer pair are modified into stiff elytra that protect the inner pair when at rest."

He barely understood a word she said. "We don't have those kinds of bugs in Texas," he snapped.

"Why, certainly you have beetles."

"Beetles? Why the hell didn't you just *say* beetles?"

"Do you know what a Pindamonhangaba beetle is?"

"Pinda—I can't even *say* it."

She clicked her tongue. *"Pronounce* is a better word choice than *say*. You cannot *pronounce* it. A Pindamonhangaba is a beetle that lives along the banks of the Pindamonhangaba River of Brazil. Dr. Wallaby's extensive studies of the beetle indicate that its saliva may contain a chemical that will cure alopecia."

"Alopecia?" He wondered what sort of dreaded disease alopecia was.

"Alopecia is baldness," Theodosia explained, "and Dr. Wallaby has honored me with his willingness to interview me for the position as his research assistant."

Roman frowned. "You're going all the way to Brazil with some old man just to study beetle spit?"

Theodosia licked her finger, then rubbed it over the spot of dust she saw on the top of her hand. "Would you have the same attitude toward Dr. Wallaby's research if you were bald? I think not. Most of the funding that Dr. Wallaby requires for his studies is given to him by bald sponsors."

Beetle spit, Roman mused. If he'd heard of anything stranger, he couldn't remember what it was. Imagine spending good money on something so stupid.

Shaking his head, he watched John the Baptist stick his beak into his water container.

The parrot flung the water every which way. "Dr. Wallaby, it is imperative that I conceive a child," he screeched. "It would please me enormously if you would consent to be his or her sire."

At the bird's statements, Roman sat up straight and stared at Theodosia. "He said—"

"I heard him."

"Who's he imitating?"

Patting her lips with the tips of her fingers, Theodosia yawned. "Me. I've been practicing those very words ever since I left the Boston depot."

Roman opened his mouth to speak again, but for a long moment words failed him. "You—are you *marrying* that skinny old scientist?"

"Marrying him?" She adjusted her pillow and lay back down on her sleeping mat. "Don't be ridiculous, Mr. Montana. I won't marry him or anyone else. I only want to bear Dr. Wallaby's child."

Roman felt like smacking his ears; surely he hadn't heard her correctly. "You don't even know the man, and you're going to sleep with him?"

Her eyes watering with weariness, she yawned again. "I am not going to *sleep* with him. I only plan to have coitus with him."

"Coitus," Roman muttered absently, completely astounded by Theodosia's plans.

Theodosia closed her eyes; exhaustion seeped through her limbs, and she felt herself drifting along the edges of slumber. "Coitus," she murmured sleepily, "is the physical union of male and female genitalia accompanied by rhythmic movements usually leading to the ejaculation of semen from the penis into the female reproductive tract."

Roman had bedded quite a few women in his lifetime, but he'd never thought of lovemaking the way Theodosia did. God, the way she described it, she made it sound like something two well-oiled machines might do when no one was looking.

He doubted seriously that Dr. Eugene Wallaby even had enough oil left in him to participate!

Roman smiled broadly, then remembered the reasons for Theodosia's plans. "Why do you want to have the professor's kid? Miss Worth?"

He saw she was fast asleep. Still grinning, he placed his Colts near his mat, lay back down, and tried to relax. But mental pictures of Theodosia, her scholarly soon-to-be-lover, and the night of scientific coupling the two of them would share held sleep at bay. He could no longer contain his mirth.

Wild, silent laughter kept him awake nearly all night long.

Chapter 4

After four hours of traveling over rolling hills and brush-strewn fields, Roman stopped to water the horses at a small creek that rippled a curving path through a shallow valley. Black willow, swamp ash, and mistletoe-drenched hackberry trees grew nearby, providing shade—and a possible place to hide.

He dismounted. Gone from his mind were all traces of the amusement that had kept him from sleeping last night. The feeling of impending danger had struck him as soon as the first shy rays of dawn had whispered through the woods, and it had nagged at him all day. "You've got fifteen minutes to rest, Miss Worth. Make the most of it, because we aren't stopping again until we've crossed the Colorado."

She climbed out of the buckboard, her feet sinking into luxurious, emerald-green grass that rose nearly to her knees. "Must you be so caustic, Mr. Montana? You have been snapping at me ever since you awakened me at dawn."

Placing one hand on the wagon for support, she removed her shoes and stockings. "Also, I do not appreciate the fact that you have been riding everywhere except *with* me. You've ridden ahead. Behind. All around in circles. Why, several times I lost sight of you completely. I could have wandered off, and you never would have realized it."

Still trying to forestall the dreaded possibility of female tears, he refused to tell her he'd been searching for signs of the three outlaws. "You wouldn't have gotten lost. All I would have had to do was follow the strains of 'Dixie.' Doesn't that pesky parrot of yours know any other song? He's been singing it nonstop for four damned hours. Why's a Yankee bird singing the Confederate anthem, anyway?"

Theodosia stooped to pick a bluebonnet, ruffled the soft petals over her fingers, then set the flower atop John the Baptist's cage, which remained on the wagon seat. " 'Dixie' may be associated with the states below the Mason-Dixon line, but the song was written by a northerner by the name of Daniel Decatur Emmett. Indeed, it was first sung in a minstrel show in New York."

"Well thank you very much for setting me straight, Miss Worth." He glared at her, trying to decide how big her brain was. Surely if it were removed from her head, it would fill a barrel. Maybe even a horse trough.

He wondered what it felt like to be as smart as she was, to know so many, many things. The extent of his own education had been four years in a country schoolhouse in north-central Texas, with a teacher whose qualifications allowed her to teach elementary reading and writing and only the fundamental basics of arithmetic.

He'd never had much time for formal learning.

There were too many chores, too many demands to fulfill, too many . . .

Too many whining women wanting too many things.

Still, he was happy with his own amount of intelligence. His knowledge served him well, and he'd never found a need to learn anything more than what he already knew.

"How delightful," Theodosia murmured, holding her hand up to her face. "A small, hemispherical member of the Coccinellidae family has alighted upon my wrist!"

He looked at the ladybug on her arm. Of course, it couldn't be a plain old ladybug to her. It had to be something scientific. "Is there anything you don't know, Miss Worth?"

With a flick of her wrist she set the ladybug free. "I do not know the impetus behind your surly disposition." She unfastened several buttons at the top of her gown, then waded into the shallow stream. Smooth stones massaged the bottoms of her feet, and cool water bubbled around her ankles. Bending, she cupped a handful of water and smoothed it onto her neck and throat. "The very least you can do is satisfy my curiosity and tell me what I have done to deserve your wrath."

Vaguely, he heard her talking to him. His concentration, however, was centered elsewhere. She'd hiked her lemon-yellow skirts and lacy petticoat up to her thighs. He had a tantalizing view of her lush cleavage too.

He watched mesmerized as she splashed water onto her face and licked off a few droplets from her bottom lip. She moved her tongue slowly, as if savoring the taste.

It took more willpower than Roman realized he had to turn around and attend to the horses.

Resigning herself to the fact that Roman was not going to discuss his sullenness, Theodosia emerged from the creek, retrieved a small, leather-bound book from her belongings, and settled down on a brilliant mass of orange-red butterfly weed beneath a slender willow. Within minutes, she was so engrossed in her reading that she failed to realize she was commenting on the text aloud.

"Man must take measures to prevent woman from having to bear his weight," she paraphrased as she scanned the page. "Must also summon patience to prepare woman for entry. Pain will be lessened for her if man begins with long session of foreplay."

Roman turned his head toward her so quickly, a sharp pain ripped through his neck. What in God's name was she talking about?

"Man positions himself between woman's thighs and begins with gentle probing," she continued. "Woman may choose to wrap her legs around man's waist. Allows for deeper penetration."

Roman's mouth dropped open to a wide O.

Theodosia turned the page. "Hips may move in a circular or back and forth motion. Maximum contact made with woman's body. If contact broken, woman deprived of stimulation required to induce orgasmic pleasure. Said pleasure heightened by . . . Well, I never even imagined!"

"Imagined what?" Roman yelled, irritated that she'd stopped talking just short of the part about pleasure.

"Why are you shouting at me?" She closed the book and stood, her yellow skirts swishing across the orange flowers. "I was merely sitting here reading, and you have no cause whatsoever to bellow—"

"What the hell kind of book are you reading?"

"A sexual treatise entitled *The Sweet Art of Passion*."

He stared at her. Hard, and without blinking. "Sex treats?"

"A *sexual treatise*. A written exposition concerning the sexual activities of human beings. It was created centuries ago by a Tibetan scholar who, at the time, was considered a leading authority on the subject. Nine years ago, it was unearthed and translated into English. It has not been revealed to the general public but has been relatively contained within the academic world."

Roman moved his unblinking stare from her face to the cover of her book. There had been many times in his life when he wished he had the ability to see through solid objects, but never more so than now.

"I have no experience with such matters," Theodosia explained nonchalantly, watching the horses amble away from the creek and begin grazing. "Therefore, I thought it judicious to educate myself."

Roman began to feel warm, and not from the heat of the day. He glanced at the creamy flesh between her breasts, wishing she'd unfastened just one more button.

"Passion is said to be an art, Mr. Montana. From what I've read in this book, some men master it and others do not. The instructions in this treatise encompass everything from the first kiss to the gen-

tlest way to deflower a virgin to several highly unusual forms of attaining sexual gratification."

Roman wondered if dead Tibetan men knew
something live American men didn't. "Uh, about
these highly unusual forms. . . . What—"

"Of course, I will proceed with my plans in an
objective manner," she added. "The pleasure that
may result from sexual relations is unimportant to
me. But even so, I should familiarize myself with
proven, effective maneuvers. Don't you agree?"

"What? Uh . . ."

Theodosia caressed the book, pondering the child
she would soon bear. "I would like to conceive a
male baby for Upton and Lillian," she murmured.

Roman felt as if his brains had been taken from
his head, scrambled like an egg, then poured back
inside. He held up his hand in an appeal for her to
stop speaking. "Wait a minute. Upton—he's your
brother-in-law. And Lillian . . . she's your sister?"

"Yes."

"And the baby you make with Dr. Wallaby—
you're giving the kid to Upton and Lillian?"

"Yes." Thinking of how much she loved Lillian
and Upton, Theodosia smiled a faraway smile.
"They are unable to have a child of their own, and
Lillian refuses to adopt. As her sister, I am the only
person in the world able to give her a child close to
her own flesh and blood. She and I are practically
mirror images of each other, and Upton and Dr.
Wallaby appear as if they were closely related as
well. Therefore, the child I conceive with Dr. Wallaby will look very much like a child Upton and
Lillian created. Not to mention the fact that Upton
and Dr. Wallaby are both brilliant. The child will
most likely inherit a profound thirst for higher

knowledge. That, of course, is another reason why Dr. Wallaby is the perfect candidate to sire the child.''

She hugged her book to her breast, excited over her own plans. "I am deeply indebted to Lillian and Upton, Mr. Montana. This is the sole opportunity I have ever had to repay their kindness and generosity in full measure. Of course, they know nothing whatsoever about my plans. If they did, they would never allow me to go through with them. Therefore, I shall give birth to their child here in Texas, deliver the infant to them in Boston, and then set forth for Brazil to join Dr. Wallaby. That is, if he accepts me as his assistant.''

She glanced at her watch. "We should depart. The fifteen-minute rest has come to an end. Actually, we have been resting for exactly seventeen minutes and thirty-two seconds.''

Roman didn't speak for a very long while. He simply stared at her, trying to understand and accept her plans with the same casual attitude that she did.

He failed. Maybe it was the vast differences in their cultures, hers northern, his southern. Perhaps it was because he was a man and she was a woman. Or maybe it was because she was a genius and he was of ordinary intelligence.

Whatever it was, the thought of a woman deliberately sacrificing her virginity and nine months of her life to get a child she was going to give away was the damnedest thing he'd ever heard of.

And the fact that she was going to do all those highly unusual lovemaking maneuvers with Dr. Wallaby to *get* the baby was—

His lips quivered with the same wild laughter that had consumed him last night.

"What do you find so amusing, Mr. Montana?" Theodosia asked coolly.

He folded his arms across his chest. "I was picturing you and Dr. Wallaby making love. Or *having coitus*, as you so scientifically put it. You and the brilliant doctor will probably consult that sex-treat book before each and every move you make. 'Page fifty-two says we aren't doing this correctly,' you'll say. You'll hold up the book, and Dr. Wallaby will read the page through the three-inch-thick lenses in his glasses. 'How right you are,' he'll say. 'We must follow the instructions precisely.' "

Roman's smile grew. "You'll stop to analyze each sentence in the book, so a single kiss will take you six weeks to accomplish. Other stuff, like learning to touch each other, will require three or four years to get right, and by the time you understand love-making perfectly, Dr. Wallaby will be too shriveled to perform!"

She sniffed in disdain. "And how long would *you* need to understand the contents of this book, Mr. Montana?"

"I wouldn't bother with the book, Miss Worth."

She refused to surrender to the warm flow of passion his announcement brought. For heaven's sake, she was a highly educated woman! Surely with a bit more discipline, she could conquer the feelings Roman so effortlessly created. "Are you saying you know everything there is to know about coitus?"

He was tempted to say yes, but the gleam in her eyes gave him the vague feeling that she was preparing to use every smidgen of her intelligence to back him into a corner out of which there was no escape. Her weapon was her brain, and in this particular instance it was far more deadly than any firearm he could think of.

So he wouldn't do battle with her mind. He'd attack her emotions instead.

He joined her by the trees, and his eyes holding hers captive, he traced the curve of her cheekbone with his finger. "I'm saying I know how to *make love* to a woman, Miss Worth. I know when to touch a woman. Where. And how."

He heard her breath quicken, and he moved in for the kill. Slowly, he drew his finger past her cheek. Over her lips. Down her throat, and finally into the valley of her breasts. She'd unfastened just enough buttons to make the task easy.

His thumb folded against his palm, he slid four fingers beneath the low-cut edge of her lacy chemise, allowing only their tips to touch the puckered velvet of her nipple. "This," he whispered, "is one way to touch a woman."

Theodosia swayed and would have fallen if Roman had not quickly captured her waist. She tried stepping away from him, but she discovered that it was not his arm that kept her to him, but her own reluctance to be parted from him. "What possesses you to think you may caress me in such a way, Mr. Montana?"

He kept his fingers exactly where they were. "What possesses you not to stop me?" He flashed her a lopsided grin and finally withdrew his hand. "We've got a lot of ground to cover if we're going to make Templeton by tomorrow. As much as I like touching you and as much as you like me touching you, we've run out of time. I guess you'll have to learn about the—uh . . . the *sweet art of passion* on your own."

For the next three hours, while she was driving the wagon, Theodosia tried to concentrate on the songs of the meadowlarks that frolicked in the branches of the oak and buckthorn trees. But the songbirds' music could not hold her attention the way Roman did.

He liked touching her. He'd said so himself. She couldn't help imagining what it would be like to touch him in a similar fashion.

She stared at Roman's back. His massive shoulders. His long black hair and thick muscular legs. He sat tall and straight in the saddle. His hips moved. Forward. Backward. To the rhythm of his horse's gait.

Hips may move in a circular or back and forth motion.

The words she'd read in the sexual treatise came back to her. Still watching the easy sway of Roman's hips, she wondered if his movements were also those a man employed when engaging in sexual relations. Was that how Dr. Wallaby would move?

Somehow she didn't think so.

Standing between his stallion and Theodosia's horse and holding the steeds' bridles, Roman watched the choppy Colorado River slosh over the sides of the ferry. He realized the current flowed more swiftly now than it had when he'd crossed the river on his way to Oates' Junction.

"This ride is precarious at best," Theodosia stated, peering over the wooden side slats of the ferry.

When Roman turned to look at her, he noticed her face was as colorless as the brisk wind that sailed through her hair. Clutching the side of the buckboard with her right hand and holding her parrot's cage in her left, she acted as though she were heading for a raging waterfall aboard nothing but a slim hope for survival.

"Ain't nothin' to be skeered of, ma'am," one of the ferrymen told her. He slackened his grip on the rope pulley and smiled at her.

Theodosia saw he had no teeth. When he opened his mouth, it looked as if someone had painted a black hole on his face.

"Nothin' a'tall to fear," the other agreed. "My brother and me've been workin' this here ferry fer many a year, and we've only lost three passengers and a mule. The men was fightin', ya see, and fighted theirsefs right into the river. The mule, well, he staggered off on account o' he was drunk as all git out."

Roman noted the alarm in Theodosia's eyes. "You aren't fighting, Miss Worth, and you aren't drunk, so stop being afraid."

His command angered her, but his deep, rich voice aroused within her an emotion that had nothing to do with ire. "Fear stems from the feeling of having no control over a specific threat," she responded, her irritation rising as she felt her cheeks warm and color with what she knew now to be desire. "Most fears are *acquired*. Indeed, it is my understanding that infants are born with only two fears, that of loud noises and loss of physical support. As they grow older, they are conditioned to feel other fears, such as fear of the dark. I have not acquired a fear of water because I learned to swim at a very early age. Therefore I do not fear water."

Roman saw the ferrymen frown in confusion. "She's from Boston," he said, as if his statement explained everything.

"Oh," they said in unison, as if his statement explained everything.

"Admit it, Miss Worth," Roman said. "You're scared as hell."

"I am simply *anxious,*" she clarified, tightening her hold on the wagon.

"If you can swim, then you don't have any reason to be anxious, either," Roman fenced stubbornly. "The worst that can happen to you right now is falling in and getting wet. Then you can swim to shore while we watch."

No sooner were the words out of his mouth than the ferry dipped sharply.

And the next thing he saw was a shiny brass birdcage flying through the misty air.

"Well, I reckon we can add a bird to the list o' passengers we've lost," the toothless ferryman said. "What kind o' bird *was* that, ma'am?"

Theodosia didn't utter a sound, but one glimpse of her face told Roman that her so-called *anxiety* had become true gut-wrenching terror. Sighing with profound aggravation, he tossed his hat to one of the ferrymen and kicked off his boots. His gunbelt hit the deck with a loud thud, right before he dove over the side of the ferry.

The cold water sucked him under. When he broke through the surface, the cage bobbed right before his face.

Crazed with fear, John the Baptist stuck his beak between the bars and bit his rescuer's nose.

"Dammit!" Anger increasing his strength, Roman twisted toward shore, and holding the cage high and using his free arm to propel himself through the rushing water, he arrived at the bank only a few minutes after the ferry.

Theodosia met him as he staggered out of the river. Quickly, she retrieved the cage and held it level with her eyes. "John the Baptist," she whispered. "John—"

"That bastard of a bird is fine!" With the back of his hand, Roman swiped dripping water off his forehead. "He bit me!"

"Bit you?"

"Two bits," the toothless ferryman announced as he sauntered toward his passengers.

Theodosia frowned at him. "Two bits, sir? Surely you mean two *bites*."

"The bird bit my nose!" Roman blasted.

"Twice?" Theodosia asked.

"Once!"

She looked at the ferryman. "You said *two* bites, sir, but Mr. Montana has only been bitten once."

"*Bits!*" Roman yelled. "Two *bits*! For God's sake, woman, he wants twenty-five cents, which has nothing to do with the fact that your pain-in-the-ass parrot bit my—"

"Weren't my aim to git y'all s'riled," the ferryman interrupted. "Mighty sorry if that's what I done. All's I want is two bits, and I'll be on my way. Got more passengers waitin' on the other side, ya see. Jest rode up."

Roman cast a glance at the opposite side of the river and saw three mounted men. They might as well have introduced themselves, for he knew exactly who they were.

His actions blurred, he grabbed Theodosia's bag, pulled it open, and snatched out a solid gold coin. "This is a damned sight more than two bits," he told the ferryman. "Your ferry is about to become disabled, understand? It's sprung a leak. The pulley's weak. I don't care what the hell kind of problem you decide to give it, but it *won't* make it across the river."

The man glanced at the three riders on the opposite shore and gave a slow nod of comprehension. "It'll probably take me and my brother nigh on a whole hour to fix the ole girl. 'Course, fer another gold piece she could stay broke fer near 'bout all day."

"Give him another gold piece, Mr. Montana," Theodosia said. "If his ferry is incapacitated, then he must have sufficient funds with which to—"

"For another gold piece, he could buy ten new ones! And his ferry's not—God, never mind!" Roman grabbed Theodosia's arm and began to lead her toward the wagon, but he stopped suddenly when he saw the three men urging their mounts into the water on the other side of the river.

Dammit, they weren't going to wait for the ferry! He swung Theodosia into his arms, carried her and her parrot to her buckboard, and tossed her into the seat.

She hit it with such force that a dull pain streamed up her spine. "Mr. Montana! What—"

"Drive up the embankment, then turn left. The road will curve around a bunch of cedars, then continue on behind them. When you can't see the river because of the trees, get out of the wagon, go into the woods, and wait for me."

"What? But—"

He reached out and clapped his hand over her mouth. "For God's sake, *listen*! I want you to hit me, got that? As soon as you do, I'll act like I'm going to hit you back. When you see me make a fist, pick up the reins and go where I told you to."

"Hit you?" she asked, her voice muffled behind his hand. "But why?"

"Dammit, do as I say!"

The sinister glitter in his eyes blazed out at her like fire looking for something to burn. This was not the sarcastic rogue with the endearing lopsided grin, she realized.

This was the Roman Montana who wore danger the way other men wore clothes.

She understood then that something was terribly wrong.

Without the slightest inkling as to why, she slapped him full across the face.

Roman drew back his fist, relieved when Theodosia immediately urged her horse up the embankment and turned her wagon to the left. Out of the corner of his eye, he saw that the three men had stopped their horses in shallow water and were watching intently.

Once back into his boots, gunbelt, and hat, he mounted, reached the top of the embankment, and directed his stallion to the right. The instant the road curled around the thicket of cedar and he knew the three men could no longer see him, he sent Secret into a wild gallop behind the trees and soon spotted Theodosia's buckboard on the road ahead.

Quickly, he dismounted, led his horse into the cedar thicket, and found Theodosia standing in the cool shadows.

"Mr. Montana, please tell me what—"

"Stay here." He pressed Secret's reins into her hand. "I'll be back to get you as soon as—as soon as I can."

"But, Mr. Mon—"

He didn't stay to hear her protest, but raced out of the woods and into her wagon. Slapping the reins over the horse's back, he coaxed the steed into an open field, knowing the buckboard would leave a wide and unmistakable trail through the long, fresh grass and scrub brush.

The surefooted mustang galloped through the meadow, slowing only when Roman sent him head-on toward a dip in the terrain. "Easy, boy," Roman murmured, guiding the horse down the slope.

"Easy, boy," John the Baptist echoed. "Passion is said to be an art. Some men master it, and others do not."

The parrot's voice startled Roman. He glared at the bird. "One more word out of you, and I'll shoot your blasted head off."

Once at the bottom of the dip in the ground he checked his Colts and sprang out of the wagon. Careful to leave an obvious path of footsteps behind him, he made his way toward a tall tangle of scrub brush and hid behind it.

His wait ended a quarter of an hour later, when he heard the distant rumble of running horses. In only moments more, the three men eased their mounts down the slope.

Roman watched the outlaws dismount. One wore a black bandana around his neck, one wore a red one, and the third wore a brown one. They all wore a veritable arsenal of weapons.

"Here's her wagon," Brown Bandana said, his pistol drawn. "But where the hell's the girl?"

"Maybe she went to meet back up with the long-haired feller," Red Bandana ventured.

Black Bandana shook his head. "She slapped him near about all the way to the moon. Then she left him. The gold's as good as ours, as soon as we find her. And if my eyes ain't foolin' me, there's her trail right there." He pointed to the path of crushed grass that led to a patch of tall scrub brush, and laughed. "May as well come on out, little lady, and bring yer gold with ya!"

Roman's fingers tightened around the triggers of his guns while he watched them walk toward him. He didn't plan on killing them if he didn't have to, but he'd for damned sure see to it that they were slowed down for a while. *Come on*, he invited silently. *Closer. Just a little closer*.

"Mr. Montana!"

Roman stiffened. He couldn't see Theodosia, but her shout sliced into his ears like the stab of a sword. Dammit, what the hell was she doing?

"Mr. Montana!" Theodosia screamed again, battling to keep her seat on the runaway stallion as he galloped toward the shallow valley ahead. "I cannot stop!"

She closed her eyes and prepared herself for a terrible fall that never came. Directly at the edge of the slope, the stallion slowed from a full gallop to a standstill. Jolted but unharmed, Theodosia opened her eyes and saw her driverless wagon. Beside it stood three armed men staring up at her. She'd seen the men earlier, once at the river and again when they'd raced their mounts across the meadow.

But where on earth was Roman? "I don't suppose the three of you invidious beings know where my escort is, do you?" She slid off the stallion and placed her hands on her hips.

Red Bandana frowned. "What'd she call us?"

"Never mind," Brown Bandana replied. "She's ridin' that long-haired feller's horse."

"They must o' traded off," Black Bandana added. "That means . . ."

Realizing the woman's male companion had tricked them, all three men spun around at once.

They met the blaze of blue eyes and the gleam of black Colts.

Roman pulled both triggers.

He hit one man in the shoulder and another in the leg, the impact of the bullets knocking them off their feet. His next bullet slammed into the third outlaw's upper arm, but the man still managed to quickly climb the embankment toward Theodosia.

Theodosia was already on her way down the slope.

The outlaw grabbed her, and pressing his gun to her temple, he dragged her down the slope. He grinned when his two cohorts retrieved their own weapons and staggered to their feet. "Ya didn't really think ya could outshoot us, did ya, Longhair?"

Roman gave a slow, easy smile, but inwardly he cursed Theodosia with every profanity he knew. "You don't really think I'm going to let you hurt the girl, do you, Red Bandana?" he countered.

"Hurt *me*?" Theodosia asked, still locked within the confines of her captor's beefy arms. "Mr. Montana, allow me to render intelligible this situation. I have never seen these men before today. They cannot possibly bear any sort of hostility toward me and therefore mustn't possess any desire to cause me physical harm. It occurs to me now that these men were following *you,* so *you* are the one who—"

"But—but we thought we was follerin' *you,*" Black Bandana said, frowning. "It's what Longhair wanted us to think. He—lady, he was tryin' to keep ya safe by leadin' us away from ya. Don't take no genius to figger that out. You must be a mite slow-minded. Don't make no never mind, though. We ain't after yer smarts. We want yer gold. Oh, and we'll be takin' Longhair's horse too. A horse who can run like that's gotta be worth some money."

Theodosia lifted one tawny eyebrow. "Indeed. Well, you may not have my gold, nor may you have Mr. Montana's stallion. Mr. Montana, do something."

"Yeah, Mr. Montana," Brown Bandana said, and laughed. "Do somethin'."

What the hell was he supposed to do? Roman fumed. One move on his part might very well end Theodosia's life, and his own as well.

Possible solutions flashed through his mind, but a sudden movement in the wagon interrupted his concentration.

John the Baptist stuck his head between the bars of his cage, craning his neck to see what was happening.

Roman dismissed the bird and pondered the situation again. For lack of a better idea, he finally decided to resort to one of the oldest tricks known to man. "You might as well give up your guns," he suggested. "My partner is right behind you and won't think twice about shooting you in the backs."

The Bandana Brothers laughed. "Ya think we're

stupid, Montana?" Red Bandana asked. "Ya ain't got no partner."

John the Baptist, still craning his neck out of the cage, squawked shrilly. "One more word out of you, and I'll shoot your blasted head off!" he shouted.

The outlaws went rigid, then dropped their revolvers and lifted their hands high above their heads.

Theodosia brushed off her skirts and turned to glare at her parrot. "John the Baptist, where on earth did you hear such a crude expression? You—"

"For God's sake, get in the wagon, Miss Worth!" Before she could announce that his so-called partner was a parrot, Roman raced out from behind the scrub brush and kicked the thieves' guns well away. He then stripped them of their other weapons. "Get going!"

Theodosia looked up at him. "Mr. Montana, these men should be taken into custody and given a fair trial. We must take them to Templeton."

"Yeah, Montana," Black Bandana agreed. "We got a right to a fair trial. 'Sides that, we're wounded!"

Roman smiled a smile that hardened his eyes. Slowly, he pulled back the hammers of his Colts. "None of your injuries are serious, and you damned well know it. And as for a fair trial . . . all right. If you get across the field and back around the cedar thicket in less than five minutes, you're innocent and I'll let you go. Take longer than that, you're guilty, and you die."

John the Baptist cracked a sunflower seed. "For God's sake, *listen*! Dammit, do as I say!" Calmly, he ate the seed. "Mr. Montana, do somethin'."

Hands still raised high, the outlaws started for their horses.

"You walk," Roman declared. "Better yet, run."

Anger scoring their faces, they began to ascend the slope, Roman right behind them. Only when they'd reached the far side of the field and disappeared behind the woods that surrounded the river did he take Secret's reins and return to Theodosia. "You aren't hurt or anything, are you?"

Theodosia climbed into the wagon and took the reins. "Other than feeling overcome with consternation, I am quite well. And you?" She examined him with her eyes. "Are you all right, Mr. Montana?"

Her question gave him pause. No one had ever asked him such a thing before. It had never made much difference to anyone whether he was all right or not.

And dammit, it probably didn't matter much to her, either. She just needed him to be all right so he could continue escorting her to Templeton. "I'm fine."

He snarled the words at her, forcing her to wonder what she'd done to anger him so. "How did you know those men were—"

"They've been following you since you left Oates' Junction. I told you not to flash your gold around." Deftly, he tied two of the outlaws' horses to the back of the wagon. He would lead the third himself and sell all three in Templeton for a tidy sum.

"You knew they were following me, and you didn't tell me?"

For a moment, he watched two sparrows. They flew low, skimming very close to the ground. He listened. The noises he heard were louder than usual and sounded closer than they actually were. And he could smell the river and the cedar thicket as if he were standing near them.

He mounted, keeping tight hold of the reins of the third horse. "I don't deal with tears well, Miss Worth."

"But why would I have wept? I wouldn't have been afraid."

He smirked. "No? Well, let me tell you something. You might know a dozen foreign languages. You might know all that psychology stuff. You might be a walking dictionary of big words, and you might know the name of every blasted star in the damned sky. But you don't have the *ordinary* sense to be afraid of three armed outlaws following you."

His retort hurt. "I wouldn't have been afraid, Mr. Montana," she said softly, "because you are with me. If you believe I have failed to pay heed to your skills, then you are mistaken. My regard for you is very real, and I speak the truth when I say I feel safe with you."

He searched her face intently, finding her faith in him echoed in the depths of her whiskey eyes. She barely knew him, but she trusted him.

She was the first woman who ever had.

Something tender tried to come to him, but then a sudden thought erased it. "Well, if you've got so much confidence in me, why'd you think you had to come help me with the thieves? Didn't you think I could handle them by myself?"

"I did see them race into the field, but I thought little of it. As you told me to do, I continued to wait in the woods. After a while, I became quite tense, and I mounted your stallion. It was my intention to walk him through the forest, but in a matter of seconds he sprang into a full gallop and ran into the meadow. I am an accomplished horsewoman, but I have never ridden a steed like yours. He is as rugged as the mustang you had me purchase in Oates' Junction, but he possesses all the speed and grace of a Thoroughbred. What can you tell me about his bloodlines?"

"Nothing," he replied, not about to reveal the precious secret. And damn her for coming so close to guessing at it! "Let's go. We can cover at least five or six more miles before the rain starts."

"Rain?" Theodosia peered at the sky. "It is not going to rain. Those are cirrostratus clouds and indicate fair weather."

He urged Secret and the third horse up the slope. She certainly had lost her faith in him quickly, he mused. "It doesn't make any difference what kind of clouds you see, Miss Worth. It's going to rain."

She smiled indulgently. It was not going to rain, but further arguing over the matter was futile.

The stubborn man would just have to realize his error himself.

Theodosia stood beside the wagon, the rim of her bonnet drooping over her forehead, her hair plastered to the sides of her face, neck, and shoulders. Cold, pelting rain drenched her clothes, seeped into her shoes, and sent shivers coursing through her. Flashes of distant lightning forced her to close her eyes.

Lightning. For years she had tried to rid herself of her fear of it. She could not. The mere mention of it brought back the day she'd seen it kill her parents.

"Miss Worth?" Though dusk had settled over the

windswept land, there remained sufficient light for
Roman to see the expression on her face. It went
beyond apprehension.

Terror gripped her.

He didn't like seeing her afraid, and the fact that
he didn't confused him. Why should he care if she
was scared?

He didn't. It was just that—well, she might start
crying, he convinced himself.

He secured the horses to the branches of a blue-
wood tree that had fallen into the rocky ravine, and
ambled toward her, noticing she'd tossed several
burlap sacks over her parrot's cage. Calmly, he
placed the cage on the ground beneath the wagon
bed.

The bird taken care of, he tried to decide what he
was supposed to do with Theodosia. The only fears
he'd ever soothed before had belonged to horses.

Wondering if a calm attitude would be contagious, he leaned against the wagon, folded his arms
across his chest, and caught raindrops on his
tongue. "Have you ever done this, Miss Worth?"

She watched rain splash onto his outstretched
tongue, and shook her head.

He could hardly believe there was really a person
in the world who had never caught raindrops on
her tongue. "Try it," he said, grinning.

His lopsided smile failed to charm her out of her
fear. "I'm afraid."

"Of rain?" He saw that her eyes were wet. With
raindrops or with tears, he didn't know. An uneasy
feeling came over him. "Look, don't cry. You said
you felt safe with me. You said—"

"I am not crying, I am not afraid of rain, and
your guns cannot protect me from what I fear."

"But what—"

"Why did you have us travel so slowly when the rain started?" she demanded. "Why couldn't we have hurried to find shelter?"

Because he knew profound fear was behind her anger, he did not react to it. "Hurrying would have overheated the horses. Then we would have stopped, they'd have stood in the cold rain, and they'd have gotten a sudden chill that might have killed them. Miss Worth, what is it that you're afraid of? What—"

Before he could question her further, another crooked finger of lightning severed the dark shadows in the sky. In the next instant he nearly lost his footing as Theodosia threw herself at him.

He enfolded her in his arms and understood then that it was lightning that frightened her. She was right; his guns couldn't hold lightning at bay.

Keeping her next to him, he retrieved a thick blanket from the sack of supplies in the back of the buckboard, then forced her to the ground and beneath the shelter of the wagon.

They lay side by side. Her shudder shaking his arms, he covered her with the blanket and gathered her close.

"Hold me," she whispered.

"I am." He frowned when she began to squirm. It was almost as if she were trying to crawl inside him. He draped his left leg over her hip.

The heavy weight of his leg somehow comforted her. She buried her face in the warm, moist crook of his shoulder and caught the fragrance of sunshine clinging to his skin. The scent not only reassured her that the storm would end, it also aroused her senses. "I've—I've never been in a man's arms before."

"Yeah? And what scientific thing are you thinking about being in mine?"

His gentle teasing deepened the feeling of security that continued to steal over her. "I'm pondering your impressive pectoralis major, deltoideus, and biceps brachii."

"Don't tell me. Let me guess. You like my arm muscles."

"And chest muscles," she added with a smile. "Mr. Montana? About the rain—how did you know?"

He slipped his fingers beneath the wet strands of hair that were stuck to her face and slid them away. "The birds were flying close to the ground, Miss Worth. The sounds were sharper, and everything smelled stronger than usual. Three sure signs of rain."

His explanation busied her mind and freed it from all lingering thoughts of the storm. "Sluggish air. Heavy air. Yes, yes. That would cause the birds to fly low, just as it would intensify odors and noises. I've never considered that possibility but have only utilized the cloud formations to forecast the weather."

In that moment she felt deeper respect for him blossom inside her. She lifted her face to him and smiled. "You have taught me something I did not know, Mr. Montana. Thank you for sharing your wisdom with me."

He'd never considered reading rain signs to be wisdom. The knowledge hadn't come from a schoolbook; he'd just sort of picked it up somehow and had always thought of it as normal sense.

She had called it wisdom. And she'd expressed gratitude for having learned it from him.

Her appreciation tugged at the same odd yet tender emotions he'd felt earlier in the afternoon. They seemed to radiate from his chest, spreading slowly and warmly through him.

Like the effects of whiskey.

He stiffened. A man lost all sense, all control, when he had too much to drink, and that was exactly how he felt now. Like a man made senseless, not by liquor, but by a *woman*.

A beautiful whiskey-eyed woman who fully planned to get herself pregnant, give the baby away, and then sail off to Brazil to discover the miracle cure for baldness within the moist and mysterious depths of beetle mouths.

And he thought he felt something for a woman like that?

He smiled at his own foolishness. It was a damned good thing he'd be rid of Theodosia by tomorrow.

Her lunacy was obviously rubbing off on him.

Chapter 5

Seated upon a small stool in the front room of Dr. Wallaby's house, Theodosia looked at the long wooden table cluttered with glass slides, scraps of paper scribbled with notes, and big clear jars that housed live specimens of various insects. No less than six microscopes were scattered throughout the tiny room, and the tall bookcases that lined the walls were filled with leather-bound volumes. On one of the two whitewashed windowsills sat bundles of dried bluebonnets, a magnifying glass, a piece of petrified wood, and a small brown package with Roman's name on it.

Dr. Wallaby was out. Wondering where he was and when he would return, she glanced at the front door.

But it was Roman who walked through it, her big blue trunk balanced on his broad shoulder. As he had in Oates' Junction, he handled the chest seemingly without effort. Only the bulge of his muscles betrayed the fact that it was exceedingly heavy.

Memories of the night filtered through her mind. She and Roman had remained beneath the wagon, and she'd slept in his arms, warm and safe in spite of the storm. Upon awakening, her first sight had been of his piercing blue eyes. She'd wondered if he'd watched her all through the night. The possibility, for some reason, had given her a thrill she'd never before experienced.

"That's the last of it," Roman said after setting the trunk down in a corner with the rest of her belongings.

His deep rich voice set her every nerve to tingling. "There's a packet on the windowsill for you, Mr. Montana."

He retrieved and opened it. Quickly, he counted the money it contained, then stuffed it into his pocket and glanced at Theodosia.

Sunshine streamed in from the window behind her, painting her hair, cheeks, and the heart-shaped ruby brooch at her throat with soft, pretty light. Her small white hands were folded in her lap, and delicate white lace encircled her wrists. She wore pink, the same color as the little flowers that grew near fence posts. He noticed those flowers sometimes. He didn't know what they were called, but he knew Theodosia would.

The pink made her look very young, and very innocent. Well, hell, he thought, she *was* very young and innocent. Her genius didn't hide that.

He shifted uneasily. Her vulnerability, like some sort of halo, glowed all around her, and he wondered if she would be all right. She knew a lot of things, but she wasn't much good at taking care of herself. She'd probably be eaten by a crocodile the second she set foot in Brazil.

He thrust his fingers through his hair. Dammit, his time was his own now! The days, weeks, months, and years of taking care of women were over. And that was what Theodosia was too. Just some daft woman he'd happened to meet and would now leave.

There was no way in hell he'd play the fool again.

He threw back his shoulders. "I'll be going now, Miss Worth. Watch out for crocodiles in Brazil." He spun toward the door.

"Would you wait with me, Mr. Montana?" Her own question startled her, as did the odd emptiness she felt inside. Had it really been only three days ago that she'd looked forward to parting company from this stubborn and arrogant man? "Dr. Wallaby isn't here, and I—"

"He's probably out looking for bugs. The man spends so much time with the damned things that he'll probably turn into one before long. And we arrived way ahead of schedule. He wasn't expecting us until tonight."

"Still, I would appreciate it if you would wait with me. We could talk for a while. You pushed the horses so hard today that we had little opportunity to converse."

"I thought you were in a hurry to get here."

"I was, but I—"

"Well, here you are, and just as soon as the King of Beetle Spit gets back, the two of you can get to work on all the things you've been planning to do. While you're waiting, why don't you memorize your sex-treat book? *One* of you should be a master at the art of lovemaking, and I can promise you now that it won't be your human fossil of a lover."

He started for the door again but stopped once more when she called to him.

"Good-bye then, Mr. Montana. And thank you

ever so much for all you have done for me." She
smiled.

Her gracious smile looked like honey to Roman,
glistening, slow-spreading, and every bit as sweet.
It drew him toward her.

Dr. Wallaby would be the first man to make love
to her.

But years from now, when she remembered her
first real kiss, he vowed she would think of Roman
Montana.

The profoundly arousing fragrance of wild flowers, warmth, and woman bathed his senses when
he reached for her. His right hand caught her chin,
and leisurely, savoring every second, he slid his left
hand up her back and to the nape of her neck.
Thus, he kept her captive for his kiss.

A barely there smile touched his lips as he
brushed his mouth over hers, in a kiss as gentle as
the play of light in her eyes. Her sigh drifted over
his tongue as he coerced her to part her lips.

He lowered his left hand to the small of her back.
She was soft to the touch, and he realized she wore
no corset. Her tiny waistline was her own, a fact
that aroused Roman further.

He urged her closer. To him. To his heat.

To the desire that the scent, taste, and feel of her
had brought to life.

She tried to pull away but was stilled instantly
when he growled with displeasure and slanted his
mouth over hers, the motions of his tongue hard,
demanding, and possessive. With increasing pressure of his hand, he kept her hips cradled within
his. She fitted his body perfectly, as if a master
sculptor had designed her especially for him.

He moved against her, into her, wanting to brand

her with the hot, hard feel of himself. He would never see her again after this day, that he knew.

But when she arched sweetly into him, mindlessly surrendering to him, he knew she would not forget him.

He ended the sensual encounter as he had begun it: gently, gradually, until his lips no longer caressed hers and their bodies touched no more.

Flashing her a lopsided grin, he fingered the soft golden curl that tumbled over her breast, turned, and walked out the door.

Theodosia knew his kiss had been his farewell.

And she realized also that she was going to miss him.

Theodosia sat at the other side of the table, watching Dr. Wallaby read the last page of the thesis she'd prepared as part of the examination. Lamplight and moonbeams washed over their supper plates, her parrot's cage, a jar of fresh bluebonnets, and Dr. Wallaby's thin, angular face.

It was true, she thought, studying the scientist. He and Upton looked like brothers. The only difference was that Dr. Wallaby was older, and the lenses in his glasses magnified his eyes to such an extent that they resembled two blue saucers stuck side by side on his face.

She remembered other blue eyes. And long black hair, a lopsided grin, and unbelievable masses of muscle.

She recalled the rhythmic rock of a certain set of hips too. Back. And forth, easy, easy.

Squirming in her chair, she forced herself to concentrate on Dr. Wallaby and wondered when she would have the opportunity to broach the subject of his siring the child. Since his return to the house a few hours ago, the scientist had discussed nothing but his research.

And she had thought of nothing but Roman's parting kiss. It remained in her mind, so real, so vivid, that she could still feel the sensation of being held by a man who desired her.

Smothering the low moan that filled her throat, she pushed a bit of fresh pear into her parrot's cage.

He nibbled at it. "Dr. Wallaby," he squawked, pear mush edging his beak, "would you be willing to impreg—"

Quickly, Theodosia pinched his beak shut and gave the puzzled scientist a weak smile.

Dr. Wallaby finished reading the last page of her two-hundred-page proposition. "This is brilliant. You've an amazing understanding of Coleoptera, Miss Worth."

"Coleoptera," Theodosia murmured, remembering that Roman had misunderstood the name and told her what he knew about Cleopatra and the snake.

"Miss Worth?"

"Yes? Oh." What on earth was the matter with her? Here she was, with the man she'd been admiring for years, and all she could think about was Roman Montana, a man she'd known for all of three days!

"It is apparent to me that you have spent a remarkable amount of time studying my findings," Dr. Wallaby declared. "I've no doubt you will prove to be an excellent assistant to me in Brazil. The position is yours."

She gasped with excitement. "Thank you so

much, Dr. Wallaby! You've no idea what this means to me."

"You are most welcome. As you know, I plan to sail back to South America as soon as I receive further funding. I hope the money will arrive soon, but such things take time. In the meantime, if you would like to return to Boston and spend a bit of time with Upton and your sister Lillian, that would be perfectly fine."

Theodosia nodded. She would return to Boston all right, but not before she had the child in her arms. "Dr. Wallaby, there is a certain matter I would like to discuss with you. A sexual matter, actually, and I—"

"Ah, so you've heard, have you?" Dr. Wallaby smiled. "Well, I suppose the news was bound to spread sooner or later."

"News?"

He laid her thesis on the table and slid a bluebonnet from the jar. *"Lupinus subcarnosus,"* he murmured pensively, twirling the stem of the blossom between his fingers. "The bluebonnet arrived in this country in the mid-1840s, either with Russian immigrants who brought it with the intention of planting it, or by accident in a shipment of flax from Germany. Their manner of arrival, however, is irrelevant. What concerns me are the flowers themselves."

Theodosia glanced at the bluebonnet, unable to comprehend the scientist's sudden decision to discuss the flower.

"While the saliva of the rare Pindamonhangaba beetle might very well provide the cure for baldness," Dr. Wallaby continued, "the common bluebonnet shows great potential for supplying the remedy for impotence in the human male."

Theodosia frowned. "Impotence, Dr. Wallaby?"

He rose, and his bony hands clasped behind his back, the bluebonnet dangling from his fingers, he paced around the room for many long moments. Finally, he stopped beside Theodosia's chair and looked down at her. "I cannot express the excitement I feel toward my initial findings. Impotence is a malady that distresses a great many men. Because I understand personally the depth of said distress, I am determined to continue with my experiments. My dilemma, however, is that I am committed to my research in Brazil and have time for little else."

Theodosia peered up at him, recalling that Upton had said Dr. Wallaby had chosen to remain unwed for personal reasons. A vague sense of foreboding darkened the bright plans she'd laid. "How is it that you are able to personally comprehend such dismay?"

He smiled a sad smile. "Although I have devoted my life to research, there was a time many years ago when I desired a wife and children. I abandoned the desire, however, because I am unable to sire children. You see, Miss Worth, I suffer the unfortunate affliction of impotence."

The early morning sunshine poured over the weather-beaten wooden sign that said WILD WINDS. Nailed to one of the red mulberry trees that lined the road, it pointed straight ahead.

Theodosia let go of the reins for a moment, retied the ribbons on her pink bonnet, and gave a quick pat to the smooth chignon at the nape of her neck.

"Wild Winds surely has its share of men, John the
Baptist. One of them might very well be qualified to
replace Dr. Wallaby. Oh, poor, poor Dr. Wallaby."

A tinge of guilt caused her to lower her head and
stare at her lap. The dear man had believed every
lie she'd told him this morning and thought it a
wonderful idea for her to study the speech habits of
the South while he waited for his research funding
to arrive. He'd been especially pleased when she
told him she'd hired Roman to escort her to the
various towns in which she would conduct her
studies. Why, Dr. Wallaby had even agreed to wait
for her in Brazil rather than Templeton if she didn't
return in time to sail with him.

Having dealt with Dr. Wallaby, she'd then set
about writing to Upton and Lillian, telling them the
same lies she'd told the scientist. Dr. Wallaby had
graciously included a letter of his own to her sister
and brother-in-law, informing them that Roman
Montana was highly capable of taking care of her
while she traveled and that they need not worry.

Theodosia sighed. "Ordinarily I am not given to
such prevarication," she murmured to her parrot.
"But my situation demands a few falsities, John the
Baptist. And when all is said and done and I have
the child for Upton and Lillian, the untruths I have
told will have little significance."

The bird spat a stream of water. It sprayed over a
mass of bluebonnets that grew at the edge of the
road. "Impotence is a malady that distresses a
great many men. Awk!"

"Yes, it is distressing," Theodosia agreed, picking
up the reins again. "As is the fact that I must now
begin an intense search for a new candidate to sire
the child."

Soon she turned the buckboard onto the main street of Wild Winds, a town she'd chosen because it was the only one she'd heard of in this area. Roman had mentioned it, and she'd gotten directions from a store owner in Templeton.

Roman. She wondered where he was, what he was doing.

"Theodosia," she scolded herself, "you will concentrate on your own activities and cease dwelling on a man you will never see again." But even as she made the vow, she knew she could not keep it.

Roman Montana had given her her first sweet taste of desire. And although she would always remain ignorant of the fulfillment to be gotten from such passion, she'd keep the memory of his kiss and embrace alive forever. In times of solitude, she would ponder it and remember.

She scanned the dusty street and spotted a small library on the left. Its presence assured her that learned people dwelled in the town. Perhaps one of the educated men would fit the physical requirements she'd set for the father of the child. The possibility revived her sagging spirits.

She registered at the Wild Winds hotel and paid two male employees to see to her horse and wagon and carry her belongings to her room, which did not meet with her approval. A small room, it was filled with lots of dust and little furniture. Still, it was a place in which she could carry out her plans.

When the men were gone, she quickly changed into a blue-and-white-striped silk dress, donned her bonnet and gloves, and set forth for the town's newspaper office.

A cluster of bells jingled when she opened the door to the Wild Winds newspaper office.

"Can I hep ya, ma'am?" the man behind the scarred old counter offered. "Name's Hamm. Simon Hamm. New in town, ain'tcha?" With ink-stained fingers, he picked up a fried chicken leg from his plate of lunch and took a huge bite. Grease glossed his thin lips, and bits of golden crust dropped into his short white beard.

Theodosia wondered if the man had ever heard of a napkin. She placed her reticule on the counter and gave a stiff nod. "Yes, you *may* help me, Mr. Hamm."

He raised his pale eyebrows. "You from England?"

"Boston. Would you be good enough to print a hundred circulars for me?"

"Would I be good enough?" Mr. Hamm pointed his chicken leg at her. "Ma'am, I'm jest about as good as they come. Why, jest last week I stayed up till near 'bout three in the mornin' with Fudd Wilkins. Fudd's dog died, y'see, and Fudd? Well, Fudd couldn't stop cryin' fer nothin'. Ain't a purty sight, ma'am, seein' a grown man cry, but Fudd loved that ole mongrel more'n he loves his wife."

He paused a moment to take another bite of chicken. "*Was* a good dog, to tell ya the truth. Name was Fudd Junior. Weren't a dog in this county who could tree a 'coon like ole Fudd Junior. Fudd had 'coon stew ever' Thursday, and I mean to tell you, Fudd can cook up some *kind* o' 'coon stew. His wife don't never cook a'tall. Lazy s'what she is. Y'ain't travelin' alone, are ya, ma'am? Best be careful if you are, on account o' the Blanco y Negro Gang's on the loose again. Busted out o' jail the way I heared it tole, and some say only the power o' God can strike 'em dead."

Theodosia studied him, thinking that perhaps the lies she'd told to Dr. Wallaby and written to Lillian and Upton wouldn't be falsehoods at all. The man's long story reinforced her desire to understand the reasons behind such rambling.

But first things first. Quickly, she took a sheet of paper and a pencil from a box on the counter and jotted down the message for the fliers. "Here is the wording I would like on the circulars," she said, and slid the piece of paper toward him.

With each word Mr. Hamm read, his eyes grew bigger and his mouth opened wider. "You—I—this—ma'am, are you sure—"

"Quite. I will wait while you print them."

He read the wording once more. "Ma'am, this ain't none o' my business, but—"

"I am in a great hurry to post the circulars, sir." She slid two gold coins across the counter. "Please make haste."

He shook his head in resignation. "All right, ma'am, but I sure hope ya know what you're gittin' yoursef into."

In the dim hallway of the hotel, a dozen men stood outside the door of Theodosia's room. Clutched in their hands were the circulars they'd come to answer:

WANTED

A tall, dark-haired, blue-eyed, and extremely intelligent man to sire a child. Willing to pay $100 in gold for services. No marriage to woman demanded, and all fatherly obligations to

resulting child will be waived.
Men meeting requirements
please contact:
Miss Theodosia Worth
Wild Winds Hotel
Room Seven
Only the qualified need apply for interview.

"Miz Worth!" one of the men shouted, and knocked on the door. "You in there?"

The second Theodosia opened the door, the men's revolting odor turned her stomach. Several were short, some had blond hair, a few had green eyes, and one had a bulbous nose that was a direct contrast to Upton's long straight one.

She gave them a polite but reserved smile. "Thank you for responding to my advertisement, gentleman. I'm afraid, however, that none of you meet the requirements I have set. Good day."

A booted foot kept her from closing the door. "I'm yer man, lady," the owner of the foot announced. "When it comes to beddin' women, there ain't no requirement I cain't meet. Now, lemme in."

"You ain't her man!" another of the applicants argued. "I am!"

The other men voiced similar declarations, and before Theodosia had time to realize what was happening, a fistfight began in the corridor. She seized the opportunity to slam and bolt the door.

The men in the hall began to bang on it, shouting curses that colored Theodosia's cheeks. She managed to move the dresser in front of the door, but only when she heard the hotel manager and his two male assistants escort the men away did she feel a small measure of safety.

"I cannot comprehend why those men thought to answer my advertisement in the first place, John the Baptist."

The parrot blinked one black eye. "I would like to conceive a male baby for Upton and Lillian," he said, then blinked his other eye. "When it comes to beddin' women, there ain't no requirement I cain't meet."

"I specified quite clearly that I was seeking intelligent candidates," Theodosia continued. "And did you hear their grammar? And their behavior—why, if not for their brawl, I might have been—"

She shuddered to think what might have happened, but she knew precisely what she would do to prevent the possibility from ever arising again.

Another circular was in order, and she had not a second to waste in having it printed and posted.

As Roman walked into the Wild Winds general store, the scents of dried apples, stale cigar smoke, leather, and sour pickles drifted around him. A fat calico cat, curled up in a pool of sunshine on the wooden floor, licked its front paw while keeping a sharp eye on a cricket that chirped on the windowsill. Roman scratched the cat's ears, then ambled to the counter and waited for the shopkeeper to finish stacking cans of food on the sagging shelves.

"Roman Montana!" Arlo exclaimed as he turned from the shelves. "Ain't seen you 'round here in almost two months. Not since you rebuilded ole man Bodine's barn. Lord o' mercy, Ben Bodine's s'damned proud o' that barn that he's tuk to sleepin' in it. Where you been?"

Roman withdrew a silky gold ribbon from a basket that sat on the counter. Twisting it between his fingers, he thought about golden hair. The ribbon was soft; Theodosia's hair was softer.

He threw the ribbon back into the basket. "I've been around, working wherever there's work." He dug into his pocket and withdrew a thin roll of bills. "Put this in my account for me, will you, Arlo?"

Arlo took the money, counted it, and then made some quick calculations in his ledger. "Let's see. This money added up with what you've already got here . . . that's a grand total of forty-two dollars and eighty-six cents, Roman. Buildin' yourself a right nice little nest egg."

Nice wasn't enough, Roman mused, deep frustration coiling inside him. Not counting the money he lacked toward the purchase of the land, he still needed money for the horses. In his head, he tried to add up how much money he had all together. Besides the money he had here in Wild Winds, he also had money saved up in seven other towns.

But adding eight figures in his head at once proved too difficult. He'd add them later, when he had paper and pencil. If he had a fair sum, he'd collect all the money and travel back to Templeton to make another payment to Señor Madrigal.

"You workin' 'round here, Roman?" Arlo asked as he ran a dust rag over a jar of multicolored jawbreakers.

Roman leaned one slim hip against the counter. "Just finished a job for Oris Brown, but I'm looking for something else. Know of anything?"

Arlo scratched his neck. "Well, there's Ralph Onslow. You know Ralph. He's got that little boot shop down the street. Seems I heard he was lookin' for somebody to go to Teak's River and fetch him a new supply o' leather. Wadja do for Oris?''

"Broke a horse for him," Roman answered, tugging at his neckcloth. "The last time I was in town, he asked me about it. I got to his place late yesterday afternoon and started. He put me up for the night, and I finished working his horse this morning."

"That fast," Arlo murmured.

Roman shrugged. He'd never understood why it took some men so long to gentle a horse. As far as he was concerned, the only secret to it was winning the animal's trust. And it was a hell of a lot easier to win a horse's trust than a person's.

The thought brought to mind Theodosia and her faith in him. For one short moment, he allowed himself to wonder if she was all right.

Arlo waved his hands in front of Roman's eyes. "Roman? Did y'hear what I jest said? There's somethin' else you might want to do to earn a little cash," he repeated, and chuckled. "Go read the poster that's hangin' over that table o' fabrics."

Curious as to what it was about the circular that so amused Arlo, Roman sauntered across the store and glanced at the flier.

The name *Theodosia Worth* fairly jumped out at him. He pulled the paper off the wall and scanned the wording.

Shock nearly knocked him off his feet. He couldn't believe the woman would go this far!

And then amusement made him smile. The woman had gone this far because she didn't have a lick of common sense to tell her not to.

Apparently, Theodosia's passionate night with Dr. Wallaby had gone awry. Maybe the scientist's brain was the only thing he had that was still in working order. "Arlo, when did you post this?"

" 'Bout noon. That Worth woman come in here askin' if she could put it up. Ain't that somethin'? You ever heared o' any woman stupid enough to actually make up a want ad for a lover? When she first come in here, I thought she was real smart. Dressed real good, talked with one o' them London, England accents, and used a lot o' big words. But for all her fancy talk, she ain't got no sense. She—"

A loud burst of laughter outside the store cut him short. "Well, what in the world? Let's go see what's goin' on, Roman."

Outside, he and Roman saw a group of men standing on the boardwalk in front of the café. A few were pointing to a sheet of paper stuck to the window, and all were nearly doubled over with laughter.

"Arlo, come see what that crazy woman done this time!" one man called. "Simon Hamm over there at the newspaper office just posted this up for her!"

The second Arlo read the flier, his laughter joined that of the other men.

But no one laughed as hard as Roman. His shoulders shaking with mirth, he looked at the circular once more and read:

WANTED IMMEDIATELY
A bodyguard to protect young woman
from unscrupulous lechers. Willing
to pay $100 in gold every month until
services no longer needed. Contact:
Miss Theodosia Worth
Wild Winds Hotel

Room Seven
Would someone *please* apply?

He reread her first flier, which he still held. Only Theodosia Worth, an empty-headed genius, could have gotten herself into such a fix.

Still, he mused while rubbing his chin, her ridiculous predicament meant one hundred dollars in gold to the man she hired as her bodyguard.

He smiled.

His horse ranch had never seemed so close to being owned.

Theodosia felt far too anxious to eat the supper she'd ordered brought to her room. Wasn't anyone going to answer her second advertisement? Surely Mr. Hamm had posted the fliers by now.

A loud knock on the door laid to rest her worry. "Well, it is about time, isn't it, John the Baptist? I was beginning to think that there existed not a single man in this town who held the qualifications for a bodyguard."

She smoothed her peach silk skirts and opened the door. In the dim corridor, his guns gleaming faintly, stood a huge man. "Have you come to apply for the position, sir?"

"Yeah."

She stepped aside so he could enter. As soon as he did, she drew away from him and struggled with disgust. The man's teeth had rotted nearly into his tobacco-stained gums, grime filled the pockmarks on his cheeks, and his hair was so greasy, it looked as though he'd combed it with a block of butter.

But she did not need her bodyguard to be attractive or clean, she reminded herself. She only needed a big, well-armed man to protect her, and this man was both.

He grinned at her. "I'm yer man, lady."

She closed the door. "I shall be the judge of that, sir. Tell me, what experience have you had?"

His black eyes glittered as he stared at her bosom. "Experience? Well, I bedded my first wench when I was fourteen and ain't let up since. Hear tell I've got some sixteen kids spread all over Texas and Mexico, so ya can be sure and certain that I'll git yer belly blowed up real fast."

"What?" Theodosia belatedly realized that this man had come in answer to her first circular, not the second. "Sir, you do not possess the intellectual characteristics I specified. What's more, you do not have blue eyes. Please leave."

Still grinning, he headed for the bed and lowered himself onto it. It groaned beneath his massive weight. "Pretend they're blue."

"I will do no such thing. You are not qualified."

"Come here, little beauty, and I'll show ya how qualified I am." He stood and fumbled with the fastening at the top of his breeches. "Some girls I know call this my blue steel throbber, but there ain't been no girl willin' to pay a hunnerd dollars in gold to get her some of it."

Keeping her gaze centered on his face, Theodosia swallowed to control her rising apprehension. "Sir, if you do not leave immediately, I shall be forced to summon the authorities and have you incarcerated. Debauched men such as yourself belong behind bars, where they can do no further harm to society."

He laughed. "Only lawman we got is Deputy Pitts, and by noon he's plumb snockered. By this

time o' the evenin', he's passed out on the floor o'
the jailhouse. Now, s'posin' ya take off that dress?
Or maybe ya need a little hep?'' He lumbered
toward her.

She grabbed her gold-filled velvet bag from the
top of the dresser and swung hard, hitting him on
the side of his face.

She might as well have hit him with a sack of
whispers. Chuckling, he heaved her over his shoulder, carried her to the bed, and laid her down.

His beefy hands snatched at her skirts. She tried
to kick him; he pinned her legs down with his own,
grabbed at her breasts, and wet her neck with great
sucking kisses.

Her all-consuming terror tore a long and desperate scream from her throat. It exploded into her
ears and shot through her body, silenced only by
the deafening crash of the door as it splintered
from its hinges.

Roman burst inside.

Theodosia only had time to see the cold fury in
his ice-blue eyes before he ripped her assailant off
the bed. Mute with surprise and horror, she
watched the man spin and slam his fist into Roman's jaw.

Instantly, Roman sent him to the floor with a
powerful kick beneath the man's chin. He allowed
the man to stagger to his feet, then grabbed his arm
and twisted it until a sickening pop assured him
he'd broken it.

The man shrieked with pain as Roman dragged
him to the window and promptly pitched him
through the glass. He hit the ground below with a
dull thud.

Roman turned from the window, and with his

lower sleeve, he wiped blood off the corner of his mouth. His shoulders heaving with exertion, he withdrew a flier from inside his shirt and held it out for Theodosia to see. "I believe you're looking for a bodyguard, Miss Worth?"

Chapter 6

It was all Theodosia could do not to throw herself into Roman's arms. Never had she been so glad to see anyone, and she was honest enough with herself to admit that his rescue was only a part of her gladness.

She'd missed him.

That now-familiar warmth shimmered through her. With wide and hungry eyes, she stared at each powerful inch of him, from the crown of his long raven hair to the tips of his dusty black boots.

"Why try to hide it, Miss Worth?" Roman asked as he approached her. "We've already talked about that heated tickle of yours. I knew what it was then, and I know what it is now. So stop all that wiggling and tell me if I've got the job."

Realizing she was squirming on the bed, she stilled. "I was not wiggling."

"You were."

John the Baptist tossed water out of his cage. "I was not wiggling. Watch out for crocodiles in Brazil. You've an amazing understanding of Coleoptera, Miss Worth."

Ignoring her parrot, Theodosia tried to calm her

breathing, which continued to come in pants. "I cannot seem to inhale properly, Mr. Montana. Please open the window."

He glanced at the shattered window. "It's about as open as it can get." Turning back to her, he gave her a crooked grin. "Think if I kiss you again you'll feel better?"

His suggestion nearly stopped her heart. "No," she answered, her voice half squeak, half whisper. "And you should not have kissed me in Templeton, either."

"I like kissing beautiful women."

She looked down at her lap. At a complete loss as to how to respond, she began removing specks of nothing from her skirts.

Roman quickly noted the crimson blush on her cheeks and the rapid pulse in her neck. Her acute sensitivity to his compliment made him suspect that no one had ever commented on her beauty before today.

What was wrong with those Bostonian men she kept company with? He understood they were her intellectual peers, but was her brain *really* the only thing they appreciated about her? If so, they were all a bunch of brilliant idiots. "Miss Worth?"

The softness in his deep voice set her to quivering, and she knew if she failed to find her poise immediately, she would freely stop struggling for it. Taking a deep breath, she hid her trembling hands within the folds of her peach skirts and forced herself to attend to the matter at hand. "Indeed I *am* looking for a bodyguard, Mr. Montana. What, may I ask, detained you from applying for the position? Had you delayed your arrival one more moment, that—that *lascivious malfeasant* might have succeeded in violating me!"

Her accusations quickly reminded him of just how irritating she could be. "If the *lascivious malfeasant* is the same slobbering son of a bitch I just pitched through the window, he didn't violate you because I got here just before he did! Dammit, woman! Instead of thanking me, you're bawling me out for—"

"I am not admonishing you but simply questioning your reasoning for postponing—"

"*My* reasoning?" He jammed his fingers through his hair. "What about *yours*? If you hadn't passed out that first flier, this never would have happened! And for your information I just got into town. I only saw your bodyguard ad ten minutes ago!"

She stood. Her eyes were level with his throat. She raised them and her chin as well. "There was nothing whatsoever wrong with my first circular. The men who answered it did not possess the intelligence to understand that they were ill-suited for the position."

"And the woman who made it doesn't have the common sense to understand that an ad like that is going to attract men who don't give a damn about qualifications but care only about being paid in gold for something *they* usually have to pay to get!"

"If you truly believe me senseless, Mr. Montana, why are you applying for the position as my bodyguard?"

He thought about how he'd worried about her after having left her in Templeton. "I need the money," he mumbled.

"I beg your pardon?"

"I need the blasted money!"

His shout hit her forehead, vibrating upon her skin. "My goodness, when you shout like that, I can see your uvula."

More anger swayed through him. "Look, I don't have the slightest inkling about what a uvula is, and I don't give the slightest damn. You—"

"Your uvula is the fleshy lobe that hangs from the soft palate at the back of your mouth. When you shout, I can see it."

"Oh, of all the stupid—"

"Your lip is bleeding. I've some salve in my bag. Would you allow me to tend to your cut?"

Her query sliced through the years, when as a boy he'd tended to all his injuries himself.

The women had always been too busy with other things.

Without thinking, he cupped Theodosia's cheek and slid his thumb across the delicate skin beneath her eye.

"Mr. Montana?" she murmured, struck by the intensity of his gaze. "Is something the matter?"

"What? No." He yanked his hand down. What the hell *was* the matter with him? "Nothing is the matter, and I don't want you rubbing some sort of stinking grease all over my—"

"Very well, we shall allow your lip to bleed. It will most certainly swell, suppurate, and cause you a fair amount of pain. Lesions to the mouth are—"

"Never mind about the damned lesion on my damned lip, dammit! What about the—"

"The job is yours, Mr. Montana. As you know, the salary is one hundred dollars a month in gold. I shall be leaving Wild Winds early in the morning and would appreciate it if you would escort me to another town. I was sadly mistaken in my belief that there were intelligent men here. But the presence of the library induced me to—"

"That isn't a library, Miss Worth. Madame Sophie had the word painted on the window so she and her girls wouldn't be bothered by the fire-and-brimstone preacher who passed through town a few months back. It's a whorehouse."

She could tell by the twinkle in his clear blue eyes that he thoroughly enjoyed taunting her over her mistake. His amusement annoyed her, as did the fact that he knew about the bawdy house. "And how is it that you are so familiar with Madame Sophie and her . . . *girls*, Mr. Montana?"

He picked his hat up off the floor and tossed it to the bed.

Theodosia watched it land atop the pillow. The hat was black, the pillow was white. The hat was Roman's, the pillow was hers.

Her senses spun again.

Roman didn't miss the sensual play of emotions in her eyes as she looked at his hat. God, he thought. It sure didn't take much to get her going. "I know about Madame Sophie and her kind, Miss Worth, because unlike you, *I* didn't have the advantage of a chapter-by-chapter sex-treat book. Since I didn't, I had to learn by hands-on experience. It doesn't bother you that I've known a few painted ladies in my lifetime, does it?"

She marched to the cracked mirror that hung on the opposite wall and smoothed back her hair. "Why should it trouble me that you choose to while away your evening hours with those demimondaines?"

He joined her across the room. Stopping directly behind her, he placed his hands on her hips and his chin on top of her head. He might not ever be her lover, he mused, but he was sure going to enjoy making her wish he was. It was only fair. She drove him insane with her genius . . .

And he would retaliate by rendering her senseless with desire.

Keeping those ends in mind, he pulled her closer.

She tried to brace herself for the flood of heat his nearness caused, but she failed. Unaware that she was slowly licking her bottom lip, she stared at his midnight hair, which curtained the sides of her face and fell over her breasts. She could smell the sun in it, and leather, and the musky odor of hard work, and some other potent fragrance that she instinctively recognized as that of the very essence of masculinity.

Only after a long moment did she notice her tongue on her bottom lip. She almost bit it in her haste to get it back into her mouth.

Roman curled his arms around her waist and caught her startled gaze in the reflection of the mirror. "About my whiling away my evening hours, Miss Worth. Maybe *coitus* can be performed only at night, but *lovemaking* . . ."

He paused just long enough to give her a slow and easy smile. "Lovemaking feels good anytime. In fact, the best time is in the morning. Make love at night, then go to sleep, and you can't remember the pleasure because you're asleep. Make love in the morning, though, and you have the whole day to think about it."

She hadn't realized that couples had sexual relations during the day. For some odd reason, she'd always believed such activities were performed at night. "And is the pleasure truly memorable?"

He knew she'd asked the question in all innocence, but he simply couldn't resist using her sweet
curiosity to his best advantage. "We could make a
few memories for you right now." He slid his hand
up her torso, stopping it only when his fingers
touched the underside of her breast. "Later, you
could think about them and decide for yourself
whether they're worth remembering."

The warmth of his hand seeped into her breast
while his sensual intentions flowed through her
thoughts. She closed her eyes for a moment, marveling over the power of desire. How she longed to
experience the full measure of its strength!

But of course, she couldn't. With every shred of
effort she possessed, she raised her own hand to
keep his still. "I was merely wondering about the
pleasure. It is only natural that I would reflect upon
that which I do not comprehend. However, as I
told you once before, the pleasure doesn't matter."

"It matters, Miss Worth," Roman said huskily.
"It matters very much, and if the circumstances
were different, I would do everything I could to
help you realize that."

"The circumstances are what they are, and I
shan't forget that." She stepped out of his embrace
and turned to face him. "Please understand that I
cannot allow my physical attraction to you to defeat my purposes. I must concentrate all my efforts
on finding the perfect man to sire the child, Mr.
Montana."

"Yeah, yeah, yeah. That tall, dark-haired, blue-
eyed *genius* of a man. What happened with the perfect Dr. Wallaby? Wasn't *he* able to concentrate all
his efforts toward giving you that child? Or maybe
he got so excited over what he read in your sex-

treat book that he fainted before reaching chapter two?"

The amusement she saw dancing in his blue eyes prompted her to recall that he'd once doubted Dr. Wallaby's ability to perform the sexual act. She decided not to give him the pleasure of gloating. "Dr. Wallaby did not meet the requirements."

"Which ones didn't he meet? What—"

"I will discuss Dr. Wallaby no further, Mr. Montana," she snipped. "Now, if you will excuse me, I—"

John the Baptist's loud squawking cut her short. "Ain't got no tea, ma'am. Bugs got in it. Oh, poor, poor Dr. Wallaby."

Roman looked at the bird. " 'Poor, poor Dr. Wallaby'? Why did he say that?"

Theodosia had never yearned for her parrot's silence more so than now. "I'm sure I haven't the faintest idea."

"Liar." Roman crossed to the cage. "Talk to me, bird."

The parrot spat a stream of water at him. "Lovemaking feels good anytime. You don't really think I'm going to let you hurt the girl, do you, Red Bandana?"

Roman wiped water off his chin. "What else, bird?"

"Mr. Montana," Theodosia said as she joined him by the cage and prepared to cover it with a cloth, "he has heard nothing at all that would be of interest to you. And even if he had, he would not respond simply because you wanted him to. He does not communicate but only mimics."

Roman snatched the cloth from her hand. "Mimic something else, bird. Go on, mimic away."

For a moment, John the Baptist preened his tail feathers. "Go on, mimic away," he said, blinking his black eyes. "It doesn't bother you that I've known a few painted ladies in my lifetime, does it?"

"No, it doesn't bother me at all," Roman answered, and chuckled. "Every male in the world, even a feathered one, craves a little wenching now and then."

"Mr. Montana!" Theodosia exclaimed. "If you don't mind—"

"Mr. Montana!" John the Baptist repeated. "You see, Miss Worth, I suffer the unfortunate affliction of impotence."

"Aha!" Roman shouted, and threw back his head to let out a great burst of laughter. "I knew it! The old guy just doesn't have it in him! I tried to tell you, but you—"

"Very well, you were correct, Mr. Montana. There now. Does my admission please you?"

He watched the rise and fall of her bosom. Dr. Wallaby had not had the chance to hold those big, full breasts. Nor had the scientist slid his wrinkled hands over her shapely white calves.

Theodosia remained a virgin, innocent of any man's touch but his own.

And yes, for some reason he didn't bother to ponder, that pleased him very much.

He retrieved his hat from the bed and walked into the corridor. "We'll spend the night here in Wild Winds and head out for Kidder Pass in the morning. Get your things together. I'm going to get us another room."

"Don't you mean two rooms?"

He slid his hat on. For the life of him, he couldn't stop smiling. "No, I mean *one*. As your bodyguard, my job is to stick to you like your own shadow. And that, Miss Worth, means we will be sleeping in the same room night . . . after . . . night . . . after . . . night."

"And create a *scandal*? We aren't married, Mr. Montana."

He gaped at her. "It didn't bother you to advertise for a lover. You even offered to pay him. And now my staying in your room is scandalous?"

She began to gather her belongings. "I should not have to explain my objections to you. If you would deliberate upon them, you would realize the vast difference between my ad and your staying in my room."

To be fair, he did what she suggested and took exactly one and a half seconds to think. "Sorry, I can't seem to realize those vast differences. Guess you'll have to explain them to me."

She slipped her gloves into her bag and closed it. "I do not plan to *enjoy* the physical attentions I must receive from the man I choose to father the child. However, I already enjoy the attention I receive from you. That, of course, makes our staying together scandalous."

He could find no sense at all in her explanation, and for that reason he realized it made perfect sense to her. "We still need to stay in a room together. And I think you know I'm right."

She did know. Indeed, after what happened this afternoon, she was afraid to stay alone. "But you will sleep on a pallet on the floor. And you must promise me, Mr. Montana, that you will do nothing to arouse me."

Laughter rumbled in his chest. "And if I give you my word, how do you know I'll keep it?"

She looked directly into his sparkling blue eyes. "Because I trust you. If you say you will do something, you will do it. If you say you won't, you won't."

Her answer silenced him.

"Mr. Montana? Do you give me your word?"

He realized he had to give her some sort of reply. But since she trusted him, he wouldn't swear not to touch her. He had every intention of touching her.

Only after a long moment did he think of what his promise would be. "I give you my word, Miss Worth, that I won't throw my hat on your pillow ever again."

With that, he vanished down the hall.

Ten miles out of Wild Winds, Roman stopped beside a grove of majestic live oaks that, because of the long, thick Spanish moss that draped from their branches, resembled wizened men dressed in gray robes. Beneath the rustling trees, winecups, sleepy daisies, and patches of bluebells created a dazzling rainbow of burgundy, yellow, and blue.

"Oh, Mr. Montana, thank you ever so much!" Theodosia exclaimed as she stopped her wagon.

"For what?"

"How sensitive of you to reflect upon my fondness for wild flowers and choose this particular spot for our picnic."

He stared at the flowers so intently that they became a blur of color before his eyes. *Had* he picked this spot for her? Was it some sort of deep-down consideration toward her that had caused him to stop here?

Well, hell, he could like flowers too, couldn't he? Just because he'd never sought them out on pur-

pose before didn't mean he didn't like being near
them.

"Those are *Callirhoe digitata*, *Eustoma
grandiflorum*, and *Xanthisma texanum*," Theodosia
announced as she climbed out of the buckboard
and gazed at the thick mass of flowers. "I do believe I shall collect a few specimens to study when I
have a bit of spare time."

Her scientific jargon aggravated him further.
"You aren't the only person in the world who likes
flowers, you know," he told her, determined to set
her straight and himself as well. "And that's what
they are. *Flowers*. Ordinary, everyday red, yellow,
and blue *flowers*. And any fat, shiny, black bugs you
see crawling around here are *beetles*. And those
clouds up there are just puffy white *clouds*. And
before you analyze my mood, let me tell you that it
is not *roinous*, got that? It's sour. It's just a plain
old sour, rotten, bad mood."

She watched him dismount. After a moment of
contemplation, she thought of a few possible reasons for his sudden irritation. Instantly, she tried to
think of a way to lead him into telling her himself.
And as she thought, excitement slid through her.

There was very little she enjoyed more than delv-
ing into the heart of an enigma, which Roman
Montana certainly was.

And yet an enigma did not wholly describe what
he was to her. Beyond her intellectual interest in
him lay something else.

Something emotional.

"What are you thinking about?" Roman demanded.

Calmly, she peered up at the sky. "The clouds.
You're right. They are not cirrostratus. They are cu-

mulus and often appear around midday on a sunny day. They are much lower than cirrus clouds, but should they become bigger and rise higher, they could turn into storm clouds. I won't worry about a possible storm, though, because you will undoubtedly hear and smell one before the clouds give notice."

She removed John the Baptist from his cage. After slipping the glittery bird collar around the parrot's neck and attaching the leash to it, she faced Roman. "And as for your mood, I wouldn't describe it as ruinous at all. It is definitely jaculiferous."

"What the hell does that mean?"

"You may look for the definition in a dictionary."

"I'm not in the habit of carrying a dictionary around in my saddlebag, Miss Worth."

"More's the pity, Mr. Montana."

He stormed through the sea of wild flowers and stopped before her. "I don't need your pity."

"How fortunate, for I pity you not at all." She removed a large basket from the back of the wagon and walked John the Baptist through the flowers. "*Jaculiferous* describes something that possesses spines," she said, and set the basket beside the trunk of an oak. "Like a porcupine."

"I'm in a porcupine mood?"

She laughed softly. "I only meant that your mood is spiny. Prickly."

"Means the same thing," he muttered. "Sour, rotten, and bad." He grabbed a blanket out of the wagon and joined her by the tree.

She helped him spread the blanket over the bed of flowers. "You've torn your shirt."

He noticed a large rip in his sleeve and shrugged.

"I've never loved a man."

Her out-of-the-blue statement set his mind spinning.

"And since I have never loved a man, I have no idea what it's like to want to marry. Tell me what it's like."

"Tell you? How the hell would I know?"

She kept her features blank, giving no indication that his response had provided her with the exact information she needed. "I cannot help the fact that I am a woman, Mr. Montana."

"What?"

She knelt and began to lay out the food for the picnic. "I cannot change my sex, but if you like, we could discuss your untoward feelings for women. Perhaps we would then be able to determine the most appropriate way for you to overcome them. Surely you do not desire to spend your life disliking the entire female race."

"What the devil are you talking about?"

She began slicing the bread, cheese, and apples. "You were in a fine mood this morning. But when I mentioned the consideration you showed by picking this spot for me, you exhibited sudden defensiveness and attacked me verbally. I believe your outburst stems from the fact that you did indeed choose this spot for me. You obviously realized that, and your own thoughtfulness toward me angered you. Such a reaction might have stemmed from the loss of a beloved sweetheart and your consequent refusal to be vulnerable to an amorous form of love again. However, when I asked you to tell me about romantic love, you demonstrated genuine ignorance of the subject. Therefore, I feel it safe to presume that you have not loved and lost a sweetheart. Sit down and eat your lunch."

"You're doing that psychology stuff again," he bit out as he sat down beside her. "Well, I can tell you right now that—"

"Furthermore, you lied to me." She handed him a piece of bread.

"Lied? But—"

"From what I understand, there is little you cannot do. Had you stayed in Oates' Junction rather than following me, you would have found other work. However, you tried to make me believe that you followed me because of the money Dr. Wallaby would pay you. That was a lie. You came after me because you knew those gold thieves were planning to rob me and that they might very well have harmed me. Your worry over me more than likely bothered you immensely."

"I needed the money, and that's the end of it!"

She smiled sweetly into the dangerous glitter in his eyes. "You suffered a negative experience with a woman sometime in your past, and as we have just discussed, the woman was not your sweetheart. Said experience must have been truly painful because it has caused you to dislike *all* women. You allow yourself to indulge in sexual activities with them, but beyond that you want nothing to do with them. That is why your consideration toward me annoys you. Open your mouth."

So startled was he by what she told him, he didn't think twice before opening his mouth and accepting the slice of apple she put into it. "How do you—"

"Know? Why, you hinted at it the first night we spent together."

He didn't remember hinting at anything of the sort. "I did not—"

"Yes, Mr. Montana, you did." She ate a bit of bread and cheese and shared some apple with John the Baptist. "You said you did not want a family."

"What's that got to do with—"

"Your animosity toward women? Really, Mr. Montana, it's quite elementary."

"Nothing is ever elementary to you, Miss Worth! You don't know what *simple* is! Everything you do, say, and think has to be connected to some sort of academic junk that normal people don't know a damned thing about!"

Calmly, she waited for him to finish raving. "To have a family, you must have a wife. You are not fond of women, so you do not want a wife. Therefore, you do not plan to raise a family on your horse ranch. That is what you told me the night we spent in the woods. Would you care for some cheese?"

"What? No, I don't want any blasted cheese! I want you to stop—"

"My goodness, what a temper," she remarked, casually examining an apple seed. "From whom did you inherit that volatile constitution? Your father or your mother?"

"I wouldn't know, and that's the last question you're going to ask me!"

She laid her hand on his knee. "I'm sorry."

"You damned sure should be. Digging into a person's mind is—"

"No, Mr. Montana. You misunderstand. I am expressing sympathy over the deaths of your parents. They must have died when you were very young, or else you would have remembered if one of them had the same temper you do. Or perhaps you never knew them at all. Whatever the case, someone else raised you. And I don't think I am wrong in believing that that someone was a woman. Whoever she was, she was uncaring toward you."

Stunned into silence, Roman stared into her eyes, wishing he could see the astonishing brain behind them. He'd told her so little, and yet she'd discovered the truth.

But not all of it. There hadn't been *an* uncaring woman; there had been *three*. He didn't like remembering them. And what he liked even less was being *forced* to remember them.

The memories made him recall his own stupidity.

Theodosia watched him squeeze his piece of bread into a dough ball. "It wasn't my intention to make you angry," she said softly. "I only wanted to know more about—"

"Angry?" He pitched the bread ball into the woods. "Are you kidding? I'm having the time of my life! Doesn't everyone enjoy having their past guessed at, carved open, and discussed by people who don't care that it's none of their business? I know you're afraid of lightning, but have I tried to find out why? No, because it's none of my business. Personally, I think being afraid of lightning is stupid. I can see being nervous about it, but you fall completely apart! Still, it's none of my business, and besides that, Miss Worth, I don't really give a damn!"

She watched the fire of fury come into his eyes. But behind the flames there glowed another emotion.

Sorrow glimmered through his wrath. His buried grief unsettled her far more than she thought reasonable. How was it possible for her to feel such profound concern for a man like Roman Montana? Besides the fact that she'd known him for only days, he wasn't at all the sort of man she ever imagined herself caring for. Not that she'd planned on involving herself with any man at all, she amended. The Brazilian research was all that mattered to her. But if she *had* considered love and romance, surely she would have sought a man whose academic background equaled hers.

Disturbed by the intensity of her own emotions, she quickly gathered the remains of the lunch and packed them away. "I suppose our feelings are very similar, really," she announced in the most normal voice she could muster. "I have not found a reason to cease fearing lightning, and you have found none to alter your dislike toward women. It occurs to me now that I have no right to question your feelings when mine parallel them. Therefore, please nurture your loathing for women, just as I will undoubtedly maintain my dread of lightning."

She picked up the basket with one hand, her parrot with the other, and stood. "There is one point I shall add, though. My terror of lightning hurts no one but myself. However, your hostility toward women will be a source of great pain for any unsuspecting woman who might fall in love with you."

He rose from the ground and loomed above her. "Let me save you the task of tricking me into telling you what I think about your point. Women don't fall in love, Miss Worth. They fall in *want*. Now, there's some food for your hungry little analytical mind, isn't there?"

She met his blazing gaze straight on. "A veritable banquet."

He didn't miss the oh-so-slight tilt of her beautiful lips. No doubt she thought she would win their verbal sparring.

He vowed she wouldn't. "Eat hearty."

"I shall stuff myself until I cannot hold another bite." She crossed to the buckboard and deposited the basket in the wagon bed and her parrot on the seat. "And when I am hungry again, I assure you, Mr. Montana, I shall come back for more."

He picked the blanket off the ground and joined her by the buckboard. "The kitchen is closed."

"Ah, but the cook often forgets to lock the door."

He stepped nearer to her, close enough that her breasts touched his chest. "You'd be entering at your own risk. The cook needs fire to work. It's hot in there." Slowly, he raised his hands and curled them around her hips. "It might melt you."

Exquisite heat flashed through her.

The second he saw her flush, he set about showing her just how hot the fire really was.

His lips came down on hers hard. His tongue slid deeply into her mouth, then he withdrew it only to thrust it between her lips again and again and again. Each time he entered her mouth, he pulled her toward him. His hands kneading her bottom, his thighs pressing against hers, he circled his hips upon hers in a rhythm he knew her body would recognize and imitate.

Theodosia began to move. Against him. With him, to the cadence he'd set. She trembled. She rocked and wavered.

He felt her soften in his arms. His lips still molded to hers, he lifted her off the ground and gently sat her in the wagon. Drawing away from her, he smoothed the tips of his fingers across her forehead. "In this mind of yours are a thousand

things. Lessons you haven't forgotten. It's time you
learned another. Where there's heat, there's fire,
Miss Worth. Fire burns"—he slid his fingers to her
breast and traced the stiff circle of her nipple—
"and it melts."

Still shaking with unappeased desire, Theodosia
watched him mount and urge his stallion back to
the road. She longed desperately to call out a
crushing comeback that would end the encounter
in her favor.

But for the first time in her life, words failed her.

Roman Montana had beaten her soundly.

Chapter 7

Theodosia padded her sleeping pallet with every article of clothing she'd brought to Texas, but she could still feel the rocky ground beneath her. She'd never been given to cursing, but as annoyed as she felt now, several colorful epithets shot through her mind.

Across from the fire a few feet away, sitting upon his own pallet and leaning against a birch tree, Roman watched her struggle. "Something the matter, Miss Worth?" He laid down the sheet of paper he'd been studying and stuck his pencil behind his ear.

"Something the matter, Miss Worth?" John the Baptist repeated, then threw water every which way. "Where there's heat, there's fire, Miss Worth."

Theodosia squirmed away from a rock pressing into her hip, only to move herself into a cluster that jabbed at her side. "You chose this spot out of pure spite, Mr. Montana. We have passed a multitude of grassy fields, leaf-strewn woods, and flowered meadows, and yet you deliberately stopped here in this—this boulder-filled pit to spend the night."

"Boulder-filled?" Roman clicked his tongue. "That is a very poor choice of words, Miss Worth.

The rocks around here aren't any bigger than my fist. And this is not a pit. It's a dried-up creek bed."

"Nevertheless, you went out of your way to find the most unwelcoming site possible. And I assure you that I know why you did."

"There's no doubt in my mind that you do. Hell, you know almost everything *else* about me, don't you?" He picked up the paper again, upon which he'd written the amounts of the savings he had in the eight different towns.

"Not only do you remain piqued over the fact that I learned a bit about your past this afternoon, but you also seek to prove to me that you have no consideration toward me whatsoever," Theodosia continued, still shifting on her lumpy bed. "You knew I would have a wretched time trying to sleep on rocks—"

"Sleep in the wagon bed."

"It is too small, and you know it."

"Then get up and push the rocks away."

"I have already attempted the process of elapidation, to no avail."

Rubbing his chin, he stared at her. "Elapidation?"

"Elapidation is the clearing away of stones."

He almost laughed. The woman had a brainy word for the simplest of things!

"Beneath one layer of rocks is another," Theodosia said, "and then another, and then—"

"When this was a creek, it was called Bedrock Creek."

"How utterly appropriate." Completely frustrated, Theodosia sat up and swiped her hair out of her face. "And just how can it be that *you* are so comfortable?"

He picked up a handful of pebbles, and one by one, he flung them toward Theodosia. When he was finished, they lay in a neat pile in her lap. "Rocks don't bother me. I've slept on them before and will probably sleep on them again. Why do you keep wearing that thick nightgown, by the way? It must be ninety degrees out here. Aren't you hot?"

John the Baptist spat another stream of water. "Well, I bedded my first wench when I was fourteen," he said, "and I ain't let up since."

At her parrot's words, Theodosia rolled her eyes, then patted the velvet ribbons that closed the front of her flannel gown. "No doubt you would like me to sleep naked, Mr. Montana."

"No doubt at all, Miss Worth."

Roman Montana embodied the truest definition of *rake*, she thought while battling anger and desire. The moment an opportunity arrived for discussing or practicing anything having to do with sensuality, he seized it instantly. "I have never slept without a nightrail on, nor will I ever do so. And I would appreciate it if you would please refrain from mentioning intimate subjects such as my nightwear."

He considered her request for exactly a half a second before rejecting it. "You've never felt cool sheets next to your skin?"

"No."

"It feels good."

"Mr. Montana, I have enjoyed restful nights with my nightgown on for many, many years. I feel it safe to presume that I will continue to enjoy them."

He shook his head. "You'll have to be naked with the guy you pick to get you with child."

Unconsciously, she crossed her hands over her breasts. "I will not."

He scratched his chin. "Then how do you plan
to—"

"I will bare my lower half."

"The man's going to want to see and touch your
upper half, too."

"He will not see any part of me, and he will most
certainly not touch me. I shall be under the blankets, there will be no light in the room, and I shall
concentrate on unrelated matters during penetration and the spilling of his seed. The entire procedure will be over in only minutes. Besides, his
wants will not concern me in the least."

Roman smiled. She was in for a shock. No man
in the world, genius or not, was going to follow her
bedding rules. Not with the kind of breasts she had,
they weren't. And if the man had a shred of talent
between the blankets, she wouldn't be concentrat-
ing on unrelated matters, either. Nor would she
want the procedure to be over in only minutes.
"Excuse me for a minute, will you? I have to add
this."

He bent his leg at the knee, placed the paper on
his upper thigh, and pretended to jot down a few
numbers. He had no intention of doing the tire-
some arithmetic. Why should he? A genius sat
straight across from him.

Because she was mad at him, she wouldn't offer
to help. But he planned to prove to her that he
knew just as much about mind tricks as she did.
And when he was through, she'd be angrier, and
he'd have the answers to the arithmetic.

"I'm adding how much money I've got now," he
said, "and how much I'll have when I'm done paying what I owe and collecting what's owed to me.

But there are eight amounts, so I'm having to separate them to—"

"Well, if you think for one moment that I am going to assist you with the mathematics after you have made me sleep on these rocks, you are sadly mistaken." Lips tightly pursed, she took hold of the sides of her nightgown and shook the pebbles out of her lap.

"I didn't ask for your help, Miss Worth. Arithmetic happened to be my best subject in school." He scribbled a few doodles on his paper. "Let's see . . . twenty-two dollars and seventy-six cents plus forty-two dollars and eighty-six cents plus eleven dollars and nineteen cents equals . . . seventy-one dollars and eighty-nine cents."

"You are off by four dollars and ninety-two cents," Theodosia informed him, totally unable to resist correcting an error of any sort.

He looked up from the paper and saw moonlight and smugness shining in her eyes. The moonlight would remain, but he vowed that the glow of chagrin would soon replace the gleam of self-satisfaction. "*I* have the paper and pencil, Miss Worth. I also have the figures right in front of my eyes. Now, if you don't mind, stop interrupting and let me finish."

Suppressing a grin, he bent over his paper again. "Where was I? I already added three amounts, and they equaled seventy-one dollars and eighty-nine cents. All right . . . seventy-one dollars and eighty-nine cents plus thirty-one dollars and two cents plus six dollars and ninety-four cents equals . . . one hundred and twelve dollars and eighty-four cents."

"You added the first set of numbers wrong, Mr.

Montana. Your first sum should have been seventy-six dollars and eighty-one cents. That added to the other amounts you just mentioned comes to one hundred and fourteen dollars and seventy-seven cents."

He feigned deafness and a frown. "One hundred and twelve dollars and eighty-four cents plus seventy-one dollars and fifty-nine cents plus twelve dollars and thirty-six cents equals the grand total of . . . two hundred and one dollars and six cents."

Theodosia shook her head and sighed in exasperation. "You are giving yourself two dollars and thirty-four cents more than you have, Mr. Montana. The total of your savings come to one hundred ninety-eight dollars and seventy-two cents."

He scratched down a few more circles and lines. "Of course, I have to settle a tab of three dollars at the Kidder Pass saloon, and a man in Caudle Corner owes me thirty dollars for a job I did for him, and I need fifteen dollars' worth of supplies. Let's see . . . zero from six is six, zero from zero is zero . . . borrow from the ten to make eleven; three from eleven—"

"Your figuring is grossly incorrect, Mr. Montana."

He raised his head slowly. "Miss Worth, please. Can't you see I'm trying to concentrate?" He dug into his pocket, withdrew a fistful of bills and some change, and counted it. "I've got thirty-seven dollars and fifty-four cents on me, so that means . . ." He scratched down more nothings on his paper.

"You will have two hundred forty-eight dollars and twenty-six cents after you have paid and collected all owed to you, all you owe, and all you will owe after purchasing your supplies. And that includes your pocket money."

As fast as he could, he wrote down the sum she'd given him. "That's the exact number I came up with," he said, smiling. "See? I told you I didn't need your help."

She could tell by his crooked grin that he was lying through those perfect white teeth of his.

Her eyes widened when she realized he'd duped her. The arrogant rogue had beaten her again! "You —you—you—"

"Having trouble coming up with a good word choice?" He folded the paper and laid it aside. "Let me help you. I outwitted you? Fooled you? Deceived you?"

"You are—"

"A trickster? Hoodwinker? Scoundrel?"

"I would like nothing better than to—"

"Slap me? Pinch me? Kick me? Bite—"

"*Would* you please stop?"

He was thoroughly enjoying making her mind spin. She'd certainly spun his enough times. "Of course I'll stop. I don't have any reason to go on. I've gotten what I wanted. Why don't you get what you want?"

"What? What do I want?"

"I thought you wanted some sleep? You don't want it anymore?"

"I—"

"Or would you like a kiss first? Consider it my way of paying you back for giving me the answer to all this confounded arithmetic."

"No, I do not want a—"

"Liar."

"Liar," John the Baptist echoed. "No doubt you would like me to sleep naked, Mr. Montana."

Laughing, Roman leaned back to look at the night sky.

Theodosia watched moonbeams flicker through his dark hair, which flowed down the white trunk of the birch tree behind him. He'd unbuttoned his shirt; the wide V provided her with a tantalizing view of his rippled chest. Moonbeams danced on his smooth brown skin too.

"If you're finished staring at my chest, Miss Worth, look at that star." He pointed to the sky.

Theodosia quickly found the star he indicated.

"Wonder why it's so much brighter than the other ones?" Roman mused aloud. "Kind of reminds you of that song, doesn't it?"

"To what song do you refer, Mr. Montana?"

"Yeah, you know. That star song. It goes like . . . uh—I can't remember the tune, but the words are, 'Twinkle, twinkle little star, how I wonder what you are, up above the world so high, like a diamond in the sky.'"

She pondered the fact that his memory of the song was so vague. "Where did you learn the song?"

He thought for a moment. It must have been his father who'd sung it to him. No other person in his life would have done such a thing with him. "I've just always known it," he hedged.

"I see." There had obviously been at least one person in his childhood who had shown a bit of kindness toward him, Theodosia mused. Someone had taken the time to teach him a song. And whoever that person was, Roman hadn't had much time with him or her. Otherwise, his memories would be sharper.

Emotion pulled at her heart as she contemplated the sad and lonely childhood he must have had.

"Don't start it," Roman warned, noticing the look of deep concentration on her face. "Whatever it is you're trying to analyze about me, keep it to yourself."

She picked up a few of the pebbles he'd tossed to her and rolled them between her fingers. "Very well. What would you like to discuss instead?"

He sought a harmless subject. "We were talking about the star."

"No, we were talking about the song."

"All right, we were talking about the song. Do you know the tune to it?"

She brushed away a leaf that floated into her hair. "I have never heard the poem sung, but I have read it. It is a child's nursery rhyme written by Ann and Jane Taylor in 1806, and I must say that I find it nonsensical. A star is not like a diamond at all. A diamond cannot shine if light is not cast upon it, for it possesses no source of light of its own. A star, on the other hand, is a ball of very hot gas that shines by its own light. The twinkling you describe is caused by disturbances in the air between the star and the earth. The unsteady air bends the light from the star, which then appears to tremble. The air also breaks up the light into the colors often seen to flash from the star."

He ignored her scientific explanation and continued to stare at the star. "You can make wishes on real bright stars like that, you know." He decided his father had told him about star wishes too.

Wishes? Theodosia repeated silently. She glanced

at the star once more. "The brightness of stars is measured by means of their magnitude, a usage that has come down from classical antiquity. A star of the first magnitude is two point five times as bright as one of the second magnitude, which in turn, is two point five times as bright as one of the third magnitude—"

"Miss Worth?"

She turned her gaze from the sky and looked at him. "Yes?"

"But what about wishing?"

"Wishing, Mr. Montana?"

"Haven't you ever wished on a star?"

She lay back down on her rocky bed. "I believe what John Adams had to say about wishing. 'Facts are stubborn things; and whatever may be our wishes, our inclinations, or the dictates of our passions, they cannot alter the state of facts and evidence.'"

Roman picked up a twig and flicked dirt with its point, then pitched the gnarled stick into the shadows. "Yeah? Well, let me tell you what I think about your Mr. John Adams. He doesn't keep me company when I'm riding on an endless stretch of road at night. Stars do. John Adams doesn't give me something to count when I can't sleep. I don't look at John Adams when I want to see something that'll take my mind off anything that's bothered me during the day. And who the hell cares about what John Adams had to say about wishing? If he'd wished more, maybe he'd've been the *first* president instead of the second."

Seeing no point in continuing with a discussion that made absolutely no sense to her, Theodosia closed her eyes and tried to sleep.

Roman watched her toss and turn. Finally, after about a quarter of an hour, she stilled, and he knew she'd fallen asleep.

He stretched out on his own pallet and looked up at the night sky again.

To Theodosia, flowers weren't things that were just plain pretty, he mused. They were to be studied, roots and all. To calm herself down, she didn't just take a deep breath; she quoted Latin words having to do with ruffled minds. She didn't know what rain tasted like, or what cool bed sheets felt like next to her bare skin. She'd never even wished on a star.

She knew a wealth of things.

But she'd missed out on a whole world of others.

Theodosia awoke with a start and saw two big blue circles a mere inch away from her face. It took her a moment to understand they were Roman's eyes. "What—"

"I didn't think you'd ever wake up." He stood but continued looking down at her. "It's almost eleven. I've already hunted, eaten, cleaned my weapons, seen to the horses, and bathed."

"Awk!" John the Baptist screeched from within his cage, which sat a few feet away from Theodosia's sleeping pallet. "I work with my hands, Miss Worth. Haven't you ever wished on a star?"

Theodosia rubbed her eyes, sat up, and raised her gaze to Roman. At the sight of him, a rhythmic pulse began to dance within the deepest part of her.

He wore nothing but his black breeches. Tan-colored sand clung to the dark skin that stretched across his broad chest. His damp hair, shining in the late morning light, fell over his broad shoulders, a few waves sticking to the thick muscles in his arms.

She lowered her gaze. Wet with what she assumed was water from the stream he'd bathed in, his breeches hugged every sleek curve and bulge in his lower torso. She realized that if she were only a bit closer to him, she'd be able to discern what each of those curves and bulges were.

The thought was highly stimulating, as was the knowing gleam in his bold and steady stare.

"Care to name the part of my anatomy that's got such a strong hold on your attention, Miss Worth?"

His husky voice worked the same magic as did the sight of his half-clothed body. "How long had you been watching me before I awakened?" Quickly, she looked away from his penetrating blue eyes and attempted to tame her emotions before he could stir them further.

God, she was beautiful in the morning, Roman thought. As if a golden cloud had descended upon her from the sky, her bright hair crowned her head in an unruly mass of fluffy curls and tumbled playfully over her slim shoulders. Her cheeks were flushed, and her thickly lashed eyes still held the luminous glaze of sleep. "For a while," he finally answered. "You snore. Not loud. Just little noises like the kind pigs make when they're rooting around."

She'd never smiled so soon after awakening. "The sound you describe is a grunt, not a snort. Snoring is a noise made during sleep when the soft palate is vibrated. A grunt is—"

"How can you think of that scientific junk so soon after waking up? What do you do, dream about it?"

"I was only—"

"Yeah, I know. You were only being a genius. Come on. I'll show you where the stream is." He reached for her hand, but when he couldn't find it, he realized it was beneath her covers. With one smooth motion, he pulled the blanket off.

Theodosia gasped.

Roman stared. Her nightgown was bunched up around her upper thighs, providing him with an unhindered view of her pale white legs.

"Mr. Montana—" She started to pull her nightgown down.

He knelt, caught her wrists, then captured her wide-eyed gaze as well.

She tried to pull her hands away; his grip was too strong. She attempted to look away from his eyes and failed at that too. "Sir, you are seeing my legs."

"Miss, I'm looking into your eyes."

"You cannot lie to me, Mr. Montana. It's true you are looking into my eyes, but your peripheral vision is allowing you to see my legs at the same time."

With a lopsided grin, he silently admitted she was right. "Peripheral vision, huh? Never knew I had any. But right now, I'm damned glad to have my fair share."

Try as she did, she couldn't keep herself from smiling. The man was filled to the very brim with a devilish charm she found no way to resist. "Yes, the sense of sight is truly remarkable. Would you free my hands now?"

"Of course." He let go of her wrists, and then, very slowly, he lowered his arm toward her legs. "I'm not aiming my hand for any special target," he informed her. "Just letting it drop wherever it will while I keep looking straight into your eyes."

The moment she felt his warm palm meet her thigh, the pulse inside her became an ache that was sweet and tormenting at once.

"Well, what do you know about that, Miss Worth? I'm still looking into your eyes, but because of good ole peripheral vision, I can see that my hand has landed right on your leg. How do people see, anyway?" he asked quickly, hoping to distract her mind while he did delicious things to her body. "I've always wanted to know about sight, but I never found anything out."

She placed her hand over his, intending to move it away. "Mr. Mon—"

"Fine, don't tell me." Gently, he wrapped his long fingers around her thigh and felt her skin quiver. "Just keep all that knowledge about eyes to yourself. I'll go through life without ever knowing how people see. I'll be lowered into my grave never having learned how—"

John the Baptist screeched and flapped his wings. *"Att Ingrid gifte sig så tidigt, gjorde det lättare för hennes far att dra sig tillbaka från affärerna,"* he declared.

Roman looked at the parrot. "What did he say?"

"He's speaking Swedish. He said, 'Ingrid's marrying so early made it easier for her father to retire from business.'"

"Who the hell is Ingrid?"

"Mr. Montana, Ingrid is only the name used in the sentence, which is a line John the Baptist must have heard me practicing when I studied Swedish last year."

"The bird speaks Swedish," Roman said. "See? Even your parrot is smarter than I am. I bet he knows everything there is to know about sight. Too bad I don't."

She laughed in spite of herself. "Do you really want to know about the sense of sight?"

"Oh, I do," Roman replied in all seriousness. "I can't remember wanting to know about something as much as I want to know about sight."

She took a deep breath. "The initial process in seeing is induced by the action of light on the highly sensitive retina. If light were to act uniformly over the entire retina—"

"Yeah, real interesting things, the eyes, huh? Come to think of it, all the senses are worth learning about. Take the sense of touch, for example. Even if I didn't have that peripheral vision, I'd still know I was touching your leg because I can feel it. How do people feel things?"

"Please take your hand off my—"

"Miss Worth, I am not a genius like you are. You've probably spent years studying the senses. Would you refuse to teach me things I don't know anything about?"

"No, but I—oh, very well. Sensory functions are carried out through a rich variety of nerve endings, which bring the primary sensory modalities of touch, heat, cold, and pain into consciousness from discrete receptor points—"

"Yeah, I think I remember reading that somewhere. Let's move on to hearing." He slid his palm down her leg, all the way to her ankle, then glided it back up again. "Well, what do you know? Not only can I see and feel that I'm touching your leg, I can hear it too. Skin against skin. Has a sound to it. How do people hear?"

She laid her hand over his to keep it still. "The

ear is considered in three parts, the outer, middle, and inner ear. The outer ear receives sounds in the atmosphere, the middle ear conducts said sounds inwards, and the inner ear, through its receptor cells, translates their effects into patterns—"

"Amazing things, ears, huh?" Slowly, he traced her earlobe with his finger.

"You are trying to arouse me, Mr. Montana."

"Miss Worth, I'm only experimenting with my senses. Arousing you is the furthest thing from my mind." He leaned nearer to her, so close that the curls around her face brushed his lips. "With just a little bit more experimenting, I'll be a professional sense-understander."

At his nearness, her breath began to come in short pants. "I can't—"

"Breathe?" he supplied, listening to her gasp. "Miss Worth, you are getting all hot and bothered by what I'm doing, and you're not supposed to. Now, please try to control yourself and let me learn about the senses."

"But—"

"Smell is a sense," Roman continued in a whisper. "Even if I shut my eyes and ears, I would still know I was near to you because I can smell you."

She yearned to ask him what she smelled like to him, but still she could not control her breathing.

He heard her unspoken question. "Flowers, but not the kind that smell strong. The kind that you have to smell real hard to smell. Ever smell flowers like that, Miss Worth? They have a perfume, but it's a barely there kind. And then, almost as soon as you've gotten hold of the scent, it fades away, and you have to wait for a while before you can smell it again. Wonder why smells go away like that?"

Theodosia struggled for a shred of composure. "Fatigue. The olfactory nerves become fatigued."

He leaned even closer to her and smiled, the corner of his lips spreading across her temple. "Don't tell me," he murmured. "Those old factory nerves are in your nose."

Heat flashed over her skin. "Your nose—um . . . brain too. Olfactory nerves—they are the pair of nerves that are the first cranial nerves, and they arise in the olfactory neurosensory cells of the ''

"Sure am glad I've got some of those smelling nerves." He nuzzled the warm satiny skin on her neck. "If I didn't, I wouldn't be able to smell the barely there flowers you wear. Handy nerves to have, huh?"

He moved his hand upward, over her hip and side, and finally to the velvet ribbons that closed the front of her nightgown. "And last, we come to the sense of taste. Another of the senses that I happen to find a lot of uses for. I probably wouldn't even want to eat if I couldn't taste what I was eating. I guess taste keeps me alive, wouldn't you say so, Miss Worth?"

She felt his other arm go around her back and instinctively leaned into it. All rational thought fled from her mind as she yielded to the power of his sensual skills.

He lowered her to her sleeping pallet, and by the time she was fully stretched out upon it, he'd already succeeded in untying the ribbons of her nightgown. "Taste," he whispered, leaning over her and touching his mouth to hers. "Tell me everything you know about taste."

His long, black hair flowed over her cheeks and neck. The feel of it upon her skin sent her reeling. Words spilled from her lips as if by their own volition, for she neither heard nor thought about anything she said. "The sense organs of taste," she whispered into his mouth, "are . . . the taste buds, which—which are goblet-shaped clusters of cells that open by a small pore to the . . . mouth cavity. The buds contain—"

"Fascinating," he murmured, then slid his tongue over her bottom lip. "Tell me more."

She closed her eyes, savoring his caresses while summoning to mind further information concerning taste. "The middle surface of the tongue is insensitive to taste, but . . . but salt sensitivity occurs around all edges, sweet sensitivity primarily at the—at the tip, sour at the sides, and bitter at the . . . back."

He lowered his kisses to her slender throat while his hand moved to open the front of her gown. "So you say I'll taste sweetness with the tip of my tongue, huh? Well now, let's see if there's any truth to what you say."

Before Theodosia could understand his intentions, she felt him lick a straight, quick path to her bare breast. When he began to circle his tongue around her stiff nipple, she arched her body directly into him, mindless to everything but the pulsing need that mounted within her.

Roman caught her by the waist and stretched out beside her. His mouth suckling one full breast, he cupped the other with his hand. It filled his palm with all the lush softness he'd known it would.

God, how he wanted her. Right here and now.

"You were right," he whispered. "The tip of the

tongue tastes sweet things. And you, Miss Worth, are the sweetest thing I've ever tasted."

She heard his voice but had no idea what he was saying to her. Longing desperately for more of the pleasure he had brought to life, she shoved her fingers through his hair, locked them behind his neck, and pulled him even nearer to her chest.

Her action nestled his face between her breasts. A man could suffocate within such succulent flesh, he thought.

But what a pleasant way to go.

His intuition telling him she wouldn't stop him if he dared to proceed further, he lowered his hand to her leg again, then slipped it slowly beneath her gown. He found no undergarments to hinder him. Moaning quietly into the valley between her breasts, he glided his fingers over the warm, soft mound nestled between her thighs.

Gasping for breath and fulfillment, Theodosia raised her hips, pressing herself against his palm. Tension, hot and irresistible, built steadily within her, and she knew instinctively that if Roman would only move his hand upon her, the tension would peak.

He knew her every thought by listening to the pelting of her heart. Wanting to see her fulfillment happen to her, he raised his head and watched her face as he began to rotate his palm against the wet silk of her femininity. "Easy," he murmured. "Slow and—"

A sudden movement to his left broke his concentration. In the next moment, he felt cold water splash against his cheek. And when he felt Theodosia stiffen, he knew water had sprinkled her as well.

His eyes narrowing, he stared at the culprit, John the Baptist.

The parrot flung a sunflower seed next. "The olfactory nerves become fatigued," he announced, blinking his round black eyes. "Every male in the world, even a feathered one, craves a little wenching now and then. I must concentrate all my efforts toward finding the perfect man to sire the child, Mr. Montana."

The words were barely out of the bird's beak when Theodosia, with one powerful movement, rolled out of Roman's arms. Infuriated with herself and the rogue whose sensual expertise had robbed her of her wits, she rose from the ground and tugged down her nightgown. "Sir, you possess a facinorous nature!"

Mad as she was, Roman decided he didn't want to know the definition of facinorous.

"Which means," Theodosia continued, "that you are exceedingly wicked. If not for John the Baptist, you—I—Mr. Montana, you might have succeeded in—"

"But I didn't because your damned parrot had to go and open his big fat beak, and—"

"How much longer will it be before we arrive at Kidder Pass? My attraction to you and my obvious inability to resist it makes finding the child's sire an extremely urgent matter. With each day—no, with each *moment* that passes, I am at further risk of—"

"Kidder Pass is a fifteen-minute ride down the road."

"What? Fifteen minutes? We were that near the town, and you had me sleep on a bed of rocks? Mr. Montana, how could you!"

He rolled to his back and stared at the sky. "How

could I? I'm facinorous. That's how could I, how would I, and how did I."

Too angry to speak, Theodosia flounced to the wagon, retrieved her clothes from her bags, and tramped out of sight to dress.

When she was gone, Roman turned to his side and glared at her parrot. "Did you know that the real John the Baptist got his head cut off?" he asked the bird. "Then it was brought to some lady on a silver platter. I'm warning you now, you mimicking, maddening, meddlesome, molting moron, that if you ever stick your beak into my business again, I will cheerfully see to it that you meet the same messy end your namesake did!"

Chapter 8

His stomach growling with hunger, Roman paced in front of the sheet Theodosia had had him string from wall to wall to partition their hotel room in Kidder Pass. Splashing sounds came from behind the sheet as well as the delicate scent of wild flowers.

In the tub, Theodosia listened to his bootheels hammer the wooden floor. "Is something the matter, Mr. Montana?"

"I'm starving! Look, I was going to take you to that fair we passed right outside town. Some of the best cooks in the world are the women who live in little towns like this one, and they cook for days before a fair. But if you don't hurry up, Miss Worth, all the food's going to be gone. You've been in there for three hours already. How long does it take to wash off a little grime, for God's sake? Just rub on some soap, rinse it off, then get out!"

She cupped some warm water in her hand and let it slide down her arm. "I have been in here for no more than half an hour, Mr. Montana. And I will have you know that I do not accumulate *grime* upon my person. I merely become a bit dusty."

He shoved his fingers through his hair. "You're taking your own sweet time in that bathtub just to get back at me for what happened this morning! But what you're forgetting is that you *liked* it!"

His reminder caused her to stiffen with frustration. Although she'd refused to dwell on the morning interlude, her body could not forget and continued to ache for the bliss she'd only begun to understand. "I, however, did not initiate the morning's encounter," she said shakily. "You did, and you should not have. And that is the last time we shall speak of it. Now, why do you suppose the newspaper office is closed today? It is a business day, and I thought to have my circulars printed—"

"The newspaper man is, at this very minute, doing exactly what I wish I was doing."

"And what is that, Mr. Montana?"

"Eating food at the fair!"

His extreme ire made her smile. "Well, at least the telegraph office was open. While you saw to the horses, Mr. Montana, I wired a message to Lillian and Upton. I assured them of my well-being, allowed you all the credit for keeping me from harm, and informed them also that I was in the scintillating depths of researching the oral meandering common to many of the people I have met during my travels through Texas. Such digressive discourse is—"

"Would you just scrub your *dust* off and get out so we can go?"

She slipped deeper into the tub. Water lapped at her lips as she smiled a contented smile. "I am not scrubbing. I am macerating."

He stopped pacing. What had she said she was

doing? Had he heard her correctly? Surely she wasn't doing *that*!

But maybe she was, he mused, a rakish smile tugging at the corners of his lips. He *had* done some rather sensuous things to her this morning. The effect he'd had on her had most likely stayed with her.

Yes, plagued with unfulfilled desire, she now had no choice but to resort to what she was doing behind that sheet.

"Mr. Montana, did you hear what I said?"

"I heard. How does it feel?"

"Oh, it feels divine. It's a pleasure that I would like to continue feeling forever."

In an effort to loosen them, Roman pulled at his pants, which were becoming rather snug due to the desire brought to life by the thought of Theodosia's sensual activity. "Yeah, I know what you mean."

"Oh? Do you enjoy macerating, too, Mr. Montana?"

"What? Uh . . ."

"Of course, one cannot truly indulge in the pleasure of macerating forever," she rambled on, trailing her warm, wet fingers across her face. "One would wrinkle terribly."

"Wrinkle?" He took a moment to think. "I've heard of going insane, blind, or growing hair on the palm of your hand, but I've never heard the one about wrinkling."

Theodosia frowned suddenly. "Who told you that to soften by soaking would cause insanity, blindness, and hair growth?"

Roman stared at the sheet. " 'Soften by soaking'?"

"To macerate is to soften by soaking, Mr. Montana. What did you think I said?"

"I . . ." He raked his fingers through his hair again. Damn the woman and her almighty vocabulary! "That's enough soaking and softening! You've got exactly three seconds to get out of that tub. Take any longer than that, and I'll come get you out myself. And if I have to do that, Miss Worth, I promise you that I will finish what I started this morning."

His vow made her light-headed with a curious combination of fear and excitement. Her eyes riveted to the sheet, she wondered if he would really do what he said he would.

"All right, here I come," Roman called. He ran his hands over the sheet, causing it to ruffle.

Theodosia nearly drowned herself in her haste to get out of the tub. "I'm out, Mr. Montana, and will be dressed and ready for the fair in only a few more moments."

Her "few more moments" turned out to be closer to an hour. By the time she finally stepped out from behind the sheet, Roman swore his empty stomach had shriveled into a dried-up knot of nothingness.

"Well, I don't sew often, but I did a fine job on that shirt," Theodosia said when she looked at him. "Even if I do say so myself."

"Shirt? What—"

"The shirt you are wearing. I mended the rip in the sleeve. You do remember that the sleeve was torn, do you not? When we got to the room, you emptied your bags on the bed and left to see to the horses. While you were gone, I began putting your things away and found that shirt. I mended it for you."

Slowly, he raised his arm and looked at his

sleeve. At the sight of the delicate stitches that closed the tear, he forgot his empty stomach.

Her caring gesture fed another sort of hunger. Indeed, he felt as if some deep void inside him had begun to fill.

"My sewing doesn't meet with your approval?" Theodosia asked after a long moment of watching him stare at his sleeve.

He lifted his gaze and met hers. "It's fine," he said softly. His brows rose in surprise when he heard the thick emotion in his own voice and realized Theodosia had heard it too. Ah, hell, he thought. If he didn't do something fast, she'd start that psychological probing of hers, forcing him to talk about things he wanted left buried.

Stuffing his hands into his pockets, he cleared his throat and gave her a good glare. "We're wasting time standing here talking about a stupid tear in my sleeve and the unmatched sewing skills that fixed it! Now, for God's sake, let's go!"

She studied him carefully. "What, may I ask, brought about your tonitruous mood, Mr. Montana?"

"Of course you *may* ask, Miss Worth. The problem, though, is that I don't know what the hell tittirons means, so I can't tell you what—"

"*Tonitruous.*"

"You say it your way, and I'll say it mine!"

"*Tonitruous* means 'explosive.' 'Thundering.'"

He saw an "I-dare-you-to-argue" expression in her eyes and quieted immediately.

Theodosia walked to the bureau, and battling the temptation to smile at Roman's agitation—which she knew was somehow related to his mended shirt-sleeve—she pinned her ruby brooch to the collar of her gown and slipped her ruffled sunbonnet over her head. "Suppose you tell me what people do at fairs. Besides eat food prepared by the best cooks in the world, that is."

He gaped at her. "You've never been to a fair?"

"No."

"They don't have fairs in Boston?"

She slid her hands into her gloves. "I'm certain they do, but I—"

"You were always too busy studying something to go." Reminded anew of the many things she'd missed out on, Roman took her hand and led her into the corridor. "You have fun at a fair, Miss Worth."

"But what form of fun, Mr. Montana?"

He smiled when he thought about what her idea of fun was. A freshly dug plant root sent the woman into rapture.

But he was going to change all that. Today he would begin to show her a world she'd never known. A world where rain had a taste and stars were made for wishing.

It was the very least he could do for the only woman on earth who had ever taken the time to mend his clothes.

After they enjoyed a dinner of flaky meat pastries, fresh crisp salad, and cold lemonade, Roman led Theodosia through the crowd of people gathered in the meadow. "There now, look at that," he said, pointing to a group of children who were dancing around a large tub filled with water and apples. "That's what you call fun."

The music of fiddles, guitars, songs, and laughter floating all around her, she watched the children take turns bobbing for the apples and clapped when one little girl succeeded in sinking her teeth into one of the floating fruits. "You did that as a child, Mr. Montana?"

"Sure did."

She felt him give her hand a squeeze and went mushy inside. Roman was definitely the most handsome man at the fair. No woman there could take her eyes off him, and several had been dragged away by their jealous husbands or irate fathers. Theodosia, for the first time, understood the pride a lady felt when her escort was the cause of such female interest.

She squeezed his hand back. "And how many turns did it take you before you got your apple?"

Her question catapulted him into the past. He hadn't had to take turns bobbing for apples because he always played the game alone. "I got my apple on the first try."

Before she could question him further, he led her toward a row of booths manned by the townswomen and urged her to examine the beautiful workmanship of the quilts, lacy tablecloths, and embroidered pillows and to sample the delicious preserves, jellies, and candies. He then escorted her to the livestock show, where she saw proud farmers exhibiting their pampered swine. She barely had time to get out of the way when one irritated hog escaped his pen, knocked over a dessert booth, and devoured two cakes before anyone could stop him.

In addition to the locals, a small traveling carnival had joined the merrymaking. A professional juggler and magician astounded one and all, as did the group of dancing monkeys. Two more carnival men had set up games of chance, which were of great interest to the townspeople because of the dazzling array of prizes and cash sums to be won.

"Well, Miss Worth?" Roman said, his fingers caressing hers as he held her hand. "What do you think about the fair?"

Her concentration centered on one of the games a carnival man was running, she didn't reply.

"Miss Worth?"

"Mr. Montana," she said, pointing to the carnival game and the man who operated it, "that number game over there is "

"Yeah, we'll play it after we get some dessert."

"But—"

He laid a finger over her lips. "We'll play the game in a minute. Now, relax and—"

"How can you expect me to embrace ataraxia when that flagitious man is committing such a blatant act of fubbery by—"

"What?"

"Mr. Montana, I cannot be calm," she translated, "because—"

"You're not having any fun, are you?" he asked, his voice tight with irritation. "And you want to know why you're not having any? Because you're too busy being a genius. Quit using those obnoxious words that only you and a dictionary have ever heard of."

"But if you would only listen—"

"Think it's warm out here?"

"What? Yes, it is a sultry day, but I—"

"Why's it so warm?" His eyes bored into hers while he waited for her answer.

She gave a delicate huff and glanced at the sky. "The sun is about ninety-three million miles away from earth, which is close enough to supply the earth with heat and light. The temperature of the sun's surface is estimated at ten thousand eight hundred degrees, and—"

"Wrong."

She blinked up at him. "Wrong, Mr. Montana?"

"It's warm outside because it's sunny. Sunshine means warmth. Period."

"But that is what I said."

"No, that's not what you said. You don't know how to say anything normal. I bet if I got you a piece of blueberry pie for dessert, you'd say to me, 'Oh, Mr. Montana, isn't this pie of blueberracocknoid simply delicious?' You wouldn't know how to just sit there and enjoy the damned pie. You'd have to tell me why it's blue. Why it stains. Then you'd launch into the history of pie. Starting from the day the Father of Pie was born, you'd work your way through his life and finally tell me how old he was when he first got the brilliant idea of filling dough with fruit. Then—"

"What is blueberracocknoid?"

"I made it up to show you just how ridiculous all those scientific names are that you tag on to everything you see. It means blueberry."

"A blueberry is of the genus *Vaccinium* and is a member of the heath family."

"Well, good for the blueberry!" He raked his fingers through his hair. "I mean it, Miss Worth. None of the scientific garbage today. Use normal words, do normal things, and think normal thoughts. Agreed?"

"Normal? But what—"

"See? You don't even know what normal is!" More determined than ever to show her the meaning of fun, he dragged her to a nearby table, upon which sat a basket of eggs. Behind the table stood a wooden rack of prizes that included costly rifles, pearl-handled knives, gold watches, bottles of French perfume, silver lockets, and porcelain dolls.

"Name's Jister," the stout carnival man behind the table introduced himself. "Burris Jister."

Theodosia stared at the man's odd hat. It appeared to have been fashioned from some sort of rodent skin. Staring at it, she finally noticed a rat's head above the man's right ear.

A rat hat. She shuddered with distaste.

His cheroot pinched tightly between his teeth, Mr. Jister squinted as smoke rose into his eyes. "Glad to see you folks. Care to guess which eggs is boiled and which is raw? A dime buys you ten guesses. Guess right ten times in a row, and y'win one o' the big prizes. Nine to one right guesses gets you a lemon drop, and no right guesses gets you a pat on the back and an offer to try again."

A crowd gathering around him, Roman slapped a dime onto the table.

"I lost thirty cents a few minutes ago," one of the townsmen warned.

"I lost fifty cents," another added. "No matter what I did, I just couldn't figure out which ones were raw and which ones were boiled."

"Mr. Montana," Theodosia said, laying her hand on his shoulder, "I—"

"Watch," he instructed her. "Just watch how much fun it is to guess."

"But Mr. Mon—"

"Miss Worth, would you just let me play the guessing game?"

She stepped away from him and gave a stiff nod.

"Very well, guess. But the odds of guessing correctly ten times in a row are—"

"I'll take ten guesses, Mr. Jister," Roman said to the egg man, blatantly ignoring Theodosia's scholarly warning. "And when I win, I want that Winchester." He pointed to the fancily engraved rifle.

Mr. Jister nodded and pushed the basket of eggs closer to the edge of the table. "Y'can do anything to the eggs 'cept break 'em. When you've picked ten, we'll crack 'em and see how good y'guessed. First wrong guess we come to, we quit breakin' 'em."

For the next fifteen minutes, Roman rolled the eggs between his palms, smelled them, shook them, held them up to the sun, and even listened to them. Finally, he separated ten from the rest. "These are all boiled," he announced.

"Well, now, let's just see about that." Over a wooden bowl, Mr. Jister began to crack the eggs.

Roman smiled when the first four proved to be boiled. The fifth was likewise boiled, and he tossed Theodosia a smug look.

She returned it when the sixth egg sluiced from its shell in a thick and glistening stream.

"Cain't have the Winchester," Mr. Jister said. "But here's a lemon drop."

Roman handed the candy to Theodosia. "I want ten more chances," he said, dropping another dime onto the table. Quickly, he picked ten more eggs, and this time he decided they were all raw.

The first egg Mr. Jister cracked was boiled. "Y'want to try again?"

Roman shook his head and took Theodosia's arm. "I didn't win, but it was fun to guess. *Fun,*

Miss Worth. Got that? Now, let's go get some dessert."

"Wait," she said, noticing a young boy approach the table. "May I stay and watch this game for a while, Mr. Montana? I . . . It is truly diverting. I might even try my hand at it." She smiled.

He didn't miss the excitement in her smile and eyes and believed she was finally understanding the meaning of fun. "All right. I'll go buy dessert and bring it back here. Good luck. And if you win, get me that Winchester." Flashing her a crooked grin, he left to buy the food.

Theodosia returned her attention to the little boy.

He slid three dimes toward the game man. "This is all the money I got, and I want a bottle o' that fancy parfume fer my mama. Today's her birthday."

Mr. Jister pocketed the three dimes. "Y'gotta win the perfume, kid. Go on and start guessin'."

Sweat broke out on the boy's freckled forehead as he began handling the eggs. His hands shaking, he finally chose thirty eggs and circled his thin arms around them to keep them from rolling off the table. "These is all raw."

One by one, Mr. Jister broke the eggs. The first six were raw, the seventh boiled. "Y'ain't gettin' no perfume, kid," he said, and laughed. "What y'get is a lemon drop."

The boy's eyes filled with tears. Head hung low, he trudged away from the table.

Moved to pity, Theodosia neared the table.

"Well now, little lady," Mr. Jister drawled, his gaze roaming over her breasts. "Y'want to try? Lot's o' nice things to win." He turned toward the enticing display of prizes, and as he gestured toward them, he saw the little boy standing by the rack. The child held a bottle of the perfume. "Hey, kid, put that back!"

"But—but I saved fer weeks to get that thirty cents! Today's my mama's birth—"

"Y'think I give a damn about when your mama was born?" Give me that bottle, or I'll—"

"I would like to play," Theodosia blurted, loath to hear the man's threat.

He snatched the perfume from the boy, then shoved him away. After placing the bottle back on the rack, he returned to the table. "How many guesses do y'want, little darlin'?"

Bristling over the endearment the game man had called her, Theodosia watched as tears rolled down the boy's cheeks. "How many eggs do you have, Mr. Jister?"

While his eyes widened, he licked his lips. "Two crates that's got two hunnerd eggs apiece in 'em."

She opened her reticule and withdrew two gold coins. "I will guess at all four hundred eggs. Will this be enough?"

One of the townsman stepped forward. "Ma'am," he said gently, staring at the gleaming gold pieces, "it's impossible to make four hundred right guesses. Are you sure you want to risk so much money?"

"I am sure, sir, but thank you for your concern." She held the coins toward Mr. Jister.

He grabbed the gold, which was more than he usually made in a month of working his game, then hoisted the two egg-filled crates up to the table. "Be my guessin' guest," he invited, his gaze dipping to her breasts again.

"If I succeed at separating each raw egg from the boiled, will I win every prize you have?"

"Oh, sure, sure," he said, grinning so broadly that the rat head above his ear moved. "Ever' last one of 'em."

Calmly, Theodosia removed her gloves and laid them over her lower arm. "Very well. Please pile all your eggs onto the ground, but keep the two crates on the table."

Almost choking on pent-up laughter, he complied.

Theodosia turned to the crowd of gaping people. "There are four hundred eggs to separate, and I would appreciate it very much if some of you would assist me."

"But we didn't guess right when we played," a woman cautioned.

Theodosia gave the woman a gracious smile. "None of us will make a wrong guess because guessing will have no part whatsoever in the choices we make. You see, there is a secret to this game, and I am delighted to be able to share it with you."

Mr. Jister frowned. "Hold on a damned minute! You—"

"The raw eggs will not spin," Theodosia quickly explained to the people, "but the boiled eggs will." Quickly, she chose three eggs from the ground and, setting them upright on the table, she tried to spin them. Two rolled to their sides, and one spun like a top. "The first two eggs are raw, and the last is boiled."

When she cracked them to prove her declaration, the crowd hummed with amazement.

"We shall put all the eggs to the test," she continued. "Those that spin we shall place in the crate on the left, and those that fail to spin but roll to their sides will go in the crate on the right. Now, let us begin."

"The game's closed!" Wildly, Mr. Jister tried to put the eggs back into the crates.

Several men in the gathering hindered his efforts while the rest of the people surged forward to test the eggs. Minutes later, the two crates were again full.

Theodosia slipped her gloves back on. "Please break the eggs now, Mr. Jister, so we may see how well we *guessed*."

When the men who held him released him, he jabbed a finger toward her. "You ain't gonna get away with this, lady."

"I already have, sir. You may break the eggs if you so desire, but I believe you and I both know they are separated correctly. And now you must keep your word and give me every prize on that rack."

"I cain't run my game without no prizes!"

"Then it appears as though I have brought you to ruin."

The fat beneath his chin shook as molten fury spewed through him. He lunged toward her, his arms stretched out before him, his hands ready to wrap around her throat.

But he never even got near her.

A solid mass of muscle appeared suddenly before him.

Roman knocked the carnival man to the ground with one blow, then, his motions blurred, whipped out his Colt. "What the hell is going on here? Miss Worth?" He scanned the crowd until he spotted her heading around the table to stand in front of the rack of prizes.

She handed a bottle of perfume to the young boy who had tried to win it. Upon further thought, she removed her bonnet, pulled a silken ribbon from it, and tied a bow around the neck of the scent flask. "There now, lad. You have a gift for your mother."

He smiled up at her when she curled her hand around his cheek, then hugged her legs before racing off to find his mother.

As Roman watched the scene, a sense of wonder came over him. How was it possible for two strangers to demonstrate such affection? It was the damnedest thing he'd ever seen.

"Lady, you ain't got no right to be givin' that perfume to the snot-nosed brat!" Mr. Jister shouted. "That was genuine French perfume made all the way in New York!"

"Miss Worth," Roman said, "would you mind telling me why I just punched this man in the face?"

"I suppose you did it because you are my hired bodyguard," she replied as she came out from behind the table. "He was about to inflict bodily harm upon me. As for why you chose to strike his face, you—"

"She tricked me!" Warily, Mr. Jister rose from the ground, his huge chest heaving.

"Mr. Jister," Theodosia began, placing her bonnet back on her head, "it was not my intention to reveal the secret of winning your egg game until you laughed over that little boy's misfortune. That not being enough to feed your hunger for cruelty, you pushed him as well. I understand that your livelihood depends on your customers' ignorance of the law of inertia. However, what I do not comprehend is the callous attitude you exhibit when people lose their money." With a turn of her head, she dismissed him and peered up at Roman. "Shall we have our dessert now, Mr. Montana?"

Roman glanced down at the boxes of food he'd dropped the moment he saw Mr. Jister attempt to attack Theodosia.

"Oh, Mr. Montana," she murmured, "when you struck Mr. Jister, you spilled our dessert."

"Well, what did you want me to do? Stuff a piece of strawberry cake up his nose? Look, I still don't understand what the hell went on here while I was gone, but you—"

"She ruined me, that's what!" Mr. Jister blasted.

Calmly, Theodosia walked among the assembly of townspeople. "In gratitude for your assistance, I would like for you to please take your pick of the prizes."

Squealing and hollering with delight, the people hurried toward the rack and promptly began stripping it of its treasures.

In an effort to salvage at least one of the valuable prizes, Mr. Jister started toward the rack, but he stopped instantly when he felt a gun barrel sink into the fat at his waist.

"Sometimes you win, Jister, and sometimes you lose," Roman said, his revolver steady in his hand. "Today you lost." With the glitter in his eyes, a stiff nod of his head, and a wave of his Colt, he ordered the game man to leave.

Mr. Jister slunk away.

"Let me congratulate you, Miss Worth," Roman said, taking her arm and leading her toward the dessert stands. "You're very talented."

"That is a very poor choice of words, Mr. Montana. Understanding the law of inertia is not a talent but an acquired skill that is the result of years of study. To explain: Centrifugal force is the pull exerted by a moving object along a circular path on the body constraining that object. The force acts outwardly away from the center of rotation. In a raw egg, the center is liquid and is therefore unevenly distributed within the confines of the shell. When spun, the raw contents slosh—"

"A thousand thanks for making all that clear to me, Miss Fountain of Knowledge. But I wasn't talking about your study habits of the past—I was talking about your amazing ability to find trouble! Didn't it ever cross that brilliant mind of yours that winning all that egg man's prizes might not sit too well with him?"

She skirted to the side when a youngster's ball came flying toward her. "No. My only concern was gaining retribution for that dear little boy who wanted the perfume for his mother."

Roman hadn't the heart to continue scolding her over her lack of judgment. To her way of thinking, she'd performed a good deed, and she had. But even so, he vowed to keep a closer watch on her.

"You aren't angry with me, are you, Mr. Montana?" Taking his hand into both of hers, she raised it to her upper chest and rested her chin upon his knuckles.

Her tender worry and gentle gesture affected him deeply. He felt vulnerable to her sweetness at that moment, as if he were standing unarmed before a benevolent, yet powerful force.

"Mr. Montana?"

He feigned a somber expression and resorted to

teasing. "Yes, as a matter of fact I *am* mad at you. I told you to get me that Winchester if you won the egg game. Instead, you let someone else have it."

"You wear two guns at your hips, have a knife strapped to your leg, and carry a rifle on your saddle. Why do you desire yet another weapon?"

"Well . . . just to have it."

How like a little boy he was at this moment, she thought, watching his crooked grin and the naughty twinkle in his eyes. On impulse, she reached up and slid her fingers through his long black hair, then trailed them down his chest. Finally, she stopped her hand at his waist and caressed the stretch of muscle in his back.

Roman stood riveted, his heartbeat the only motion in his entire body. She'd never touched him like this before, and judging by the innocence in her eyes, he knew she had no idea that her simple caresses were arousing him to such a degree that it was all he could do not to ravish her in front of the whole township of Kidder Pass.

He had to be alone with her. Now. Right now. And when he had her all to himself, he knew exactly what he would do.

She hadn't mentioned her sex-treat book in a while, but he hadn't forgotten about those highly unusual things the dead Tibetan men had practiced. Maybe reviewing *The Sweet Art of Passion* with Theodosia would lead to some highly unusual fun. "Miss Worth, why don't we go back to the room now?"

She dropped her hand from his waist, then picked a bit of lint off his shirt. "May we savor a bit more diversion first? I've a mind to see that number game."

He couldn't deny the pretty plea glistening in her eyes and resigned himself to waiting awhile longer before exploring the Tibetan sex secrets. In truth, perhaps it was better that he had a chance to cool down. "The number game, huh?" He looked at the booth.

Sensing he was in accordance, Theodosia picked up her skirts and headed toward the other carnival game, and Roman followed.

When they arrived, Roman saw that Burris Jister had joined the number game man. The men resembled each other, and both wore matching rat hats, leading him to realize they were brothers. He knew, too, that the other Jister brother was probably just as crafty as Burris.

"That's her, Gordie!" Burris shouted. "Close down the game, and—"

"Well, afternoon to you, miss," Gordie said. Smiling, he pushed Burris into a chair. "Hear tell y'ruined my brother."

"She won his prizes fairly," Roman stated, his voice a growl.

"Yeah, she sure did," Gordie agreed, shoving his brother's shoulder when Burris tried to get out of the chair. "Fair and square. And y'know? That's how I run *my* game—fair and square."

"Well, Mr. Montana," Theodosia said, smiling, "we have finally come upon a fair game. One in which we may trust our own abilities."

Roman studied the setup of the game. Strung along a clothesline were a multitude of wooden clothespins, and on each pin was painted a number. "All right, what's the scientific secret to this game, Miss Worth?"

"There ain't nothin' scientific!" Burris yelled.

"Mr. Jister is correct," Theodosia said. "There is nothing scientific about this game. All one needs to win is a good aim and a good memory."

"Really?" Roman asked.

"That's right," Gordie said, sliding a sly look his brother's way. "I run a real honest game. Y'want to play, mister?"

Before Roman could reply, a young couple approached the booth.

"I'd like to play," the man said, patting his sweetheart's hand. "Where are the prizes?"

"This is a bettin' game, sir," Gordie explained. "Put up your money, and if y'win, I'll match what you've bet."

The man dug two dollars from his pocket and laid them on the stand. "What are the rules?"

Gordie turned and winked at Burris, who refused to take his eyes off the blond woman who had destroyed him. "As you can see," Gordie said to his customer, "on seven o' these pins is written number nine, sixteen, eighteen, sixty-one, sixty-six, eighty-nine, and ninety-eight." With a cane, he pointed to the seven specific pins. "Them's the winnin' numbers. Get a good look at where they are, because I'm gonna turn all the pins over. Now, to win all's y'gotta do is remember where one o' the winnin' numbers is and then toss a ring over it. If y'ring it, you'll walk away with four dollars in your pocket. If y'don't, I keep your money, and y'get—"

"A lemon drop," Roman broke in.

"No, cherry," Gordie said. He handed his customer a wooden ring. "Tell me when you're ready for me to turn the numbers over."

Aware that a crowd was gathering around the

booth, the man studied the pins carefully, then nodded.

By means of a handle attached to one end of the
clothesline, Gordie turned the pins so that their
numbers faced the back of the booth.

"I'm going to ring number eighty-nine," the man
told his girl. "I know exactly where it is." He threw
the ring and shouted triumphantly when it landed
over a pin.

The people watching clapped wildly.

Gordie removed the pin from the line and turned
it over. "We got a winner, Burris! He got number
eighty-nine. Hate to part with my cash, sir, but
y'won fair. Here's your money."

The man beamed as he accepted the bills from
the game operator and a kiss on the cheek from his
sweetheart.

"My escort would like to play now," Theodosia
said when the couple left. "He will bet all the
money he has."

Roman frowned. *"All* the money I—"

"How much money do you have?" she asked.

"What? Uh—I don't know. About thirty dollars or
so. But I—"

"Really, Mr. Montana," Theodosia said, looking
up into his wide blue eyes. "You witnessed yourself
how easy it is to win this game. Knowing what you
know about it, why would you bet a measly sum?"
She turned back to the number game operator.
"He'll bet one hundred and thirty dollars, sir."

Gordie almost fell down. "A hunnerd and thirty
dollars?"

Upon hearing the high stakes, the throng of people moved closer.

Roman took Theodosia's elbow. "Are you crazy? I—"

"Can you match a hundred and thirty dollars, sir?" she asked the game man.

"Sure can," Gordie replied. His hands shaking with excitement, he retrieved a cash box from beneath the booth, opened it, and showed her the money. "I've got just about two hunnerd here."

"Put your money down, Mr. Montana."

Roman led her a few feet away from the stand. "Miss, Worth, I just told you that I only have about thirty—"

"But I've yet to pay you your salary." Swiftly, she removed a hundred dollars in gold from her bag, returned to the counter, and laid the money down in front of Gordie. "Now add what you have, Mr. Montana."

He saw more people swarm around the booth, some announcing they'd won at the number game, others complaining that they'd lost. Their comments convinced him that the game truly was one of skill.

"Mr. Montana?" Theodosia prompted him.

He stared at the glittering pile on the wooden counter. The gold, added to the money he already had in the various banks, brought his total savings up to almost three hundred and fifty dollars. That meant he was only a hundred and fifty dollars away from being able to pay Señor Madrigal the balance on the land. It seemed ridiculous to take the risk of losing a hundred and thirty dollars on some stupid number game.

But if he managed to ring a winning number by means of his own abilities, he'd walk away from the booth with two hundred and sixty dollars . . .

And the ranch would finally be his.

He studied the game's setup again. Theodosia had said all it took to win was a good memory and a good throw.

He had both. "All right." He added thirty dollars to the heap of gold and picked up a wooden ring.

Gordie turned the numbers back over so his customer could see them. "Tell me when you're ready."

Roman memorized where number sixteen was. "I'm ready."

Gordie spun the numbers over. "Good luck, mister."

"Don't miss," Theodosia added. She gave his arm a gentle squeeze and stepped back.

A hush fell over the crowd as everyone held their breath and waited for him to throw the ring. Roman ignored his large audience and targeted every ounce of his concentration on the game. The only thing in the world that mattered at that moment was the wooden pin he'd chosen.

And then, with one fluid motion, he threw the ring and watched it neatly circle the all-important pin.

"You did it, Mr. Montana!" Clapping, Theodosia joined him in front of the counter. "Give him his money, sir."

"Well now, we gotta see if he got a winnin' number first," Gordie said.

"I got number sixteen," Roman declared.

Struggling with laughter, Gordie winked at Burris again, then removed the pin from the clothesline and showed it to his customer.

Roman stared at the number on the pin. A potent mixture of disbelief, confusion, and bitter regret caused him to pound his fist on the counter.

He'd lost.

Chapter 9

"Dammit!" Roman shouted.

"If my eyes ain't foolin' me," Gordie said calmly, "this here pin y'ringed is number ninety-one. 'Pears your memory ain't as good as you thought it was. Y'lose, but it was a pleasure doin' business with you." Deftly, he scooped the heap of money into his cash box.

Murmurs of sympathy rippled through the assembly of spectators until Theodosia's bright laughter silenced them.

"What the hell do you think is so funny, woman?" Roman thundered. "I just lost a hundred and thirty dollars! Dammit, if I hadn't let you talk me into playing this stupid—"

"You did not lose, Mr. Montana, and I suggest you get that money box before the Jisters take it away."

The merry sparkle in her beautiful eyes alerted him to something he'd yet to understand. Quick as a striking serpent, he grabbed the game operator's hand.

"Hey!" Gordie hollered as his cash box crashed

back to the counter. "Just what the hell do you think you're—"

"He did not lose, sir," Theodosia insisted, "and you know it."

Burris grabbed his brother's shoulder. "I tried to tell you, Gordie! That woman is—"

"Allow me to see the pin my escort rang," Theodosia said, snatching it from the game man's hand before he had time to stop her. "There are two ways of looking at this pin, Mr. Montana. Hold it thus, and you do indeed see number ninety-one. But if you hold it upside down like this—" She turned the pin upside down.

Number sixteen met Roman's eyes.

Theodosia laid the pin down. "The seven winning numbers, nine, sixteen, eighteen, sixty-one, sixty-six, eighty-nine, and ninety-eight, may all be turned upside down so that they read six, ninety-one, eighty-one, nineteen, ninety-nine, and eighty-six. The customer can win only if the operator chooses to allow him to do so. So you see? There is nothing at all scientific about the game. It only requires a good memory and aim—and a bit of observation concerning numbers."

"Well, I'll be damned," Roman murmured.

"The number man cheated us!" a man shouted. "I want my three dollars back!"

"Me too!" another man echoed.

Frantically, Gordie and Burris tried to escape the horde of people. Burris fell in the dirt, Gordie fell on top of him, and several of the townsmen quickly captured them. "Somebody fetch the sheriff!" one of the men ordered.

Satisfied the men could handle the Jisters, Roman opened the cash box and removed his winnings. He then handed the box to a young man standing beside him. "You can divide the rest."

"We ain't gonna forget what you done, lady," Gordie warned as the sheriff and deputy of Kidder Pass arrived.

"Damned right we ain't," Burris added. "Somewhere, sometime, we're gonna meet up again. And when we do—"

"When you do, you'll meet up with me, too, Jister," Roman reminded him.

"They'll be incarcerated, won't they?" Theodosia asked as the lawmen led the Jisters away.

"I doubt it," Roman muttered. "The sheriff'll probably just run them out of town and warn them not to come back."

But the Jisters would be back, he knew. Both had promised to exact revenge on Theodosia, and the cold hatred in their eyes had echoed their vow.

God, Roman thought. In Oates' Junction, Theodosia's lack of *common sense* had placed her in danger with the three gold thieves. Here in Kidder Pass her *genius* had earned her the hatred of two carnival thugs who had not only seen her gold, but had a thirst for retaliation that would haunt them until it was fulfilled.

Daft or brilliant, it didn't seem to matter which Theodosia was. She invariably attracted danger.

Roman decided to leave Kidder Pass in the dead of night when no one in town would notice their departure and no one outside town would expect to find them. The more miles he put between Theodosia and the Jisters, the safer she would be.

"Mr. Montana, those game men should be jailed. They—"

"Their games aren't illegal. Shady, yes, but not

illegal. Most people don't put up much money to play the Jisters' games, so when they don't win, they don't lose a lot. Of course, most people don't have a genius to help them beat the odds." He looked down at the money in his hand. "I . . . thank you," he whispered. He wished he could say more, but he wasn't certain how to express feelings he couldn't decipher.

Theodosia smiled and drew her hand down his muscular arm. Her mind warned her to stop touching him so often and so intimately.

But the tender emotions in her heart impelled her to caress him whenever she had the opportunity. Indeed, she felt like hugging him.

"Will we be making another trip to Templeton, Mr. Montana?" she asked, unable to find the courage to hug him the way she wanted. "After ten years of working toward your dream, you must be thrilled to be able to give Señor Madrigal the final payment and obtain the deed to your land."

Roman didn't know what to say. Her insight into his thoughts and feelings . . . her understanding of how important his land was to him . . . her willingness to postpone her own plans and return to Templeton with him . . .

He felt like giving her a hug. Only a plain and simple thank-you hug, of course. After all, he felt nothing but gratitude toward her. Nothing more, and that was that.

But she'd probably read some profound thing into his plain and simple hug, he realized. She'd think he was infatuated with her, or maybe that he was falling in love with her.

He wouldn't hug her. It was a stupid idea in the

first place, and he was damned glad he hadn't given in to the urge.

"Mr. Montana?"

He stuffed his money into his pocket. "I'll get to Templeton sometime," he finally answered her question. "I still have to collect the savings I have in the other towns before I can make the last payment on the land. Are you ready to go back to the room now?"

Maybe he'd hug her in the room, he thought suddenly. And maybe he'd kiss her there too. That way she'd know his attentions had everything to do with desire and nothing to do with emotions.

Which was the absolute truth.

"May we seek out more fun before returning to the hotel, Mr. Montana?" Theodosia asked, her interest piqued by the carnival magician performing a short distance away. "If I could only watch that man a bit more closely, I believe I could understand what tricks he uses to make those doves disappear." She began walking toward the magician.

Roman caught her hand and led her purposefully toward town. "Miss Worth, I think you've had enough fun for one day."

Two minutes after he and Theodosia returned to their hotel room, Roman hung his hat and gunbelt on the hatstand and announced he was bored.

In the act of removing her gloves, Theodosia stopped. "Bored?"

"To death." Hands clasped behind his back, he began pacing around the room, stopping every now and then to stare out of the window and sigh heavily into the windowpane.

John the Baptist stretched his leg out between

the bars of his cage. "Of course, one cannot truly
indulge in the pleasure of macerating forever," he
called out.

"We could return to the fair in a while," Theodosia suggested to Roman. She took her bonnet and
shoes off and filled her parrot's food and water con-
tainers.

Roman shook his head and shrugged out of his
shirt. "I'm hot," he explained upon seeing the startled look on her face. "Hot and bored." He pretended a huge yawn.

Theodosia could not keep herself from staring at
him. The sleek muscles in his chest stretched and
coiled as if he had snakes beneath his skin. She
took her fill of the sexy sight he presented, and only
when the first warm tingles came to life inside her
did she turn and settle into the hard, high-backed
chair in front of the small writing desk. "Why don't
you indulge in a short nap?"

"I'm not sleepy. I'm bored, and sleeping is the
most boring activity I can think of. Name some
things we could do, and I'll pick one." He knew
what one of her suggestions would be and hoped it
wouldn't take her long to suggest it.

"We might order a light repast. Some fruit, perhaps."

"We just ate a few hours ago." For effect, he
stopped before the small throw rug by the bed and
began pushing at it with the toe of his boot. "God,
I'm bored."

"Well, would you like to converse?"

He stared at the ceiling. "I feel like doing something quiet. Something . . . I don't know. Something peaceful. I want to sit here and relax, but I
don't want to sit here doing nothing."

She thought for a moment. "We could read for a while."

Triumph soared through him. "Read? Well, I guess we could. But I don't have anything to read."

"Oh, that's not a problem at all, Mr. Montana." Smiling, Theodosia rose and opened one of her trunks.

Roman saw her withdraw several thick volumes, none of which was the sex-treat book. "What are those?"

She carried them to the bed and spread them out upon the mattress. "This one," she said, pointing to the biggest book, "contains the complete works of Shakespeare. This second one is a history of the Great Sphinx, which is an awesome sculpture in Egypt."

Seeing that his response was less than enthusiastic, she reached for the third book. "And this one is a detailed and extremely interesting textbook about the human spleen!"

"Spleen?"

She caressed the book's spine. "The spleen is a highly vascular, ductless organ near the stomach or intestines of most vertebrates. It is concerned with final destruction of blood cells, storage of blood, and—"

"Yeah, I know all about spleens." *Spleens?* God, talk about something that really *would* bore him to death!

She frowned slightly. "You are familiar with spleens?"

"Oh, sure. A spleen is—well, you know. It's that intestinal cell that destroys the stomach. I've always felt really sorry for people who have spleens."

"But—"

"I also know everything there is to know about Shakespeare. He's the one who wrote the story about that woman named Julie. She drank poison and died when her lover, Hamlet, couldn't get that damned spot of blood off his hands. And you want to know how the Great Stinks got its name? It stinks, that's why, and no wonder. There's probably a thousand Egyptian kings buried inside it. If those Egyptians would only bury their dead in the ground the way we do, they wouldn't have had to name that sculpture the Great Stinks. Now, what else do you have to read?"

Theodosia burst into laughter. She simply couldn't help it. "You, sir, are the most amazing storyteller I have ever chanced to meet."

Her laughter gladdened Roman, for he didn't hear it often. He liked seeing her this way, happy and carefree.

Of course, he also liked seeing her in the throes of desire, unable to catch her breath or resist his caresses.

With those ends in mind, he looked at the books she'd shown him and screwed up his facial features. "Don't you have anything else I could read?"

She laid down the medical volume about the human spleen. "I have the sexual enchiridion."

"Enchiridion? What's—"

"The handbook," she translated. *The Sweet Art of Passion*. But when once I asked you how long you would need to understand its contents, you led me to believe that you were already well versed in the art of passion."

His mind whirled. "I am. Versed, that is, and very well. Passion—I know everything about it. You name it, I've done it. It's just that—well, skilled at the art as I am, I'm curious about whether those Tibetan sex scholars knew as much as I do. They might have made a lot of it up, just to impress the Tibetan girls."

"Mr. Montana, are you serious about your desire to review the treatise?"

Desire was the key word, Roman mused. "I'm very serious, Miss Worth."

Nodding, she collected the other books he didn't want to read, put them away, and unpacked the sexual treatise.

Roman fairly grabbed it out of her hand and stretched out on the bed to read.

"Perhaps we could discuss sections of the treatise later," Theodosia proposed as she gathered writing materials with which to pen a letter to Upton and Lillian while Roman read. "I would be exceedingly interested to know how you compare the Tibetan practices with those you may have employed yourself in the past. I'm certain there will be a wealth of cultural differences."

Her suggestion aroused him instantly. Damn! He hadn't read the first word of the sex-treat book yet, and he was already raring to go!

So she wouldn't see his reaction, he opened the book and laid it over his hips. He then tried to think of an academic-sounding reply to her proposal. "Uh—yes. Yes, of course, Miss Worth. I would be more than scientifically glad to teach you the differences between Tibetan moves and American moves."

"*Teach*, Mr. Montana?"

"Show. I mean . . ."

"*Discuss*, I think, is the word you seek."

Discuss, hell, he thought, but said aloud, "Yeah, that's what I meant."

Satisfied, Theodosia returned to her letter.

Still swollen with desire, Roman turned to his side, giving her his back while he opened the book.

The first page was tri-folded. As he began to unfold the paper, he realized it was folded because it was much longer than the other pages of the book. When he had it completely unfolded, he saw it showed a diagram of a fully erect male member, which by his best estimation was about twelve inches long and the width of his fist. Beneath the diagram a caption said, "Woe is the man who is not endowed thus, for he will never satisfy a woman's passion."

Roman stared at the diagram, wondering if it was a self-portrait of the Tibetan sex scholar's own lower anatomy. If so, the man was a damned liar. Either that, or he'd had a horny elephant pose for the drawing.

Relieved by his own hypothesis, Roman refolded the diagram, turned the page, and saw another sketch, this one of a couple in the act of making love in a flower garden.

Roman frowned. The man and woman's limbs were so twisted together, he couldn't tell which legs and arms belonged to whom, or which two ends were which. Thinking perhaps he was studying the drawing wrong, he turned the book upside down, but that way made it look as though the couple were going at it in the sky.

Damn, he thought. A man had to be a contortionist to make love to Tibetan women.

Engrossed as he was by the bizarre sketch, he failed to hear Theodosia approach the bed. The slight touch of her hand on his shoulder startled him so badly, he let out a shriek and dropped the book. "For God's sake, Miss Worth, don't sneak up on me like that!"

"But I was only wondering what your initial thoughts were concerning the Tibetan scholar."

He sat up and dragged his fingers through his hair. "He was a lying acrobat, that's what I think! You don't really believe the stuff in this stupid book, do you?"

Thoroughly intrigued by his obvious rejection of the treatise, she sat down on the bed and picked up the book. Thumbing through it, she scanned a few pages. "Actually . . . well, yes. I had no reason to believe otherwise until now. Why do you say the treatise is stupid, Mr. Montana?"

"For one thing—" He broke off and took the book away from her. Opening it to the page that showed the couple making love, he jabbed his finger at it. "If this is one of those highly unusual forms you talked about one time—this isn't highly unusual. It's *impossible*!"

"It is?"

"These two have practically turned themselves inside out! People don't make love this way, Miss Worth. If they tried, they'd never get untangled!"

She glanced at the drawing again. "That is but one of the positions described. There are others, and the majority of them seem quite comfortable, to my way of thinking."

He decided she'd taken acrobatic lessons sometime in her youth.

"How far did you read, Mr. Montana?"

"I haven't read anything except that I will never be able to satisfy a woman's passion." He unfolded the folded page and held it up for her to see. "What is Tibet? A land of giants?"

"The diagram isn't correct?" She leaned forward for a better look.

"I thought you'd studied human anatomy."

She drew away, but her gaze remained on the diagram. "I have studied anatomy, but I've never seen a penis—well, I *have* seen one. A few years ago I took an art class, and one of my assignments was to sketch a nude male. The model posed without clothes, of course, but his penis was in a state of repose." Frowning in consternation, she looked up at him. "Are you saying this diagram isn't a true reproduction of—"

"Hell no!"

His shout and the glitter of ire in his eyes injured her feelings. "I apologize," she whispered, "for my ignorance."

"I didn't mean to yell," he said quickly. "It's just that I can't believe you thought this diagram was a true-to-life drawing. Why didn't your brother-in-law set you straight?"

"Oh, Upton doesn't know I have the book. One of the assistant librarians at Harvard loaned it to me."

"Then why didn't *he* set you straight?"

"Miss Biddington is a woman. A very dear woman who is fast approaching the age of seventy."

An old spinster, Roman mused. That explained why the woman hadn't set Theodosia straight concerning the diagram. He could only imagine the fantasies dear Miss Biddington must have entertained while staring at the drawing.

"Since you haven't begun to read, I shall leave

you to do so now, Mr. Montana." Theodosia began to rise.

Roman caught her by her waist. "We could read together. That way we can discuss what we read as we go along." And what a perfect place for the so-called *discussion*, he thought—the bed. "It'll save time."

"Well . . ."

He gave her a serious look. "You said yourself that the reason you've been reading this book is so you can understand what will happen when you finally find the perfect man to father the child. Seems to me that you would want me to explain these passionate things to you. Or would you rather the man you choose tells you about them? If you'd rather a complete stranger explain—"

"I have no intention of being passionate with the man. I've told you before that my relations with him will be strictly—"

"Then you should know about these passionate things in case the guy tries to start them," Roman fenced, drumming his fingers upon the book. "That way, you can stop him before he gets very far. The more knowledge you have, the more you'll be able to control your doings with him."

Toying with a lock of her hair, she contemplated his reasoning. "All right, Mr. Montana. I see your point."

He patted the space beside him, moving over for her when she settled next to him and leaned into the mound of pillows propped against the headboard. " 'Chapter one,' " he said, turning to the beginning of the chapter and scanning the page. "Oh, this part explains the preparations for lovemaking. Touching, kissing, and stuff like that. You won't be doing any of those things with the candidate you choose, but maybe we should talk about them anyway. Just so you'll have a full understanding.''

Theodosia read the page. She'd read it before, but reading it with Roman made the words much more meaningful . . .

And erotic.

He heard her breath quicken and smiled inwardly. If this was the way she responded to the touching and kissing paragraph of the first chapter, he certainly looked forward to what she would do when he got to the really good parts. ''A man *could* begin to make love to a woman by kissing her, but that's not the way I do it.''

''Oh?'' She turned her face toward him and looked into his eyes. ''How do you do it? I—of course, I need to know so I will be able to recognize such foreplay should the chosen candidate attempt it.''

His inward smile grew. She was the worst liar he'd ever encountered. ''Well, I like to touch a woman's face. Glide my finger along her chin and up to her temples, and smooth my thumb across her eyelids. Sometimes I put my hand around her neck and move it down to her throat and then over her shoulder. I also like to push my fingers into her hair. And while one hand is doing those things, I have my other hand curled around her waist. Gradually, I bring her closer to me, so close she can feel the effect she's having on me. You know what I mean, don't you, Miss Worth?''

She remembered the afternoon in Dr. Wallaby's house, when he'd pulled her tightly next to his body. She had indeed felt the proof of his desire. ''Yes,'' she whispered. Hearing her own throaty whisper, she looked away from his sky blue eyes and glanced down at the book.

At her action, Roman reminded himself to go slowly. Casually, he toyed with the dainty gold chains that hung from the bottom of her heart-shaped ruby brooch, then turned a page in the book and began to read aloud. " 'Before the removal of the clothes, much time must be taken by the man to ready the woman for the sight of his nakedness. A virgin is likely to be frightened by her first encounter with a man's arousal and will resist his advances if her fear is not quickly put to rest. To soothe a maiden's worry and incite her sweet passions, a man must take the greatest care to kiss her in an unhurried manner.' "

He stared into space, as if in deep contemplation. "True," he announced, "but not before touching her face, throat, and shoulder, like I just explained. And once a man's kissing a woman, he should do everything he can to get her to open her mouth. Kissing pursed lips is like pressing your mouth against a juicy peach but not being able to bite into it. You know that if you could only sink into it, you'd get a taste of heaven. You know what I mean by that, too, don't you?"

So mesmerized was she by what he was saying to her, she didn't realize she'd leaned into him. Nor was she aware that he had lifted his arm over her shoulder so she could rest against the side of his bare chest.

All she could think about was her growing desire to feel his mouth upon hers.

Roman read her every thought within the depths of her smoldering brown eyes, but his intentions included much more than kissing her. " 'Once a woman parts her lips for a man, he must use his tongue to imitate the movements of lovemaking,' " he continued to read. " 'He should use slow and shallow strokes at first and eventually employ full and deep thrusts. If he is successful in his endeavors, the woman should reciprocate at this point and use her own tongue to mate with his. While engaged in the kiss, the man must then begin to fondle the woman's breasts. He should not grab such succulent treasures, but handle them with the utmost reverence. While caressing the breasts with one hand, a man must then place his other against the woman's belly and gradually lower it until he is cupping the soft mound between her legs. The feel of his touch upon the dwelling place of her womanly passion will cause her to breathe heavily, and perhaps she will follow each breath by a low moan that will be a lovely sound to his ears. When she does these things, the man will know she is prepared to accept and enjoy the more intense preparations for lovemaking.' "

As he finished reading the passage and Theodosia pushed her hips into his side, Roman's need heightened. He didn't know who was more excited by the sensual instructions, Theodosia or himself.

Knowing she would follow his actions, he moved his body downward until he was no longer sitting but fully reclined on the bed. His own breathing became labored when Theodosia lay down beside him and rested her head on his shoulder.

Her face was only inches away from his. He glided his finger along her chin and up to her temple, finally smoothing it across her eyelids.

When she didn't resist, he pushed his fingers into her hair. It filled his hand with golden softness,

bringing every nerve in his palm to life. Liking the
way the delicate locks shimmered next to his dark
skin, he played with them for a while before gently
curling his hand around her neck and feeling her
pulse throb against his fingers.

"Theodosia," he said softly.

She'd never heard him address her thus. The
sound of her name on his lips and the desire she
heard in his husky voice increased her yearning for
his kiss.

When she tilted her face higher, Roman gently
took hold of her chin and caressed her bottom lip
with his thumb. Gazing into her eyes, he gave her a
slow and easy grin.

She couldn't resist his charm and smiled back.

He kissed her smile, surprised but delighted
when she parted her lips. And when she tentatively
touched her tongue to his, his desire escalated so
quickly, he thought his loins had been turned to
stone by the wave of some magic wand.

He could wait no longer to see the whole of her
beauty.

Reaching around her, he started the task of un-
fastening the buttons at the back of her gown. To
keep her mind off what his hand was doing, he held
her gaze and moved his hips toward hers in a slow
and steady rhythm he knew would beckon to the
virgin inside her.

His fiery intent closing over her, Theodosia felt
heat melt through her. Finding the strength to battle his power over her seemed as impossible as sub-
duing a dragon with a needle. Surrendering, she
matched the movements of his hips, meeting each
of his gentle thrusts with a timid one of her own.

In a few more moments, Roman had the buttons

unfastened. Continuing the slight motions of his hips, he slid one shoulder of her gown down and off her arm. The tiny ribbons closing her sleeveless chemise presented little trouble, and in the next moment he bared her breast.

"The man might try this, Theodosia," he warned quietly. "Be on your guard."

When she felt his big warm hand close over her breast, she quickly pulled it away.

Roman felt the sting of defeat until she pushed her upper torso into his chest. He understood then that she wanted to feel his bare skin next to hers. Swiftly, he turned her slightly to the side and pulled down the other side of her dress and her chemise. When both her breasts were freed, he gathered her into his arms and held her close.

Theodosia sighed. The feel of Roman's skin and muscles next to her softness overwhelmed her with a sense of wonder. She closed her eyes and savored the incredible feelings.

Roman didn't have to guess to understand how she felt. Theodosia trembled in his arms, her contentment so real, he imagined he could smell its sweet scent.

Pressing warm airy kisses to her cheek, he untied the drawstring of her embroidered petticoat, then tugged her gown, chemise, and slip down to her knees. With his arm beneath her thighs, he lifted her legs until her dress and underthings fell past her calves and off her feet. That accomplished, he then removed her stockings.

Theodosia moved restlessly against him, sensual hunger making her ache with the need for fulfillment. "I am powerless to understand this hold you have on me," she said softly, staring into the blue pools of his eyes. "Vitally aware though I am of what you are doing, I—I cannot find the will to deny myself the pleasure of your touch."

Her honesty made his throat tighten with emotion. He'd never known a woman like her, a woman who trusted him enough to tell him the truth about her feelings.

"Theodosia," he began, caressing her breasts and the smooth skin of her belly, "the pleasure has only just started."

She raised her hand and pressed her fingers into the hard muscle beneath his nipple. Fascinated by his strength, she moved her hand upward, over his massive shoulder, through his long raven hair, and down his bulging arm.

Her touch nearly drove him insane. A low groan of intense need rumbled in his throat as he wrestled for whatever last drop of control he could find within the storm of desire that raged through him.

At the sound of his barely leashed passion, Theodosia dropped her hand from his arm. "You will not impregnate me." She searched his face for evidence that he would not. "Will you?"

"No." The word left his lips on a hot, tight breath. "You're a virgin now, and I promise you still will be when I'm through. There are other ways."

His declaration confused and excited her at once. "What are they?"

His gaze never leaving hers, he untied the drawstring of her lacy drawers and drew them slowly down her smooth white legs.

A hint of anxiety leaped through her veins as he slid the last of her garments off her body. She lay before him completely naked—and had never felt so vulnerable or uncertain in her life.

Roman watched her worry come into her eyes and alleviated it with a deep and leisurely kiss that soon had her writhing beneath him once more. Only then did he raise his head and behold the unveiled splendor of her body.

He couldn't speak. Couldn't breathe. He could only stare.

Never had he seen such perfection.

Long moments passed before he could talk to her. "Beautiful," he whispered. "God, you are so beautiful, Theodosia."

She could not miss the sincerity in his eyes. It shone forth with all the intensity of the star he'd once pointed out to her. Profoundly moved, she felt her own eyes fill with tears.

The moment Roman saw them, he stiffened, old and uncomfortable memories slithering through him.

But the disagreeable recollections vanished instantly when Theodosia turned into him, pressing her body against his in a plea for the pleasure he'd promised her.

He laid his hand on her hip and gently rolled her to her back. Slowly, ever-ready to soothe her should apprehension return to her, he moved his hand to her inner thigh and caressed the velvety flesh he found there. While his fingers slid across her skin, his thumb swept into the silken folds of her femininity.

Theodosia nearly came off the bed. Short but steady waves of pleasure wafting through her, she arched her hips toward the promise of pleasure.

Watching the play of growing rapture on her

face, Roman slipped two fingers into her. Instantly, his own need began to pound through him, causing him to grit his teeth.

God, she was tight. And hot. And wet.

And he was about to burst out of his breeches. "This," he rasped, "is a hint of what lovemaking is all about."

Surprise jolted her when his fingers began a pumping motion and his thumb circled softly upon her. "Roman." She moaned his name, then reached for him.

The moment his broad chest met her breasts and his hair fell over her throat and stomach, the first spark of bliss glimmered deeply inside her. She gasped as the unfamiliar feelings grew, but the tender look in Roman's eyes assured her that he knew what she felt and was in total control of everything happening to her. Her gaze enfolded within his, she gave herself up to him and lifted her hips into his hand, the source of the incredible feelings coming to life inside her.

Her surrender deepened her pleasure. Something wonderful whirled within the depths of her womanhood. Tensing with anticipation as the delicious feelings spread slowly through every part of her, she realized the sensations would peak and that it was Roman who guided her toward the sensual crest.

And then she was there. The warm and gentle pleasure quickly intensified. Like a flower opening to the splendor of the sun, ecstasy too beautiful to fathom blossomed inside her. She savored the feelings in complete awe, her body trembling with wonder.

She lay motionless for a long while, wrapped in

Roman's attention as the rapture he so skillfully mastered mellowed into a warm, sweet pulse that left her so satiated, she could think of nothing in the world she still wanted.

A smile touched her lips when she saw Roman watching her, his eyes following every emotion and feeling that passed over her features. He looked as pleased as she felt, and his satisfaction somehow increased her fulfillment.

"Roman," she whispered. Overcome with emotion, she smoothed her hands over the hard muscles in his back and began to kiss his shoulder, chest, and throat.

Her sweet and innocent caresses made him want to hold her forever and never let her go. Instead, he withdrew his hand from her, and while he pressed his lips to her moist forehead, he dwelled on the fact that he'd pleasured her. Shown her a taste of sensual joy. He'd been the first man to do so.

And that meant more to him than he cared to ponder.

He sat up, and sliding his hands beneath her, he lifted her into his lap and held her close to his chest. Unappeased desire continued to torment him, but he ignored it and concentrated on the beautiful woman in his arms.

"Tell me you're not sorry, Theodosia," he demanded quietly.

The glint of potential regret she noted in his eyes tugged tenderness forth from her heart. She said nothing, but only stared at him, memorizing every line, curve, and shadow on his face.

He'd come to mean a lot to her, had become very special to her. She could not understand how it was possible for her to feel such fondness for a man like

Roman Montana, but she could not deny her own affection for him.

And she could not imagine how she would feel when the day came that they would part.

"Theodosia?"

Gently, she touched the cleft in his chin, then slipped her fingers through the raven silk of his hair. "Tell me when I gave you permission to address me by my first name."

He grinned down at her. "Calling you *Miss Worth* while practicing the sweet art of passion just didn't seem to occur to me. What about you? You called me by my first name too."

"Did you know," she murmured, her hand still lost within his thick hair, contentment still whispering through her, "that the name *Roman* is from the Latin word *Romanus*? It means 'a person from Rome.' "

"Don't tell me—the name *Theodosia* is from the Latin word *Theoknowsia*, which means 'a person who knows everything.' "

She lowered her hand to his chest and drew lazy circles around his dark nipple. "*Theodosia* is Greek, meaning 'divine gift.' When my sister Lillian was sixteen years old, my parents despaired of ever having more children. When I was born, they thought of me as a present from heaven. Thus, their choice for my name."

Her explanation caused him to realize how little she'd told him about her past. She'd certainly delved into his past enough times, but she didn't offer to share her own memories with him. He decided it might be fun to coerce her into talking about them.

But not now. Later, after he'd made sure she

wasn't sorry about what they'd done. "I asked you a question, and you haven't answered it."

She laid her head on his shoulder, marveling over the fact that she was completely naked and felt no shame or timidity. "No, Roman, I am not sorry. The pleasure satisfied my physical need as well as my curiosity, which has continued to build ever since you first mentioned the importance of sexual fulfillment. Once again, you have taught me something that I did not know, and for that I am truly grateful."

As it had in the past, her gratitude pulled at something in his chest that was beginning to feel a lot like his heart. "Why did you cry, Theodosia?" he asked, absently running his hand through the warm moist hollow between her breasts.

She recalled her eyes filling with tears. He'd told her she was beautiful. She'd never imagined how much the words would mean to her. Indeed, before she'd met Roman she'd rarely thought about her looks but had concentrated only on her studies. Smiling, she felt the corner of her mouth spread against his smooth skin. "I wept because you made me happy, Roman. The happiest I have ever been in my life."

Her admission of happiness, the first any woman had ever spoken to him, strengthened the tug he felt in his heart.

And when she snuggled closer to his chest and wiggled in his arms, he thought about how right it felt to have her there.

Chapter 10

With Secret tied to the back of the wagon, Roman drove the buckboard down the moonlit dirt road, Theodosia fast asleep at his side. As he'd vowed to do, he'd taken her out of Kidder Pass in the middle of the night. Sleepy as she'd been, she'd voiced little objection but had quietly done as he'd asked.

When they reached the town of Singing Creek at dawn the next morning, he carried her into the hotel. She never woke up, not even when he took off her clothes and tucked her into bed. After seeing to the wagon and horses, he joined her and promptly fell asleep beside her.

Hours later, when Theodosia awakened, she found herself in a strange room. She had no clothes on and was lying in bed next to Roman. Her first thought was that he was as naked as she was, but the feel of his buckskin-clad legs assured her he was not.

"What is Tibet?" John the Baptist asked from within his cage, which sat atop the small table in front of the window. "A land of giants? Who the hell is Ingrid?"

Theodosia watched her bird fling water onto the

windowpane. Where on earth were they? she wondered, examining the small but clean and well-furnished room. She remembered Roman waking her up in Kidder Pass and telling her something about throwing the Jisters off the trail, and she had vague memories of traveling down a long stretch of dark road. But beyond those things, she had no further memory of the night's activities.

Sweeping her gaze over Roman's face, she decided her confusion didn't matter. She was fine. Safe and sound. Roman had seen to that.

Warmed by her own thoughts and the heat of his body, she looked at his hat and gunbelt, which hung on the hatstand near the door. The familiar sight made her smile. Closing her eyes, she allowed her thoughts to drift through her mind like a gentle mist through lazy sunshine, and she wondered what it would be like to wake up beside Roman every morning for the rest of her life.

Married to him.

Her eyes opened. She gasped so quickly that she almost choked. Jerking herself away from him, she shook her head to clear it of such a ludicrous thought.

"Oh, Theodosia," she whispered. *"Married to him?"*

It was one thing to enjoy Roman's company and attentions and to worry about the inner wounds his disturbing past had inflicted. It was even permissible for her to feel warm regard for him.

But it was quite another thing altogether to fantasize about being his *wife*!

What in heaven's name was happening to her? It wasn't like her at all to indulge in daydreaming. Such fanciful thinking had no bearing at all on reality, and she'd always prided herself for keeping both her feet firmly on the ground.

She'd misplaced her wits, that was what. So flattered was she by this devastatingly handsome man's compliments and passion for her—so touched was she by the tender feelings he drew forth from her—that she'd lost complete sight of her all-important objectives.

Resolve hit her as if someone had shot it at her.

The time had come to direct all her concentration toward her plans. She had to remember Lillian and Upton's child. Had to intensify her efforts to find a man whose intelligence equaled Upton's. She couldn't forget her deep desire to travel to Brazil, either. And how could she have forgotten Roman's own dreams? He didn't want a wife. He wanted a horse ranch!

Dear God, things had gone much too far between them.

She sat up, and careful not to awaken Roman, she crawled to the end of the bed on her hands and knees.

Her round, white bottom was the first thing Roman saw when he opened his eyes. God, what a great way to start the day! he mused, reaching for her and hauling her back into bed with him.

"Roman, release me this very instant." Both hands planted on his chest, she pushed with all her might.

The real anger he heard in her voice bewildered him. Taking hold of her shoulders, he gave her no quarter as she tried to escape him. "What—"

"I must get dressed and begin my plans—"

"You don't even know where you are, Theodosia. How can you make plans?"

"I have made them." She wouldn't look into his eyes, knowing that if she did, she'd be completely lost. "And it doesn't matter that I don't know where I am. Whatever town this is, I'm certain that a newspaper office is a part of it. I must have my circulars printed and posted. If all goes well, I will begin conducting interviews by late this afternoon."

He no longer found her advertisements for a lover as amusing as he once had. Letting go of her shoulders, he lay back down and glared at the brass hatstand across the room.

Theodosia got out of bed, opened one of her bags, and quickly donned a silk wrapper. "We slept together. In the same bed." She glanced at him and immediately wished she hadn't.

His long ebony hair flowed over the pillow and pooled on the mattress, providing a captivating contrast to the pristine sheets.

His size never failed to amaze her. Even from where she stood, she could see each ripple of his muscles, each masculine line of his thick, long body. One of his thighs was almost as big as her waist!

She couldn't understand how they'd both fit in the bed. He filled it completely.

"It was late when we got here," Roman told her, still staring at the hatstand but feeling her gaze traveling over him. "There's only one bed, and I sure as hell didn't want to sleep on the floor."

"You didn't have to take my clothes off."

"You didn't mind when I took them off yesterday." He swung his feet off the bed and stood.

Her heart swooped. Tantalized by the sheer grace

locked within his tremendous frame, she could do nothing but stare as he walked toward her.

"For God's sake, Theodosia, tell me what happened between yesterday and now that is making you act this way."

I dreamed of being your wife.

"Answer me!"

"I have not been devoting sufficient time and energy to my goals, and do not shout at me." Flustered, she folded her arms across her breasts, dropped them back down to her sides, then folded them across her breasts again.

"When I—when I am with you . . ." she faltered, her fingers tapping the backs of her arms, "you make me forget my aims. In all honesty, I do enjoy your attentions, and as I told you yesterday, I have no immunity whatsoever against—against your *sexual sorcery*. But I cannot, *must* not forget my ambitions. Lillian and Upton's child is—"

"You said you didn't regret what happened yesterday." He flung the words at her as if he were pitching stones.

She cast her gaze to the floor. "I didn't. I don't. But it was terribly unfair of me to allow you such liberties. In hindsight, I realize that my willingness gave you to believe that we would continue such intimate activities, which is not the case at all. I apologize for having misled you."

He didn't want her apology. He wanted to feel her in his arms again.

"Roman, I understand why you slept with me last night, but the time will soon come when I . . . Once I choose the man to sire the child . . ." She lifted her gaze and met his. "When I find him, you will have to sleep elsewhere, and I will tell you now that it will be for more than one night. I have no intention of failing in my endeavors and will avail myself of the man's services until I have conceived Lillian and Upton's child."

Roman's eyelids narrowed so tightly that he could barely see. Thousands of men lived in Texas, and not all of them were like the greasy son-of-a-bitch he'd pitched out of the window in Wild Winds. It was entirely possible she *would* find a suitable father for the baby.

"Do you understand, Roman?"

His mouth twisted, but he conquered his ire. "I understand, Theodosia." Quickly, he dressed. "Now let me tell *you* something I hope *you* will understand," he said, buckling his gunbelt around his hips. "Your plans are your own business. The only thing that concerns me is getting the rest of the money I need for my ranch."

"I beg your pardon? But you already have the money to buy—"

"I don't have any horses," he snapped. "How can I call my ranch a horse ranch without horses? Pay me my salary when you're supposed to, and I won't care if you *avail yourself* of the services of every male genius from here to China."

He stormed out of the room, slammed the door behind him, and headed straight for the saloon.

He had whiskey for breakfast, more for his mid-day meal, and by the time he'd had his fill and left the saloon, Theodosia's circulars fluttered from every post in Singing Creek.

Though the cluster of men outside her door waited quietly, Theodosia had no intention of beginning the interviews until Roman returned.

How could he do this to her? she asked herself for the thousandth time since the candidates had begun to arrive. Had it escaped his memory that she'd hired him to be her bodyguard? And to think she'd paid him a hundred dollars in gold in advance!

She crossed to the window and peered down at the dusty street below but saw no sign of the irresponsible rake. Anger spread through her like slow-working poison.

A sudden pounding on the door nearly made her knees buckle. Deeply startled, she spun away from the window and clutched the bodice of her gown. "I have already announced that the interviews have not yet begun!" she shouted at whichever one of the candidates was banging on the door. "If you will only be patient for a few more—"

"It's me! Open the damned door!"

At the sound of Roman's deep voice, relief filled every part of her. She hurried to let him into the room.

As soon as she opened the door, one of the candidates shouldered his way through the group of other men. "We were here first! Why are you letting *him* in?"

Before Theodosia could answer, Roman snatched out his Colt and pressed the barrel between the man's eyes. Slowly, as if enjoying every tense second, he pulled back the hammer. "I could see to it that you *never* get in."

Alarmed by the violence of Roman's action and warning, Theodosia tried to understand what was the matter with him. True, he wasn't above using force when he deemed it necessary, but threatening murder wasn't like him at all. "Roman," she said gently, placing her hand on his shoulder, "he only wants his turn, which is no reason to kill him."

Roman lowered his gun and walked into the room.

As he passed her, Theodosia smelled whiskey. He reeked of it! Her anger returning with a vengeance, she watched him open John the Baptist's cage and remove the parrot. He then sat on the bed, and the wall against his back, he settled her pet in his lap and began to stroke the bird's head.

Theodosia longed to give him a piece of her mind. How dare he return inebriated! Oh, what she would tell him when she'd finished the interviews!

With a wave of her hand, she invited into the room the first applicant, a tall blue-eyed man with wavy black hair. "Please be seated, sir," she said, indicating the two overstuffed chairs by the window.

As soon as the man sat down, Roman began a conversation with the parrot. "So, bird, what do you know?"

John the Baptist pecked at a button on Roman's shirt. "Sir, you are seeing my legs."

Roman glanced at the bird's scrawny legs. "Yeah, and they're sexy as hell."

"Roman," Theodosia bit out, "would you please—"

"Do you enjoy macerating, too, Mr. Montana?" John the Baptist asked, lifting his right wing.

Roman nodded. "Every chance I get. And no matter how often I do it, I never go blind or insane, and no hair has ever grown on the palm of my hand."

Swallowing her fury, Theodosia sat down in the

other chair and gave her full attention to the candidate. "May I know your name, sir?"

"Andrew Colby."

"Well, Mr. Colby, I can see that you meet the physical requirements, so we shall advance to the intellectual—"

"You, Miss Worth, are the sweetest thing I've ever tasted," John the Baptist declared, his voice screeching through the room. "While engaged in the kiss, the man must then begin to fondle the woman's breasts."

Roman pounded the bed with his fist and laughed uproariously.

Andrew's mouth dropped open so wide, Theodosia heard his jaw pop. "Mr. Colby, please try to ignore the two irritants on the bed and reveal to me the extent of your academic background."

Andrew closed his mouth and thought for a moment. "I started school here in Singing Creek, but when I was fourteen, my father sent me to a boys' school in Illinois. It was his hope that I would study medicine, but by the time I turned eighteen I knew I wanted to enter law school. Unfortunately, Father didn't have the money to send me. I returned to Singing Creek and am now employed by Mr. Victor Rammings, an attorney. I've learned a great deal about law while working for him, but I have not yet saved enough money to pay for my education. That's why I answered your—"

Roman interrupted with a loud rendition of "Dixie." John the Baptist echoed the song but in a totally different pitch. The result was an ear-splitting cacophony of sour notes.

Theodosia had reached the limit of her patience.

She fairly flew out of the chair and stalked toward the bed.

But before she could get the first word of admonishment out of her mouth, someone pushed the door open with such force that it banged against the wall.

In marched a middle-aged woman wearing a black silk dress and a furious expression. Once in the room, she whirled back toward the door and pointed a toothpick finger at the five men waiting in the hall. "Bricky Borden, just you wait until I tell Sissy that you were one of the men who answered the disgusting advertisement this Miss Worth posted! Sissy will never consent to marry you now! And Hogan Grappy, rest assured that Iris will soon know about *your* afternoon's activities! She'll have you thrown out of the house before supper! And *you*, Cleavon Dirter! Your mother is going to hear about this, and so is yours, Rufus Hardy!"

The men in the corridor vanished, as did Andrew Colby.

A feeling of foreboding rolling through her, Theodosia approached the woman who'd barged into the room and examined her closely.

The woman had her silver hair pulled into such a tight bun that her eyes were slanted. Her nose—long, thin, and pointed—had a black mole right on the tip, and her wrinkled mouth was so pursed, Theodosia wondered if she had just finished sucking on a pickle. "Who—"

"I am Miss Edith Fowler, and my brother, Campbell, is the mayor of Singing Creek. Ten minutes ago, as I left choir practice at the church, I saw and read one of your sordid circulars, and I have come to demand that you leave Singing Creek immediately. We do not abide women of your kind. I am certain that my brother will fully support my demand, so it would behoove you to make utter haste!"

John the Baptist hopped off the bed and waddled across the floor, stopping directly before Miss Fowler. "Even if I shut my eyes and ears, I would still know I was near to you because I can smell you," he said.

Completely unconcerned with the situation, Roman kicked off his boots, chuckling all the while.

Theodosia threw him an irate look, then turned back to the prim, proper, and prudish Miss Fowler. "It is not my intention to disturb the sensibilities of the people who reside in Singing Creek, Miss Fowler. If you understood the full circumstances that induced me to post my advertisement, I feel sure you would be willing to allow me to stay in your town. Please sit down, and I shall explain my desperate situation."

Her curiosity and the fact that she would soon have a wealth of gossip to share with the ladies of the Singing Creek sewing circle led Miss Fowler to relent. She gave a stiff nod and proceeded to sit down in one of the chairs by the window.

John the Baptist followed her, stopping by the toes of her shoes. "I have never slept without a nightrail on, nor will I ever do so."

Roman snickered again. "You've never felt cool sheets against your skin—er . . . feathers?" he egged the parrot on, ignoring Theodosia's glare.

The bird craned his neck up to Miss Fowler. "I'm only experimenting with my senses. You're a virgin now, and I promise you still will be when I'm through."

When Roman doubled over with laughter again, Theodosia closed her eyes and counted the seconds in an effort to maintain her poise. "Miss Fowler—"

"I have never been so shocked in all my life," Miss Fowler said, her silver eyebrows knit together. She moved her feet away from the parrot, glad when her skirts swished across the bird's face.

Startled, John the Baptist leaped into the air. Flapping his wings, he managed to fly into Miss Fowler's lap.

Her actions automatic, she reached out to fend him off.

He avoided her flying arms and sprang to the back of the chair. More secure now, he leaned over, placed his beak next to Miss Fowler's ear, and said, "I've never seen a penis."

Her complexion completely void of color, Miss Fowler grabbed the arms of the chair and squeezed so hard that her arms shook.

"I cannot find the will to deny myself the pleasure of your touch," John the Baptist continued, rubbing his head across her temple. "This is a hint of what lovemaking is all about."

Miss Fowler screamed.

Her ears ringing, Theodosia hurried to retrieve her parrot. Keeping her pet snugly under her arm, she looked at Miss Fowler and started to apologize.

But John the Baptist wasn't finished talking. "I believe you're looking for a bodyguard, Miss Worth? Much time must be taken by the man to ready the woman for the sight of his nakedness."

Clutching her reticule tightly to her sagging bosom, Miss Fowler jumped from the chair and nearly fell down in her haste to remove herself from the scene of such carnal discussion.

Roman could not control himself. He laughed so hard that his stomach began to cramp.

"How *could* you?" Theodosia demanded. "Only this morning I reiterated to you the importance of my goals, and yet you paid no heed whatsoever to what I said to you. On the contrary, you saw fit to drown yourself with liquor, and when you returned to me, you did your level best to ruin the interviews! And to make matters as unpleasant as they could possibly be, you offered me no assistance at all with that busybody Miss Fowler. Indeed, knowing that John the Baptist will not cease his mimicking once he starts, you did everything you could compel him into one of his loquacious moods!"

Roman watched the rise and fall of her big full breasts. "Come here," he said, his voice brimming with the sound of his sensual intentions.

She remained exactly where she stood, beside the chair Miss Fowler had occupied. "How much whiskey did you consume?"

"Sixty-four and a half bottles. Now come here."

At his gross exaggeration, given in the face of her dilemma, her anger rose. "I am leaving Singing Creek." She heard the fury in her own voice, but saw that it had little effect on Roman. The man had stretched out on the bed and closed his eyes!

"Yeah, we'll leave in just a minute," he muttered, his head beginning to pound with the aftereffects of whiskey. "Start getting your things together."

The next sound she heard from him was a snore that reverberated throughout the room. As if meted out by the swing of an ax, rage cut through her with such force, she almost lost her breath.

Within ten minutes she had all her belongings packed. In ten more minutes she had several hotel employees carry her baggage downstairs. The wait for her horse and wagon to be delivered to the hotel entailed another ten minutes.

Half an hour after Roman began to snore, Theodosia headed out of town.

Roman damned the blackness of the night. With no moonlight to guide him, he couldn't find a hint of Theodosia's trail. Self-condemnation and apprehension clawing at his insides, he continued heading southwest, which was the direction the Singing Creek stableman said Theodosia had taken. As he traveled through the heavy night mist, he called out her name, but to no avail.

He traveled for the rest of the night, and when dawn unveiled no sign of her, a stream of curses left the taste of rust in his mouth. Turning Secret around, he rode a little over five miles before spotting wagon tracks. A sprinkling of sunflower seed hulls assured him he'd located Theodosia's trail, and an hour later he found her asleep beneath the buckboard.

He'd come upon her not a second too soon.

Red wolves circled silently around the wagon, their noses to the ground. Several crept within a few feet of where she lay, while others slunk toward her horse, who remained hitched to the wagon with his reins looped over a mere sassafras sapling.

Roman realized instantly that if he shot at the wolves, he would frighten the horse, who was already showing signs of panic. If the mustang chose to bolt, the slender tree trunk and supple branches would bend, and the reins would slip right over them. The wagon would then run over Theodosia.

The sole way to keep that from happening was to

catch the horse before the steed understood what was happening. Speed was of the essence.

And speed flowed from Secret's very soul. In the next instant, the tremendous gray stallion responded to his master's command and sprang forward.

As his horse raced directly toward the wolves, Roman had never been so glad for the trust the steed had in him.

Most of the wolves scattered, but the braver animals stayed to defend their prey. His eyes on the mustang, his senses trained on the snarling wolves, Roman leaped out of the saddle and grabbed the mustang's bridle before the horse had a chance to escape. Drawing his Colt, he prepared to shoot the wolves.

But before he could fire the first shot, the mustang began to rear. Lifted off the ground by the terrified horse's actions, Roman could barely keep the wagon from moving, much less aim his gun accurately.

Dammit, he couldn't shoot! The hungry wolves skulked too close to Theodosia, and he refused to take the risk of hitting her with a stray bullet. Doing his best to keep the rearing mustang still, he shot into the air, kicking pebbles and shouting at the hungry wolves.

Coming out of a dead sleep, Theodosia became wide awake, and a terrible scream came from her throat. Her heart pounding with fear, her mind swimming with confusion, she sat straight up, forgetting she was beneath the wagon. The moment her head crashed into the hard wood, a dizzying pain dulled her senses, and darkness fell before her eyes. The last thing she understood before she lost consciousness was that someone was shouting her name.

"Theodosia!" Roman yelled again. He'd heard her scream, but because of her spot beneath the wagon, he couldn't see her. Horrified over the possibility that she might have been bitten, he threw his empty gun toward the cluster of slinking wolves.

The largest of the wolves howled with pain, and its tail tucked beneath its legs, it turned and ran into the grove of oak and pecan trees. When the other wolves followed suit, Roman realized he'd struck the leader of the pack.

Only moments after the animals fled, the mustang began to calm. Roman let out a long shrill whistle that brought Secret cantering out of the woods. The stallion stopped in front of the mustang. Counting on Secret's presence to further soothe the mustang and keep it from running, Roman lunged toward the wagon and threw himself beneath it. His action upset John the Baptist's cage, but he paid little attention to the mishap.

"Oh, God," he whispered upon getting his first close look at Theodosia and the blood that oozed from a wound to her temple. Carefully, he slipped her out from beneath the buckboard, then scooped her into his arms. Her body flowed over his arms as if something hot had melted her over them. Fighting back a rush of alarm, Roman carried her to the edge of the woods and laid her down on a soft bed of dew-moistened leaves.

Judging by the large red bump that swelled near her temple, Roman knew she had not been bitten by a wolf. She'd hit her head, probably by sitting up beneath the wagon.

He found no further injuries and quickly set about building a huge fire, knowing that if the wolves remained near, the flames would keep them at bay. After retrieving the few medical supplies he kept in his saddlebag, he proceeded to tend to Theodosia's wound.

Her head in his lap, he bathed the injury with clean water while boiling a pan of witch hazel leaves over the fire. A short while later, when the witch hazel had cooled, he drenched the wound with the pungent astringent, relieved that the soothing liquid promptly began to reduce the swelling.

But when Theodosia remained unconscious, his worry returned. Continuing to keep her forehead moist with cool water, he held her close. "Theodosia, wake up. Wake up now, Theodosia."

His anxiety mounted when she did not respond. Quickly, he unbuttoned the back of her bodice, pulled her gown down to her waist, and emptied his canteen upon her chest.

It seeped through her chemise, wetting her thoroughly. She stirred.

"Theodosia," Roman said loudly, patting her cheek. "For God's sake, wake up! Open your eyes! Look at me, Theodosia."

Consciousness returned to her in fragments. A deep but distant voice came to her first, followed by the feeling of being wet and cold. She began to notice a pounding ache in her head and extreme soreness near her temple.

Eventually, she felt something big and warm next to her right side. A beat sounded in her right ear, a rhythmic noise she soon recognized as a heartbeat. Someone was holding her.

She couldn't find the strength to open her eyes. Lying in the dark, she tried to understand what had happened and who was holding her. She remembered the sound of gunfire and feeling afraid and disoriented. Someone . . . a man had shouted her name. Beyond that, she couldn't remember anything.

The beat next to her ear increased in tempo, sounding through her mind almost like a drum roll. The deep voice came to her again. Strong, long arms tightened around her.

"Roman."

She'd yet to open her eyes, but when she whispered his name, Roman knew she was coming around. He continued to pat her cheek. "Wake up, sweetheart."

The endearment escaped before he thought to say it. *Sweetheart?* he repeated silently. He'd never called a woman by that name in all his life! "All right," he barked down at her, "enough is enough. Wake up!"

She opened her eyes and saw two Romans staring down at her. Blinking, she tried to adjust her vision, but a long moment passed before she could see clearly.

Roman's eyes were the first part of him she saw. Chips of clear blue sky, she thought, managing a small smile and then looking at his mouth.

Her smile faded. If his lips were any indication, he was in a terrible frame of mind. "Roman? What hap—"

"Just be still," he gritted out. "Don't talk."

"But I only want to—"

"You knocked yourself unconscious." Now that he had proof that she would be all right, anger began to take the place of apprehension. "But first you left your bodyguard asleep in Singing Creek. Then you traveled alone all night. Of course, you had to pick a *moonless* night, so that your trail would be next to impossible to find. Then you tied your horse to a sapling as round as my toe and didn't unhitch him from the wagon. You then went to sleep under the buckboard without bothering to make a campfire. After all that, you almost became breakfast for a damned pack of wolves, which had no reason to fear coming near to you because you didn't make a fire. That's when you finally knocked yourself unconscious. Best as I can figure, you sat up while you were under the wagon and hit your head."

Her head reeling, she needed almost five whole minutes to understand completely. "But you called me sweetheart."

He frowned. So she'd heard that, had she? Damn her! "What's that got to do with—"

"How is it possible for you to think of me as a sweetheart and then be so angry with me?"

Gently, he laid her on the ground and rose to his feet. "I didn't mean to call you sweetheart, got that? It—it's one of those worried words. Those stupid words people say when they're nervous. Well, hell, Theodosia, you had passed out, and you wouldn't wake up! The word just slipped out. That's all there is to it, so forget I ever said it."

A shiver passed through her, causing her to realize she was wet and partially unclothed. Indeed, her bosom was clearly visible through the clinging chemise. "You pulled my dress down."

He saw suspicion floating in her huge brown eyes. "Yeah, and then I ravished you. I'm wanted in five states for violating unconscious women." He stalked toward the wagon to retrieve the Colt he'd thrown at the wolf. God, to think he'd thrown one of his precious weapons at a damned wolf! He'd never committed such an atrocity in all his days of carrying a gun.

And all because of a woman. *A woman!*

Mumbling profanities, he reloaded both weapons and took one to Theodosia. "The last time you ate was yesterday at the fair. You need something in your stomach, or you're going to get dizzier. I'm going hunting. I won't be far, and while I'm gone, stay exactly where you are. If anything happens, fire two shots into the air. You do know how to shoot a gun, don't you?"

She cocked the revolver, pointed the gun toward the sky, and pulled the trigger.

In the next moment, a slender branch fell on top of her, causing her to shriek with surprise.

Shaking his head, Roman left to find breakfast.

When he returned a short while later, Theodosia was fast asleep. Her hand on her chest, she still held the gun, pointing it directly at her face.

"Oh, of all the . . ." Roman muttered, taking the gun and stuffing it back into his belt. "You don't have the sense God gave a hammer."

The smell of food soon awakened Theodosia. Opening her eyes, she saw Roman stirring a pot over the fire. "What are you making?"

"Soup. We've got provisions in the wagon, but nothing I can make fresh soup out of. I doubt you can keep down much more than this."

Holding the side of her head, Theodosia sat up. A

moment passed before the pain subsided sufficiently for her to speak. "What kind of soup is it?"

"Prairie chicken. I got three."

"Prairie chicken?"

He threw some salt into the soup. "I've also heard them called grouse, but the name never stuck with me."

"I've never eaten a decoction of *Tympanuchus cupido pinnatus* for breakfast."

He gave her a sideways glance. "Is that scientificaneeze for prairie chicken soup?"

"Scientificaneeze?"

"That's the name of the language you speak when you're off on one of your genius runs."

She ignored his barb. "A decoction of *Tympanuchus cupido pinnatus* is indeed prairie chicken soup."

The bump to her head obviously hadn't done anything to her brain, he mused. "How's it possible for you to think of anything intellectual about three buck-naked, simmering prairie chickens?"

"I—"

"Never mind. Here." He dished out a bowl of the broth and handed it to her. For himself, he made a plate of the meat.

"I thought I'd done well," Theodosia said after finishing the soup. "After I left Singing Creek, I tried to do everything I thought you would do."

He tossed a prairie chicken leg into the fire. "Yeah? Well, I never would have laid myself out like a damned banquet and invited wolves to come eat me."

Gingerly, she lay back down on the leaves. "I would not have placed myself in such a predicament had you not infuriated me with your temulency yesterday. You—"

"I might have gotten drunk yesterday, but I did not temulent you!" He wasn't exactly sure what *temulency* meant, but it sounded like something sexual.

"*Temulency* means drunkenness, Roman. After Miss Fowler left the room, I told you I was leaving Singing Creek. But due to your state of inebriation, you possessed neither the will nor the ability to accompany me. Did you really expect to find me in the room when you awakened?"

"I sure as hell didn't expect to find you out here in wolf kingdom! Where did you think you were going, anyway?"

She picked up a handful of sand and let it trickle through her fingers. "To a town."

"*What* town?"

"The first one I came to."

He stood. "You were heading southwest, Theodosia. In four or five days time you would have been in the damned desert, with nothing but cacti, mesquite, and rattlesnakes for company." He crossed to the wagon and began scrounging through Theodosia's bags.

When he brought her her nightgown, she frowned. "What—"

"Put it on. You're not going anywhere today, tomorrow, or the day after that. In fact, you're staying put until I think you're fit to travel, and you might as well be comfortable while you're at it."

She drew the gown over her head, pulled it down, then removed her clothes from beneath it. "You are wrong about my not having company while I journey," she said, slipping her arms into the sleeves of her nightgown. "I have John the Baptist, who is superb company. *He* does not belittle me, nor does he shout at me. Would you bring him to me, please?"

Shoving his fingers through his hair, Roman swiped her clothes off the ground, threw them into the wagon bed, then bent to get the cage out from beneath the vehicle. As he straightened, the cage door swung open.

John the Baptist was not inside.

"Roman? Will you bring him to me, please?" Theodosia asked again, wondering why he was standing so still.

His back to her, Roman held the cage to his chest and frantically tried to decide what to do. If he told her the bird was gone, she'd make him go look for it. She'd want to go with him, of course. She'd have to go, since there was no way in hell he'd leave her here unprotected.

But what about her head injury? She couldn't travel.

He wouldn't tell her that her bird was gone.

But if he didn't tell her, the parrot would wander farther away. Theodosia would never forgive him if something happened to her pet.

Dammit!

"Roman?"

"Uh . . . he's asleep." Roman placed the cage on the wagon bed so Theodosia couldn't see it. "Dead to the world. He—didn't I just tell you that you had to rest today? Go to sleep!" Still refusing to look at her, he walked around the buckboard, his gaze sweeping over every inch of dirt he passed as he looked for signs of John the Baptist.

Theodosia didn't care for the distress she heard

in his voice. Something was wrong. Determined to find out what it was, she struggled to her feet, resisting the wave of weakness that passed through her. One slow step at a time, she approached the wagon.

"John," she whispered upon seeing the empty cage. Clutching the side of the buckboard for support, she picked up the cage.

When Roman turned around, the first thing he saw was the telltale shine in her eyes. "Don't cry. I'll find him. God, just don't cry."

She nodded mutely, then began to sway. The cage crashed to the ground.

In an instant, Roman swept her into his arms. "I swear I'll find him, Theodosia, but I won't go out looking for him right now. I can't leave you here, and I can't take you with me. You're about to pass out again, and I—"

"The wolves," she whispered. "What if the wolves got him?"

"They didn't. They didn't get him. Got that?" God, he hoped the wolves hadn't gotten the parrot.

"Please find him, Roman."

Her voice shook. With pain or fear, Roman didn't know. "I will, but—"

"I'll be fine. I can drive the wagon while you ride Secret. I'll follow you."

"The hell you will!" He regretted shouting the second he saw more tears fill her eyes. "I told you not to—"

"I cannot stem my tears," she whimpered, feeling several tears trickle over her lips. "John the Baptist is more than a pet to me, Roman. He's— well, how would you feel if Secret were lost, and the only person who could find him refused to co-operate?''

The moment the question was out of her mouth, Roman knew he was defeated. Truth was, if Secret were ever lost, he'd scour every inch of the earth until he found the stallion.

And the parrot *had* played a part in keeping Theodosia safe from those Bandana Brothers, he recalled.

Roman gave a great sigh. He was going to track an African parrot through the Texas wilds while tending to an injured genius from Boston who was wearing nothing but a flannel nightgown.

This was the stupidest thing he'd ever been forced to do.

Without another word of argument, he placed Theodosia into the back of the wagon and made a bed for her. "I'll lead your mustang. You stay here on the pallet. I know you don't have a lot of room, but you can curl up or something." He stared at her until she crawled into the bed.

After kicking dirt over the campfire and tying Secret to the back of the buckboard, he resumed his search for clues as to which direction the parrot had taken.

"You aren't going to ride?" Theodosia asked, watching him examine the ground all around the wagon.

"The parrot isn't heavy enough to make tracks I can see while mounted. I've got to be close to the ground. He can't fly, right?"

"Only for short distances." She grimaced as pain shot through her head. "His wings are clipped."

"You sliced his wings?" Roman asked disbelievingly. There was no love lost between him and the bird, but he didn't like thinking about the parrot being cut into.

"I only snipped a few of his feathers off. The ones he needs to fly. He experienced no pain during the procedure." With a will so strong that it surprised her, she fought and conquered the terrible weakness that continued to seep through her limbs. "How long do you think he's been gone?"

Roman remembered knocking the cage over when he'd dragged Theodosia out from beneath the wagon. "About three hours."

"Three hours? Oh, Roman—"

"He's a parrot, for God's sake, not a roadrunner! He couldn't have gotten very far, especially since he can't fly."

She forced herself to remain calm.

"Here's a bird footprint," Roman muttered, his eyes following the prints until they stopped at a patch of grass. "Sand," he said, bending over the grass. "There's sand stuck to this grass." Rising, he looked out over the distance. "He went that way."

"How do you—"

"If you start feeling the least bit bad, you have to tell me, Theodosia. Promise me you will, or I won't make the first move to find your bird."

She knew he'd keep his vow. "I promise."

Satisfied, Roman took hold of the mustang's bridle and began to walk, his gaze never lifting from the ground.

"What is it you see?" Theodosia held the wagon's sides while watching Roman in action.

"There was a heavy dew last night. When John the Baptist walked through this grass this morning, he had sand on his feet, and it came off on the wet grass. We're lucky that the grass grows in patches surrounded by sand. Every time your parrot left grass, he got into more sand, and then into more wet grass. The dew is dried now, but sand is still stuck to the grass. We have a trail to follow."

Though fear for her parrot and pain from her head wound continued to plague her, Roman's explanation amazed her. While living in Boston, she'd spent thousands of hours in the company of brilliant people, but she'd never once come across anyone who possessed the marvelous skills Roman demonstrated now.

She knew then that if it was at all possible for someone to find John the Baptist, that someone was Roman Montana.

An hour later, he proved her right. Theodosia spotted John the Baptist. Although he resembled little more than a gray blob in the far distance, she knew it was he. His red tail feathers acted like a beacon.

The bird sat perched on the horn of a steer skeleton, calmly preening his feathers. "Roman, there he is! Oh, please, let's go collect him before he meanders away again!"

Roman didn't move. Something wasn't right. He saw nothing alarming, but his every instinct warned that danger lurked just ahead. Still as steel, he watched and waited for evidence of the peril.

It came in the form of a man. Hidden in an oak thicket and blending in with his rustic surroundings, a Comanche warrior pointed a lance straight at John the Baptist.

Chapter 11

Roman reacted instantly and retrieved his rifle from the sling on Secret's saddle. In the next moment he fitted the weapon to his shoulder, narrowed his eyes, and sighted along the rifle barrel.

Theodosia watched him point the gun at John the Baptist. "Roman! Dear God, what are you doing?" Pulling herself to her knees, she tried to grab his shoulder.

She caught thin air and toppled out of the wagon.

Deaf to her horrified screams, Roman curled his finger around the trigger and fired just as the lance left the warrior's hand.

Frightened into speechlessness by the sharp crack of gunfire, Theodosia raised her head from the ground and watched something long and slender fly out of the oak forest. She couldn't determine what it was but knew only that it sped directly toward John the Baptist.

Before she could scream again, the sailing object came apart in the air, splintering into two pieces that fell harmlessly to the ground.

Roman lowered his rifle, and keeping his gaze directed straight at the warrior, he assisted The-

odosia back into the wagon bed. "Why'd you throw
yourself out of the buckboard?"

"I did not throw myself out, Roman. I fell out
while trying to keep you from shooting John the
Baptist. You—"

"I spent a whole damned hour following bits of
sand to find him for you! Why would I have gone
through all that and then killed him?" God, would
he ever get used to her complete lack of common
sense?

She nodded and swept her hair out of her eyes.
"Yes. Yes, of course you're right. You wouldn't have
shot John the Baptist, but I—I panicked, Roman. I
wasn't rationalizing. It all happened so quickly,
and I couldn't understand what you—" She looked
into his eyes. "What *was* that thing you shot?"

Roman watched the Indian vanish into the
woods, but the man's disappearance in no way settled his apprehension. The warrior was without a
mount, which was highly unusual for a Comanche
brave. And from what Roman had been able to see,
the warrior's lance had been his sole weapon.

With no horse or arms, the warrior would surely
attempt to get those necessities somehow.

Dammit! Roman raged. This morning he'd bat-
tled a pack of wolves, and he suspected that he
would soon be forced to fight a Comanche warrior.

"Roman?"

"I shot a Comanche lance. The warrior was going to kill John the Baptist, probably out of fear. I
doubt seriously that he'd ever seen an African parrot before today, and Indians are—well, they're
suspicious of things they don't recognize."

"A Comanche warrior?" Theodosia scanned the

entire area but saw no sign of the Indian. "How did you see him? Where—"

"Sunlight hit the metal tip of his lance. When I saw the flash, I saw the warrior."

"You—Roman, you shot the lance," she whispered as if in prayer.

"Would you rather I'd shot the warrior?"

"What? No. No, of course I wouldn't have wanted you to shoot the warrior. But you—"

"I aimed for the lance because I knew the warrior was just about to throw it."

She couldn't fathom his blasé attitude. For goodness' sake, he'd hit a flying lance from a distance of at least a hundred yards! Another man would have bragged about and celebrated such marksmanship.

But not Roman. He made use of his skills when he had to, and when he had no further need of them, he put them away, like a shirt he didn't feel like wearing anymore.

Her profuse admiration for him moved her to embrace him.

Instantly, Roman thrust her away. "Theodosia, get down in the wagon."

She started. His voice sounded like wheels churning through gravel, and she realized immediately that he would stand for no argument on her part. As she slipped into the pallet he'd made for her in the wagon bed, her heart skipped several beats when it dawned on her that Roman had spotted the Indian again.

"Stay there," Roman instructed her. His fingers whitening around his rifle, he watched the Comanche warrior step out of the thicket and walk toward the wagon, a small bundle in his arms.

By heading straight toward a white man's loaded

rifle, the Indian showed incredible bravery, stupidity, or desperation, Roman thought. He tensed in preparation for whatever he would have to do to protect Theodosia.

Finally, the Comanche stopped near the wagon, knelt, and slowly placed the bundle on the ground. His black eyes never leaving the armed white man in front of him, he unwrapped the parcel and then stood.

Roman saw a Comanche infant lying amidst the cloth. "Well, I'll be damned," he muttered when the baby began to wail.

Disturbed by the sound of the infant's wailing and Roman's curse, Theodosia sat up. One look at the warrior caused her to gasp with surprise. Wearing nothing but a buckskin breechcloth and the cloak of his thick black hair, he stared directly into her eyes. Taken aback by the intensity of his dark gaze, she looked away and glanced at the baby at his feet. The naked male child appeared to be about four months old, and as Theodosia listened to his cries, her heart went out to him.

"Roman," she murmured, "the baby—"

"He's probably the warrior's son," Roman replied. "The mother must have died somehow."

Filled with pity, Theodosia held her aching head and began to climb out of the wagon. But she stilled instantly when the warrior spoke.

"Mamante," he warrior said, laying his hand on his chest. "Mamante."

"His name must be Mamante," Theodosia said. She tapped her own chest. "I'm Theodosia. And this man, is Roman. Roman, tell him who we are."

"You just did, Theodosia. Now get back down in the wagon."

Mamante pointed to the mustang hitched to the wagon.

"He wants my horse," Theodosia speculated.

Mamante patted his belly, then crouched to rub the baby's belly as well.

"He wants to eat my horse," Theodosia added.

Roman resisted the urge to roll his eyes. "He doesn't want to eat your horse. He wants to *ride* your horse and get food from us. Now, for the last time, get back down in the wagon."

When Roman made no move to assist the Comanche, Theodosia struggled to her knees. "Aren't you—Roman, aren't you going to supply him with the things he needs?"

Roman heard the disbelief in her voice, but he concentrated on the warrior, noticing that dark bruises shadowed Mamante's chest and abdomen. Defeat shone from the brave's somber eyes. His arms dangling at his sides, his shoulders slumped forward, he presented a vivid picture of a man bereft of all strength, stripped of all pride.

Roman handed his rifle to Theodosia, slipped his knife out of the sheath tied to his thigh, and assumed a fighting stance.

"Roman! You cannot mean to battle this unarmed man with a knife!"

"Stay out of this, Theodosia."

She had no time to object further. Mamante moved away from the infant, Roman stalked him, and the fight began.

Roman swung the dagger in an arc, barely missing Mamante's face. He then lunged forward, ramming his head into Mamante's stomach and causing the warrior to double over. Before Mamante could catch his breath and straighten, Roman knocked him to the ground with a powerful side kick to the chest.

Flat on his back, Mamante clutched handfuls of dirt and closed his eyes. A long moment passed before he struggled to his feet. Heaving, he staggered as if intoxicated, swinging his fists through empty air.

Theodosia felt nauseated by Roman's vicious treatment of the weakened Indian. "Roman, stop this madness! You're going to *kill* him!"

In answer, Roman slammed his fist into Mamante's jaw, causing the brave to spin in the dirt and fall once more. Again, Mamante rose from the ground. He stood motionless, his back bowed, his head hung low.

In an effort to force Mamante to summon the strength to fight back, Roman moved toward the squalling infant. When he reached the baby, he stood directly over him and gave Mamante a grim smile.

Fear for the child froze Mamante to the spot for one short moment. And then, fury radiating from each part of him, he released an ear-splitting war cry and sprang forward, knocking Roman well away from the child.

Still on his feet, Roman raised the dagger directly above Mamante's head, anticipating the Indian's response. Instantly, the warrior grabbed and squeezed Roman's wrist.

Having received the exact reaction he wanted, Roman pretended to struggle for possession of the blade, then jammed his knee into Mamante's belly. As Mamante slipped to the ground, Roman fell with him. Rolling in the dirt the two men continued the battle for the knife.

Finally, Roman slowly unfurled his fingers from around the hilt.

Screaming a second war cry, Mamante yanked the knife from Roman's hand. Both men rose. Roman stood still, but Mamante leaped backward. His black eyes gleaming, he threw himself back to the ground and somersaulted toward his adversary.

As Mamante rolled past him, Roman tensed in preparation for the sharp pain to come. Though he knew it would happen, he made no move to prevent it, and in the next second he felt a sharp pain rip through his thigh. Clutching the knife wound, he turned in time to see Mamante charging toward him again, dagger in hand. Roman took one long step to the side, and just as Mamante raced by, he took hold of the warrior's arm. Leaning backward, he shoved his foot into Mamante's belly and allowed himself to fall on his back, thus tossing the brave over his head.

Dazed, Mamante stared at the sky for a moment before realizing he'd dropped the blade.

Get the knife, dammit! Roman demanded silently.

Mamante lifted his body from the ground with his left arm and stretched his right arm out toward the weapon, but he fell back to the dirt when Roman kicked his supporting arm. Panting, Mamante curled into a ball and rolled directly onto the dagger. Clutching it with both hands, he bolted to his feet and slowly began to circle Roman.

Though he knew full well that the Comanche would fight to the death, Roman had no intention of allowing the battle to continue. Mamante's exhaustion was obvious, and Roman would not force the courageous warrior to expend what little strength he had left.

It was time to be defeated.

He charged toward Mamante, who responded by leaping into the air and kicking both feet into Roman's chest. When Roman fell, Mamante knelt by his head, grabbed his hair, and held the knife to his throat.

Roman lay still and silent, pretending a wild-eyed expression he hoped Mamante would interpret as fear.

"Roman," Theodosia called, her voice almost a whisper. "Mamante." Standing in the shade beneath a massive oak tree, she held the Indian baby close to her breast, and with a wealth of emotion in her eyes, she begged the men to cease fighting.

They looked at her and saw her tears, which trickled down her cheeks and fell upon the infant in her arms.

Silently, Roman congratulated her. He realized she had no idea how poignant her tears and helplessness appeared as she cuddled the baby while witnessing such violence, but he knew the Comanche warrior would be deeply moved by her concern for his son.

"Please stop," Theodosia murmured. Pale with the horror of what she'd seen, she lifted the baby to her face and wept into his soft black hair.

Swiftly, Mamante stood. Staring down at Roman, he flung the knife down.

It impaled the ground beside Roman's left ear. Roman didn't flinch but only gazed up at the warrior. The renewed pride he saw flashing in Mamante's eyes convinced him he'd done well by forcing the Comanche to fight him.

Roman pulled the dagger out of the dirt and got

to his feet. "Theodosia, put the baby down, and make a bag of food."

She walked slowly toward the Comanche warrior, laid the child in his arms, and adjusted the infant's blanket before crossing to the wagon. There she filled a bag with bacon, dried beans, apples, cornmeal, several jars of preserved vegetables, a loaf of bread, and a generous quantity of sugar.

While she finished preparing the sack of food, Roman fashioned a bridle with a length of rope he carried on his saddle. He then unhitched the mustang from the wagon and slipped the bridle over the horse's head.

His shoulders back, his chin lifted high, Mamante accepted his winnings and took the rope reins from Roman's hand. While Theodosia held the baby, he swung himself onto his new mount, then slipped the food bag strings over his shoulder. Theodosia gave him the infant, but his face remained void of emotion until Roman held out his rifle and an ample supply of ammunition.

The gleam of arrogance in his eyes mellowed into a soft shine of gratitude then. Smiling broadly, he took the rifle and ammunition and quickly sent the mustang cantering into the field.

In moments, he disappeared.

"Why, Roman?" Theodosia demanded. She took tight hold of his upper arm and tried to shake him. "Didn't you see his bruises? Didn't you notice he was weak with hunger and fatigue? *Why* did you have to fight him?"

Roman turned to her and drew his fingers down the sticky trail her tears had left upon her cheeks. "No man, white or Indian, wants to beg, Theodosia. When Mamante—a Comanche warrior—didn't try to steal the supplies he needed but came and begged for them instead, I knew he'd lost all self-respect, all strength of heart. Making him fight me for the things he needed was the only way I could think of to give him back his pride."

His explanation humbled her. For all her years of studying the workings of the human mind, she'd failed to understand that Mamante's most serious affliction was not his hunger or bruises but his loss of self-esteem. Roman had not only sensed the Comanche's deepest misery but had effectively soothed it.

"Roman?"

Without answering, Roman walked swiftly into the distance and retrieved John the Baptist. When he returned to Theodosia, he handed the parrot to her.

She caressed her pet with the back of her hand and caressed Roman with her eyes. "You let Mamante win the fight, didn't you, Roman?" she asked softly.

He didn't answer, but she knew his silence meant yes. "I am impressed beyond measure by the extent of your abilities. Your physical skills, your understanding of the human spirit, your compassion . . . you are a remarkable man, Roman, and I am fortunate to know you."

He waited for the tenderness he knew her words would awaken. As soon as the gentle feelings began whispering through him, he thought about how accustomed he'd become to anticipating and experiencing them.

He would miss the emotions when they came no more. After he and Theodosia parted for their separate ways, there would be no one in his life to make him feel the way he did now.

He raked his fingers through his hair, pondering the fact that he'd always believed his ranch and horses would fulfill every longing he had.

He wasn't so sure anymore.

Sitting on the soft bed Roman had made for her, Theodosia sorted through her belongings. She'd packed with such haste in Singing Creek that her gowns were quite wrinkled, her gloves were crushed, her underthings were wadded into tight balls, and her jewelry had spilled all through her various bags.

She made a glittering pile of her jewelry, then looked up to watch Roman groom Secret. His guns gleamed faintly in the firelight, as did the metal buckle on his belt. Twigs, dead leaves, and brittle pecan shells crunched beneath his bootheels, and moonbeams glinted off his hair as he walked around his stallion.

Memories of the afternoon came back to her. Closing her eyes, she relived the events in her mind and smiled faintly as she recalled the skills Roman had demonstrated while tracking John the Baptist, and the wisdom he'd shown in his dealings with the Comanche warrior.

She felt a pull at her heart, a gentle tug that released a flood of affection into every part of her. Opening her eyes, she saw Roman watching her. His bold and steady stare made her blush. "Is your wound troubling you at all?"

He patted the bandage beneath his breeches. "I imagine I'll live. How about you?"

She realized he thought the knife wound nothing

but a scratch. His unconcerned attitude relieved her of all worry. Gingerly, she touched her temple. "I'll be fine."

"Playing with your wealth?" Roman teased, noticing the mound of her shining jewelry.

She picked up her ruby brooch. As she held the pin up for Roman to see, firelight twinkled through the bloodred stone and over the delicate gold chains that hung from the bottom. "Have you ever heard the term *heartstrings*, Roman?"

"Have you ever heard the term *heartstrings*, Roman?" John the Baptist repeated, and splashed water out of his cage.

Roman leaned against Secret's barrel. "Heartstrings? Yeah, I've heard of heartstrings. Are they real?"

"It is only an expression." Theodosia shook the brooch, watching as the dangling gold chains swayed. "This pin belonged to my mother, and I have treasured it all these years. It's a ruby heart, and attached to its bottom are tiny gold chains. They're the heartstrings."

Roman looked at the gleaming heart-shaped pin.

"*Heartstrings* is an interesting term," Theodosia murmured, still watching firelight burn within the facets of the ruby brooch. "Back in the fifteenth century, the heartstring was believed to be a nerve that sustained the heart. Presently the expression is used to describe deep emotion and affection, and one is said to feel a tug at the heart when so touched. I am charmed by both the beauty of the word and the definition."

Roman ran his hand over the currycomb he held. Was it only the brooch that had prompted Theodosia to talk about heartstrings, or had she been thinking about her own feelings? Her own affection? If so, was her fondness for him?

How *did* Theodosia feel about him? She spoke of her sexual attraction, her gratitude, and her admiration, but did she harbor any other emotions toward him?

He longed to ask.

But he didn't. If he prompted her to discuss her feelings, she would prompt him to do the same.

And he sure as hell didn't want that to happen. Truth was, he didn't know how he felt about her. She drove him insane most of the time, but other times . . .

"I apologize for my irrational behavior in Singing Creek, Roman. I should not have left the town without you."

He turned back to Secret and ran the currycomb down the stallion's sleek flank. "Everything I've ever seen you do was irrational, Theodosia," he teased. "Why are you apologizing now?"

Smiling, Theodosia stretched out on her bed. "How long have you had Secret?"

"Eleven years. Now go to sleep. I told you this afternoon that we aren't moving from here until I think you're ready to travel. If you don't start resting now, we'll be here forever." He began working on Secret's tangled mane.

"I'm not doing anything but lying here, Roman." She watched him tend his horse for a while longer. "I believe I understand why you call your stallion Secret. He is an unusual horse, and you've no intention of revealing his bloodlines to anyone. But he is the breed you will raise on your ranch."

"Maybe." Finished with untangling Secret's mane, Roman moved to the stallion's tail and wondered how it might feel to share his ideas with Theodosia. It had never been easy to keep such exciting plans to himself.

"Will you tell me about him?" Theodosia asked. "I promise to keep your secrets as well as you have."

Roman didn't answer but only continued to work at removing dried mud from Secret's tail.

"You are not the only one who knows about his bloodlines, Roman. Whoever you purchased him from knows as well." Glad his back was to her, she smiled slyly.

"I didn't buy him, Theodosia."

"You bred him yourself."

"Exactly. Now go to sleep."

She sat straight up and glared at his back. "Roman, you are being extremely unfair. I have trusted you with my very *life*, and you do not trust me to keep a secret about your *horse*. I am well aware of the fact that you stand to become wealthy by breeding horses like Secret. Do you truly believe that I would reveal his bloodlines to anyone when I know that to do so would risk your chances of making the fortune you've worked so hard to attain?"

He heard true hurt in her voice, and when he turned, he saw her wounded feelings mirrored in her eyes. Smoothing his hand over his stallion's back, he tried to think of one valid reason why he shouldn't trust her with his secrets.

No reason came to him, and he knew in his heart he could trust her with the information he'd never revealed to another soul.

He grinned. Trust a *woman*? Either he'd lost his mind, or something had happened to change his views concerning the female race.

One member of the female race, anyway.

Still smiling, he looked straight into Theodosia's eyes. "Secret had a mustang dam and an English Thoroughbred sire. I bred the two horses in the dead of night out of sheer curiosity."

At his admission, her eyes widened with pleasure. It wasn't so much *what* he'd told her, but the fact that he'd *told* her. "Why in the dead of night?"

Remembering his youthful transgression, Roman bowed his head and chuckled. "The mustang mare belonged to me, but the English Thoroughbred did not. If I'd asked the Thoroughbred's owner for permission to breed the horses, he would have either said no or charged me a stud fee. So I bred the horses in secret."

"That is stealing," Theodosia said, but smiled back at him.

"The owner couldn't possibly have missed what I stole from him, and the stallion thoroughly enjoyed my stealing it."

Theodosia's smile turned into soft laughter.

"My horses are going to be every cattle rancher's dream come true," Roman explained, thrilled by the mere thought. "To rope a runaway steer, a man needs a horse that can reach a full gallop in only a few strides, Theodosia. The horse should be able to keep running at a tremendous speed for at least a quarter of a mile."

"And Secret is a horse capable of both things," Theodosia realized aloud. "Oh, how exciting!"

Her genuine enthusiasm warmed him all over. "It's the combination of mustang stamina and Thoroughbred speed, nimbleness, and intelligence. But I won't be stocking mustangs. I'm going to buy Spanish mares down in Mexico. Although mustangs are throwback cousins to the Spanish mares and are free for the taking to any man who wants to round them up, Spanish mares are bigger, healthier, and more reliable. So if a scraggly mustang can produce a horse like Secret, imagine how much better a Spanish mare can do. And as for the Thoroughbred stallions, I hear the best Thoroughbred farms are in Kentucky. I'll—"

"Oh, but you're wrong, Roman." Theodosia shook her head. "The best Thoroughbred farm in the country is in New York. My father—"

"Yeah, I've heard of some good farms in New England too. I'll visit all of them until I find the horses I want. They won't come cheap, though. The finest cost anywhere from six hundred to seven hundred dollars."

"That's true, but if you knew the owner of the horse farm, you could negotiate the price—"

"I don't know a damned one of them."

"But Roman, I—"

"Look, Theodosia, it doesn't matter how many of them you know. By the time I've got the money to buy the stallions, you'll be up to your neck in Brazilian beetle spit."

"Roman, if you would only allow me to explain about my father's business—" She broke off suddenly when thunder rumbled in the distance.

Aware of her fear of storms, Roman quickly crossed to her pallet and sat down beside her. "It's not going to rain. Not here, anyway. You won't be seeing any lightning. I promise."

She couldn't suppress a small shiver.

"How come you're so afraid of lightning?" He moved her hair away from her face so he could see her eyes.

"My parents were killed by lightning when I was five."

Shock almost knocked Roman to the ground. He'd never dreamed her dread of lightning was connected to something so terrible. "You don't have to tell me."

"I want to." She gave him a soft smile when he put his arms around her shoulders and pulled her close. "Chancellor and Genevieve," she began quietly. "Those were my parents' names. The day they died, we were picnicking. While I gathered flowers into a basket, they watched from beneath a large tree. The sky became suddenly dark as a storm blew over the area, and Father called that it was time for us to return home. Just as I started toward the tree, lightning struck it. Mother and Father died instantly. I've been terrified of lightning ever since and have found no way of ridding myself of the fear."

Roman took her hand and thought about how horrible it must have been for a five-year-old to watch her parents die so suddenly and by such stunning means. "I'm sorry that happened to you, Theodosia."

A flood of affection washed through her as she listened to the sincerity in his deep voice. She squeezed his hand in gratitude.

"What happened after the accident?" Roman probed gently, surprised by his own intense interest.

"I was devastated, of course, and very frightened about what would happen to me without my parents. But Upton and Lillian traveled to New York and took me back to Boston with them. They raised me as if I were their own daughter, Roman, lavishing upon me everything they had to give, most especially their love. If not for their kindness, I would not have recovered from the terrible ordeal of watching Mother and Father die.

"As I've told you once before," she continued, "I am deeply indebted to them, and that is one of the reasons why I have resolved to give them a child."

"One of the reasons?"

"Guilt is another. You see, Lillian and Upton wanted to devote all their time to me while I was small, and so they postponed having children of their own. When they began trying to start a family, Lillian had great difficulty conceiving, and then she suffered four miscarriages. Her physicians have said that she should have begun a family long before she began to try. If she could possibly manage to carry a child past the first three months, her chances of delivering a healthy infant are significantly higher, but unfortunately she does not seem capable of remaining with child for longer than seven or eight weeks."

"And you think it's your fault."

Theodosia let go of his hand, picked up a stick, and drew circles in the soft dirt beside his boots. "It *is* my fault, Roman, and the sole way I can ease Lillian's heartache is to bear a child for her. A baby of her own flesh and blood would mean the world to Lillian, and I am the only person who can make her dream come true."

For a while, Roman said nothing but only watched her draw in the dirt. "I understand that you want to do something nice for your sister, but isn't having a baby for her taking it a bit too far? I mean, people just don't do that kind of thing, Theodosia."

His question and statement filled every corner of
her mind. In only a few moments a startling, yet
sad realization came to her.

"When you truly love someone, Roman, no sacrifice is too great to make."

He made no reply to her revelation; she offered
no further comment.

In the warm quiet, Theodosia pondered the fact
that Roman had never known real love . . .

. . . and Roman wondered what such unselfish
love felt like.

Chapter 12

Pulling aside the curtains that draped one of the windows in the lobby of the Red Wolf hotel, Roman watched the newspaper boy pass out Theodosia's fliers on the street outside. The lad distributed the freshly printed circulars to young and old alike, but no matter the age of the man who received one, he saw, not a single one of them failed to cast a glance toward the second floor of the hotel.

Roman hoped Theodosia wasn't dressing for supper in front of an open window, but he suspected she probably was. She didn't have enough sense not to.

He glared at the crowd of men outside for a moment longer, then snatched the curtain closed. As soon as the dark of night fell to hide their activities, the whole slew of randy bastards would come slithering into the hotel like hungry snakes after a chick. And why wouldn't they?

There wasn't a man alive who would willingly turn down the chance to receive a hundred dollars in gold for sleeping with a woman as beautiful as Theodosia.

He wondered what she would say if he told her

she wasn't well enough to go through with her plans yet. Maybe he could lie and say that head wounds got worse when the injured person tried to engage in anything sexual. He could say it caused rotting of the brain.

Rubbing his chin, he mulled over the idea, then rejected it when he remembered he'd already used it. For a solid week and a half after the encounter with the Comanche warrior, he'd successfully kept Theodosia out in the middle of nowhere, well away from any towns. It was true that he'd wanted her wound to heal before he allowed her to travel, but he admitted to himself that a full ten days was overdoing it a bit. After all, her head had a bump on it, not a bullet in it.

During the ten days, Theodosia had done nothing but sleep, eat, bathe, read, and share her intellect with him. And he'd done nothing but sleep, eat, bathe, hunt, and be aggravated by her intellect. Finally, after a week and a half of resting, she'd dressed, climbed into her wagon, and started driving, giving him no choice but to follow and then lead her to the next town.

Once in Red Wolf, her shoes had barely touched the street dust before she'd hurried off to the newspaper office to have her dumb fliers printed.

Roman had always liked Red Wolf, and he visited the town whenever he had the chance. He decided now, however, that he didn't like the town anymore. God, he'd never realized how many womanizers lived here!

He kicked a potted plant that sat by the window and ignored the hotel manager's loud throat-clearing. In deep contemplation, he ambled toward a large velvet chair, sank into it, and stretched out his long legs.

Why the hell did it bother him that Theodosia would soon give herself to some horny genius? It wasn't as if he were being forced to share her. To share something, one had to own it.

And Theodosia did not belong to him.

"I don't want her to belong to me anyway," he muttered.

"Pardon me?" the hotel manager said, looking up from the registration desk. "My name's Parks. Oliver Parks. Did you say something to me, Mr. Montana?"

Roman looked at Mr. Parks without even seeing him. "She's not the woman for me. Hell, I don't *like* women! But even if I did, she wouldn't be the one I'd pick. Well, what man do you know who would want a woman who doesn't understand how to have fun? Oh, she said she had fun at the fair in Kidder Pass, but you want to know what kind of fun she had? Intelligent fun, that's what. Yeah, the only reason why she had a good time was because she found ways to use her damned genius."

"Of course, Mr. Montana," Mr. Parks said, repositioning the inkwell that sat on the desk. "Yes, of course. Whatever you say. Oh, by the way, if you plan to ride out of town anytime soon, be careful. Word has it that the Blanco y Negro Gang is in the area. We just got the news this morning that they shot and killed three people over in Kane's Crossing, and one of them was a fifteen-year-old girl."

Mr. Parks shook his head. "You ever heard of any men more dangerous and arrogant than the five in that gang? I've never seen them, but I hear tell they wear black from head to toe and they all ride white

horses. Sure hope to God they don't come here to
Red Wolf. Thirty bounty hunters have been chasing
them since they broke out of jail, but not a one has
gotten them. I guess it'll take a wish granted from
heaven to get rid of them. That, or the Devil himself.''

Roman nodded, but his thoughts remained on
Theodosia. "How many men do you reckon live in
Red Wolf, Mr. Parks?"

"What?" Mr. Parks scratched his whiskered
cheek. "Oh, I don't know. About a hundred and
seventy-five or so. Maybe two hundred."

Two hundred! The number spun through Roman's mind like a tumbleweed caught in a dust
devil.

He ran his thumb over the butt of his Colt, silently vowing that if a single one of the Red Wolf
applicants met the requirements for Theodosia's
lover, that man would sorely wish he'd been born
short, blond-haired, green-eyed, and extremely stupid.

When Theodosia heard the door open, she spun
away from the window and watched Roman walk
into the room.

"Let's go, Theodosia. I'm hungry."

"Roman, did you see?" she asked, pointing to the
street below. "A little boy is already passing out my
circulars. Why, he has even posted them on the
front of various buildings."

Fondling his gun again, Roman slid his gaze
down her body, savoring each beautiful part of her.

He'd never seen her wear her hair the way she
wore it tonight. She'd arranged little braids on top
of her head and stuck green-velvet flowers in it. A

few shimmering curls lay upon her slender neck, touching the strand of pearls there. Pearls almost the same pale hue as her skin.

The color of her silky dress reminded him of dawn. Kind of pink, kind of orange, kind of yellow. And just the way those soft colors clung to the morning sky, the dress molded to Theodosia's curves.

The gown dipped low in the front. Roman suspected that if she sneezed, coughed, or even laughed, she'd spill right out of it.

He wondered what amusing thing he could tell her that would make her laugh.

"What are you staring at, Roman?" Even as Theodosia asked the question, she stared back at him. He'd changed into a black suit and stark white shirt, which looked even whiter next to his dark skin. He wore a black string tie. Its ends fell over his broad chest, as did his thick charcoal hair.

But his dinner clothes did nothing to conceal the raw power that coiled through every part of his massive frame. Indeed, his formal attire emphasized it.

A sweet ache pulsed warmly within her.

"What are you thinking about, Theodosia?"

She noted his crooked yet knowing smile. "You are already aware of my thoughts. Therefore, I see no need to discuss them." She smoothed her peach skirts. "Upton and Lillian bought this gown for me in Paris. Do you like it?"

He traced her curves with his eyes again. She wore her beauty the way other women wore perfume, he mused. He doubted a man in the world could resist her charms.

The thought made him remember that he would

not be the only man enjoying the gorgeous vision she presented tonight. Red Wolf's townsmen would be treated as well.

Horny bastards all of them, and as her bodyguard, it was his duty to put an end to trouble before it even began.

He folded his arms across his chest, his stance rigid as a frozen tree. "No, I don't like the dress, and you aren't wearing it. Put something else on."

"Something else?" She picked up her skirts and swept them outward. "But Roman, this gown is perfectly suitable to wear to supper."

He glared at the gown, trying to think of something wrong with it. "It's too tight. You won't be able to eat—"

"I will be able to eat just fine."

He watched the play of shadow between her lush cleavage. "Button up the front."

She looked at the bodice. "This dress has no buttons on the front."

He stared at the gown again. "It's dragging the ground. The streets are dusty."

"I can have it laundered."

"Well, the chairs at Victoria's are full of splinters. *Jagged* splinters. They'll rip that dress to shreds when you sit down, so take it off and put something else—"

"Victoria's?"

"Victoria's Café. It's the only restaurant in Red Wolf, and the chairs aren't fit for more than firewood!"

She slid her gloves on. "Roman, perhaps you should tell me the truth about what is bothering you about my appearance."

He suspected if he didn't tell her, she'd analyze it

out of him. "All right. The truth is that that dress is going to attract every ruttish son-of-a-bitch in Red Wolf. You've already had your ridiculous fliers distributed, Theodosia, and the men here have already read them. You're probably the only new woman in town, so they'll know right away that you're Theodosia Worth and are willing to pay gold to be bedded. They're going to crowd around you—"

"As my hired bodyguard, you will take the proper measures to—"

"I can't fend off a whole damned herd of panting—"

"A herd?" Theodosia smiled. "Really, Roman, you exaggerate." Still smiling, she draped her lacy shawl over her shoulders and headed out the door.

Roman followed, growling curses all the way. Before they'd even left the hotel, he'd glared down three men, elbowed another four out of the way, and revealed his Colts to two others.

"I don't know why we couldn't have eaten in the room," he muttered, escorting her down the boardwalk.

She slipped her gloved hand into the crook of his elbow. "I thought it would be nice to dine in a restaurant, but let's not linger. It's possible a few men will come to the room later, in answer to my circular, and I must be there to meet them."

Roman decided he would keep her out well past midnight. He'd order a twenty-course meal, then relax for hours over coffee. After that, he'd walk her around the town and show her . . . Show her what?

Damn Red Wolf for being such a boring place!

"This is it," he said, stopping her in front of Victoria's Café and escorting her inside.

The small restaurant charmed Theodosia. Clean, well-starched tablecloths of yellow-and-white gingham and small terra-cotta vases filled with red poppies covered every table. Shiny copper pots and pans, baskets, and paintings of flower gardens hung on the bright yellow walls, and someone had swept the polished wooden floor clean of all debris.

"Judging by this restaurant, I would venture to guess that there dwell civil people in Red Wolf, Roman. That, of course, raises the odds that a few intelligent men will be calling on me."

Roman scanned the gathering of people in the café, his gaze meeting that of every man who looked at Theodosia. Some turned back to their meals, but others defied his silent warnings and ogled the woman at his side. "They all look pretty damned stupid to me."

"Roman!" a woman called from across the room.

Theodosia watched as the well-endowed woman sashayed toward Roman. When the lady reached him, she circled her arms around his waist and kissed him full on the mouth.

A totally unfamiliar emotion sizzled through Theodosia, melting the smile from her lips. She tried to step away.

Roman wouldn't let her. "Theodosia, this is Victoria Langley. Victoria owns the café."

Theodosia decided the woman thought she owned Roman as well. "How do you do, Miss Langley. I am Theodosia Worth."

Victoria's painted eyebrows rose. "The same Miz Worth who's willin' to pay gold for stud services?"

Theodosia's own brow rose higher. "The words *stud services* are not accurate descriptions of—"

Victoria's throaty laughter filled the café. "I ain't

above takin' a little thank-you money from my own lovers, but I'll be damned if I'll ever pay any of *them*!"

Theodosia bristled. "Miss Langley—"

"You from England, Miz Worth?"

"Boston." Goodness, Theodosia thought. Why did everyone in Texas assume England was her home?

Victoria waved to a young girl across the room. "Meg, show Roman and the lady to a table!"

Once the waitress had seated and left them to study the menus, Theodosia gave rein to her irritation. "Am I wrong in thinking that *you* are one of the men who has given that woman a little *thank-you* money, Roman?"

"Wrong as wrong can be."

Mollified, she glanced back down at the menu.

"Why should I pay Victoria for what she gives to me for free?"

She had no chance to release her stinging rejoinder. The waitress arrived to take their orders. "I would like a small portion of chicken and a plate of fresh fruit," she said. "Oh, and would you mind removing the skin from the chicken, please?"

The girl's freckled nose wrinkled. "It's fried chicken, ma'am."

"Still, I prefer that the skin be removed."

Roman leaned over the table. "Why have fried chicken if you aren't going to eat the skin? That's the best part."

"I don't care for the skin."

"Ordering fried chicken when you don't like the fried skin doesn't make any sense!"

"Why don't you concentrate on your own order?"

Shaking his head, he looked at the menu again.
"I'll have fried chicken *with* the skin, roast beef,
catfish, and baked ham. Creamed potatoes, corn on
the cob, turnip greens, cowpeas, butter beans,
stewed okra, and baked squash. Biscuits and corn-
bread too. And for dessert, I want peach cobbler,
blueberry pie, and apple cake. And coffee. *Lots* of
coffee."

He handed his menu back to the waitress, saw
Theodosia staring at him, and began to drum his
fingers on the table. "I'm hungry."

"But you are not a bottomless pit. You cannot
possibly eat—"

"I'll eat it."

"It will take you hours."

He certainly hoped so.

"You Miz Worth?" a man asked as he arrived at
the table.

In his haste to stand Roman knocked over a glass
of water.

It spilled into Theodosia's lap. "Roman!"

"What do you want?" Roman demanded of the
man.

"I come in answer to her ad."

"Here?" Roman blasted. "In a restaurant? The
ad says to go to room nine in the hotel. Can't you
read?" He stuffed his hand into the pocket of his
trousers, thus revealing one gleaming Colt.

The man looked at the gun, then laid his hand
over his own. He lowered his eyes down to Theodosia. "I'm tall, dark-haired, blue-eyed, and smart."

"Yeah?" Roman challenged. "What's nine hundred and fifty-seven times three hundred and
twenty-six?"

The man scowled. "I need paper to figure that out."

"Then you fail the interview," Roman announced.

"You ain't the one who posted the ad."

In answer, Roman drew his gun and cocked it. "No, but I'm the one pointing this Colt at you."

"Roman, please," Theodosia said, then turned her face up to the man. "Sir, I'm afraid you are not qualified. Thank you for your interest, though."

Roman didn't sit back down until the man had left the table.

"What's the answer, Roman?"

"Answer to what?"

"What does nine hundred and fifty-seven times three hundred and twenty-six equal?"

"Damned if I know, damned if I care, and dammit, here comes another one!"

"Good evening," a short, stocky man said as he arrived at the table.

"For the love of God," Roman muttered. Once again, he stood, his Colt steady in his hand. "Get the hell away from the lady. Can't you see she's trying to get some supper? Besides that, you're short!"

"I beg your pardon?" the man asked.

Roman stared at the man's clothing. It was all black, except for the stiff white collar of his shirt. Gritting his teeth, he replaced his revolver in his belt and sat back down.

"I am Reverend Sommers," the man said. "You, sir, look a bit familiar to me, but I don't believe I have ever seen *you* here in Red Wolf, miss. I assume you are visiting, and I wanted to invite you to Sunday services."

Theodosia gifted the minister with a brilliant smile. "How do you do, Reverend? I am—"

"She's Irma," Roman blurted, and gave Theodosia a look of warning. "Irma Sue Montana. And I'm Roman Montana."

"Well, Mr. and Mrs. Montana, I hope to see you on Sunday. Enjoy your meal."

When the minister left, Roman glowered at Theodosia. "Are you crazy? You were about to tell him your name!"

"And how does that make me deranged?"

"For God's sake, you're *Theodosia Worth*, the woman who posted the fliers! You'd have shocked him right out of his collar!"

"Shocking him would have been better than killing him, which is what you almost did. Honestly, Roman, what is the matter with you tonight? You are as agitated as I have ever seen you."

He was saved from having to answer when the waitress brought their meals. Roman had ordered so much food, a second table was necessary to hold it.

But before he could take the first bite, he saw two men standing in the corner across the room.

Both held Theodosia's fliers, and both were watching her. In the next moment, both began ambling toward her.

Roman had had all he could take. He stood and quickly gathered all the fried chicken, bread, corn, fruit, and cake into napkins.

"Roman, what on earth are you—"

"We're leaving." He tossed a few bills onto the table and took her hand.

She yanked it from his grasp. "I am not leaving,

and I do not comprehend your—" She stopped speaking abruptly as Victoria sidled up to the table.

"Mind if I join y'all?" Victoria asked.

"I'm sorry, Miss Langley, but we were just leaving," Theodosia said. "Roman?" She took his hand and dragged him out of the restaurant. Once outside, she started for the hotel.

"Wrong way," Roman said, pulling her in the opposite direction.

"But earlier you said you wanted to eat in the room."

"Well, now I want to eat outside!" Clutching her hand, he escorted her into an open field that edged the town. There, he sat her down in a cool mound of bluebonnets and tossed the bulging napkins down beside her.

Theodosia looked up at him. "Would you care to divulge the reasons for your anger, Roman?"

"I am *not* angry!"

She leaned against the cluster of large rocks at her back and opened the napkins. "Then would you care to eat now?"

"I'm too mad to eat!" He gave her his back, stuffed his hands into his pockets, and stared at the dusky sky. "I told you what would happen, Theodosia. But did you listen? Hell, no. You didn't listen!"

"What happened?"

"What happened?" He spun to face her. "Didn't you see all those—" He paused, trying to remember the name Theodosia had called the man who had attacked her in Wild Winds. "Didn't you see all those *lackivating meaflarants* back there, for God's sake?"

"Lackivating meaflarants? What—oh." She

smiled a secret smile. "I believe the description you seek is *lascivious malfeasants.*"

"Call them whatever you want! They were lined up wall-to-wall, just waiting—"

"Roman, they were doing no such thing. Granted, one man approached the table, but you dealt with him. The second man was Reverend—"

"Look, Theodosia," he said, pointing his finger at her, "I'm your bodyguard. In order for me to do my job, you have to follow my rules. Rule number one is that you don't wear what I tell you not to wear. Rule number two is that you never forget rule number one. Rule number three is—"

"I do not appreciate your domineering attitude."

"Yeah? Well, I don't give a damn whether you like it or not!"

Calmly, Theodosia removed the skin from a piece of chicken and ate the meat. She then picked up a strawberry.

Still scowling, Roman watched her bite into the ripe fruit. The contrast of the crimson berry against her cloud-white skin fascinated him. She kept the berry between her soft full lips, and he could tell by the way her cheeks moved that she was sucking the juice.

Desire slammed into him with such force, he began to sweat.

"Roman, aren't you going to eat?"

"What? Uh, yeah." His loins aching fiercely, he sat down beside her, then noticed the vivid contrast of her peach skirts, the thick emerald grass, and the brilliant bluebonnets. God, she looked so pretty sitting there eating her strawberry.

"Here." She handed him a slice of watermelon. He bit into it and felt juice dribble over his chin.

Smiling, Theodosia dabbed at it with a napkin.

Her caring gesture tempered his desire. In passion's place rose that same tender something she often managed to rouse within him.

"Have you ever had a friend, Roman?"

The sound of her voice brought him out of the daze her beauty had led him into. Mentally shaking himself, he laid down the watermelon and bit into a chicken breast. "I've met some people here and there," he slurred.

"Meeting people isn't the same as having them for friends. I've met several people since my arrival to Texas, but I do not know enough about them to call them my friends. Therefore they are only acquaintances."

He got the feeling she was leading up to something. Whatever it was, he probably wouldn't like it.

He resolved to throw her off track. "I don't know a lot about you, either. Reckon that makes you only an acquaintance."

She flicked the green stem of her strawberry into the moonlit field. "You wound me, sir. You know more about me than anyone else in Texas."

He ate more chicken and thought about what she had said. "I don't know hardly anything about you."

"Truly?" She tilted her head toward her shoulder. "Well, I really *haven't* told you much, have I? It wasn't my intention to keep anything from you, though. I can only assume that I've been so profoundly interested in knowing more about you, that it slipped my mind to talk about myself. Later this evening, I promise to answer any question you might ask. But for now I must return to the hotel."

She began gathering the food back into the napkins.

"Where were you born?" he blurted, determined to ask her a couple hundred questions before allowing her to go back to the room.

"New York."

Roman grabbed more chicken from the napkin she held and tore into it as if he hadn't eaten in days. "I'm not done eating yet, Theodosia."

"Oh, very well." She laid the napkins back down. "But please hurry."

He chewed so slowly that the chicken turned to mush in his mouth. "What's your favorite color?"

"I am fond of several colors. I like green, blue, and pink. Are you finished now?"

"No." He ate some corn on the cob next, trying his best to get a lot stuck between his teeth so he could spend time getting it out again. "Did you have any dolls when you were a little girl?"

"A collection of over three hundred."

At least she'd had some dolls, he mused. That was *one* thing normal about her. "Did you play with them every day?"

"Oh, I didn't play with them at all. They were antiques and much too valuable to handle."

So much for the one normal thing about her, Roman thought. "Who's the most famous person you've ever met?"

She leaned back against the rocks again and took a deep breath of the cool, flower-scented air. "I met Ebenezer Butterick once."

"Who the hell is Ebenezer Butterick?"

"He developed the first paper dress patterns. I have also met William Crooks, who discovered thallium, and Joseph Bertrand, who wrote a treatise concerning differential and integral calculus.''

Roman had never heard of any of the men she claimed were so famous. Of course, he didn't travel through the same social circles she did, either. "I met Darling Delight a few years ago. Got her autograph too. She wrote it right on my . . . uh—she has good handwriting. Best handwriting I ever saw.''

"Darling Delight? Who is she?''

"Only the most famous showgirl in the world.'' He slid a hunk of apple cake into his mouth and licked vanilla icing off his bottom lip. "You know what Darling Delight does?''

"No, and I am not altogether certain I desire to know.''

"She takes off her clothes.''

Theodosia retrieved the napkins again. "I have heard enough. We shall we return to the hotel—''

"She pastes yellow, orange, and red streamers onto her breasts, then moves up and down so the streamers start twirling. When I first saw them spin, I thought she'd caught on fire.''

Theodosia stared at him. "Miss Darling Delight is to be highly commended for her worthy contribution to mankind.'' She rose from the ground and brushed bits of grass off her skirts.

"I'm still eating, Theodosia.''

"Roman, I am returning to the hotel now. You may stay out here and enjoy the rest of your meal at your leisure, or you may come with me and perform your job as my protector. The choice is yours.''

Some choice, he thought.

Grumbling every step of the way, he escorted her back to town.

"All you have to do is look into that man's eyes to know he's not the right man to father the baby, Theodosia," Roman whispered into her ear. Sitting in a chair directly behind hers, he had a clear view of each man she interviewed and an objection to all of them.

Theodosia lifted a sheet of paper in front of her face so the candidate sitting across from her could not read her lips. "You didn't like the first man's weak chin, Roman," she whispered in reply to his comment. "You said the second man's pale complexion indicated poor blood that would certainly be passed on to the baby. The third man had a limp that you claimed would inhibit his coital abilities. Now, what in heaven's name is wrong with *this* man's eyes?"

"They're messed up. Look close, and you'll see for yourself. His problem isn't real bad yet, but I've seen this before, Theodosia, and I can tell you that in a few years this poor guy will be completely wall-eyed."

Theodosia lowered the paper and gave the candidate a smile while searching the depths of his eyes. She saw nothing about them that suggested any sort of disorder.

But Roman's suspicions twisted through her mind like an impenetrable mass of vines. "I am sorry, sir," she said to the man, "but you do not meet the requirements. I do thank you, however, for your interest. Good evening."

Frowning, the man stayed seated. "What's wrong

with me? I'm tall, my eyes are blue, and I have black hair."

Roman bolted out of his chair. "And I have two Colts that say there's going to be *a lot* wrong with you if you aren't out of here in three seconds!" He drew both guns. "One, two—"

The man stormed out of the room. Roman slid his guns back into his belt and sat back down, but he remained stiff with irritation as the fifth candidate walked into the room. "Tell him to leave before he even gets a chance to sit down, Theodosia," he whispered.

"What? But—"

"I saw this man earlier," Roman lied quietly. "He stepped out of the saloon and pissed right in the street. You don't want someone so ill-mannered to sire the baby, do you?"

Theodosia frowned in disgust. "Sir," she said to the man as he reached the chair, "I'm afraid you are a bit short in stature."

"What?" the man asked.

"You look like a short statue," Roman translated, "so get out."

Shaking his head in confusion, the man departed.

"Roman, I did not say that man looked like a short statue," Theodosia clarified. "I said he was—"

"Never mind." Roman watched as the next candidate entered the room. Tall, with black hair and blue eyes, the man possessed all the physical requirements.

Running low on his supply of the lies he could tell about the candidates, Roman prayed this sixth man was an idiot.

"Good evening, Miss Worth," the man said. He sat down and ran a long finger across his full moustache. "I am Melvin Priestly. I am twenty-six years old and am the schoolmaster in Red Wolf."

The man was not an idiot, Roman seethed. "Theodosia," he whispered. "He—"

"Roman, please." She studied the candidate, highly pleased with his looks. "How long have you been teaching school, Mr. Priestly?"

"Four years, and please call me Melvin."

Roman glowered. "She'll call you Mr. Priestly, and you damn well better call her Miss—"

"Roman." Theodosia swiveled in her chair toward him. "Please!"

"I'm only trying to make him respect you," Roman explained. "The two of you have known each other for less than five minutes, and he already wants to use first names, for God's sake. Listen, Theodosia. If you don't get respect from these guys, they'll—"

"I am receiving very little from *you*," she snapped, turning back around. "Melvin, please tell me about your interests."

Melvin crossed his legs.

"Look at that, Theodosia," Roman whispered. "He's sitting like a woman. I think he's . . . well, you know. I bet he wears pink underdrawers."

As imperceptibly as possible, Theodosia reached around the chair, intending to pinch Roman's arm. But the second her fingers touched him, she knew it was not his arm she'd found.

Blushing, she snatched her hand away from his groin.

Roman leaned near to her again. "If you want me, all you had to do was tell me. I'll be glad to accommodate you, but we'll have to get rid of Melvin here first."

Theodosia had to curb the urge to fan her face, for she felt unbearably hot. "Your interests, Melvin?"

Melvin rubbed his chin while deliberating. "I read a great deal, and I especially enjoy philosophy."

"Philosophy?" Theodosia leaned forward. "Any philosopher in particular?"

When Roman saw Melvin's gaze dip to Theodosia's breasts, he realized the bastard was getting an eyeful of creamy cleavage. Quickly, he curled his hand around her shoulder and pulled her back into her chair. "You were slouching. Hasn't anyone ever told you that slouching will make your back crooked?"

"I am quite fond of Aristotle," Melvin announced, puzzled by Theodosia's companion's continued whispering. "Pardon me, sir, but are you whispering about me, by any chance?"

Roman raised one black brow. "As a matter of fact, yeah. What was Aristotle's middle name?"

"His middle name?" Melvin repeated, running his finger across his moustache again.

"Roman," Theodosia murmured, "Aristotle was born in 384 B.C., and during that time period people were not given middle—"

"I'm not asking you anything, Theodosia," he interrupted. "I'm asking Melvin."

"Aristotle did not have a middle name, sir," Melvin stated.

"Yeah?" Roman stood and folded his arms across his chest. "Shows how much *you* know. Get out."

Theodosia bowed her head. Staring at her lap,

she willed herself to remain poised. "Roman," she said, lifting her head, "what was Aristotle's middle name?"

Roman didn't miss the smug look that flashed across Melvin's face. Trying frantically to think of a good middle name for Aristotle, he looked around the room and spotted a painting whose artist had signed the right-hand corner. "Egbert," he declared firmly, having read the name *Egbert Booker* on the painting. "His middle name was Egbert, and they called him Eggy for short. Not many people know that. It's one of those rare facts that get lost in the pages of history, and since you failed to find it, Melvin, get out."

Theodosia closed her eyes for a brief moment, then opened them. "Roman, Egbert is an Anglo-Saxon name. Aristotle was Greek."

"Aristotle Egbert's father was from Anglo-Saxon," came Roman's swift reply.

"Sir," Melvin began, "Anglo-Saxon refers not to a dwelling place but to the Germanic people who conquered England in the fifth century A.D. and formed the ruling class until the Norman conquest. An Anglo-Saxon may also be described as a person descended from the Anglo-Saxons, or a white gentile of an English-speaking nation."

Roman walked out from behind Theodosia's chair.

Sensing his black mood, Theodosia rose and stepped in front of him. "Melvin, will you meet with me again tomorrow? I would enjoy a more in-depth conversation with you. Perhaps we could breakfast together?"

"Nothing would give me more pleasure, Theodosia." Melvin stood. "I shall come for you at seven-thirty. I hope that's not too early, but I must be at the schoolhouse by nine."

Theodosia inclined her head. "Seven-thirty is fine."

"Good evening to you both." With that, Melvin showed himself out of the room.

The second the door clicked closed, Theodosia whirled on Roman. *"Egbert*, Roman? *Egbert?"*

Without a word, he crossed the room and disappeared behind the dressing screen.

Theodosia began to follow him but stopped suddenly when his string tie and shirt came flying over the top of the screen. "Roman, are you going to bathe?"

"Yeah. Want to join me?"

She did her best to ignore the rush of warmth his invitation created within her. "I have already bathed in the water that is in the tub. If you must bathe, then you should send for clean—"

"You do not accumulate grime upon your person, Theodosia, but only become a bit dusty. Isn't that what you told me one time?"

"Yes, but—"

"Then this water is clean enough for me." He struggled to pull off his boots.

Theodosia heard them hit the floor and decided that since Roman was behind the screen, she would take the opportunity to change into her nightgown. "Roman, why did you treat Melvin Priestly the way you did?" she asked while undressing.

Because I don't want so much as one of his moustache hairs getting anywhere near you, he answered silently.

"Roman?"

He tugged off his stockings, then removed his gunbelt and laid it over the top of the screen.

"Roman, it was painfully obvious that you did not care for Melvin," Theodosia declared, withdrawing her nightrail from a drawer in the bureau. "I, however, thought him a very proper and intelligent gentleman, and I feel certain that after breakfast tomorrow you will be of the same mind."

He took off his pants.

"Roman, are you listening to me?"

With one smooth motion he tossed his pants over the screen.

They landed at Theodosia's feet just as she slipped into her nightgown. Unable to resist the temptation, she picked the pants up.

They were still warm with the heat of Roman's body. She held them close to her breasts, and the heat swirled into her. Desire flared to life so quickly, she gasped.

Roman heard the small sound and smiled. "Sure you don't want to join me, Theodosia?" he asked, stepping into the tub. "You probably got some dust on you while we ate in that meadow." He lowered himself into the cool water and leaned back against the tub.

She heard him splashing. *Roman was naked.* "Naked," she whispered.

"What was that you said?" Roman called out. *Naked.* That's what she'd said. Chuckling softly, he grabbed the bar of soap and quickly ran it over his body. "Soap up the old arms, Roman," he pretended to talk to himself. "Yeah, that's it. Over the shoulders, down the chest, and around the belly. Stand," he continued, and stood. "Now for the legs. One leg, two legs. Up the thighs . . .

and . . . right in between them. Ah, feels good. Feels damned good."

Theodosia clutched his pants so tightly that her arms trembled. She couldn't see Roman, but just the thought of where his hands were . . . the very idea that he was touching himself . . . holding himself . . . feeling himself . . .

"Hey, Theodosia!"

What? she answered, then frowned when she realized she hadn't spoken the word aloud. "What?"

"You know when I made you rest for those ten days before we traveled to Red Wolf? Well, I didn't tell you this, but sometimes at night when you were asleep, I read that sex-treat book of yours. Guess what that Tibetan guy called a certain part of the male anatomy?"

Weak with desire, Theodosia barely made it to the chair across the room.

"He called it a 'seeking manroot'!" Roman continued merrily. " 'A thrusting sword of passion,' which is, of course, to be sheathed by the 'wet warm velvet of the woman's femininity.' Oh, and get this one—'a flaming spike with which to gently impale the quivering virgin'!"

Theodosia listened as his deep rich laughter filled the room. She realized he thought the Tibetan scholar's descriptions ridiculous, but *she* found them so erotic that she began squirming in her chair.

"I'm getting out now," Roman said. "But don't worry. I'll cover up my throbbing masculinity with a towel." He rinsed the soap from his body, stepped out of the tub, and wrapped a towel around his waist.

Theodosia nearly fell out of her chair when he

walked out from behind the screen. Lampshine shot through his long black hair like bolts of lightning through a midnight sky, and trickles of water glistened on his tanned skin, highlighting swells of muscle that bulged and stretched as he sauntered toward her.

She'd never seen his bare legs before, but she saw every inch of them now, for the towel barely covered his sex. Indeed, as he moved she caught glimpses of the dark shadows between his thick, wet thighs.

"You look a little warm, Theodosia," Roman murmured as he stopped before her. Reaching out, he cupped her cheek and slid his fingers over her temple and around the curve of her ear. "Do you want me to open the window?"

"I will." She jumped from the chair as if flames had suddenly burst from its seat. Her quick action brought her into direct contact with Roman's body, and as she brushed against him, she felt something slide down her legs and land on the tips of her shoes.

There was only one thing she could think of that could have fallen.

"My towel fell off," Roman announced, thoroughly enjoying the blend of desire and apprehension he saw brimming in her huge whiskey eyes.

Theodosia kept her gaze centered on his lopsided grin. "Put it back on," she whispered.

"Why? Don't you want to see the hard, jutting length of my desire?"

Her knees wobbled. "No."

"Sweet little liar, you do *so* want to see it. You're curious as hell to see for yourself what a real-life lunging lance looks like."

"Roman, I am going to hide the sexual treatise so you cannot read any more of it. Now, please pick up the towel and put it back on."

He slid his arm around her waist. "I've got a lot of the book memorized, Theodosia. For example: 'When a man lies with a willing virgin, he must remember that she has entrusted to him her entire future of lovemaking. He must hold her gently, fondle her tenderly, and speak sweet words to her so she will let go of her fears and become moist and well prepared to accept his pulsing staff.' "

Theodosia hadn't the strength to object when he drew her close to him. As he had just described, his sex pulsed against her, and she felt herself moisten with a desire so intense that all she could think about was Roman fulfilling it.

Somehow, she thought of one weak protest. "Roman, have you forgotten what I told you in Singing Creek?"

"What was that?"

"That my willingness led you to believe that we would continue such intimate activities—"

"Oh, that. Yeah, I forgot it. I still can't remember much of it."

"Roman, it is extremely unfair of me to allow you such liberties because—"

"Theodosia, believe me. I see nothing at all unfair about what we're doing. And now that we have that little worry of yours taken care of, let's get back to what I read in your book," Roman murmured. "The man has to hold the woman gently. Like this." He curled his other arm around her and traced her spine with the tips of his fingers. "And he has to fondle her gently. Like this." He brought his right arm around to her front and took her warm, full breast into his hand. "And now for the sweet words."

Bending so that his mouth was but a sigh away from her ear, he pressed a soft kiss to her earlobe and tried to remember some of the sensual lines he'd read in the sexual treatise. He failed to recall any of them and realized that he'd been so absorbed by the passages concerning techniques of lovemaking that he'd only skimmed the parts that concerned flattering a woman.

So he'd make up his own sweet words. "I like your eyes," he whispered. "They're the color of tree bark. The color of a well-worn saddle. The color of whiskey, Theodosia, and if I look into them for a long while, I feel drunk."

Theodosia barely heard him. She could only concentrate on the fact that he was naked, fully aroused, and pressing himself into her.

It was too late to stop him now, she knew. How could she ever have thought it possible to withstand the power of Roman's magnetism in the first place? She could no more escape his hold on her than she could if she were bound to him with ropes.

Roman smiled when she went soft in his arms. "And your lips . . . pink as Secret's tongue. As boiled gulf shrimp. Pink as dawn, Theodosia, and just as pretty."

Turning his head, he kissed a path to her mouth.

She parted her lips for him in sweet welcome. Reveling in his deep, unhurried kiss, she laid her hands on his broad shoulders and emitted a soft sound that was half moan, half whisper, and all surrender.

Roman lifted her into his arms, carried her to the bed, and gently laid her down. His eyes never leaving hers, he straightened, and as he stood beside the mattress, he silently demanded that she look at and know each part of him.

And Theodosia obeyed his sensual command. . . .

Chapter 13

His male beauty brought forth emotions she'd never realized existed. She felt more than astonished, more than captivated.

Wonder enveloped her, an all-consuming sense of awe that defied her to resist the yearning to touch him. Slowly, as if prolonging the pleasurable anticipation, she reached out her hand and slid her fingers into the thick black hair between his hips.

The sight of her pale skin against his darkness both startled and amazed her. Unaware that she was licking her bottom lip, she trailed one finger down his rigid masculinity.

Roman shuddered violently. His head fell back over his shoulders, and a tortured groan ripped from deep inside his chest. Raising his head again, he captured Theodosia with a look that bade her to watch his every move.

She did.

He cupped the soft pouch that hung between his thighs, and then slowly, slowly, closed his fingers around his thick arousal.

In total fascination, Theodosia watched as he

glided his hands up and down. Suddenly, she comprehended what it was he wanted her to do.

She took him gently into her hand. Her own action filled her with a desire so deep, she swore she felt the beginnings of the sexual rapture Roman had once given her.

She lifted her gaze up to his face. "How I can feel the early tremors of pleasure before you have even touched me is beyond my comprehension, but I do feel them, Roman."

He smiled at her, pondering the fact that one of the things he'd always detested about women was their penchant for deception.

Theodosia possessed no such fault. On the contrary, she always spoke honestly about her desire, knowing that he would help her to understand the unfamiliar feelings she experienced when with him.

So as not to startle her, he lowered his massive frame onto the bed as slowly as possible. Stretched out and lying on his side beside her, he curled his hand over her smooth thigh and smiled at her again.

She laid her hand on top of his and felt something right about the moment. Something comforting, as if she belonged right where she was . . .

In his arms, basking in the warmth of his smile.

"Desire—all by itself—feels good, Theodosia," Roman explained. "And now that you've sampled a big part of the pleasure that can be had between a man and a woman, your body recognizes it and—well, I guess you start the pleasure all on your own just by thinking about it."

"I've sampled a big part of the pleasure," Theodosia mused aloud. "I take that to mean that I have not gone full circle."

"No."

She understood what he meant. Without realizing it, she began to fantasize about making love with Roman. Being intimately joined with him— and ultimately creating a child with him.

Her thoughts proved so beautiful that she didn't want to let them go.

But memories of Lillian forced her to do so. She pulled the fantasies from her mind and reminded herself that the child was not to be her own. It would be Lillian's, and Lillian's preference in men was obvious in Upton. Her sister hadn't fallen in love with and married a rugged Texan who wore revolvers at his hips and could track anything under the sun. Lillian had married a brilliant Harvard professor who had dozens of academic awards to his credit.

She could not make love with Roman and risk conceiving. Period.

"You can't get with child by touching me, Theodosia," Roman whispered, seeing her every thought within the depths of her eyes. "And it won't happen by my touching you, either. You know that."

She did know. Moving away from him so she could see him in his entirety, she dropped her gaze and reached out to hold him again. The instant she touched him, the initial pleasure she'd felt only moments ago became an ache that she knew only Roman could soothe.

"Roman?"

He didn't answer but waited patiently for her to

complete her intimate exploration. Only then would he fulfill her need.

He moved his hips slightly forward, coaxing her to continue.

Her eyes tracing the path her fingers took, Theodosia slid her hand up and down, savoring the incredible feel of him.

She thought him velvet, she thought him stone.

She thought him magnificent.

Raising her gaze to his face, she sent him a silent plea.

He rose to his knees and gently pushed her shoulder until she was lying on her back. Lifting his leg over her hip, he straddled her thighs.

Theodosia lay motionless, staring at him so intently that his image etched itself in every crevice of her mind.

Looming above her, keeping her captured between his legs, and gazing down at her with smoldering intent in his vivid blue eyes, he presented a majestic picture of strength and masculinity. She waited in sheer awe for whatever he would do to her.

Slowly, carefully, he lay upon her, covering her body with his own. Desire pumped steadily through him. God, she felt good beneath him. All soft and warm and willing.

Without realizing her own actions, Theodosia parted her legs and lifted her hips into his. His rigid manhood pushed into her belly, and although the sensation sent her to greater heights of desire, she knew something wasn't right.

She wanted to feel him lower. Closer to the ache that continued to throb throughout her womanhood.

With her hands on the mattress, she tried to push herself toward the headboard of the bed.

Roman was well aware that she struggled to position herself in such a way as to feel him poised between her thighs. The woman had no willpower. Impossible as it seemed to be, he would have to be strong enough for both of them.

He took a deep, ragged breath, closed his eyes, and forced himself to concentrate upon the fact that if he made love to her, Theodosia would later hate herself and him too.

The possibility of that happening appalled him so suddenly, he stiffened.

"Roman?" She writhed beneath him again.

"Be still, Theodosia," he whispered, his lips moving within the mass of her fragrant hair, his body ablaze with desire he could barely keep leashed.

"But I—"

"I know." Raising his head, he looked down at her and smiled. "I'm going to do something new. Don't be afraid."

She kissed his shoulder. "I could never be frightened of you, Roman."

Her admission tightened his chest with what he now identified as tenderness. Taking hold of one of the thick, fluffy bed pillows, he rolled to the mattress, then sat up. "Easy, sweetheart," he cooed to her when she reached for him. Smiling gently at her, he slipped his hand under the small of her back, lifted her lower torso off the bed, then positioned the pillow beneath her bottom.

Quickly, he stretched out upon her again and threaded his fingers through her luxurious golden hair. Holding her luminous gaze, he moved his body down hers until he felt his chin glide across the softness curled upon the mound of her femininity.

His warm breath skimmed across her belly. Staring down at him, Theodosia saw that his thick charcoal hair streamed over her white hips and upper thighs, and the sight struck her as one of the most sensual things she'd ever seen. Her breath came in shallow pants, her body trembled, all in silent supplication for Roman to appease her.

In answer, Roman edged down lower. His hands at the backs of her thighs, he lifted her legs so that her knees touched the sides of his head.

Theodosia gasped with sharp pleasure when she felt him lay his tongue flat against the pulsing entry to her body. *Roman. Roman.* His name sang through her veins like a fluid song, somehow increasing the bliss that rose steadily inside her.

Before she even thought to do so, she raised her legs toward her chest, thus assisting Roman in his efforts to open her completely. Stretching out her arms between the V of her thighs, she took his powerful shoulders into her hands, unaware that her nails scored his back.

For a moment, Roman could only stare at her legs, which lay neatly over her chest. Her agility was not only astonishing, it provided him with unhindered access to her female sweetness.

Her position and the impetus of passion behind it made him even more determined to take her to the highest pinnacle of ecstasy. He swept his tongue upward, spreading her slick inner folds with motions that were gentle yet demanding at once.

The feel of her . . . taste . . . the scent of her . . .

Everything about her was exquisite.

Dear God, how he wanted to please this beautiful woman! And as he pondered his desire to sire her pleasure, he realized her fulfillment was more important to him than his own release.

That end in mind, he flicked his tongue over the tiny swell hidden within her woman's flesh. Within seconds, he sensed the early flutters of her climax, and he watched as her bliss swept over her face.

It seemed to Theodosia that the pleasure had no end. Even when the ecstasy crested, it continued for long moments that had her writhing wildly beneath Roman's masterful touch.

Finally, it began to ebb gently away, leaving Theodosia in a state of complete and perfect contentment.

"Thank you, Roman," she whispered. Opening her eyes, she looked down at him and smiled.

He laid his head on her thigh and reached up to caress her breast. Only when he saw that her breathing had returned to normal did he speak. "It didn't hurt when you stretched your legs up like that?" he asked, curious as hell as to how she could have done such a thing without the slightest show of pain.

"Yoga," she answered dreamily. "It's Hindu theistic philosophy. A system of exercises, if you will, for attaining bodily and mental control and wellbeing. There is a lot of stretching involved, and over the years, I have become quite agile."

Roman wasn't quite sure what Hindu exercises were, but he decided the Hindus probably had as much fun making love as the Tibetans.

"I scratched you," Theodosia said, noticing the long red marks on his shoulder. "I'm sorry."

"Don't be." He moved to lie beside her, then took her into his arms.

His sex felt like fire on her skin, making her realize that although *she* had found fulfillment, *he* had not. "You remain in a thoroughly aroused state, Roman."

He held his breath, wondering if she planned to do something about his problem.

But in the next instant he dismissed the idea. He suspected she would comply if he asked, but every instinct he possessed warned that she wasn't ready for anything more tonight.

He planted a small kiss on her forehead. "Being in this state is nothing new to me, Theodosia." *Especially since I met you,* he added silently.

"But I could—although I am not certain how—perhaps if you showed me—"

"No." He held her more tightly, pondering her sweet proposal and the generosity behind it. The other women he'd known in his life had always demanded and taken from him. They'd never given back.

Theodosia was the first who had ever even offered.

He kissed her forehead again.

At his tender gesture, her affection for him rose. Again, she thought about how she longed for him to take her full circle. For him to make true love to her. Their union would be glorious, she knew.

She closed her eyes tightly, frustration twisting inside her. Roman could not be her lover. He could be her friend and nothing more.

And if she continued to forget that fact, she would never see Lillian holding a child.

Struggling to subdue the sadness that suddenly

darkened her mood, she opened her eyes. "Roman, when we were in the meadow," she whispered, "I asked if you'd ever had a friend. You failed to answer me."

He suspected she was doing that psychology thing on him again and waited to feel irritated.

No irritation came to him. Instead, he knew a genuine desire to be as honest with her as she had been with him.

"No, Theodosia," he murmured, drawing his fingers up and down her arm. "I've known a lot of people, but I've never stayed in any one place long enough to make a real friend. What about you?"

She kneaded the muscle beneath his nipple and continued to struggle with frustration and melancholy. "Like you, I am acquainted with a great many people. I study with them. I hold discussions with them. Until I met you, I considered them friends. I understand now, however, that I erred in my judgment. A friend is a favored companion, and although I enjoyed the company of the people I know in Boston, I enjoy yours ever so much more. I like being with you."

Her admission made him feel beyond wonderful.

"Roman?" She buried her face in the thick black satin of his hair. "Would you consider . . . What I mean to say is that—" She paused for a moment, dwelling on her special feelings for him. "I think of you as a friend. And I would like to be your friend as well. A friendship usually exists without verbal proclamation, but—well, taking into account your negative feelings toward women, I feel the need to verify the actuality of such an affectionate association."

He couldn't answer and feigned sleep.

Disbelief pumped through him as he lay there with his eyes closed.

The first real friend he'd ever had was a woman.

While driving the wagon out of the town of Red Wolf, Theodosia skimmed Melvin Priestly's letter once more:

> Miss Worth,
>   Please forgive me for the inconvenience I have caused, but I will be unable to meet you for breakfast this morning. Moreover, I fear I must withdraw my application for the position of siring the child.
>   Sincerely,
>   Melvin Priestly

Her brow furrowed in consternation. "I cannot imagine why Melvin changed his mind," she said to Roman's back. "He gave no reason whatsoever in his note."

Roman rode ahead, glad she couldn't see his smile. "How's your new horse?"

Theodosia glanced at the small horse she'd purchased to replace the one Mamante had taken. "Fine," she replied absently, still pondering the oddness of Melvin's sudden decision.

Another part of her, however, some deep place within her breast, felt relieved that Melvin hadn't shown up. She told herself that her relief stemmed from the fact that she was not yet ready to submit to being bedded. That she needed a bit more time to dwell on the things she would be doing with the man who mirrored Upton in every way.

But that same deep place within her breast also sheltered the truth. Her feelings for Roman had a

great deal to do with her reluctance to lie with another man, and although she knew she would eventually go through with her original plans when she
found a replica of Upton, she knew also that it
would be the most difficult thing she'd ever done.

"Roman, what do you suppose happened to Melvin?" she made herself ask.

Roman's grin grew as he wondered if anyone in
Red Wolf had found Melvin Priestly yet. Having
found Melvin before the man reached the hotel,
he'd forced him to pen the note of cancellation to
Theodosia and had then bound, gagged, and stuffed
him into a shed behind the schoolhouse.

"Roman?"

"What? Oh. Uh, he probably just got tied up.
Don't worry about it. We'll make it to Enchanted
Hill by tonight. There are a lot of men there."

He grinned again. Enchanted Hill had its share
of men, all right, but most of them were uneducated farmers who ventured into town only when
they needed supplies. Roman had met most of the
townsmen and knew that in one way or another
none would satisfy Theodosia's requirements.

And the schoolteacher was an elderly woman for
whom he'd once built a desk.

"You'll get to see Enchanted Hill when we get to
the town, Theodosia," he called. Slowing his stallion, he waited for her to catch up with him. "Leg-
end has it that the hill has the power to grant
wishes."

She gazed up at him, thinking his eyes much
bluer than the sky. "I have told you before what I
think about wishing."

He stopped Secret abruptly, deciding there was
no time like now to change a bit of Theodosia's

thinking. "Are you in a real hurry to get to Enchanted Hill? I mean, is it all right if we get there sometime tonight instead of this afternoon? Today's Sunday, anyway, so you can't get those fliers of yours printed. The newspaper office'll be closed."

She brought the wagon to a halt. "Why would you delay our arrival?"

He didn't answer, but the telltale twinkle of mischief she saw in his eyes fairly blinded her.

Holding on to the tree trunk, Theodosia swallowed the last of her raisin sandwich and looked down to watch her bare feet swing through the air. The ground lay at least twenty feet below. She'd never been in a tree before, and she'd certainly never been in a tree dressed in only her chemise and petticoats.

She smiled, thinking of how she'd gotten up in the tree. Like a big male gorilla, Roman had had her hang on to his back while he'd scaled the tree. He'd brought John the Baptist's cage up into the tree as well, claiming the bird needed to get back into his natural habitat every now and then.

The man was certainly in a silly mood today.

"Having fun?" His arms stretched out to his sides for balance, Roman walked the length of the thick oak limb upon which Theodosia sat, then returned to her.

She cringed as he dodged a thin branch that the wind blew toward his face. "I am not convinced that *fun* is quite the word that describes what I am feeling at this moment, Roman. But I will say that sitting on a tree limb while feasting upon raisin sandwiches is undoubtedly the *oddest* experience I have ever had. What possessed you to suggest we do such a bizarre thing?"

John the Baptist pecked at a few leaves that brushed the side of his cage. "You look like a short statue, so get out," he said, then squawked loudly. "What possessed you to suggest we do such a bizarre thing?"

With the greatest of grace, Roman sat down beside Theodosia and tickled the bottom of her foot with his toes. "I used to do this all the time when I was a kid. Up in a tree is the best place to hide from people you don't want to find you."

"I see." She picked a leaf from a slender branch and twirled its stem between her fingers. "And the raisin sandwiches you took with you, they strike me as a lonely food. Something one would eat only in solitude. Did you eat them often?"

"You're hinting, aren't you, Theodosia?"

"Would you rather I be frank?"

"I knew a Frank once, and I didn't like him much. No, I'd rather you be Theodosia."

She watched him slap his leg as he laughed at his own joke. Biting her bottom lip, she tried to maintain what little composure could be had while sitting in a tree dressed in her underthings. After all, *someone* had to keep foolishness in check.

A second later, she realized that that *someone* was not her. She burst into laughter, laughter that gradually tapered into giggles, which finally became a soft smile.

Roman could not stop staring at her. He'd always thought her beautiful, but her laughter enhanced her beauty to such a degree that she seemed almost unreal. As if she'd come from a dream, or a wish.

But she wasn't a fantasy, and to reassure himself

of that fact he reached for her hand and felt her warmth permeate his senses. "You're enjoying being up in this tree, huh?"

"Strange though it is to me, yes." Her smile widening, she reached out and drew her finger across his bottom lip. "I don't suppose you would tell me who it was you were hiding from when you climbed into trees, would you, Roman?" she asked, her voice as soft as the rustling of the tree branches.

He looked down at the ground, watching as the breeze blew through dead leaves. "The bad guys."

"Bad guys?"

"They were three women." He raked his fingers through his hair. "Well, one was a woman and the other two were girls who grew up into women."

Three! Theodosia thought. "Will you tell me about them?"

He heard tenderness playing through the sound of her voice and remembered she was his friend, as he was hers. He squeezed her hand and nodded. "Yes."

She hadn't expected him to yield so quickly. A thrill spun through her. "Truly? Why?"

"Why? That's a strange question."

"Be that as it may, I'd still like to know why."

"Who the hell knows?"

"But surely there must be a reason."

"I just feel like it! God, why does there have to be a reason for everything, Theodosia? Can't you just accept things the way they are without picking them apart?"

"You don't have to shout, Roman."

He felt immediately contrite. She couldn't help her inquisitiveness. It was as much a part of her as his hot temper was of him. "I shouted so you could see my uvula," he said, hoping to soothe her with a bit of teasing. "Don't you like the look of my uvula?"

"You—"

"I'll have you know that I have the sexiest uvula in all of Texas, Theodosia. Maybe in all the country. Hell, probably in the entire world."

"Roman, you are—"

"Handsome?"

She stared at him blankly for a moment before recovering from the surprise his question caused. "Yes, you are very handsome, but you are also—"

"What do you think is handsome about me? My face?" He turned his face so she could see his profile. "My muscles?" He flexed his arm muscles for her.

"Everything about you is handsome, Roman, but you would do well to know that you are incorrigible. Unmanageable, if you will."

"Is that a compliment?"

She couldn't resist laying her hand on his chest. His heart beat steadily beneath her palm, and she loved the feeling.

If Roman behaved any way other than the way he behaved, she mused, he would not be the Roman with whom she was so taken. "Yes, Roman, your being incorrigible is a compliment."

Smiling smugly, he took her leaf from her fingers and folded it. Holding it to his mouth, he blew into it.

His action created a loud whistle that so startled Theodosia, she almost fell off the limb.

Roman steadied her instantly. "Want to try?" He folded another leaf and handed it to her.

Blowing into a leaf was the farthest thing from her mind, but she tried it anyway.

Roman laughed when the noise she produced sounded more like a snorting hog than a sharp clear whistle.

"I have not had the practice you have, Roman," she said. "Perhaps if I had spent youthful days hiding in trees and eating raisin sandwiches, I would be as proficient at leaf-whistling as you are."

He slid his knife from the sheath tied around his leg and used it to scratch into the limb.

Bits of bark flying into her lap, Theodosia waited for Roman to begin his story. She sensed his need to ponder his memories for a while and so summoned all the patience she possessed.

Her silence had a sound to Roman. Strange as it was, he could hear her understanding, her very real interest in him.

He felt as though he were hearing a song he'd never heard before. A beautiful song whose melody and lyrics had been written especially for him. And he knew then that sharing his past with the beautiful composer of that song would bring him a peace he'd longed to feel for years.

"Flora was her name," he murmured. "She was my stepmother for thirteen of the longest years time has ever made. And then there was Cordelia. And Veronica. They were her daughters, my stepsisters. Cordelia was eight when they came to live on the farm, and Veronica was nine. I was five."

He dug his knife into the tree limb for a while before continuing. "My mother died soon after I was born. I don't know how my father met Flora, but I know he died about a year or so after he married her. Unlike you, I didn't have any blood relatives to go to, so I had to stay with Flora and her daughters."

Just the sound of Roman's voice convinced Theodosia that his memories were going to be as sad to her as they were to him. She swallowed, trying to prepare herself.

"I don't remember a whole lot about those early years, but one thing I recall well is that Flora and her daughters cried all the time. God, they never stopped." Roman paused and ran his fingers over the marks he'd scratched into the limb. "Whenever something didn't go their way, they cried. Flora didn't make any sound when she cried, but Cordelia and Veronica wailed so loud that sometimes I thought they were in horrible pain. I guess I used to cry when I was little, but after I met Flora and her girls, I never cried again."

He continued digging the tip of his blade into the limb. "Pa's name was Bo. Bo Montana. Sometimes, if I don't think real hard and just let the thoughts come, I can sort of remember what he looked like. He had black hair, and he was tall. I can't recall what color his eyes were, but maybe they were blue like mine.

"Before Pa married Flora, he'd had a woman come to cook, clean, mend, and all that other stuff for us. She made big meals and lots of pies. When Flora moved in, the pie lady never came back again.

"I guess Flora started doing everything then. A year later, when Pa was gone, things changed. Flora gave Cordelia my bedroom. I must have been seven then. Before that, Cordelia and Veronica had shared a room. I had a collection of snakeskins on my bedroom wall, a squirrel-and-raccoon-tail rug on the floor, and rows of strange rocks on my windowsill. Cordelia took all my things out of the room. Flora wouldn't let me put them anywhere else in the house, so I ended up taking them to the barn. Anyway, I started sleeping in the front room, and I slept there for thirteen years. But sometimes in the summer I slept outside."

Though her eyes stung, Theodosia successfully won her battle with tears. "Who did all the chores when your father was gone, Roman?" she asked softly.

"I did the ones I could. Flora had some man come do the heavier jobs. But as soon as I was nine . . . or maybe I was ten . . . I don't remember, anyway, around that time Flora gave me more to do so she wouldn't have to pay the man as much money. We had our horse, a few cows, some pigs and chickens, a couple of turkeys, a vegetable garden, and small crops of corn and sorghum to tend to. I got up early and finished as much as possible, and then I went to school with Cordelia and Veronica. After school, I'd come home and work until night made it impossible to see."

Theodosia could see by his scowl that his mood was steadily darkening. "How long were you able to stay in school?"

"Not long. Four years was all. I guess I was about fifteen when Flora decided I was old enough to take on the farm by myself. After that, I didn't have time for school anymore. Cordelia and Veronica had a lot of books, though, and I'd borrow a few every now and then without them knowing. I'd read when I could, but God, there was always so much to do. So many chores, and Flora and her girls wanted so many things, made so many demands—"

He broke off as years-old bitterness erupted inside him, and took a moment to control his heated emotions. "They were three of the greediest people ever born. They had to have new furniture, a bigger porch, a better wagon, wider windows. Some of the things they wanted I made myself, but others I had to buy. To get the money, I started working for neighbors. By the time I was sixteen, I'd done all sorts of work and there was very little I didn't know how to do. When I was seventeen, I rebuilt the house and added three new rooms. Flora used one as a tea parlor, one as a study for her girls, and the other for her own personal sitting room."

Theodosia felt real fury toward the three women she'd never even met. Three rooms! she raged. And Roman hadn't been given a one of them!

"But Flora and her daughters were never satisfied," Roman went on, still carving the limb with his knife. "It didn't matter how hard I tried to please them, they never said thank you. Instead, they complained. If I made them a table, they said it wasn't big enough, or smooth enough, or high enough. The wagon I was able to get them wasn't fancy enough, so they decided they wanted a carriage with velvet seats. I wasn't able to get them that carriage, and they never let me forget it. I bet they cried over that for a solid six months."

For a while he watched a bright red cardinal hop along a higher branch. "Maybe the worst thing, though, was that I always felt like they didn't trust me to do things right. I tried so hard, Theodosia, but they never had any confidence in me, not even when I'd finished a big job well."

Theodosia curled her hand around his shoulder. "Did Flora ever hurt you physically?"

"No, but you know what? She ignored me so much that a spanking every now and then might have been nice. Sounds strange, huh?"

"No, Roman," Theodosia whispered, her heart in her throat. "It isn't strange at all. A spanking, although negative, would have been a bit of attention, and that is what you were seeking."

He saw the cardinal spring off the branch and watched until the bird flew out of sight. "Yeah, well, Flora never spanked me. Except for when she told me what she wanted me to do, she acted like I didn't exist, and so did her daughters."

Theodosia remembered his reaction to the shirt-sleeve she'd mended for him and realized then that Flora Montana had never performed such menial tasks for her stepson. Whatever Roman had needed, he'd provided for himself.

"It occurred to me once that maybe they acted like that because they didn't know me well," Roman added quietly, and sighed. "So I started trying to tell them about the things I thought about. Things I wanted to do one day. Even before I had Secret, I'd wanted to raise horses. I told Flora about my dream of turning the farm into a horse ranch, and she said my plan was a castle in the air. She told me that I would never amount to much more than a dirt farmer. After that, I never told her anything again."

Theodosia closed her eyes. So many bewildering questions had been answered that she didn't know which one to ponder first.

Finally, one settled in her mind, and she dwelled upon Roman's ignorance of unselfish love. Raised by demanding women, he had no way of understanding that giving was as much a part of love as receiving.

The thought caused her to remember his refusal to consider marriage. She knew now that his hesitation stemmed not only from his adverse feelings toward women but because after thirteen years of providing for his thankless stepmother and stepsisters, he simply could not bear the idea of having to take care of another woman.

And then there was his reluctance to discuss his goals. Yes, he'd eventually told her about them, but she suspected he'd never revealed them to anyone else. He was right to keep such lucrative plans to himself, but his secrecy involved more than that. Talking about his ambitions would have made him vulnerable to the same ridicule and lack of faith his stepmother had shown him.

Sighing, she opened her eyes again and saw that Roman was watching her. "Why didn't you leave Flora and her daughters, Roman? I realize you were young, but as proficient as you were, you could have made your way in the world."

The very real sorrow he heard in her voice touched him so deeply that he could not answer immediately. "I thought the farm would belong to me one day. Flora always said it would pass to me when I was eighteen. God, I loved that farm, Theodosia," he murmured, clenching his hand into a fist. "It was home to me, and both Ma and Pa were buried on it. I couldn't imagine ever leaving it, especially when I believed it would be mine. And I wanted to show Flora what I'd do with it. She said I'd be a dirt farmer, so I was hell-bent on becoming a rancher right before her eyes."

Theodosia watched his fingers turn white around

the hilt of his knife. "You didn't get the farm, did you, Roman?" she asked achingly.

He turned away for a moment, his pain so agonizing that he didn't want her to witness it. "No. I didn't get the farm. She lied, Flora did. Pa hadn't left a will. So when he died, the farm and everything on it passed to Flora. She lied to me to keep me there working for her. I've asked myself a million times why I didn't ever ask to see Pa's will, but I can never think of an answer. I don't know why I believed Flora. I just don't know. But I'll tell you one thing. I've felt damned stupid over it for a long, long time. Every time I think about it, I curse myself for a fool."

Theodosia realized Roman had every reason in the world to distrust women. Flora Montana had been beneath contempt, and the betrayal he'd suffered at her hands was unconscionable. "Roman," she began, summoning every shred of the knowledge she'd gained from her years of intense study, "the human mind is incredible in many ways. Sometimes, when it senses the possibility of terrible grief, it devises a sort of defense mechanism to protect its own sanity."

He turned back to look at her again.

She saw the hope in his eyes. Hope that she would somehow make him feel better.

And she knew then that she was speaking not only to Roman the troubled man, but to Roman the hurt little boy as well.

Taking a shaky breath, she chose her words with the greatest and most tender of care. "I think perhaps that you allowed yourself to trust Flora's promise because you simply could not conceive the possibility of losing the land that meant so much to you. You shut away the terrible prospect to keep the worry from tormenting you. And you loved the land far more than you hated Flora. It was that love that gave you the strength to bear her cold treatment of you. Such feelings do not label you a fool, Roman, but a man with a gentle heart full of wonderful dreams."

As he listened to her speak, tranquillity lit up a dark place inside him. He'd teased her about her genius in the past, but at this moment he felt grateful for her intelligence, for in the space of only a moment her wisdom laid to rest his years' old self-condemnation.

"Roman," Theodosia pressed gently, "how did you come to learn the farm was not to be yours?"

He met her gaze and kissed her with his eyes. "After Flora met a man by the name of Rexford Driscoll in the nearby town of Hawk Point. She took one look at him and practically threw herself at his feet. Driscoll had recently gambled away his land in a game of cards and was on his way back east. I think he said he was from Virginia.

"Anyway, when he saw our house and farm, he asked Flora to marry him. She did. I didn't go to the wedding, but after the ceremony she came looking for me. She found me in the corn field, and she still had her wedding dress on when she told me she was selling the farm. I had a basket of corn in my arms, and I dropped it. She didn't seem to notice, but went on to inform me that Pa hadn't left a will and that the farm was hers to sell."

Viciously, he dug his blade into the tree branch. "I stayed awake all night, walking all over the land I had thought would belong to me. But no matter how hard I thought . . . no matter how fast or far

I walked, I couldn't understand how I could get Flora to let me keep the farm. I didn't have any money, and I knew she wouldn't give me the farm out of the kindness of her heart. By late afternoon the next day, she'd sold the farm to a merchant from Hawk Point. The man had plans to raise peacocks. Said they fetched a good price from wealthy people who wanted something elegant and exotic strutting around their gardens. My land— peacocks."

Shaking his head, he massaged the back of his neck and the muscles in his shoulder. "I don't know how much Flora sold the farm for, but I reckon she did well with the sale. It wasn't a big farm, but it was good land. With the money in his pocket, Driscoll took Flora, Cordelia, and Veronica back east with him. I never heard from any of them again, but sometimes I wonder how long Driscoll put up with those three women."

"Flora didn't leave anything for you?" Theodosia asked, appalled. "Nothing at all?"

"Our mustang mare," Roman answered, and smiled. "But the only reason she left the horse to me was that she thought it was worthless. The mare's name was Angel. She was Secret's dam, and his sire was Driscoll's Thoroughbred. Like I told you before, I bred the horses one night when everyone was asleep. The way I see it, Driscoll and Flora didn't leave me with nothing. They left me with the knowledge of exactly what breed of horses I would raise on my ranch, and I've been working toward that goal ever since."

The depth of his strength and determination astonished Theodosia to such an extent that tears threatened to spill again. "Do you realize how remarkable it is that you have become the man you are, Roman? Many people whose childhoods were similar to yours live their entire lives wallowing in self-pity. Constantly doubting themselves, they are afraid to decide upon a dream, much less attempt to reach it. You not only know what you want, but you have very nearly attained it."

At her praise, his tranquillity deepened and mingled with the relief he felt over having finally shared his past with someone who cared enough to really listen.

He finished carving the tree limb and slid his knife back into its sheath. "The memories I just told you about are the bad ones, Theodosia, but I have some good ones too. It's true I was on my own when I was a kid, but I did a lot of fun stuff to keep myself busy. Whenever I could escape, I'd spend hours playing away from the house."

She imagined him as a little boy, running all over the farm and investigating everything he encountered. Her daydream touched her heart. "What sort of play did you indulge in?"

He didn't reply. *Telling* Theodosia about the fun he'd had wouldn't accomplish a thing. No, he would show her—and urge her to participate. He didn't think it would be difficult.

After all, he'd already succeeded in getting the prim little genius up into a tree.

Smiling, he tapped the bars of John the Baptist's cage.

The parrot responded by splashing water every which way. "I'm going to buy Spanish mares down in Mexico," he stated.

"Yeah?" Roman said. "What a coincidence. So am I."

The bird blinked. "I read a great deal, and I especially enjoy philosophy."

"I like to read about sex," Roman declared.

John the Baptist ate a peanut. "What do you think is handsome about me? My face?"

"Don't get him started, Roman," Theodosia scolded. She reached for her parrot's cage, then tried to rise.

"Just sit there for a minute," Roman advised, standing. He stepped over her, hunkered down, and got a firm hold on the tree trunk. "All right, now get on."

Holding her bird cage with one hand, she positioned herself on Roman's back, wrapped her legs around his waist, and curled her arm around his neck. Just as he began his descent, she caught a glimpse of what he'd carved into the tree limb.

Her heart stirred.

She'd seen her name engraved upon scrolled diplomas, gold jewelry, and a wide variety of other elegant items.

But she'd never seen it carved in the wood of a live oak tree.

Chapter 14

As Roman walked out of the Enchanted Hill hotel the next morning, he found the hotel owner polishing the brass urns that sat beside the door.

"Good morning, Mr. Montana," the man said.

Roman nodded. "When you get a chance, could you put a new doorknob on room two? The one that's on the door now is hard to open."

"Lord have mercy, I meant to have that thing fixed last week. The last person that stayed in that room couldn't get out at all and was locked inside until someone finally heard him screamin'."

"Then you'll fix it?"

"Sure thing, Mr. Montana. Sure thing."

Satisfied, Roman walked out into the street, but the bustle of activity that met his eyes stopped him short.

Many of the townsmen were busy scrubbing the fronts and sides of buildings. Women swept the boardwalks, washed windows, and planted bright red geraniums in barrels that decorated the sides of the street. A group of adolescents beat dust from carpets they'd carried out of various buildings. Even the children worked. Smiling and laughing, they raced around the street hanging red, white, and blue ribbons on every available post in the town.

Roman decided some dignitary was passing through. Or maybe it was the mayor's birthday. Shrugging, he headed into the telegraph office and sent Theodosia's latest message to her sister and brother-in-law. She wired Lillian and Upton whenever she had the chance, and when she couldn't she posted letters. All her messages concerned her continued studies of oral meandering. Roman had no idea what oral meandering meant but decided it was too boring a subject to bother himself with.

Next, he visited the general store with a specific idea of what he wanted to buy. Fifteen minutes later, he bought a new rifle to replace the one he'd given Mamante, and also purchased another very special item. He had the storekeeper's daughter wrap the item in yellow paper and tie it up with a bright red satin ribbon. With the rifle and the pretty box under his arm, he walked out of the mercantile, whereupon a young boy promptly handed him the daily newspaper.

One look at the headline not only explained the reasons for the townspeople's efforts to spruce up the town, it sent foreboding speeding through him.

ENGLISH ARISTOCRATS ARRIVE TONIGHT!

"Ain't that somethin', mister?" an elderly man commented as he sat rocking in a chair beside the store door. "Lord, ain't nothin' like this ever happened in little ole Enchanted Hill. Did y'git to read the story yet?"

"No," Roman gritted out.

The man rubbed his grizzled cheek and crossed his bony legs. "Well, as I understand it, some seven

Englishmen got their heads together and decided they didn't want to take some Grand Tour thing over there in Europe. Wanted to take a tour of our own Southwest instead, and once they got here to Texas, somebody tole 'em about Enchanted Hill. I reckon they's a-comin' to make a few wishes on the hill, jest like ever'body else does who passes through. Anyhow, they sent a real dignified committee ahead of 'em to see to their hotel reservations, train and stage schedules, and things like that. Them English 'ristycrats is all rich, y'know."

Rich was not the only thing those English dandies were, Roman seethed. They were educated. *Highly* educated, just like Theodosia. And with seven of them coming, it was very likely that at least one would be tall, dark-haired, and blue-eyed. Wealthy as they were, they wouldn't care about getting Theodosia's gold, but they for damned sure wouldn't refuse a string of long and passionate nights in her arms.

Dammit, he had to coerce her into leaving Enchanted Hill before she got a look at the newspaper!

He bolted back toward the hotel, raced through the lobby, and flew up the stairs that led to the rooms. When he reached his and Theodosia's room, his palms sweated as he grasped the doorknob.

It wouldn't turn until he exerted all his strength on it. Finally the door opened, and he saw her. She stood beside a table, upon which sat a bowl of apples, oranges, and several ripe lemons.

"Roman," Theodosia whispered. "Have you seen this?" She held up the newspaper so he could read the headline emblazoned across the top of the page.

"A hotel employee slipped the paper under the door shortly after you left. I—you—do you realize what this means?"

He knew exactly what it meant. She had the same thoughts about the aristocrats that he did. Nothing he did or said would keep her from meeting with the Englishmen.

But feelings he couldn't understand, couldn't name, made it imperative that he try.

He tossed his new rifle and the yellow box to the bed and drew himself up to his full height. "We're leaving Enchanted Hill right now, and I don't want to hear a word of argument." He crossed to the closet and pulled out her trunks. "Get your things packed."

"Roman—"

"For God's sake, there's a contagious disease spreading through town," he lied desperately. "If we stay a second longer, we might catch it. Pack your bags."

She stared at him. "What kind of disease?"

"Measles," he blurted.

"I had a terrible case of the measles when I was seven. Therefore I am now immune to the disease."

He stuffed his hands into his pockets, summoning more lies. "Yeah? Well, I've never had a single measle anywhere on me. But even if I had, these are rare measles, Theodosia. They just got discovered. Could be that those sickly Englishmen are the ones who brought these measles over here from Europe, so we're leaving."

Hope soared within him when she joined him in front of the closet. "I'll help you pack your dresses." He grabbed a few of her gowns from the

closet, wadded them up, and stuffed them into one
of her trunks.

"Roman, wait." Theodosia stayed his hand as he
reached for more of her clothes. "Please, let's talk
about this."

He had no inkling of how to discuss his raging
emotions. All he could understand was that Theodosia was not going to leave Enchanted Hill willingly. And he knew intuitively that if she stayed
here, by tonight she would find the perfect man to
sire the child.

Fury blasted through him like a horrible scream.

His silence deafened Theodosia to everything but
the sound of his anger and hurt. She lowered her
head and stared at his boots.

He didn't want her sleeping with one of the Englishmen any more than she wanted to do it, she
thought. And why *would* he support such a thing?
The intimacy they'd shared had resulted in *her*
pleasure, but never his. He'd respected her refusal
to allow him to make love to her, had honored her
reasons for denying him.

But the fact remained that he had wanted her,
desired her every bit as much as she did him.

And now, after he'd shown such incredible control and understanding, she was going to freely give
herself to another man.

She'd never felt more selfish in all her life.

Awash with guilt, she lifted her head and centered her gaze on his chest. "I'm sorry, Roman,"
she whispered.

He stared into her eyes, trying desperately to find
something within them that would convince him
that she felt the same inner turmoil he did.

When she looked away, he knew that if indeed

her emotions paralleled his, she was not going to allow them to decide her actions.

He stepped away from her. "Sorry, Theodosia?" he flared. "About what?"

She frowned softly. "For—for hurting you."

"Hurting me?" He feigned an expression of deliberation, then a look of sudden comprehension. "You think you'll hurt me by going to bed with one of those English guys?" he asked, forcing disbelief into his voice. "Why would that hurt me?"

"I . . ."

"Let me explain something to you," Roman continued hotly. "I liked the feel of your body, but what I liked more was seeing if I could get you to let me touch you. Your denials and protests were like dares, and I don't turn down dares, not ever. The only thing I ever cared about was trying to get the innocent little genius into bed with her clothes off. I did it, and as far as lovemaking goes, hell, I don't care whose thighs I lie between. The ends are always the same."

He forced a smug smile and ambled toward the door. "You're nothing but a job to me. Got that? We'll stay in Enchanted Hill for as long as you want, and you can do whatever the hell you feel like doing."

He twisted the doorknob forcefully and left the room.

Theodosia stared at the door.

You're nothing but a job to me. . . .

Part of her knew he'd spat the words only to disguise his hurt. But another part of her recognized the truth of what he'd said. They'd become close friends, yes, and they'd shared some beautiful moments together. But the fact remained that she *was* a job to him, a means by which he could obtain the rest of the money he needed to start his ranch. And considering the vast differences in their dreams, she would never be anything more to him.

Sorrow clutched at her heart. She swore she could feel it bleed.

Before she realized it, she was hurrying to the door with every intention of going after Roman and making him believe that *he* was the man to whom she wanted to give her innocence, not some Englishman passing through town.

But she stopped abruptly when the scent of fresh lemons assaulted her senses. Startled, she glanced at the bowl on the table and noticed the ripe lemons.

Lemons. Lemon verbena.

Lillian.

She curled her hands into fists by her sides, swallowed a cry of frustration, and tried to rationalize. "Theodosia," she whispered to herself vehemently, "if you fail to maintain a firm presence of mind, your heart will surely guide your actions. For Lillian's sake, you mustn't let that happen. You *mustn't.*"

Her mind. Her heart. A real battle had begun between her intellect and her emotions.

She knew which would win.

The powerful pull of the mind was far more decisive than the simple little tug of the heartstrings.

With gay sounds of laughter and lively music surrounding him, Roman leaned against one of the posts of a whitewashed picket fence and watched Theodosia swirl around the town square.

She outshone every woman present. Moonbeams

and lamplight flickered through her golden hair, shimmered over her mint-green satin gown, and glowed within the depths of her dark emeralds. But it was not the light or her jewels that caused her to shine.

It was her sparkling beauty, and the tall man holding her in his arms was completely captivated by her.

His name was Llewellyn. Hammond Charles Alexander Llewellyn. The second son of a rich and powerful English duke, he had wavy black hair, clear blue eyes, and wore a diamond the size of a horse's eye on his right hand. Roman decided the guy was as obnoxious as his name.

It certainly hadn't taken Theodosia long to make her choice, he ranted silently. Of course, the group of Englishmen had made things easy for her. She'd stood in the hotel lobby, watching as they entered. After only one look at her, all seven of them had headed straight for her, and each of them had asked for her company at tonight's welcome dance.

She'd given her company to all of them, but had spent the most time with Hammond Llewellyn. Yes, Hammond was the one, Roman knew.

The one who would know Theodosia in the most intimate way possible for a man to know a woman.

Roman wished she would get herself in some sort of risky situation so he could draw his gun, shoot, and accidentally hit Hammond Llewellyn.

He straightened when he saw her leave the dancing area and make her way through the crowd. She walked straight toward him.

So did Hammond. The Englishman walked with quick light steps, as if he were treading barefoot upon sharp rocks. He wore a black suit on his lanky body, and Roman thought he looked like a burned candle wick.

"Roman," Theodosia said when she reached him, "I thought you should know that Hammond and I are going for a stroll."

She hated informing him of her plans with Hammond, feeling as if she were flaunting her relationship with the nobleman. But Roman had insisted on performing his duties as her protector tonight, and she knew she had to tell him where she was going and what she was going to do.

While waiting for his reply to her statement, she took her fill of him. Dressed in a beige shirt that stretched tightly across his chest and black breeches that left nothing to her imagination, he caused her to forget to take her next breath. He appeared so casual, she thought, so totally at ease.

But she knew that behind that relaxed facade existed lethal power that could uncoil with the speed of a striking serpent.

Her admiration and affection for him filled her so quickly, she became light-headed. Without realizing her actions, she reached for the fence post to steady herself.

Reacting instantly, Roman shot out his hand and took her arm.

His touch made her breathing difficult once more. "Roman?" she murmured. "Are you coming with us?"

He wondered if her breathlessness was caused by dancing or by her attraction to Hammond. Stifling anger, he gave a stiff nod.

"Do you mean to say that he is joining us on our walk, Theodosia?" Hammond queried.

Roman pinned the Englishman with a glare. "You got a problem with that?"

Hammond stared at the tall, extremely well-muscled man whom Theodosia had earlier introduced as her bodyguard. In the long-haired gunslinger's eyes glittered a look of danger, the like of which Hammond had never previously encountered. The man appeared sufficiently sinister to belong to that horrid Blanco y Negro Gang he'd heard so much about since his arrival in Texas.

Dear Lord, these Texans were crude, Hammond thought to himself. Indeed, he'd regretted ever having traveled to this uncivilized part of America until he'd set eyes on Theodosia Worth, a woman who possessed all the grace of the noblewomen he knew in England.

Hungry for the sight of elegance after journeying through so many seedy areas throughout Texas, he'd been struck by Theodosia's beauty and poise the moment he'd seen her standing in the hotel lobby. Unfortunately, his six companions had likewise been attracted to her, but that no longer seemed to be a problem. Theodosia had obviously decided he was the best of the lot, which proved her intelligence, to his way of thinking.

Glancing at her, he wondered what proposition it was that she said she'd put to him during their walk. She'd refused to discuss it here at the dance but had insisted they wait until they could speak privately.

Hammond brushed a speck of lint off his coat sleeve and glanced down his nose at Roman. "Do forgive me, sir, but I cannot seem to remember your name."

Roman folded his arms across his chest. Was he

so inconsequential to this British womanizer that the man could not even recall his name? "Montana. Roman Montana. How long are you here for, Hamm?"

Hammond bristled. "My name is not Hamm. It is Hammond."

"Roman has been the most marvelous company for me during my travels through Texas, Hammond," Theodosia quickly commented, feeling an instant desire to defend Roman from Hammond's obvious dislike. "Since meeting him, I have learned a wealth of information concerning—"

"Concerning the art of making a campfire?" Hammond taunted. "Concerning skinning squirrels, or hacking down trees for the building of log cabins, perhaps?"

"Hammond," Theodosia said, "please."

"I haven't taught Theodosia how to make a campfire, skin a squirrel, or fell trees for a cabin, Hamm," Roman began, his eyes narrowed. "But I've taught her a few other things you didn't mention. Why don't you ask her what they are?"

When Hammond looked at her, Theodosia felt her cheeks begin to burn. "Roman has demonstrated many new skills to me," she answered lamely.

"I see." Hammond deliberated upon her flustered expression and the fact that she had defended the gunslinger. It dawned on him then that there was more to her relationship with Roman than she would have him believe.

It maddened him that she would exhibit her fondness for an uneducated backwoodsman while in *his* presence. Why, *he* was a blueblood!

He faced Roman again. "Theodosia has no further need of your skills or services tonight, Mr. Montana. I shall see that no harm comes to her. Why don't you go to the saloon and drink, or whatever it is you Texas gunmen do to entertain yourselves? Off you go, now."

Roman smiled. "What we *Texas gunmen* do to entertain ourselves is kill people, Hamm." For effect, he slid one of his Colts from his belt and couldn't resist spinning it in his fingers. He performed the feat so quickly that the shape of the weapon vanished, and it appeared as though he held nothing more than a flashing gleam.

And then, in less than a second, the gun stilled completely in his hand, its barrel pointed straight at Hammond. "I think I'll go along with you and Theodosia. Maybe I'll entertain myself by killing a few people while we stroll along."

A moment passed before Hammond recovered from his astonishment and apprehension. "Theodosia," he said with all the authority he believed was afforded to a man of his aristocratic status, "one need not know cheap gun tricks to shoot straight, my dear. Such sleight-of-hand foolishness can be found in any circus. You do not need your bodyguard tonight. I am wearing a pistol, and I assure you that I am an expert marksman."

"I'm certain you are, Hammond," she replied tightly. "But Roman is—"

"Oh, very well," Hammond snipped, loath to hear her praise Roman further. "Shall we stroll now? I am ever so impatient to escape the sound of this homespun Texas music and discuss the proposition you mentioned earlier." Without so much as a glance at Roman, he led Theodosia away from the revelry.

Not bothering to keep a discreet distance, Roman followed them to a creek that bubbled beside a cluster of oak trees. A gentle breeze rustled through the leaves, moonlight washed over the swaying grass, and the air smelled of the roses that grew in the well-kept garden near the edge of town.

What a perfect setting for romance, Roman decided, moving to stand directly behind Theodosia.

"If you do not mind, Mr. Montana," Hammond said, "Theodosia and I would prefer to speak alone. Your standing behind her like some sort of guardian angel inhibits our privacy."

"I *am* her guardian, Hamm, but I assure you that I'm no angel."

Hammond snorted delicately. "All right, but I must ask that you step far enough away so as to be unable to eavesdrop upon our conversation."

"I don't have to eavesdrop," Roman retorted. "I know exactly what she's going to say to you." He laid his hand on Theodosia's back and urged her closer to Hammond. "Well, Theodosia? This is the moment you've been waiting for. Get on with it."

She parted her lips to speak but could not find her voice. Roman was right. This *was* the moment she'd been waiting for. Aside from his physical looks, Hammond Llewellyn possessed degrees in Greek and Latin literature and had graduated with honors from Oxford University. He fit her requirements as smoothly as her glove fit her hand.

"What's the matter?" Roman murmured into her ear. "Have you changed your mind?" He spoke the words with a caustic edge to his voice, but every part of him hoped they were true.

Theodosia trembled when Roman's long thick hair brushed her cheek and his warmth drifted into her. She caught his scent of fresh air, leather, and earth and remembered the security and tender contentment she gained by his nearness.

God help her, she yearned to turn and feel him take her into his arms.

"Theodosia?" Hammond took her hand, lifted it to his mouth, and kissed it. "Do not keep me in such suspense, my dear. If indeed there is something with which I may assist you, you've but to ask."

"Yes," she said softly, struggling to tame the wild emotions Roman evoked. "You—there is something with which you may assist me. I . . ."

She paused. To find the courage she needed, she concentrated on the memory of Lillian lying in bed the morning she lost her fourth child. She recalled her sister's tears and the look of utter defeat in her eyes.

And she remembered her own profound desire to give Upton and Lillian the one thing no one else could give them.

"Hammond, I have resolved to give my childless sister a baby," she blurted, then continued quickly. "I shall bear the child for her, but until this afternoon I met with no success in finding the man who met the requirements I set concerning the paternity of the babe. I sought a man who resembled my sister's husband both physically and intellectually. You, Hammond, exceed my expectations, and I—" She closed her eyes. "I would like you to impregnate me. Should you agree to my proposal, all fatherly obligations toward the child will be waived, and I shall pay you in gold for your services."

When she finished, Hammond took off his coat

and held it close to his stomach so as to allow it to drape the front of his lower torso.

But his efforts were for naught. Roman had already seen the distinct bulge between Hammond's legs. He turned, walked away, and peered into shadows as black as his mood.

"What an unusual gift for your sister," Hammond said, his voice quaking with amazement and desire. "She is extremely fortunate to have a sister who is as generous as you are, Theodosia. Does she resemble you?"

Theodosia opened her eyes but kept her gaze cast to the leaf-strewn ground. "Very much so."

"Ah, then I gather you are endeavoring to give her a child who will be most like a child she and her husband might have created together."

"Yes." To keep her hands from shaking, Theodosia clasped them together. "I would have your answer now, Hammond."

He smiled at her. "Theodosia, I am honored to have qualified to sire such a special child, and I accept your proposition."

It was done, she thought. The father would be Hammond Llewellyn. She would lie with the British aristocrat and conceive his child.

Her mind spun with so many thoughts that she became suddenly dizzy. Taking a step backward, she sought to encounter Roman's hard warm body, and lean against him.

She met with empty air. After a glance over shoulder, she saw Roman standing well away from her, and felt his distance keenly.

When she turned back around, the disquiet Hammond noted in her eyes reminded him of the affection she harbored for Roman. What she saw in that vulgar gunslinger, he couldn't fathom.

He dismissed his own irritation, however, upon remembering that the beautiful Theodosia Worth had chosen *him* to take to her bed, not the ignorant Roman Montana. "Did you have a date and time in mind, my dear?" He hoped fervently that she planned to begin trying for the child this very night, for he'd wanted her ever since he first spotted her this afternoon.

"Not tonight," Theodosia said, surprised by her own quick answer. "I . . . I'm afraid I am much too weary, Hammond. Roman and I have been traveling, and I—"

"I understand." He kissed her hand once more. "Of course, you must rest. I shall collect you in the morning at eleven, whereupon we can enjoy a late breakfast together and become further acquainted with one another. And now, please allow me to escort you to your hotel room."

As she walked back toward town at Hammond's side, she heard Roman's footsteps behind her. Before this night, he'd gone ahead of her, leading and protecting her with his skills. Now he trailed in her shadow.

A deep sense of sorrow gathered in the center of her chest, and she was suddenly glad Roman walked behind her.

That way he couldn't see her tears.

"You didn't sleep last night." Roman stood in the middle of the room, watching as Theodosia emerged from behind the dressing screen. "I heard you tossing."

She stopped beside one of the two beds in the

room and stared blankly at the patchwork quilt. "You did not sleep, either, Roman. I watched you rise from your bed and pace."

He didn't reply but waited to see if she had more to say to him.

She said nothing until she noticed his belongings beside the door. "What—"

"I'm moving to another room," Roman explained upon seeing her look of confusion. "I can't stay in here with you, and you damned well know it. It wasn't so long ago that you informed me that I would have to sleep somewhere else once you'd picked the man to father the child. You do remember saying that, don't you?"

Her eyes burned, but she allowed not a single tear to fall. Holding Roman's intense gaze, she nodded.

He stared back at her.

Silence clung to the air like choking humidity until a loud knocking at the door finally broke it.

"He's here," Roman said. *Mr. Perfect*, he added silently.

"Are you—are you joining us for breakfast?"

Roman swore the tension between them was thick enough to slice. "I think you'll be safe enough with Sir Blueblood and his fine little English pistol. If any dragons come along, he'll rescue—"

The knock sounded again. "Theodosia?" Hammond called from the corridor. He knocked again.

Theodosia crossed to the bureau to retrieve her gloves and bonnet.

Each time Hammond knocked, Roman's agitation rose. He glared at the door. "I'll go keep him company while you finish dressing." Quickly, he

moved toward the door, struggled with the doorknob, and stepped into the hall.

Hammond watched him shut the door. "Is Theodosia—"

"She's not ready yet." Roman leaned one shoulder against the wall and crossed his arms over his
chest.

"I see." Hammond fondled the large diamond on
his finger. "And do the two of you always share a
room?"

"Yeah."

"The same bed as well?"

Roman smiled. "That's none of your business."

Flustered, Hammond patted his carefully
combed hair. "I presume you will be tagging along
for breakfast?"

"Where Theodosia goes, I go."

Hammond scowled. "You will not be present
when I perform the services Theodosia has chosen
me to execute, will you?"

Roman raised one black eyebrow. "Only if you
need a man there to tell you how to perform them,
Hamm."

At the blatant insult, Hammond slapped his
gloves across Roman's cheek.

Roman didn't flinch.

"Have you nothing to say about the fact that I
slapped you, sir?" Hammond asked incredulously.

Roman sent a dangerous smile into Hammond's
eyes. "Ouch."

"Sir, by slapping your cheek with my glove, I
have issued a challenge to you," Hammond explained, his irritation growing to anger.

Roman laughed. "You challenge men with gloves

in England? What do you sissies do when the fight comes? Throw socks at each other?''

Hammond knew a fury that transcended all thought of civil behavior. Instantly, he reached inside his coat.

But before he had time to even touch the metal of his pistol, Roman whipped out his Colt, cocked it, and aimed it at Hammond's chest.

Hammond paled with fear.

Roman decided the man looked as if he'd dipped his face into hot white wax and let it harden there. ''If you can't bed a woman any better than you can pull a gun, Hamm, then I think it'd be a damned good idea for me to be there while you attempt to get Theodosia with child. I could sit across the room and call out step-by-step instructions.''

Hammond had no chance to form a reply. From inside the room, Theodosia was trying to open the door. ''Roman, are you out there? The door won't open.''

Hammond took the knob but failed to turn it. ''It seems to be jammed, my dear. Give me a moment, and I will bring the manager.''

Roman moved Hammond's hand away and forced the doorknob to turn.

As soon as the door opened, Theodosia saw Roman's heavy revolver in hand and understood that the two men had had words.

''This savage drew his gun on me,'' Hammond announced.

Theodosia waited for Roman to elaborate.

He only met her gaze.

She read the truth in his brilliant blue eyes.

Watching their silent exchange, Hammond was reminded anew of their simmering attraction to each other. As he had last night, he tried to convince himself that their emotions didn't matter, that *he* was the man who would bed Theodosia.

But his injured pride demanded reprisal, and after a moment of thought, he knew precisely how he could gain such satisfaction.

He threw back his bony shoulders. "Theodosia, I simply cannot endure this man's presence. His thunderous expressions, dripping sarcasm, and fondness for violence have taken their toll on me. Indeed, my sensibilities have been tormented to such an extent that I must reconsider accepting your proposition."

Theodosia laid her hand on his arm. "Hammond, surely you do not mean to—"

"Yes, my dear, I do. I am afraid that I will be unable to assist you in the fulfillment of your goals. I understand your unwavering desire to present your beloved sister with the child she has been unable to have, and I do apologize for having caused this inconvenience. I shall, however, stand firm in my decision. Good day to you both."

Roman watched the nobleman march down the corridor, then turned back to Theodosia. He saw bewilderment in her beautiful eyes, and shock, and panic.

He saw defeat, and he understood that as she watched Hammond vanish down the hall, she was watching her goal disappear as well.

Something happened inside him at that moment. He couldn't name it, but it made him resolve to prevent Theodosia from losing what she'd worked so hard to attain.

He leaned against the wall again and folded his

arms across his chest. "Well, you win some, and you lose some."

Slowly, Theodosia moved her gaze from Hammond's back to Roman's face. "I beg your pardon?"

"You lost, Theodosia. Failed with your plans. You aren't going to get a kid for your sister. It's just as well, though. It was a dumb idea in the first place, and it got even dumber when you picked that aristocratic ass."

His callous attitude hurt her. She realized he didn't want her sleeping with Hammond Llewellyn, but he didn't have to gloat over the fact that her plans had fallen to ruin. "Roman—"

"I'll see you later." Roman tipped his hat and started down the hall. "I saw a few Thoroughbreds at the livery, and I'm going to go take a closer look at them. I've got a ranch to buy and horses to put on it, in case you've forgotten. You might have failed with *your* plans, but I'm for damned sure not going to fail with *mine*."

Still pretending smugness, he continued to stroll down the hall. When he reached the stairs, however, he raced down them, reached the lobby within seconds, then hid behind a tall potted plant by one of the windows.

In a few moments he saw Theodosia enter the lobby. She crossed through the room, exited the hotel, and stepped outside.

He watched her from the window. She spotted Hammond walking down the boardwalk and hastened to catch up with him.

The nobleman took her hand, brought it to his lips, and kissed it.

And the place inside Roman that Theodosia had managed to light up went dark again.

Chapter 15

Theodosia turned up the lamp and chose the chair farthest away from the one in which Hammond sat. They'd spent the day together. Hammond had driven her to Enchanted Hill. He'd made a wish; she had not. The day was over now.

Night had fallen.

Was it her imagination, or did the bed seem to be getting bigger? Every time she looked at it, it appeared to have grown, as if to remind her what she was supposed to be doing in it.

A shiver of apprehension skimmed down her spine.

Folding her hands together on her lap, she examined her hotel room as though she'd never seen it before. It *did* seem different, she thought. No bullet-studded gunbelt or black hat hung on the hatstand, and no boots lay in the middle of the floor. The closet contained her gowns, but not a single man's shirt, and atop the dresser lay scattered a bit of her jewelry, her lacy handkerchief, and her reticule, but no sheathed dagger.

The room even smelled different. She couldn't detect the scent of sunshine or steel or leather or the musky scent of hard work. She recognized only the fragrance of her wildflower perfume and Hammond's spicy cologne.

The room contained nothing that might have reminded her of Roman.

"Theodosia, please do not be anxious." Hammond tried to reassure her but could not help wondering when she would allow him to take her to bed. "I am a gentleman, and I shall be quite content to wait until you are sufficiently comfortable to proceed with your plans. We—"

He broke off suddenly when the sound of wagon wheels filled the room. Turning toward the window, he saw a parrot perched in a cage and realized the bird had made the sound.

John the Baptist threw peanut shells and water at the windowpane. "Did you know the real John the Baptist got his head cut off?" he called.

Hammond rose and approached the window. "A *Psittacus erithacus*. And what a handsome African gray he is too. From whom did he hear the story of John the Baptist, Theodosia?"

Glad for the distraction her parrot had provided, Theodosia unfolded her hands and smoothed her chocolate-brown skirts. "His name is John the Baptist, but as for what he just said, I imagine Roman told him the story in a moment of anger. Roman has been at odds with my parrot on several occasions." She smiled, remembering not only Roman's habit of arguing with the bird as if the parrot could understand, but the two times Roman had saved John the Baptist's life as well.

She recalled Roman's crooked grin too. His quick temper, his unmatched survival skills, his boundless common sense, his deep, rich laughter, and all his hard-earned dreams.

She had so many memories of Roman Montana. "Theodosia?"

She blinked and saw Hammond staring at her. "Yes?"

"My goodness, what are you dreaming about? The look on your face suggests you are in another world."

Another world, she mused. Yes, the world she'd shared with Roman. "I was thinking about Brazil." She smoothed her skirts again.

Hammond nodded but didn't believe her. Oh, she'd told him about Brazil and the estimable Dr. Eugene Wallaby, but Hammond knew it was not the scientist or the Pindamonhangaba beetles that filled her thoughts.

It was that long-haired savage she'd been running around with. What a bloody nuisance the gunslinger was! Even when the man was not in Theodosia's presence, he was with her in spirit. Of course, Theodosia being in the same room she'd shared with Roman Montana did not help matters, Hammond realized. No doubt she "saw" him in every corner.

"Yes, well," he said to her, "while you were daydreaming about Brazil, I asked you how your parrot has fared on the journey through Texas."

"He has fared well, Hammond, thank you."

John the Baptist pecked at a bar on his cage. *Vulgare amici nomen, sed rara est fides.*

"'The name of friend is common, but true friendship is rare,'" Hammond translated. "He's listened to Latin quotations, I see."

"I had a collection of snakeskins on my bedroom

wall," John the Baptist announced. "He has fared well, Hammond, thank you."

Theodosia felt a sudden sense of foreboding when she remembered how much her parrot had heard Roman say in the past. "Hammond, please sit down, so that we may—"

"I am a gentleman," John the Baptist interrupted. "I'm going to raise horses!"

"My, but he is loquacious, isn't he?" Hammond commented.

John the Baptist lifted his right wing. "I was thinking of Brazil. Don't you like the look of my uvula?"

Theodosia stood and hurried to the window. "John the Baptist hears a great many things, Hammond, and more often than not I have not an inkling as to where he has heard them. He—"

"When Flora moved in, the pie lady never came back," John the Baptist continued.

Hammond leaned down to the cage for a closer look at the bird.

The parrot squawked. "Why the hell is he talking about beetroot? I'll cover up my throbbing masculinity with a towel."

Hammond gasped. The bird was imitating Roman Montana, he realized. The curse and indecent sexual comment convinced him of that.

Throbbing masculinity. Hammond felt a surge of jealous anger. "Fascinating bird," he forced himself to say. "Simply fascinating."

"I told Flora about my dream of turning the farm into a horse ranch," John the Baptist screeched, "and she said my plan was a castle in the air."

Theodosia quickly covered the cage with a cloth. Her parrot protested immediately by throwing water on the cloth. "I've heard of going insane, blind, or growing hair on the palm of your hand. Awk! She was Secret's dam, and his sire was Driscoll's Thoroughbred."

Hammond didn't miss the look of dread that leaped into Theodosia's eyes, nor did he ignore the fact that she'd swiftly covered the cage. The parrot was most definitely repeating what it had heard Roman say in the past, and Theodosia apparently considered the statements exceedingly private.

He straightened and led her back to her chair. "Well, my dear, how do you feel?"

She knew precisely what he meant. Hammond was ready to proceed with the bedding. "I . . ."

"Would you care to converse for a while longer?"

His suggestion relieved her immensely. "Yes. Yes, I would."

He smiled. "What shall we talk about? We've been together all day and have already discussed a wealth of subjects." He looked around the room, pretending to deliberate upon a possible conversation. "Why don't we discuss a few of the things your parrot mentioned? I must say that he is quite astonishing. What has he heard about a pie lady, for goodness sake? And who does he know named Flora?"

She was saved from having to answer when someone knocked on the door. "Excuse me." She stood and advanced to the door. "It's not locked, but it won't open," she said when the doorknob wouldn't turn.

Standing in the corridor, Roman grasped the knob and forced the door open.

Theodosia drank in the sight of him. She hadn't seen him since that morning, and although the uncaring attitude he'd shown over the possible failure of her plans continued to sting her feelings, she'd thought about him all day. "Roman."

He'd never seen her wear the dress she had on tonight. The same color as her eyes, it looked beautiful next to her pale skin and flaxen hair.

He wondered if she'd put the pretty gown on especially for Hammond. He wondered, too, when she would be taking it off for Hammond.

He knew he shouldn't have come to her room, but he hadn't been able to stay away. "I left some things in one of the dresser drawers. Can I get them?"

Hammond snorted. *"May* you get them," he corrected imperiously, then stiffened when an ice-blue gaze sliced across the room and stabbed into him.

Never taking his eyes away from Hammond, Roman strode into the room, his Colts sliding upon his thighs. Taking his time, he removed a shirt, a razor, and a black kerchief from the dresser drawer.

Hammond cleared his throat to get Theodosia's attention and stifled a vindictive smile. "While Mr. Montana is collecting his things, why don't you sit back down so that we may continue our conversation, my dear? I believe a few of the subjects mentioned were a pie lady, a person named Flora, the unattainable dream of turning a farm into a horse ranch, and a certain Thoroughbred who belonged to Driscoll. Those were the topics we were about to discuss, were they not?"

Roman went completely rigid. Only his eyes moved as he settled his gaze on the sole person in the world in whom he'd ever confided.

Theodosia.

She'd betrayed him.

His silent fury blasted into her like a fireball. "Roman, you don't under—"

"I do understand, Miss Worth."

She watched contempt blaze into his eyes as he continued to stare at her. But his loathing did not grieve her as deeply as the profound pain she saw there as well.

She rushed toward him, desperate to allay his suspicions.

He walked straight past her and stopped at the door, which remained wide open. "I met a man this afternoon who offered me a job down in Morgan's Grove. I came in here to get the rest of my things because I'm leaving Enchanted Hill."

Shock flew through Theodosia. She grappled for the top of the dresser to steady herself, then started toward him again.

He gave her a look that expressed his every feeling.

She stopped, suddenly comprehending how his enemies felt when confronted by the stark look of danger he was capable of presenting. It was frightening enough to stop a heartbeat.

Satisfied that she understood his silent warning not to cross him, Roman left the room and closed the door behind him.

"Theodosia, what happened?" Hammond asked, feigning total confusion. "Mr. Montana appeared rather irritated." He walked to where she stood and laid his hand on her shoulder. "Theodosia?"

She couldn't answer. Panic gripped her as if with crushing fists.

"Theodosia, what—"

"I have to stop him," she whispered. "I have to

stop him!" She threw herself toward the door and grabbed the doorknob.

She pulled, pushed, and pounded it, but it would not budge. "Hammond, help me with the door!"

"Of course." He ambled to the door and took a moment to examine the knob. Slowly, he curled his fingers around it and gave it a few token jiggles. "I cannot understand why the hotel management has not repaired—"

"Hammond, please!"

For a full ten minutes, Hammond made a great show of trying to force the doorknob to turn. "Theodosia, I am afraid we are imprisoned in this room."

She began to bang on the door with her fists. "Someone open the door! Is there anyone out there? Someone open the door!"

It seemed to her that all of eternity passed before the hotel manager finally arrived and opened the door. "Miss Worth," he said, "I'm sorry I forgot to fix—"

"Which room does Roman Montana occupy?" she demanded.

"Mr. Montana? He was in room eight, but my wife checked him out about fifteen minutes ago."

Theodosia raced out of the room, ignoring Hammond's shouts for her to stop. When she reached the end of the corridor, she dashed down the stairs, hastened through the lobby, and ran into the street. Frantically, she scanned the town. When she didn't see Roman anywhere, she ran to the livery.

There she found her wagon and her own horse.

But Secret was gone.

* * *

"I have a surprise for you, my dear." Sitting beside Theodosia on a bench in the town's sunny rose garden, Hammond patted the top of her hand and utilized every speck of the gentlemanly behavior that had been bred into him.

Inside him, however, dwelled an ever-growing impatience. Theodosia had refused to allow him back into her room last night after Roman Montana had left town, and she had remained in her room until well past noon today, pining away for the ignorant gunslinger.

But Hammond felt positive that if she would only allow him to perform the services for which she'd chosen him, she would forget Roman Montana's very existence. He prided himself on his sexual prowess. Indeed, none of his three mistresses in London ever had cause to complain.

Theodosia wouldn't either, he vowed. Oh, she'd explained what the intimate nights would entail, and although he'd said nothing at the time, he had no intention of following her rules.

Coitus in a pitch-dark room, indeed! Theodosia lifting her nightgown only to her hips! No kissing! No caressing!

Just swift penetration and the spilling of his seed.

How ludicrous, Hammond mused. With each passing moment in Theodosia's company, his desire for her increased, and it had become almost impossible for him to keep his hands off her. "What have you to say?"

"A surprise," Theodosia murmured, fiddling with the heart-shaped ruby brooch at the throat of her gown. "How nice, Hammond." Good manners dictated that she look at Hammond's face while he talked to her, and she did. But it was not Hammond she saw.

Roman's image hovered in her mind. Indeed, she'd thought of nothing else since his sudden departure last night.

Tears burned the backs of her eyes. She couldn't understand how it was possible to have any left to shed.

"Theodosia, I feel I owe you an apology, my dear. I offer one now, and I hope you will accept it."

So intense were her thoughts of Roman that a moment passed before Theodosia understood what Hammond had said to her. "An apology?"

He nodded. "I am not certain what it was I said last night that so disturbed Mr. Montana, but I assure you that it was not my intention to ruffle him," he said, forcing sincerity into his voice. "Why, I was not even speaking to him but to you. I truly am sorry, Theodosia, for whatever it was that I might have done that led him to leave."

She bowed her head.

"I understand how you must feel," Hammond continued. "You and Mr. Montana spent a great deal of time together, and you miss him. But Theodosia, do you forget your ambitions? Bearing a child for your sister is not your sole objective. There is also your research in Brazil, which is a truly laudable undertaking in the interest of mankind. And I am certain that Mr. Montana has goals of his own. You did not believe you would remain in his company for an indefinite period of time, did you?"

Theodosia forced herself to concentrate on what Hammond said. "No." The word escaped her on the same whisper that blew the truth through her mind. Hammond was right. The day would have come when she and Roman would go their separate ways in search of their separate dreams.

She just hadn't expected the day to come so soon, and she certainly hadn't expected it to bring Roman such pain.

"I believe I have the remedy for what troubles you, Theodosia," Hammond said, patting her hand again. "It occurred to me last night that there are a great many things in town that must remind you of Mr. Montana. After all, the two of you arrived here together and stayed in the same room."

Theodosia closed her eyes for a moment. *Roman.* His name echoed through her while she wondered where he was, what he was doing. Did he hate her now? Would he curse her memory forever?

Realizing she was dreaming about Roman, Hammond decided that the sooner he put his plans into action, the sooner he would taste Theodosia's kisses, caress her soft body, and feel her writhing beneath him.

The very thought made him tremble with lust.

He helped her off the bench and escorted her to the carriage he'd rented. "I shall show you the surprise now, Theodosia. I've no doubt it will ease your distress considerably." Handing her into the vehicle, he had to suppress a smile of excitement.

"Where are we going?" Theodosia asked as he drove into the countryside surrounding the town.

"You will see for yourself when we arrive."

Twenty minutes later, when he stopped the carriage before a quaint cabin not far from the legendary Enchanted Hill, Theodosia remained bewildered.

Hammond alighted from the carriage, then assisted Theodosia. "This is the surprise," he said, gesturing toward the cabin.

She examined the log cabin. Emerald-green ivy climbed along one side of the structure, a blue swing hung from the porch roof, and the garden of brilliant red zinnias that edged the front had attracted the attention of two hummingbirds. Theodosia watched the tiny birds for a moment, then looked at Hammond. "The cabin is quite lovely, but I'm afraid I do not understand why you brought me here."

He took her elbow and led her into the house.

Theodosia stopped short in the front room. Her trunks and bags lay on the floor near one of the three windows. On a small table near the fireplace sat John the Baptist, asleep in his cage with his head beneath his wing.

"Your horse and wagon are safe in a shed behind the cabin," Hammond informed her. He removed his gloves and laid them on the top of a small pie safe. "I spotted this cabin yesterday when you and I visited Enchanted Hill. Of course, I thought little of it until this morning, when I realized it would be just the thing to take your mind off your depression. After renting it from the man who owns it, I took the liberty of having all your belongings moved here while you and I enjoyed our midday meal and conversed in the rose garden earlier. I have also hired one of the townswomen to bring us three hot meals a day so that we do not have to trouble ourselves by going into town to dine."

Theodosia turned to face him. "I gather that you wish us to live here, but what I do not comprehend is why."

"It's quite simple, my dear," he replied, glancing

at her lush round breasts. "As I said before, many things in town remind you of Mr. Montana. You and he never came to this cabin together, so there is nothing here that could possibly cause you to remember him. I am only trying to help lessen your sadness so that you will feel more at ease while accomplishing your dream of conceiving a child for your poor sister."

She almost told him that she could be on the other side of the world and still think of Roman. She needed no reminders to remember the man who had somehow carved his name on her heart, just the way he had carved hers on the oak tree.

She walked into the small bedroom in the back of the house and glanced at the bed.

Roman was gone. Missing him would not bring him back.

He'd reach his dreams. Soon. She had all the faith in the world that he would.

And she would attain hers as well.

She peered up at Hammond, who had followed her into the bedroom and now stood beside her. He was the perfect sire, and so she would lie with him as quickly and frequently as possible until she conceived. Then she would bear the child and get on with her life, which had been her plan all along.

She looked at the bed again. "Tonight, Hammond," she murmured. "When darkness has fallen, I will lie with you."

Roman kicked dirt over the remaining embers of the campfire he'd made a few miles outside Enchanted Hill. By his best estimation, it was around noon. He'd meant to be long gone by now, but had not found the will or the effort to hurry. Instead, he'd cleaned his weapons and tack, groomed Secret, washed his clothes, and polished his boots.

He kicked more dirt over the dead campfire and noticed an oak sapling growing nearby. Someday the tiny tree would be huge. And perhaps a man would climb it and carve a woman's name into one of the branches.

He looked into the woods, in the direction where Enchanted Hill lay. Had she gone through with it and let Hammond Llewellyn into her bed?

Pain radiated from his chest like streaks of poison from an infected wound. He raked his fingers through his hair, then mounted Secret.

No job had actually existed in Morgan's Grove. With no specific place to go, he allowed Secret to choose the way. The stallion tossed his head and ambled down a woodsy path that led south.

Before long, the path gave way to a long stretch of rocky dirt. A green lizard slithered off the warm dirt and into a mass of thorny vines. Roman paid no attention to the reptile.

Why? he asked himself for the thousandth time since last night. Why had she discussed him with Hammond Llewellyn? The question swarmed through his mind just as a cloud of gnats swarmed around his face.

Several hours passed. The buzz of the gnats grew louder, sounding more like bumblebees. Roman took off his hat, rubbed the back of his hand over his sweating forehead, and breathed air saturated with sharp odors.

He stopped Secret and sat straight and still in the saddle.

A powerful storm was brewing.

Hammond Llewellyn was a highly educated British nobleman, but he had no knowledge of Theodosia's terror of lightning.

Roman did.

Hammond counted the hours for nighttime to arrive. As he and Theodosia strolled away from the cabin and through the windswept meadow, he glanced at the bright sky. Would the merciless Texas sun never set?

"Here we are," he said when they finally reached the huge oak tree that grew in the same field that featured the famous wishing hill. "Would you care to dine now, Theodosia? I'm sure the lady from town packed a delicious supper for us. I instructed her to prepare only the finest meals." He held up the picnic basket the townswoman had brought to the cabin a short while ago.

Theodosia sat down on the ground beneath the shelter of the oak branches. Fondling the heart-shaped ruby brooch nestled amidst the froth of lace at her throat, she remembered that the last time she'd eaten near an oak tree, she'd been up *in* it, not below it.

Hammond sat down beside her and handed her a plate of thinly sliced roast beef, tiny new potatoes, tender green beans, and fluffy biscuits.

She accepted the plate but remembered raisin sandwiches. A strong force pulled at her heart, drawing forth tender emotions that almost made her weep.

"My fellow companions departed Enchanted Hill this morning," Hammond said, and took a bite of his biscuit. "I am to join them in a small town by the name of Rolling Ridge, whereupon we shall prepare for our return to London. But do not fret,

my dear. My companions will not reach Rolling
Ridge for another month, so you and I have ample
time together."

When Theodosia remained silent, Hammond became more determined to draw her into conversation. If he couldn't make love to her yet, he could at
least fill the hours with lively discourse. "I saw a
smattering of Comanche Indians recently, Theodosia. My companions and I were visiting a town by
the name of King's Cove when a group of soldiers
passed through with their Comanche captives. As I
recall, there were five or six warriors and one
squaw with a baby. The red-skinned devils were almost dead, but do you know their black eyes continued to smolder with the promise of violence?
The soldiers executed them that very night, but
from what I understand two escaped, a warrior
and his son."

At that, Theodosia gave him her undivided attention, her heart thrashing against her ribs and spine
as thoughts of Mamante and his child returned to
her memory. "A warrior and his son?"

Made smug by the fact that his conversation had
so seized her interest, Hammond ate another bite
of biscuit, took his time chewing, and nodded. "The
soldiers hunted everywhere, but failed to find the
brave who escaped with the child. The warrior
might have been able to fashion some sort of crude
weapon after he escaped, but he'd been beaten se-
verely. And without food or a mount, he and his
child most likely perished. Their deaths are a bless-
ing, as I see it. Anyone with a jot of intelligence
comprehends the fact that this country can never
live up to its full potential while there is a single

one of those horrible Indians alive, and I, for one, fully support their eradication."

Theodosia recalled Roman's deep compassion and gentle understanding toward Mamante. The Comanche warrior of whom Hammond spoke might not have been Mamante, but it didn't matter.

Hammond's insensitive views repulsed her.

"Don't you agree, Theodosia?" Smiling, Hammond dabbed the corners of his mouth with a red-and-white-checkered napkin.

"No, Hammond, I do not agree," she snapped. "Furthermore, I find your lack of compassion grossly unsettling."

He almost choked on a mouthful of potatoes. "Compassion? For an *Indian*?"

Her anger increased, as did her understanding of Hammond Charles Alexander Llewellyn. Did she really want this cold-hearted man to father a baby for her kind-hearted gentle sister and brother-in-law?

What if the child inherited Hammond's cruelty?

"The Indians are people, Hammond, not animals to be slaughtered at the will of white men. They possess the same emotions as other human beings, and pride is among the feelings they experience. You have no right to celebrate the killing of such a proud people. Nor have you the right to hope for the eradication of an entire race. Why, you hoped for the death of an *infant*, Hammond! An innocent *baby*!"

"But I—"

"And while we are on the subject of your personal opinions, I shall take this opportunity to inform you that Roman's ability with his weapons is not sleight-of-hand foolishness. You, Sir Blueblood,

would do well to master the same skills he possesses. Moreover, I will have you know that Roman
Montana is not a savage but a man whose kindness
is of such astonishing depth that I fear it goes well
beyond your realm of comprehension."

Hammond reddened with fury. "You prefer that
ill-bred gunslinger to me!"

Theodosia presented him her back and looked
out over the wide open field ahead. The orange,
blue, and lavender wild flowers splashed vivid colors through the long, verdant grass, and sunbeams
spread shimmering goldness upon everything they
touched. A few sparrows skimmed directly above
the flowers. They flew so low that it appeared to
Theodosia that the vegetation brushed across their
feathered breasts.

A hot breeze swept past her, bringing with it an
unusually loud sound of crickets. She listened to
the sharp noise for a moment, then breathed deeply
of the humid air, discovering it to be filled with an
especially strong scent of cedar.

An eerie sensation crawled over her, like insects
creeping upon her skin.

"Theodosia," Hammond flared, "I allowed my
companions to continue their tour without me because you and I had an agreement. I have spent a
goodly amount of money renting the cabin and paying the townswoman to bring our meals. I must
insist that you honor the bargain we made."

She continued to stare into the meadow. Her om-
inous feelings intensified.

Through her mind drifted a conversation she'd
once had with Roman.

*Mr. Montana? About the rain—how did you
know?*

The birds were flying close to the ground, Miss Worth. The sounds were sharper, and everything smelled stronger than usual. Three sure signs of rain.

The sparrows in the meadow, she thought. The cricket sounds, and the strong scent of cedar.

She looked up into the oak tree.

A storm was gathering.

She was sitting beneath a tree.

Picnicking.

She scrambled off the ground, and just as she began to run, black clouds moved in front of the sun. A dark shadow veiled the ground, and a wicked fork of lightning stabbed through the somber sky.

Theodosia could barely see through her tears. Having no idea in which direction she fled, she continued blindly through the meadow.

Hammond chased her. "Theodosia! Theodosia, stop!"

She heard him calling to her, but a deep, loud rumble overcame his voice. She thought it was thunder, until five white horses galloped into the distance ahead.

Upon each snowy steed sat a black-garbed man.

"Theodosia!" Hammond shouted again. He continued racing after her but stopped suddenly when he saw the five mounted men on the other side of the field. Horror consumed him. He'd heard enough about the outlaws to know exactly who they were. "Theodosia, it's the Blanco y Negro Gang!"

With no further consideration for Theodosia's safety, he turned and fled toward town.

Theodosia slowed her frantic pace long enough to look over her shoulder and see Hammond leaving her. Alone beneath a sky that continued to siz-

zle with dangerous lightning, and at the mercy of
five criminals whose horses now sped toward her,
she felt a sickening terror rise into her throat, cut-
ting off her breath and almost gagging her.

Real thunder joined the roar of the horses' hoofbeats. As the terrible noises hammered through
her, she ran. Rain began to pelt her face and
drench her skirts. The soggy fabric clung to her
legs, slowing her flight.

Lightning crackled above her, and the horses galloped behind her. She saw Enchanted Hill and
stumbled toward the small knoll. There she fell
facedown, and the horses stopped all around her.
One pawed the earth near her feet.

"Get up, woman."

Lightning continued to flash, followed by terrible
thunder that shook the ground on which she lay.
Her tears slipped into the sodden grass.

"I said get up!"

A moment later, she felt strong hands grab her by
the waist and haul her to her feet. When the man
spun her around, she saw a jagged scar on his forehead, as jagged as the lightning.

He pushed her against the hill. "Well now, look
at these big brown eyes. Big tits too. And hair the
color of our gold. Purty, ain't she?"

The other four men dismounted. Rain and tears
impairing her vision, Theodosia could hardly see
them. They were but black blurs coming toward
her.

She dug her fingers into the side of Enchanted
Hill, feeling dirt squeeze under her nails. A wish—
the first she'd ever made—filled every corner of her
heart.

The men gathered around her, touching her. She

felt millions of hands on her, and twice that many groping fingers. Quaking with fear and the knowledge that she was going to die, she closed her eyes but could still see the glare of lightning.

She heard the ripping of fabric and more thunder.

Rain beat upon her bare breasts.

Gunfire rent the air, loud enough to overcome the thunder. Theodosia gasped, waiting to feel the burning pain of bullets smashing into her body. She felt nothing but the sting of the rain as it continued to batter her breasts.

The crack of more gunshots exploded in her ears. The men around her began to shout and move away from her.

She opened her eyes and watched two of the outlaws crash to the ground beside her. One had a moustache, and the other was the man with the jagged scar on his forehead. Blood splattered her hand and the side of her skirts.

She looked up. Into the meadow.

Through the silver drift of rain, a gray stallion charged toward the hill, his hooves ripping up the wet ground and leaving a spray of mud in his wake.

And astride the extraordinary steed, both his guns drawn and his long ebony hair flowing like a black banner behind him, was her wish come true.

Roman Montana.

Chapter 16

A violent madness had come over Roman as he watched the Blanco y Negro Gang pin Theodosia to the side of the hill. He swore that in only minutes, they would all be dead.

His vow burned into his heart as if branded there.

His powerful legs his only means of staying on Secret's back, his potent rage unleashing every shred of skill he possessed, he let go of the reins, fitted his rifle to his shoulder, and took careful aim. He had no worry of hitting Theodosia; Secret's smooth, steady gait enabled him to aim with deadly accuracy.

He shot twice. When he saw two men fall at Theodosia's feet, he knew they were dead.

The other three outlaws returned fire, but Secret's speed made Roman a target too fast to hit. In seconds the magnificent stallion reached the hill.

Roman quickly shot a third man, then threw himself off Secret's back. While he was still in the air, he snatched his dagger from its sheath, and as he fell, he plunged the knife into the belly of the man directly before him.

The man staggered, but retained enough strength to kick the knife out of Roman's hand. Roman saw him raise a revolver and rolled to the side in time to dodge the bullet.

He bolted to his feet and grabbed the outlaw. One arm around the man's neck, his other curled around the top of the man's head, he gave one strong heave.

The man fell, his neck broken.

Heaving with fury and exertion, Roman looked up and saw the fifth man riding into the meadow. The other four white horses followed.

Roman whipped out his Colts.

"Lightning."

The soft voice, like the glimmer of a single star in a midnight sky, broke through his savage craze. He lowered his guns and stared at the four dead men lying in the mud.

The infamous Blanco y Negro Gang. Dead. He'd killed them. They'd tried to hurt Theodosia.

But one had escaped.

Again, he raised his guns toward the outlaw riding out of the rain-swept field.

Something touched his back. Fingers. They trembled.

"Roman."

He groaned, spun in the mud, and lifted Theodosia into his arms. With one mighty motion, he set her upon Secret's back, then collected his fallen weapons and swung into the saddle.

Theodosia laid her head on his chest and wrapped her arms around him as he urged Secret into a ground-eating gallop. She could still hear the thunder, rain smacked her skin, and the stallion's hooves made a battering noise.

But the loudest sound of all was the beat of Roman's heart.

Her breath warmed Roman's chest. He held her tighter and felt her shake. She was so wet, he thought. Her breath was warm, but her breasts were cold.

And bare.

Anger erupted inside him again. He wanted to scream. Instead, he kept Secret on a swift and steady course toward the small cabin in the near distance. When he finally pulled on the reins, the stallion came to an abrupt but smooth halt.

Theodosia in his arms, Roman dismounted and raced toward the cabin. One firm kick opened the door; another closed it.

He stopped in the front room. One look at it told him exactly what had happened.

Theodosia's belongings lay scattered all over the floor, and Roman knew her gold was gone. Apparently, the Blanco y Negro Gang had found the cabin before they'd found Theodosia.

He stared at the empty fireplace, knowing he had to voice the question in his mind but dreading its answer. "Did they rape you?"

She heard nothing but his heartbeat. It sounded through her, releasing a twisted torrent of memories. "The Comanches," she said, speaking into his chest. "Hammond was glad they killed the Indians, Roman."

He frowned. What the hell was she talking about?

"One escaped," Theodosia whispered, "with a baby. Hammond hoped they died, but perhaps they were Mamante and his son. You gave them food. A horse, and a rifle. But first you fought Mamante.

You returned his pride. He hired the lady from town to bring the picnic. Hammond did."

She clawed at his shirt when she saw more lightning through the window. "I tried to find you last night, but the door wouldn't open. Secret was gone, and I knew you were too. The lady made roast beef, but I could only think of raisin sandwiches."

Realizing she was incoherent, Roman carried her into the bedroom and laid her down on the bed. The sight of her bare breasts made him clench his fists.

But with a gentleness that belied his brutal fury, he began to remove her wet clothes. When she was naked, he drew a quilt over her body, gathered her in his arms, and held her close.

"He said it was a surprise," Theodosia whispered. "This cabin. But I would have remembered you, no matter where he took me. He wasn't the one, Roman. I could not have lain with him."

Roman understood then that she had not lost her innocence to Hammond Llewellyn. But what about the Blanco y Negro Gang? "Theodosia—"

"I smelled the storm. Heard it. The sparrows flew low over the meadow. I imagined the blossoms skimmed their bellies. Beneath the tree. Roman, we were beneath the tree. Picnicking. With all the lightning. Just like my parents. I—I have never known such terror."

She made no sound, but he felt her tears wet his cold damp shirt.

"I was afraid, Roman, and so was he. He left me. And then I was by myself with the lightning and those men. I ran, as quickly as I could. But the lightning chased me, and so did those men. I made a wish. Not on a star, but on Enchanted Hill. And then you came."

"So they didn't—"

"No. You killed them before they could. One got away."

He didn't speak for a long while. "I'm sorry for leaving you last night."

His apology warmed her far more than did the quilt he'd wrapped around her. "It was John the Baptist," she whispered. "Please believe me, Roman. It was John the Baptist."

He understood instantly. She hadn't betrayed him. Her parrot had.

The heavy burden of guilt pressed down on him. "I'm sorry," he said again. "God, I was just so mad, Theodosia. I never took time to think that it might have been the bird and not you."

"Anger has a way of relieving us of rational thought."

Her intellectual statement assured him that she was calming down.

She blinked up at him. "Why did you come back?"

He moved a wet lock of her hair off her forehead, then watched rain slide down the windowpane. "The storm. Llewellyn didn't know how scared you are of lightning. I hated thinking that, so I came back. The manager at the hotel told me you and Llewellyn had checked out and that Llewellyn had hired a few men to move your things to this cabin. I'd planned to keep you safe from the lightning. Instead, I found you at the hands of the Blanco y Negro Gang."

She felt him kiss her bare shoulder and pondered what he'd told her. Still believing she'd spilled his secrets to Hammond, he'd ridden straight into a barrage of bullets for her. He'd killed four men for her.

He might have died for her.

Such profound feelings came over her that she lost her breath entirely.

A loud squawk tore through her thoughts and caused her to gasp in air. Shifting, she peered over Roman's shoulder and saw John the Baptist waddle into the room.

"They must have turned his cage over when they ransacked the place," Roman mused aloud. "At least they didn't hurt him."

"Ransacked? Who—"

"Didn't you see the front room? Your things are thrown all over the place."

"What?"

"Your gold is gone, Theodosia," he said softly, hating to tell her but knowing he had no choice. "Your jewelry probably is, too, except for the heartstrings brooch that's still pinned to what's left of your gown. The gang was here before they found you in the meadow."

Her tears trickled onto his hand, shining up at him like wet diamonds. Staring down at them, he discovered that the tears themselves brought him no dismal feelings.

But Theodosia's sorrow tormented him.

"What shall I do now?" Theodosia squeaked. "Roman, without money, how shall I—"

He silenced her with a long and tender kiss. And then, his lips still caressing hers, he whispered words he never believed he'd tell to any woman.

"I'll take care of you, Theodosia."

* * *

She had no idea where Roman would take her. Drained as she was, she didn't care. When he brought her wagon around to the front of the cabin and handed her into it, she took the reins and prepared to follow him wherever he led.

Starlight and moonbeams lit the way. The storm had died, and the rain had left a fresh scent in the night air. She concentrated on the sweet fragrance and the swing of Roman's hair across his broad back.

Several hours later he stopped Secret beside a glade through which a creek bubbled. "We'll sleep here," he said, dismounting.

She climbed out of the wagon and began to make her bed. When she finished, she watched Roman tend to the fire, and felt a deep security over doing the things that had become so familiar to her since having met him.

"Hungry?" he asked.

She nodded.

He made her a raisin sandwich.

Accepting it, she smiled and held it as though it were the last and most precious food on earth.

"Where do you want to go, Theodosia?"

"I was under the impression that you had a place in mind."

He finished his sandwich in three bites. "All I thought about was getting you away from that cabin and the town of Enchanted Hill. The next town is Sundt, about five miles west of here. Do you want to go there to find—to have your fliers printed—" He paused, battling angry frustration. "Well, to do what you always do when you get to towns."

Stretching out upon her bed, she watched tree

branches sway. Droplets of water splashed to her face, but she didn't care. "Without my gold, I cannot pay—one hundred dollars in gold was to be payment for . . ." She closed her eyes. In light of all that had happened, how was she to conceive a child for Lillian? "I cannot pay you either," she whispered.

"One day I'll send you a bill," he said softly, and smiled.

She tried to return his smile, but failed. "I do not know what to do now, Roman. The child . . . I simply do not know what to do."

He moved to where she lay and kneaded the tense muscles in her slim shoulders. "Go to sleep."

"I shall awaken in the morning and still not know what to do."

Lying down beside her, he took her into his arms. "Then don't do anything, Theodosia. Just be with me for a while."

She looked into his eyes, which shone with moonglow and blue twinkles. Perhaps he was right, she mused. In time, maybe she would know what to do about her dilemma.

Cuddling closer to him, she breathed deeply of his familiar scent. "What shall we do together, Roman?"

"Nothing," he replied, smiling tenderly. "And everything."

Theodosia finished her two hotcakes well before Roman finished his stack of ten. She couldn't imagine what he had in mind for their first day of doing nothing and everything, but counted on his ideas to ease the confusion she continued to feel over her plight.

That thought in mind, she decided to hurry the morning along by cleaning up the pan she and Roman had used to cook the hotcakes. Using a small, thick towel to guard her hand from the hot metal, she reached for the pan handle, then prepared to pour stray bits of hotcakes onto the ground.

"Stop!" Roman shouted.

His shout so startled her, she dropped the pan. "Roman, what on earth—"

"There are still hotcakes left in the pan."

She glanced at the empty pan and his full plate. "Roman—"

"You were going to throw away the baby hotcakes," he explained. "They're the best part of a hotcake breakfast." He pointed to the tiny round cakes still left in the pan. "Those are the ones that drip off the spoon after you're finished pouring out the big ones. Come on, Theodosia, don't tell me you've never eaten baby hotcakes. I thought everyone had done that."

She picked up one of the dime-size hotcakes and popped it into her mouth. It crunched between her teeth, but held the same flavor as the larger ones. "There now, Roman, I have sampled a baby hotcake. Are you satisfied now?"

"Good, huh?"

She realized he was not going to drop the subject of baby hotcakes until she confessed to feeling the same way about them as he did. "I do not recall ever having dined upon a more savory food. Why, I am surprised that the best restaurants in Boston do not serve such delicacies."

"Go ahead. Make fun."

She wondered if she'd hurt his feelings. "I am not making fun, Roman. I—"

"You should be."

"Should be what?"

"Making fun. Inventing fun. Having fun. You know what else you can do with baby hotcakes besides eat them?"

She couldn't think of a single use for the hotcake scraps, but suspected Roman knew of thousands.

Roman reached for a few of the small cakes, then examined the area and spotted the exact thing he'd been looking for. "Watch this." He lay on his belly and dropped a few tiny hotcakes beside the anthill he'd found.

Curious, Theodosia lay down beside him

"Look at the ants take the cakes into the mound," Roman said, his gaze riveted to the industrious ants. "I used to watch ants for hours on end. I still like watching them."

"Ants are one of several groups of social insects that belong to the order *Hymenoptera*," Theodosia explained. "The known species of ants are classified in seven subfamilies of *Formicidae*. The ancestors of ants are believed to have been solitary, fossorial wasps—"

"Theodosia?"

"Yes?"

"Shut up and watch the ants."

She did, and before long she, too, began dropping bits of hotcakes for the ants to carry into their mound. When one cake proved too bulky for them to haul, she assisted them by picking up the food scrap and dropping it directly into the mound's opening.

Roman didn't say a word while she played with the ants. He simply watched her, feeling a deep sat-

isfaction when he saw the fascination and contentment in her beautiful whiskey-colored eyes.

Finally, after over an hour of playing, Theodosia
straightened into a sitting position and saw Roman
taking off his boots and stockings.

He sank his bare toes into a mud puddle.

She watched the dark, sticky mud ooze all over
his feet. "Why are you doing that?"

He shrugged. "It feels good, but if you want to try
it, you have to find your own puddle. This one's
mine."

She couldn't fathom why *anyone* would want to
bury their feet into mud. "I don't care to try it."

"Suit yourself." He leaned forward and pushed
his hands into the mud as well. Sinking them deep,
he grabbed as much mud as he could hold, then
pulled it out of the puddle.

Theodosia saw little bubbles rise and pop on the
surface of the mud he held, then an earthworm
squirmed over his thumb. She couldn't resist moving over to where he sat. "You have found a member of the *Lumbricidae* family, Roman, which is a
hermaphroditic worm that moves through the soil
by means of setae—"

"Nope. You're wrong. This is not lubmicditty."

"Lumbricidae."

"Whatever." He lifted the worm level with Theodosia's eyes. "This is Ernie. Yeah, good ol' Ernie
Earthworm, and he moves through dirt by squirming, got that?" He began looking for more worms
and soon had a whole handful.

Theodosia reached for one.

He yanked his hand away. "My worms."

His crooked grin caught her full attention. How
she loved that naughty expression of his.

"If you want a worm, Theodosia, you have to find one yourself."

She glanced at the mud puddle.

He almost laughed at the look of disgust on her face. "I guess to someone who only becomes a bit dusty, the thought of sticking your hands into a mud puddle is about the worst thing you can think of, huh? Tell you what, Lady Immaculate . . . how about we take a bath after we finish playing in the mud?"

"Together?"

"Is that shock I see in your eyes, or excitement?"

His question made her blush. "I have not been playing in the mud, Roman, therefore I do not need to bathe."

She regretted her words the second they left her lips.

Roman released the worms, slopped up some more mud, and smeared her left cheek. "That's more than a bit of dust you've got on you. You need a bath."

She saw mud drip to the bodice of her dress. "Roman, look what you did to me."

He found her dismay highly amusing. "Aren't you going to get back at me?"

Her head still bent over her chest, she raised her eyes to him, then immersed her hands into the mud and drew forth two great globs of the cold slosh.

He saw real mischief sparkling in her narrowed gaze and looked forward to seeing what she would do to him. "Go on," he pressed. "I dare you. I double-dare you. Hell, I quadruple-dare you."

The mud sliding beneath her sleeves and down her arms, Theodosia suppressed a shiver. She knew if she threw the mud at Roman, he'd throw more back at her. Becoming so totally filthy was not a pleasant thought, but backing down from Roman's quadruple challenge was far worse.

He ducked just as she flung the mud at him. "Ha-ha, you missed!"

The mud fight became serious business to her then. Resolute in her efforts to muddy him, Theodosia withdrew more mud from the puddle, but lost her chance to toss it at him when he rose from the ground, pulled something out of his saddlebag, and ran into the woods.

She followed, but at a much slower pace. "Roman?" Listening for sounds that would tell her where he was, she peered all through the thicket. "Roman?"

The loud caw of a crow startled her into dropping her mud. "Roman, I do not find this hiding game of yours at all diverting. Make your presence known at once, or I shall—"

She stopped speaking. Or she would what? she wondered. What threat could she give him?

"Roman, if you do not show yourself this very instant, I shall cease to play with you."

Nothing. No sound, no movement, no Roman. "Very well," she called into the woods, "I am returning to camp." She turned, took a few steps, then stopped abruptly.

Fear lashed through her like a thousand whips. At the base of the tree that grew not a foot away from where she stood lay a rattlesnake, its thick body coiled, its tail clattering in deadly warning.

"Roman," she whispered without moving her lips. "Roman."

She'd barely finished saying his name a second time, when all of a sudden he was there. It seemed to her that he'd fallen from the sky and landed directly upon the dangerous serpent.

In the next moment he held the writhing reptile out in front of her, his fingers clasped firmly behind its head. "Want to pet him?"

She moved well away. "No."

"Aw, come on, Theodosia, pet him. There aren't many people in the world who can say they've petted a live rattler. Pet him." He stepped toward her. "Pet him." He advanced toward her again. "Pet him."

She knew he wasn't going to give up. "You'll hold him tightly, won't you."

"If he shows one sign of trying to bite you, I'll bite him myself."

Trying to take some small measure of comfort in his absurd promise, she slid one finger down the squirming snake's back. "All right, I petted him."

"You did good, Theodosia. Real good."

She almost corrected his grammar from "good" to "well," but found his mistake strangely soothing. "Where were you, Roman?"

Using the snake's head as a pointer, he raised his arm and gestured toward the branches of the tree. "I saw the snake before you did and was just getting ready to warn you, when you turned around and nearly stepped right on it. Leave it to you, Theodosia, to walk straight into danger."

She watched him carry the snake deep into the glade. He returned without the reptile, and she realized he'd set it free. "Another man might have killed the rattlesnake."

Roman flicked a bit of dried mud off his thumbnail. "I kill for food and defense. I didn't want to eat that snake, and it wasn't going to hurt me."

With that, he pulled from his pocket the bar of soap he'd taken out of his saddlebag, and headed toward the creek.

She knew where he was going, knew what he planned to do there, and knew she shouldn't follow.

She followed.

"You look like Santa Claus."

Roman gave his long full soap-beard a final pat, and swished his sudsy hands in the cool creek water. "And you look like you have a white owl on your head."

"This is a hat, Roman. An ermine hat." She reached up and reshaped her soap-hat.

He sat down in the creek, doing his best to study her lather creation and not her gorgeous bare body. "What's an ermine?"

"A large European weasel." A rivulet of soap tickled her breasts as it slid over her chest. "In actuality I have a pile of soap on my head, Roman."

"It looks more like a weasel hat. Say it's a weasel hat."

"I already have." She sank into the water beside him. "Oh, my goodness. These creek pebbles—"

"They feel good on your bare bottom, huh?" He reached for her and pulled her closer. "All round and smooth."

"Round and smooth," she mused aloud, looking at him from the corner of her eye. "My bottom or the pebbles?"

He saw an alluring smile in her eyes. "I know an invitation when I hear one, Theodosia," he murmured huskily.

"Sir, I do not know what you're talking about."

"No? Well, let me show you, miss."

She moaned with deep excitement when he scooped her into his arms and laid her over his lap. His skin was so warm, the water so cool.

He threaded his long fingers through her hair, and she felt her soap hat spill off. His lather beard dripped to her chest. She cupped her breasts, smoothing the suds around and around and around. . . .

The sight of her caressing her own breasts caused Roman to shudder with desire. His arm beneath her neck, he lifted her face to his, and as he kissed her, he slipped his hand between her thighs and his fingers into her womanly depths.

She'd been prepared to savor the slow delicious journey toward pleasure, but her bliss peaked instantly, rippling all through her body as the creek water rippled over her skin. She arched high, her head dipping into the water.

Roman decided she would have drowned if he hadn't been holding her. "God, Theodosia," he said when she finally stilled in his arms, "I'm sorry you weren't ready. I should have spent more time getting you going."

She had the grace to give him an embarrassed expression but felt no shame at all. Her body responded to Roman's sensual skills like a musical instrument in the hands of a master, and the resulting melody was too beautiful to resist or hold back.

Gazing into his eyes, she realized she wanted to give him the same pleasure he'd offered her. It didn't matter that she was uncertain about how to go about it; she knew he would teach her.

She wriggled off his lap and sat in front of him.

Her hands around his waist, she rubbed her
thumbs gently across his tight belly, then glanced
downward. "Roman, your lance is lunging completely out of the water."

He threw back his head and laughed. "Yeah, the
old sword of passion is definitely thrusting, huh?"

Carefully, she took him into her hand, loving the
soft groan her action caused him. "It's throbbing."

"Masculinities have a way of doing that when
touched by a beautiful woman."

She smiled. "I think perhaps that I shall conduct
an experiment, Roman."

The suggestive tone in her voice set him afire.
"What kind of experiment?"

"An experiment in the name of science. Sexy science," she added, tightening her hold on him. "It
has already been proven that flaming spikes have
the ability to throb, but I shall now attempt to discover what else they are capable of doing."

He couldn't answer right away. He gritted his
teeth. He took deep breaths. He tried to think of
everything but what she was saying, doing, planning.

Finally, he replied. "Theodosia, I am about to ex-
plode in your hand," he warned.

She saw the tight expression on his face. "But I
haven't even done anything yet."

"You don't have to. Just the thought . . . just the
feel of your hand . . . for God's sake, woman, just
the sound of your voice is driving me insane."

"You look as though you are in extreme pain."

"I am."

"Ah, then I shall seek a remedy."

He dug his fingers into the rocky creek bed when
she began to glide her hand up and down. He

wanted to hold back. He wanted it to happen slowly.

He knew it was going to happen fast.

When he reached for her, Theodosia got to her knees and pressed her breasts against his chest, but did not slow her caresses. He pushed his hips toward her, capturing her hand between her belly and his. He became hotter in her hand. Harder. He pulsed. Her gaze traveling over every part of his face, she watched his release begin even while she felt its strength in her hand.

Witnessing this wonderful man's ecstasy was the most beautiful thing she'd ever seen. And to know that *she* had given him such pleasure brought her a happiness so deep that she realized it stemmed from her very soul.

"Theodosia," Roman whispered. Breathing heavily, he buried his face between her breasts and felt her heartbeat on his lips. A wealth of emotions caught hold of him. He tried to name them but could only concentrate on the way they made him feel.

God, he felt so good. *She* made him feel so good. He wanted to hug her as hard as he could, but he forced himself to remember his own strength.

Tenderly, he sat her in his lap again and spread soft kisses over her throat and shoulders. "You didn't have to do that."

"I wanted to."

"Why?"

Here was the little boy inside him again, she mused. The child who had given but who had not received. "Roman," she murmured, caressing the muscles in his arms, "you have pleasured me in the past. It was important to me to pleasure you as well. I assure you that it made me as happy as it did you."

Her explanation sought, found, and warmed a place so deep inside him, he couldn't understand what that place was. "Thank you."

She slipped her hands into his hair, loving the sight of her pale fingers lost within such blackness. "You're welcome," she whispered, then fell into a long lapse of silence.

"What are you thinking about, sweetheart?" Roman murmured.

She cupped a handful of water, dropped it over his shoulder, and watched it trickle over the muscles in his chest. "I was thinking about the definition of *fun*, which is 'something that provides amusement or enjoyment.' It is also 'playful, often boisterous action or speech.' I have decided, however, that I no longer think that definition is correct."

He lifted his head and looked into her eyes. "Are you saying you're going to change the meaning of a word?"

She nodded and stretched up to kiss the cleft in his chin. "The new definition of *fun* is 'Roman Montana.'"

"I cannot do it, Roman," Theodosia said, cracker crumbs spraying over her lap as she spoke.

Mounted, Roman leaned down and handed her another cracker. "Try again."

She stopped the wagon, took the cracker, and bit into it. But her lips were so dry, she could hardly get them to pucker. This cracker challenge was yet another new experience Roman had decided she needed. During the past week of traveling, he'd had her catching minnows with her bare hands, leaving scraps of bread near bird nests for the mother birds to find, and filling her mouth with jawbreakers to see how many would fit at one time. She'd even participated in her first pillow fight, which Roman won, but only because his pillow casing was of thicker fabric than hers.

And now he wanted her to whistle through cracker-crumb-coated lips. "May I have a bit of water first?"

"No." To prove the feat could be done, Roman ate four crackers, and with dry crumbs peppering his lips, he whistled loud and long. "See? It's not impossible to eat crackers and whistle."

She tried to lick her lips but failed. "Roman, I am very thirsty. And the sunset is upon us. Might we stop for the night, preferably near water?"

John the Baptist stuck his beak out from the bars of his cage and snatched the cracker from Theodosia's hand. "I had a terrible case of the measles when I was seven," he called shrilly. "The sunset is upon us."

"There's a stream ahead," Roman relented, urging Secret toward a woodsy area in the near distance. "But if you think I'm going to forget about making you do the cracker whistle, you're wrong."

Smiling, Theodosia followed him and drove the wagon into a beautiful glade through which a sparkling stream ran.

But her smile faded when she saw horse tracks all around the ground. "A gang," she squeaked.

Roman saw the fear on her face as she looked at the tracks, and he knew she was remembering the Blanco y Negro Gang. "No, Theodosia. The horses that made these tracks aren't shod, so they aren't white men's horses." He dismounted and walked well away from the stream, studying the trail of tracks. "They're wild mustangs."

Her fear vanished instantly. "How do you know? Couldn't they have been Indian ponies?"

He knew she wasn't questioning him; she only wanted to learn. Pointing, he gestured toward several neat piles of horse manure. "The horses that were here stopped to relieve themselves. An Indian war party keeps its horses moving, so manure is scattered. Indians moving with their families transport their belongings with them. They carry their lodge poles, which leave marks in the dirt as the Indians travel. There aren't any pole marks anywhere around here. Wild mustangs often pass under branches that a mounted man would be unable to dodge. See the tracks under those low branches over there?"

She did indeed see the tracks he indicated, and she marveled over how quickly he'd determined that they'd been made by a harmless herd of wild mustangs.

She climbed out of the wagon, drank her fill of the clean sweet stream water and sat down in a thick bed of grass and wild flowers. Watching Roman lead the horses to water, she let her thoughts wander.

She remembered long library aisles filled with old books and the tiring afternoons she'd spent walking down the musty-smelling aisles in search of some elusive piece of information. She recalled elderly professors with their beards, spectacles, and long bony fingers. She could even remember how the professors smelled—like dust, probably from walking down the same musty-smelling library aisles.

She strolled through aisles now, too—endless stretches of dirt roads surrounded by fresh greenery and happy birds and clean fragrant breezes. Her professor wore no beard and no spectacles, and his fingers, though long, were thick and brown and felt wonderful intertwined with hers. He didn't smell like dust. He was sun and leather, and he possessed knowledge not found within the yellowed pages of books.

He smiled often while sharing his wisdom with her. She smiled back at him and drank in his teachings as if each drop were more precious than the last.

He was Roman, and the world he showed her proved so beautiful, she wondered how she would ever be able to leave it.

The thought occupied her mind with such intensity that Roman noticed. "Why so quiet?"

She ran her hand through the luxurious mass of grass and flowers. "I'm thinking."

Her answer disturbed him. He'd done his best to get her mind off her future plans, and he'd done well. But he knew it was only a matter of time before she began dwelling on her goals again. "You're thinking about the baby. Brazil. About Dr. Wallaby and the research." He sat down beside her and absently began to pick the blossoms that grew all around him.

She watched him stick his thumbnail through each of the flower stems to make thin slits through which he inserted individual stems until he'd created a long chain of blossoms.

"Ever done this, Theodosia?" He tied the two ends together, forming a posie necklace.

"No, Roman, I never have."

He slipped the necklace over her head, and as he arranged it around her shoulders, an iridescent butterfly floated past her face. "Sometimes I'd make these chains and have my mare, Angel, wear them around her neck. Eventually, she'd eat them off."

Theodosia made a flower necklace of her own, a small one, then crowned Roman's head with it. "There. Now you are His Majesty, King Roman."

He leaned toward her and kissed her soft cheek. "When I first met you, you never would have pretended I was King Roman."

"When I first met you, I did not know how to pretend," she replied, gliding her hand down his thick arm. "I have done quite a few things since then that I have never done before."

And there are so many more things I want to show you, Theodosia. He urged her to lie down on the ground, then he lay beside her. "Close your eyes and stare at the sun through your eyelids. After a while you'll start seeing a bunch of colors swirling around."

She did as he asked and saw the colors he'd said she would. It was a simple thing—watching colors twirl around behind her eyelids.

But it brought her such peace.

"Roman," she murmured, her eyes still closed.

He kept his shut, too. "What?"

"I wasn't pondering the baby, Brazil, Dr. Wallaby, or the research. I was thinking about how much I've enjoyed this time with you." She paused, trying to stem the sudden sadness that rose within her. "I shall miss you, Roman Montana."

Her declaration strengthened his suspicions that she was preparing to commence with her plans and then return to her own world. A world he could never share with her.

He sat up, and for a moment he watched the horses drink from the stream. One day soon he would watch only one horse drink from streams. Secret would be his sole company.

"I have something for you, Theodosia."

She opened her eyes and sat up beside him.

"I got it for you in Enchanted Hill," Roman said, taking her hand and caressing her slender fingers, "but—well, I got mad and didn't give it to you."

He rose, crossed to the stream where Secret stood, and took a yellow box out of his saddlebag. Sunlight shimmered over the bright red bow, and he felt glad he'd had the present wrapped.

"What is it?" Theodosia asked when he handed her the box.

He stuffed his hands into his pockets and grinned down at her. "We could sit here for a few weeks while you guess. Or you could do what makes the most sense and open it."

At his sarcasm she stuck her tongue out at him.

He'd never seen her do that before and liked seeing her do it now. "Well?"

She began to open the gift.

When five whole minutes had passed and she had yet to untie the tight red bow, Roman had to restrain himself from grabbing the box and ripping the paper off. "For God's sake, Theodosia, do you want the damned gift or not?"

His impatience made her giggle. "I am savoring

this moment, Roman." Just to irritate him further, she stopped trying to open the present and glided her finger across the yellow paper. Only when the spark of aggravation in his eyes became the glitter of real anger did she finish opening the gift.

Inside the box lay a doll. Her face was a plump walnut, upon which were painted her tiny features. Golden straw made her hair, and beneath her blue-and-orange-calico dress she had a soft body of feather-filled burlap.

"She's *not* a valuable antique. Got that?" Roman announced. "You don't put that kind of doll behind some glass case and stare at her. You play with her, and you don't worry about her breaking. Probably the worst that might happen to her is that her head could fall off. If that happens, you just glue it right back on."

"You are wrong, Roman."

He frowned. "Wrong? About what?"

Theodosia fondled the doll's stiff straw hair. "She is valuable—because *you* gave her to me." Recalling that she'd once told him she'd had a collection of three hundred dolls that she couldn't play with, she understood the significance of his gift. "Would it upset you if I wept?"

"Looks to me like you already are," he answered, watching a few of her tears splash to the doll's wrinkled brown face.

Holding the doll tightly to her breast, Theodosia gazed up at the thoughtful man who'd given it to her. His long raven hair shone in the late afternoon sunshine, as did his eyes, which were even bluer than the heaven above him. She looked at the deep cleft in his chin and the lopsided slant of his smile. His height and size always amazed her, and as she admired his physique, she dwelled upon his astonishing skills and knowledge as well. The man had little formal education, and yet . . .

And yet Roman Montana was one of the smartest men she'd ever known.

Some men, she mused, used their intelligence within the walls of a laboratory. There was little they didn't know or understand within their scientific realm.

Roman's laboratory was the world. No walls closed around him, and there was little he didn't know or understand within his natural domain.

She pondered the fact that wisdom was not confined to the pages of books. Was not always something that could be taught.

And genius, she realized, was not necessarily measured by academic awards. Was not necessarily—

Genius. The word took complete control of Theodosia's thoughts. A genius, she remembered, was a person endowed with extraordinary mental capacity. With superior power of the mind. One could be a genius at mathematics, science, and other academic areas . . .

Or one could show true genius with horses. Survival skills. People.

It dawned on her then that Roman Montana was a genius in every sense of the word.

She dropped her doll.

"Theodosia?" Roman said, noting the incredulous expression on her face. He knelt down beside her and cupped her cheek in his palm. "What's the matter?"

Her wide-eyed gaze locked with his. For weeks she'd been traveling from town to town, posting circulars and interviewing strange men in an effort to find a man as intelligent as Upton. And all along, Roman had been right by her side, guiding her with his own special brand of genius and taking tender care of her.

Brilliant and kind. That's what Upton was.

And so was Roman Montana.

Dear God, why hadn't she caught the similarities before now? Had her search for academic intelligence blinded her to everything else?

Her heartbeat staggered, like something dead brought back to vibrant life. "Roman," she whispered, "I . . ." She paused and laid her hand on his chest. "Roman, would you—would you consent to be the man to sire the child?"

Chapter 17

Her question leaped into Roman's heart and traveled through his every vein. He didn't dare answer right away, afraid if he did, he'd wake up and the dream would be over before he'd seen how it ended.

Before he'd made love to her.

His silence caused Theodosia to bow her head in embarrassment. She knew what he was thinking. How could she have forgotten? "I'm sorry, Roman," she said, her voice as fragile as the delicate flower necklace he'd made for her. "The gold. I failed to remember that I no longer have the means with which to pay you. I do have my ruby brooch—"

"I don't want your gold or your brooch, Theodosia."

She looked up and saw the truth of his words in the azure depths of his eyes. "Do you accept?" she whispered.

He could see nothing but her beauty, could hear nothing but her beautiful request. "Yes."

The reality of the situation fell over her. Once

upon a time she'd planned to have coitus with some stranger in a darkened hotel room.

Instead, she was going to make love with Roman Montana beneath a canopy of trees.

Joy rose in her heart like a beautiful sunrise. She reached out her arms for him.

Roman brought her to him, next to his chest, and he held her as though someone might come and take her away from him in the next moment. Smiling into her soft hair, he urged her to the ground again but continued to hold her.

And hold her.

Nighttime found them still on the ground, ensconced within the cocoon of each other's arms, the thick bed of grass and flowers, and the knowledge of what would soon happen.

"It's dark," Roman whispered.

Theodosia couldn't breathe, much less reply. The time had come, she mused. In a short while she would cease to be a maiden.

The thought brought her a tinge of worry. "You will be gentle, Roman."

She spoke the words as if they were a statement, but he heard the question in them. "Yes."

She rose from the ground, retrieved one of her bags out of the back of the buckboard, and disappeared behind a mass of brush.

His own breathing a little ragged, Roman built a fire within the shelter of the nearby oak glade. He then prepared a bit of stew with dried meat, onion, and potatoes. Food was the last thing on earth he wanted, but he remembered that Theodosia hadn't eaten since noon.

When the food was simmering over the fire, he saw Theodosia watching him. Dressed in her flannel nightgown, she sat against the trunk of a large tree, firelight dancing over her long golden hair and the purple violets embroidered on her gown. "I made some supper."

She could smell the stew but could see only Roman.

He'd removed his shirt, boots, and stockings and wore only his tight black breeches. His dark chest rippled and gleamed and enticed.

He was going to take off those tight black breeches and make love to her. Tonight.

She fondled the knowledge as if holding it in her hand.

"Do you want to eat, Theodosia?"

Mute with anticipation, she could only shake her head.

He sensed her excitement, but he reminded himself that a whisper of trepidation edged her desire. Casually, he picked up a spoon and began to stir the stew. "Nervous?"

"No," she said a bit too quickly.

He smiled.

She saw the crooked slant of his grin and realized he knew she lied. "Yes, Roman, I am a bit anxious," she admitted, gliding her finger across one of the purple violets on her gown. "But only because tonight will be the first time I . . . I—"

"Have coitus?" Still smiling, he continued to stir the stew and remained determined to do his best to relax her. "But I thought it was just a scientific procedure. Didn't you tell me one time that it was only the joining of male and female gentiles that move in rhythm—"

"It is the physical union of male and female *genitalia* accompanied by rhythmic movements, usually leading to the ejaculation of semen from the penis into the female reproductive tract. But Roman, I—"

"Yeah, yeah, I know. The bedding rules. I haven't forgotten them. I'll make our bed in the pitch-dark woods, away from the fire. I won't kiss you, I won't touch you. I'll only wait for you to bare your lower half. You can close your eyes and think of unrelated matters, and I'll be done in two minutes. Maybe less. I don't even have to take my breeches off if you don't want me to. I could just open up the front."

"Two minutes?" she repeated disbelievingly.

Her distress amused the hell out of him. "Theodosia, I am only trying to do this the way you once told me you wanted it done." He removed the stew from the fire and rose.

Theodosia watched him remove blankets from the back of her wagon and amble toward her. Moonlight poured over him; sensuality radiated from him. Just the sight of him sent pleasure wafting through her.

She could only imagine what bliss it would be to feel him inside her.

The thought so excited her, she squeezed handfuls of the leaves scattered around her. "Roman, we must make haste. If we do not, I fear my anticipation will push me toward the fringes of insanity."

He stopped before her. "I thought you were nervous."

"I am feeling many emotions at this moment. Nervousness is but one of them."

"I see." Stifling laughter, he set about making their bed.

She knew she should help him, but could not move from her spot by the tree.

He was making their bed. Upon that pile of soft blankets, she would surrender her virginity to him.

She would become a woman in Roman's arms.

He heard her soft moan and saw the expression of intense pleasure on her face. God, were her fantasies so real that she'd found ecstasy alone? "Hey, wait for me," he teased. "We're supposed to do this together, remember?"

She stood and slowly untied the front of her gown.

Roman sobered instantly. Purple violets cascaded down her lush figure as the gown slipped to the ground. He'd seen her naked before, but tonight was different.

Tonight he would know every inch of that pale and perfect body.

But contrary to her demand, he would know her slowly.

He picked up her gown and slipped it back over her head.

"Roman, what—"

"The rules," he reminded her. "Lie down."

She did and gazed up at him.

"Cover yourself with the blankets."

Again, she obeyed.

"Pull your nightgown up to your waist, close your eyes, and think of anything but what I'm going to do to you."

She started to do as he asked but stopped in midaction. "Roman, cease this play."

He narrowed his eyes. "Do what I told you to do, Theodosia."

He wasn't playing. The devastatingly sexy sound in his voice assured her of that. She pulled her nightgown up to her waist and closed her eyes.

"You wanted total darkness, you get total darkness," Roman explained. "No matter what, keep your eyes shut." He knelt beside her. "Do you want my breeches on or off? I can do this either way."

His question deepened her yearning for him. "Off."

He withdrew her arms from beneath the blankets. His thumbs caressing the back of her hands, he placed her palms upon the fastening of his breeches. "I burned my hands making the stew and can't deal with these buttons. You'll have to do it."

She started to open her eyes in surprise, but in the next moment she felt Roman's hand covering them.

"I told you to keep your eyes shut, Theodosia."

She fumbled with the button for a moment, then felt it open. Heat fairly consumed her. She swore flames licked at her fingers and that they blazed straight from Roman's hard body.

"Theodosia," he pressed.

She undid the other buttons, and then, with her hands at the waist of his pants, she rolled his breeches and undergarments off his hips and down to his knees. When she heard him shift, she knew he'd discarded the clothing entirely.

He was naked now.

She moved to touch him intimately.

He caught her hand. "No touching, and don't you dare open your eyes."

Such frustration consumed her that she groaned. "You are naked, and I am not."

"I know."

"But—"

"I'm going to penetrate you, Theodosia," he whispered into her ear. "I'm going to spill my seed inside you. And you, my little scientific sweetheart, are going to think totally unrelated thoughts."

She tried to open her eyes. Again, he laid his hand over them. "Roman—"

"Penetrate you," he murmured once more. "Like this."

She felt his long fingers slide into her and cried out with delight.

"You aren't thinking about unrelated things, Theodosia," Roman cooed, moving his thumb over the most sensitive spot of her female flesh. "If you were, you'd feel no pleasure. Think about—um, think about spleens."

She longed to chide him, but the pleasure he gave made speaking impossible. Instead, she moved restlessly against his hand.

"Of course, I don't plan to penetrate you only with my fingers," Roman continued, drawing nearer to her.

She felt his arousal burn into the side of her thigh. "Dear God, Roman—"

"Think of olfactory nerves, Theodosia," he suggested softly, pressing himself against her in a rhythm he knew would bring her body to fever pitch. "Think of Shakespeare."

Gently, he parted her thighs, then settled his hips between them. Her rigid-nippled breasts pressed into his chest, her soft whimpers flowed into his mind, and fire scorched through his every vein. Kissing and nuzzling her neck and throat, he positioned himself so that his hot maleness skimmed across her feminine moistness. "I'm going to penetrate you now," he warned huskily. "While I do, think of the magnitude of stars."

She felt the velvety tip of his masculinity press

lightly at the pulsing entrance to her body. Reacting instinctively, she reached around Roman's back, placed her hands on his bottom, and tried to shove him forward.

He resisted her efforts. "Think of the laws of inertia."

He entered her slightly, giving her just enough time to crave the full length of him before withdrawing completely and then repeating the same tormenting procedure once more.

"Theodosia, open your eyes."

She opened them and saw the very essence of passion in his blazing gaze. He pushed his hips forward slowly . . . slowly, and it was with sweet leisure that she experienced her first sensation of being joined with a man.

He felt thick, but her body stretched to accommodate his size. He felt long, but she wanted all of him.

She tried to raise her hips, but his weight kept her pinned to the ground.

"Think of me, Theodosia," Roman whispered, keeping steady hold of her smoldering gaze. "Think of me."

In the next instant he filled her mind and her body. A flash of pain shot through her as he drove his full length into her, but the wondrous feeling of having him inside her quickly overcame her discomfort.

"Theodosia," Roman groaned. "Oh, God, Theodosia." He stilled, savoring the long-awaited pleasure of being buried inside her silky wet tightness.

Theodosia was not willing to allow him to be still. She writhed beneath him, impatient for him to bring her the rapture he'd so skillfully given her in the past.

With one swift motion Roman pulled her nightgown above her head and off her arms, then tossed it into the shadows. Taking her stiff nipple into his mouth, he began to show her the true meaning of lovemaking. "You're going full circle tonight, Theodosia, and I'm going with you. Move with me, sweetheart."

Though she had never lain with a man before this night, her body knew precisely what to do. Each time he slid out of her, she pressed her hips toward the ground, then raised them to join with him again.

Lost to everything but him, she listened as he murmured endearments and words of encouragement to her. His deep, rich voice caressing her senses, she gave herself up to him in complete abandon.

Her total surrender to him brought Roman a fresh surge of desire, and a more profound determination to take her to the highest pinnacle of ecstasy possible. Keeping his strokes long, deep, and steady, he moved to claim her mouth with his own, and while he drove his tongue between her soft lips, he circled his palm upon the stiff nipples of her erect breasts.

His skillful attentions to so many places on her body at once gave Theodosia the deepest pleasure she had yet to experience, and as her ecstasy rose, she felt her tight passage clutch at Roman, as if embracing him in tiny, rhythmic hugs. His presence inside her enhancing her fulfillment, her senses spinning, and her body bucking beneath him, she screamed out his name.

Her sensual contractions kindled a blaze within Roman's loins. His hard slick body strained for control, but she pulsed so tightly, so sweetly around him that he ceased to fight back the bliss she offered but instead allowed her to bring him into the same fire of pleasure that consumed her.

Flames of bliss shot through his frame and caught his very soul afire. Shuddering from the extraordinary feelings he'd found in Theodosia's arms, he kissed her with more passion than he'd ever before shown her. . . .

And spilled his seed inside her.

Theodosia lay in the crook of Roman's arm, her body glistening with the dew of lovemaking and the sheen of moonbeams. A swath of ebony hair cascaded over her breasts, warm, thick, and soft as satin.

Lazily, she looked into her lover's heavy-lidded eyes. "Was it as beautiful for you as it was for me?" she whispered.

Her question floated through him like a feather on a breeze. "Yes."

"I will never forget this night, Roman."

He trailed his hand down the curve of her back and over her bottom, finally resting it upon her smooth thigh. "Just in case you do, I'll remind you in the morning."

Realizing he meant to make love to her again when they awakened, she sighed in contentment. "I did not know," she whispered. "Lovemaking. How could I ever have thought lovemaking to be a mere scientific procedure?"

He spread his kisses to her cheek and eyelids. "You believe everything you read. You should read to wonder. To wonder whether what you're reading is true or not." He tucked her more closely into the warm shelter of his body, then drew a blanket over her so the evening breeze would not chill her damp skin.

Read to wonder. Theodosia found the advice both wise and beautiful.

She lost herself in his deep blue eyes again and allowed her thoughts to take her where they would.

They kept her with Roman.

He was not only her friend, she mused, and not only her lover.

He'd become something more.

She glided her fingers into the silk black of his hair, dwelling upon the fact that she'd never doubted Brazil and her research would satisfy every yearning she'd ever had.

She was no longer so certain.

At dawn the sound of crunching leaves broke through Roman's dream. He had his Colt in hand even before he opened his eyes. "Quiet," he ordered when Theodosia began to stir beside him.

"Don't shoot," a man's voice called out from the thicket. "I ain't here to do nary a bit o' harm. Jest wanted a jag o' breakfast if you've got any to share."

Holding his revolver steady, Roman watched a man with a shock of white hair trudge out of the woods. The man led a swaybacked mule, upon whose back were piled burlap sacks and a small gray-faced dog.

"How do," he man greeted, stopping beside the remains of the campfire. "I'm Oble Smott. I seed your wagon through the woods."

Theodosia sat up in alarm, clutching the blankets to her breasts.

"Oh, pardon me, ma'am," Oble said, tipping his hat. "I seed your wagon through the woods, but I shore didn't see that y'all was nekkid. I'll turn my back fer a spell whilst y'all git your clothes on."

Sensing that Oble Smott was but a harmless wanderer, Roman handed Theodosia her flannel nightgown, then rose and donned his breeches.

"This here's Stub," Oble said, scratching his mule's long ears. "Stub fer stubborn. And my dog's Chaparito. That's Mexican fer Little Feller. I got ole Chaparito when I was down in Mexico some ten years ago. I ain't never been back since on account o' I couldn't get me no food a'tall that weren't swimmin' in them chili gravies. Lord o' mercy, them chili gravies give me some *kind* o' powerful wind. I near 'bout blowed mysef right off the saddle whilst tryin' to ride out o' Mexico. Y'all dressed yit?"

Roman glanced at Theodosia and saw her tying the last ribbon on her nightgown. "We're dressed."

Oble turned back around and commenced to restart the fire. "Y'all look to be a right happy couple. Who are you?"

So as not to embarrass Theodosia, Roman said, "Mr. and Mrs. Montana. I'm Roman, and my wife is Theodosia."

"I knowed a Theodosia once," Oble said. "She had the biggest, purtiest brown eyes y'ever seed in your whole life. And when she blinked them long lashes at me, I'd fall plumb to pieces. Someone stole her, though. Pro'bly et her. I always knowed she'd make fer some good eatin', but I couldn't never bring mysef to eat her. Best cow that ever lived, ole Theodosia.''

Theodosia smiled, then burst into loud laughter.

The happy sound of her laughter had Roman chuckling too. Smiling, he set about fetching the food for breakfast. With Theodosia's help, he soon had a batch of small meat pies frying over the fire.

"Much obliged," Oble said after he and Chaparito had consumed most of the pies themselves. Patting his tight belly, he leaned back against Stub's legs, then yelped in surprise when cold water splashed his face.

John the Baptist tossed a second beakful out of his cage. "Much obliged," he said. "His middle name was Egbert, and they called him Eggy for short. I shore didn't see that y'all was nekkid.''

Oble howled with laughter. "Lord, that's one o' them talkin' birds! I ain't never seed one, but I've heared of 'em. How y'gittin' along, bird?''

The parrot cracked a sunflower seed. "If you want a worm, Theodosia, you have to find one yourself. Pull your nightgown up to your waist.''

Quickly, Roman reached for the cage.

"I'm going to spill my seed inside you," John the Baptist called merrily.

Seeing the flustered expressions on Roman and Theodosia's faces, Oble laughed again. "Ain't no need to git all red-faced with me, y'all. If it weren't fer nightgowns gittin' pulled up and seed gittin' spilt, there wouldn't be no people in the world. Set your minds at ease and tell me where you're headed.''

Roman set John the Baptist's cage behind Theodosia and gave the parrot a glare. "Nowhere," he answered.

"That's the best place to go," Oble stated. "Been there mysef many a time. Most folks I meet up with is always hurryin' around to git to where they're goin'. They got things to do, places to see, and they cain't stand wastin' nary a second gittin' there to do whatever it is they think cain't wait to git done or seed. Folks orter slow down some and quit frettin' over tomorrow when somethin's starin' 'em right in the face today."

He pulled a burr off Chaparito's stubby tail. "Me? Well, I ain't done nothin' earth-shatterin' important in my life, but I'll tell you the truth, I've enjoyed ever' minute o' ever' one o' my simple days. 'Specially my days with my beloved Jeweleen. She was my wife fer twenty-two years. We never did git us no young'uns, but we was shore happy. I still miss her, and times come when I wake up in the middle o' the night and still reach fer her. 'Course, she ain't never there, and that's a real deep-down-sad feelin'. Ole Jeweleen, she used to wear flowers in her hair. I'll always remember her with flowers in her hair. She growed them flowers hersef, and one time she won a prize at a church festival fer growin' the purple-est posy."

He paused, recalling the day at the festival. "I started out havin' a good time at that church festival, but I got bit by a squirrel right after Jeweleen won her posy prize. That critter sank them teeth o' his straight through my thumbnail, and it ain't growed right since. I weren't tryin' to do nothin' to the dang thing but feed him a peanut. Y'know, y'don't never think about how useful thumbnails is till somethin' goes wrong with the one y'use the most. I used to use this here bent thumbnail fer cleanin' out my ears. Cain't use it fer that no more, and sometimes I wonder if the reason why I cain't hear like I used to is on account o' my ears is s'dirty."

He stood, brushed off his pants, and lifted Chaparito upon Stub's back. "Well, I'd best be goin' now. Hold on tight to each other, hear? Love good, laugh a lot, and y'all'll have a real fine life together."

When Oble disappeared into the woods, Theodosia stared after him. "He still reaches for his wife at night," she whispered.

She wondered if she would reach for Roman while sleeping in the jungles of Brazil. And while asleep in the master bedroom of his ranch house, would Roman reach for her?

A painful emptiness tore through her breast, causing her to lay her hand on her chest in an effort to soothe the hurt.

"Theodosia? Are you all right?" Roman asked, noting the look of deep despair etching her fine features.

"What? Yes. Yes, of course I'm all right, Roman. I was only thinking about Mr. Smott." Quickly, she thought of something completely unrelated to her true thoughts. "He possesses a penchant for rambling speech. Why do people converse in such a manner here in Texas?"

Roman cleaned out the frying pan. "Rambling speech?"

She couldn't believe he didn't know what she was talking about. "At one point, Mr. Smott began by telling us that he had done nothing important in his life, and he ended by wondering if his bent thumbnail was the cause of his dirty ears. I do not comprehend the reasons behind such oral meandering."

Roman smiled. So *that's* what oral meandering was. "You're from a city. All you have to do to see people is step out your front door. But out here people usually live far apart. They don't see each other often, so when they get together, they have so much to say that one subject just naturally leads into another and another. They talk about anything and everything, and when the socializing's over they go home and start saving up more stuff to talk about when they're all together again. After a while, that kind of talking becomes a habit, so if country folk ever move to a town they still talk about anything and everything. And it's not called oral meandering, Theodosia. It's called chatting."

"Chatting," she murmured. "But how does one begin country chatting?"

"By saying anything in the world and then waiting to see what your mind thinks of next. But you're from the North. You probably can't do it," he challenged.

She concentrated on the first statement she would make. "Oble Smott had white hair."

Roman anticipated her next sentence, but she said nothing. "And?"

She simply could not think of anything else to say.

"Did his white hair remind you of anything?" Roman offered.

She closed her eyes and saw something white flash through her mind. "His hair was as white as the bedspread I used to have on my bed when I was a little girl."

"Good, good. Now, what does the bedspread make you think about?"

"I spilled tea on that bedspread and tried to hide it with a quilt, but Mrs. Singleton found the stain. Mrs. Singleton was my governess, and she always smelled of peppermint because her pockets were full of the candies. Once she and I went on an outing to the park, and we fell asleep on the bench. I woke up first and tickled Mrs. Singleton awake by brushing a dandelion under her nose. She sneezed so hard that her spectacles flew off and landed in the grass. A man stepped on and broke them, so I had to lead poor Mrs. Singleton home."

When she opened her eyes she saw Roman smiling at her.

"Tell me what Mrs. Singleton's spectacles have to do with Oble Smott's white hair, Theodosia."

"Nothing."

"That's country chatting."

She realized there was nothing to analyze about the oral meandering after all. Such manner of talk was a simple matter of putting memories into a string of oddly connected, but friendly chatter. And strange though the chatter seemed to her intellectual ears, she'd somehow become accustomed to it and found it rather soothing.

She thought about all the things Oble Smott had chatted about: his mule, dog, and problems with the food in Mexico. He disagreed with hurrying. He'd not done anything of vital importance in his life, but he'd lived his simple days happily.

Hold on tight to each other, hear? he'd advised. *Love good, laugh a lot, and y'all'll have a real fine life together.*

Fine lives, she thought. Separate lives—Roman's in Texas, hers in Brazil.

There wouldn't be anyone in Brazil with whom she could practice country chatting. Dr. Wallaby wouldn't understand it and wouldn't have time to learn it. If not for Roman, *she* wouldn't have understood or taken the time to learn it, either.

She wondered how many, many other things he could teach her that she would never have the opportunity to learn, and the painful emptiness filled her once more.

"Theodosia, did you hear what I said?"

"What? No. No, I'm sorry, Roman, I did not."

"I asked if you'd forgotten about last night. Judging by that blank look on your face, you have. I swore I'd remind you in the morning, and I always keep my promises."

She crossed her hands over her breasts. "Roman, Oble Smott will see—"

"He's long gone," Roman said, pulling at the ribbons on the front of her gown. "Besides, I'm sure he suspected we were going to indulge in a little nightgown-pulling-upping and seed-spilling as soon as he left. He won't come back."

He lifted her into his arms and carried her back to their sleeping pallet. There he laid her down and stretched out beside her. "He's right, you know. Oble Smott is. People do hurry too much, Theodosia. I'm going to take his advice and make slow, slow love to you."

She turned into his arms, deciding that she, too, would heed Oble's sage advice. Dismissing thoughts of tomorrow, she concentrated on what was before her very eyes.

And oh, what a sexy sight it was. Roman's gaze

flickered with blue fire, and his desire became her own.

She didn't remember him taking her nightrail off, nor could she recall him shrugging out of his breeches. Her recollections started when his lips met the soft sensitive flesh at the hollow of her throat and he began to kiss her body.

And while he so thoroughly caressed her with his mouth, his heavy male hardness slid upon her as well. His lips . . . his hands . . . the cascade of his long raven hair . . . his hot arousal . . .

Every part of him touched every part of her. She bucked beneath his skillful stroking, her body trembling for the feel of hard male flesh inside her.

Sensitive to her need though he was, Roman wanted her hotter. He lifted her to her knees, then lay down with his head propped up on the mound of thick pillows. With his hands, he showed her what he wanted her to do.

When she realized her dark and compelling lover's intentions, Theodosia gasped with surprise but, with the most profound anticipation lending strength to her quivering muscles, she submitted to the urgings of his hands and moved to kneel over his face.

One hand kneading her breast and the other fondling her bottom, Roman nuzzled with his lips the soft pale hair between her thighs, then began to tease her wet female flesh with the tip of his tongue. He knew where to touch her, knew precisely how to set her ablaze with deeper need.

His sensual caresses spread fire through Theodosia's every nerve. She arched her back; her head fell over her shoulders, and her flaxen hair pooled on Roman's smooth brown chest. Circling her hips over his warm mouth, she abandoned herself to the glorious pleasure.

Vitally aware of each small tremor of rising bliss he brought to her, Roman continued pleasuring her until he knew she'd almost reached the pinnacle of ecstasy. And then, with one strong, fluid motion, he took hold of her hips and pushed her downward.

Before Theodosia had time to realize what he was doing, she felt him thrust into her, his thick masculinity impaling her fully. So smooth were his actions that her climax never faltered, but rose to such an incredible height that when the final burst of rapture shot through her, she screamed Roman's name with all the fervent passion his magic had drawn forth from her.

"Again," Roman whispered hotly into her ear. "Again."

She barely heard him, barely understood him until he began pumping wildly. The thick hair between his hips brushed against her slick femininity as he ground into her. Immediately, she felt herself spiraling into a second encounter with sweet all-consuming bliss.

Her climax gripped him tightly, luring and beckoning him toward his own fiery release. Hot spasms exploded through his body, rippling through his muscled frame like thunderbolts through the sky.

Exhausted but fully sated, Theodosia stilled upon his chest, her cheek pressed against his moist shoulder. She could not move, didn't want to.

And neither did Roman.

Morning sunshine drifting over them, they lay quietly, their bodies still joined in sensual union, the beats of their hearts meshed as one.

* * *

As the days wandered into weeks, Theodosia discovered she could no longer recall what date of the month it was. She tried to keep count, but time eluded her and soon ceased to hold any meaning for her at all.

Only Roman mattered. In the wonderful world he'd introduced to her, she played with him. Beneath trees and open skies. She danced with him, and he swirled her across ballrooms of forest floors and flower-strewn meadows. She sang with him, nature's music the hauntingly beautiful symphony that accompanied them.

She loved with him. Sheltered within tall emerald grass, upon soft beds of leaves, or in sparkling streams, she surrendered to him at dawn, in the sultry heat of noon, and lying under the twinkling stars of cool nights.

She was never without him. By day he was at her side, by night he filled her every dream.

And her happiness knew no bounds.

"I'm sorry you're in such a bad mood, Theodosia," Roman teased one evening. Standing with his back against a tree, he cleaned his knife with a soft rag and listened to Theodosia's bright laughter fill the air as she played with the baby possum he'd managed to catch for her. She laughed all the time now, he mused. Any silly little thing set her off.

Sitting beside the fire upon a stack of folded blankets, Theodosia laughed harder when the tiny animal wrapped its long tail around her bare back and began pulling her hair with its small grappling paws. "I cannot believe there was a time in my life when I refused to sleep without a nightgown on," she said, stroking the possum's back and smiling when it hissed with pleasure. "Now I walk through woods and fields as naked as—"

"As naked as I like you to be," Roman finished for her. His body was as bare as hers, as they hadn't bothered to dress after their bath in the nearby pond. "You have to admit, though, it feels good not having to wear clothes all the time."

She touched the possum's pink nose. "It does," she agreed with a smile. "Indeed, I think perhaps that I will find my garments exceedingly uncomfortable the next time I am forced to wear them for any length of time."

Roman finished with his knife and returned it to its leather sheath. "Then don't wear them for any length of time. Now there's an idea. How about if we stay here for a while and live naked?"

"We'll be Adam and Eve, and this will be our Eden."

"Want to read for a while, Eve?" Grinning the crooked smile she so loved to see, he retrieved two books from one of her bags in the bed of the buckboard. "Spleens or sex-treats?" he asked, holding up the two volumes.

"Spleens, please."

He studied the covers of the books. "I'm not in the mood for spleens tonight."

"All right. Sex-treats."

He threw the medical textbook back into the wagon, ambled toward the fire, and sat down beside her. "Your friend is too young to be around while we read this, Eve."

She caressed the possum's soft fur for a short while longer, placed it on the ground, then watched it waddle into the forest shadows.

"You're beautiful, you know that?" Roman

asked, watching the fireshine shimmer over her pale body and through her long gold hair.

His compliment brought her a rush of emotion. She leaned toward him, drawn to him by more than desire, more than passion. "I am seized by an unfamiliar feeling," she whispered.

She explained no further.

She didn't have to. Roman knew the same odd, yet powerful feeling. But if Theodosia had no name for it, he wouldn't try to name it, either.

All he knew was that the profound emotion made him want to possess her body and soul.

"The book," she murmured, her lips a breath away from his. "We were going to read the book."

"Yeah, the book." Pulling himself from the powerful spell of feeling cast over him, he dipped his thumbs into the pages and haphazardly opened the volume to whatever section fate decreed.

Looking down at the page staring up at them, he and Theodosia examined the detailed picture of a man who, by means of his tongue, hands, feet, and manhood, was making love to no less than six women at the same time.

"I think I'll move to Tibet," Roman quipped. He turned the page, upon which was illustrated another picture.

The diagram showed a man with ropes tied around each of his wrists and ankles. He hung suspended from a ceiling beam, and with his swollen shaft poised and four men handling his ropes, he was being lowered toward a spread-eagled woman on the floor.

"I think I'll stay in Texas," Roman decided aloud.

Giggling, Theodosia thumbed through more pages, then stopped at one. "Let's try this."

Roman scowled. The picture displayed a couple making love in a sitting position with their feet locked behind their heads. "Are you crazy? I can't get my feet around the back of my neck like that."

"Try."

"No."

"Why not?"

He stared at her. Was this sexual daredevil really the same prudish woman who had vowed to have a brief, unfeeling bout of coitus in a pitch-dark room? "Look, Theodosia, even if I were able to get my feet crossed behind my head like that, I'd never be able to get them down again. I'd be forced to go through life inching along the ground on my bare—"

"Oh, very well." She turned to another page. "How about this?"

In the picture she indicated, a man in a standing position made love to a woman while holding her off the floor. They were face-to-face, and the woman's body was folded in a jackknife pose with the backs of her legs pressed against the man's chest, her feet resting upon his shoulders, and her hands grasping the back of his neck. To further support her, the man had his hands beneath her bottom.

Roman remembered how far Theodosia had stretched her legs above her head during their sexual encounter in Red Wolf and suspected the unusual form of lovemaking wouldn't be impossible for her. "This position has definite possibilities."

When he rose from the ground, Theodosia saw he was fully erect and ready to begin. The sight increased her own desire, and she eagerly took his hand when he held it down to her.

Roman helped her to her feet, then clasped her

waist. "On the count of three jump aboard. One
. . . two . . . three."

She hopped up and into him, curling her legs
around his back.

"This is all wrong," Roman said, staring into her
twinkling whiskey eyes. "Your legs are supposed to
be on my chest and your feet are supposed to be on
my shoulders."

"But I can see no way of moving my legs upward
while you are holding me like this. Your arms are in
the way."

"Did you see directions written anywhere on that
page that shows the drawing?"

She shook her head and kissed the tip of his nose.
"I believe we shall have to determine the procedure
ourselves."

Roman thought for a moment. "I have an idea."
He set her back on the ground, then lay down on
his back. "All right, sit on my stomach and stretch
your legs over my chest."

Carefully, she sat on his belly and adjusted her
legs before her so that her feet dangled just past his
shoulders.

Her position afforded Roman a tantalizing view
of pure femininity. "Why don't we just stay like this
for a while?" he suggested, his hands stroking the
tops of her thighs, the tips of his fingers pressing
lightly into the sweet treasure between her legs.

Theodosia leaned over and locked her hands behind his neck. "Up, my magnificent Tibetan lover."

Holding her behind the small of her back, Roman
slowly sat up. Theodosia's legs rose with him. "Are
you sure this isn't hurting you anywhere?"

She sighed. "I feel a long, delicious stretch at the

backs of my thighs, and the sweet ache of desire inside my—well, you know."

He did indeed know. The thought nearly rendered him senseless with longing for her. "All right, I'm going to stand up now. Hold on."

Standing proved more difficult than he'd imagined. Most of Theodosia's weight pushed into his torso, and what with her sitting between his chest and bent knees, he was off balance and could not get enough weight pushed toward his legs to be able to stand without rolling backward.

"I'm going to have to rock to my feet," he informed her. "You just sit still."

He began to rock back and forth. The sounds of crunching leaves and his own heaves of exertion filled the quiet of the night, but he soon shifted enough weight forward to be able to stand. Quickly, he slid his hands downward and supported Theodosia by holding her bottom. "It's a wonder those Tibetan men can even perform after the work out of trying to stand up with their women hanging off their necks."

Theodosia grinned into his eyes. "While you were rocking, I thought of the means they probably employ to arrive in this standing position. It occurred to me that the woman lies on her back upon a high bed or table and raises her legs toward her shoulders. The man then leans over her and slips his arms around her back while the woman wraps hers around his neck. Thus, the man simply straightens."

"Now you tell me. We could have used the back of the wagon to do that. What good is your genius if you don't use it in time?" Turning his head to both sides, he kissed each of her ankles.

She felt his swollen sex stir against her lower back. "Make love to me, Roman."

Her request and the peculiar but highly provocative, wide-open position she was in brought him such fierce desire that a low growl of passion reverberated through his chest. Lifting her higher, he attempted to situate her so that he could lower her directly upon his rigid masculinity.

But he couldn't see what he was doing and felt his member slide straight through Theodosia's legs and slide up over her belly.

She looked down and smiled. "You missed."

"Well, dammit, I can't see! And since I'm holding you up with both hands, I can't feel what I'm doing either. It's like trying to hit the bull's-eye while blindfolded and with my hands tied behind my back."

" 'Twould give me unprecedented pleasure to assist thee, O helpless one," Theodosia offered sweetly. She released her right hand from around his neck and took firm hold of his pulsing arousal. "Lift me once more."

When he did as she asked, she guided him. Her position allowed him to sink more deeply into her than he ever had. "Oh!" she cried softly. Nestling her face in the thick black hair that streamed over his shoulder, she concentrated on the wonderful feeling of being so completely filled by him. "Oh, Roman."

He couldn't answer. Gritting his teeth, he tried to stem the pleasure flowing swiftly through his loins. She'd taken all of him, and he was buried so deeply inside her that he could feel her womb. It was the most incredible sensation he'd ever experienced.

Cautiously, afraid to hurt her, he began to move,

inching his hips upward while lifting and lowering Theodosia.

The gentle care he took with her merely frustrated her. "Roman, please." Raising her head from his shoulder, she pressed her lips to his and slipped her tongue deeply into his mouth.

Her passion freed him from all worry, and he drove into her with all the strength his raging desire lent to him.

But he stilled abruptly when he heard a snapping sound. Dear God, had he or Theodosia cracked something important? "Something broke. Was it something of mine, or something of yours?"

Though she yearned for the sensual peak of the pleasure she'd begun to feel, Theodosia couldn't stifle her laughter. Her profound amusement burst through her in great churning waves.

Roman was hard pressed to keep a firm hold on her. She quaked in his arms, and the convulsive movements not only caused him to stagger as he struggled to maintain his balance but made him a little worried over the safety and well-being of his highly vulnerable and deeply buried man parts. He lifted Theodosia high and felt himself slide out of her depths, just as a fresh seizure of laughter rolled through her. "For God's sake, Theodosia! Stop—"

The rest of his command was lost in a loud groan as he tripped over an exposed tree root and fell toward the ground. Instantly, he twisted his body and landed on his back so Theodosia would not be hurt.

Startled, she ceased laughing. "Are you all right?" she asked, sitting on his belly.

He took a moment to retrieve his breath, which had blown completely out of his chest. "Are you kidding?" he managed to answer. "Falling flat on my back on a tree root, with you coming down hard on my belly was such a pleasant experience that I think we should do it again."

His sarcasm assured her he wasn't injured. She moved so that she was lying full length upon him. "Roman," she began, smiling into his steady gaze, "the cracking sound you heard was caused by your stepping on a brittle stick. I am truly sorry I laughed, but when you asked if one of us had broken something, I simply could not—the thought struck me as—you were so serious, that I—"

He watched laughter come into her eyes again, and this time he joined her in her merriment. Holding her tenderly to him, he laughed into her soft fragrant hair and couldn't remember ever having so much fun.

"Roman," Theodosia whispered when her fit of amusement had finally subsided, "we have yet to finish what we started."

He lifted an ebony eyebrow. "Can we do it—I mean, *may* we do it the American way?"

She smiled. "Yes, Roman, we may."

He swept his fingers into the hair at the sides of her head and studied her beauty as if tonight would be the last time he had the pleasure of seeing her. Profoundly tender emotions thrumming through him, he rolled her to her back, and covered her body with his own.

Theodosia gloried in his lovemaking. He pleasured her gently, slowly, and so sweetly that her happiness became a joy so overwhelming, it brought tears to her eyes.

And when at last he was through and he held her next to his warm and powerful body, Theodosia gazed into the fireflames and allowed every memory she had of him to filter through her mind. With each one that came to her, a single truth grew in the heart of her heart, and she slowly came to understand the unfamiliar feeling whose name had eluded her earlier.

She suspected the emotion had come into existence long ago, on the day he'd first settled that glittering sapphire gaze of his upon her.

She'd fallen in love with Roman Montana.

Chapter 18

As summer slipped silently into the edge of autumn, Theodosia kept her love for Roman silent as well. Although he seemed to enjoy her company, he'd never once spoken about his feelings, and so she could not bring herself to admit to her own.

But when time revealed a second secret to her, she knew it was one she could not keep from him. Her woman's flow was more than a month late.

She had conceived Roman's child.

If only Roman returned her love, she thought every time he took her into his arms. If only he'd marry her, take her to his ranch, and give her a dozen more children in the years to come. She'd forget every thought of Dr. Wallaby. Every thought of the Brazilian research.

Every thought but the one of Lillian and Upton. Her vow to give them the child they so longed to have haunted her.

Had bearing a child for them not been her plan for months?

She withdrew into herself for long periods of time, deliberating, rationalizing, trying her hardest to see and understand her dilemma in the right light.

And when the answer finally came to her, it caused her great sorrow. But even so, she knew it was the only possible one.

Roman did not love her. She couldn't make him love her. He was not going to marry her, he was not going to take her to his ranch, and he was not going to give her a dozen more children.

He didn't want a wife and family. He never had.

She had to concentrate on the well-being of the child she carried.

She did, and imagined Lillian holding the babe while Upton stroked its downy head. The image became so vivid and real in her mind that she could almost smell Lillian's lemon verbena. Could almost see her sister's brilliant smile.

The babe deserved to live in a loving home with parents who were not only married . . .

. . . but who were totally devoted to each other.

The child belonged with Lillian and Upton.

Roman led the way into Willow Patch, a small town in which he would purchase needed supplies. As he dismounted and tied Secret to a post in front of the whitewashed hotel, he tried to ignore the persistent feeling that something was wrong with Theodosia.

But every time he looked at her, his instincts about her deepened. Something *was* wrong, and whatever it was, it had been bothering her for the past two days.

He wouldn't wait for a third day to pass before understanding the reasons for her quiet dismay, for he hated seeing her upset.

And he missed her smile and laughter.

They would spend the night here in the Willow Patch hotel, he decided, and he would confront her as soon as she'd settled in the room.

As it turned out, he couldn't even wait for her to remove her bonnet before beginning the interrogation. "All right, let's have it," he said the second he'd escorted her into their room and closed the door. "I know damned well something's wrong with you, and I want to know what it is. *Right now.*"

Her gaze darted around the room, sweeping past the gleaming mahogany bureau, the blue-and-red-braided throw rug, a collection of framed paintings, and the red ruffled curtains hanging on the two small windows. Parting her lips to speak, she unconsciously cupped her lower abdomen.

Roman watched her. Gently, as if afraid she would shatter into a million bits, she laid her hand on her stomach.

Realization crashed through him like a stone through glass. Stunned, he stared at her belly.

There, behind her hand, deep inside her, slept a tiny life.

His baby.

He could not have been more sure of its existence if he held it in his arms.

He raked his fingers through his hair, trying desperately to sort through the explosion of thoughts that took hold of him at that moment.

He thought of the lives he'd taken.

He'd never created one.

He thought of his own life. What righteous thing had he done with it? He'd worked and saved money, yes, but he'd yet to see his dreams come true. Had yet to attain the proof of his success.

The baby was no notion, no unfulfilled objective. It was real, alive, a miracle he'd had a part in bringing about.

He thought of kin. He had none. No relatives anywhere in the entire world.

He did now. The baby was his own flesh and blood.

He thought a thousand things and connected all of them to the small life dwelling inside Theodosia's womb. The precious life he and Theodosia had created together.

"Roman," Theodosia murmured, her head bowed, "what I set out to do has been done. I have conceived."

He tried to reply but remained too astonished to speak.

"I am grateful for all you have done for me," Theodosia continued, still staring at the hardwood floor. Anguish filled every corner of her heart, but she valiantly resisted tears. "And I wish you happiness and success in all your endeavors."

The meaning behind her words struck him instantly.

She was leaving him.

He couldn't understand, couldn't comprehend why she was leaving. What about their baby? he wondered frantically.

Their baby.

No.

God. He'd forgotten. He'd been so totally involved with Theodosia herself that he'd forgotten what she wanted from him.

A baby.

He'd given one to her, and now she was going to give it to her sister and brother-in-law! Was going to bear the child and hand it over to two people he'd never met. Then she'd set sail for Brazil and wade in some beetle-infested river for the rest of her life.

Those had been her intentions all along, and *she* hadn't forgotten them. But in light of all that had happened between them . . . in light of all the times they'd shared, how could she continue to hold on to her original intentions?

He wasn't exactly sure what the shared times had meant to him, but they'd meant *something*. Apparently, though, they'd meant absolutely nothing to Theodosia. If they had, she wouldn't be so eager to return to another life without him.

He wasn't good enough for her, he realized suddenly. Wasn't smart enough for her. He'd been but the chosen candidate to her, the man who'd satisfied her needs and wants.

Just as he'd been for Flora. He'd never been good enough for Flora, either. She'd used him, then sold everything he'd thought belonged to him. She'd left him with nothing but a dream.

And now Theodosia was about to take away the baby that belonged to him and leave him with the same unfulfilled dream Flora had.

Everything bad . . . all the terrible things that happened years ago were happening again.

Rage burned straight through his heart and consumed his very soul.

And at that moment a vibrant truth flared to life inside him, so bright, so strong he shook with its intensity.

"No way in hell," he seethed aloud. "No way in hell, Theodosia!"

He stormed toward her. "It's *my* baby, too, got that?"

His shout thundered through her. Confusion fairly overcame her. "Roman—"

"You are *not* giving the baby to your sister!"

"*What?*" Her mind spinning, she stepped backward until the backs of her legs hit the bed.

You are not giving the baby to your sister! His words shouted through her endlessly, and her heart skipped so many beats, she felt sure she would collapse and die.

Did he want her and the child? Would he tell her he loved her? Would he marry her, take her to his ranch, and give her a dozen more children?

Her chest tightened in anticipation of what he would next say.

"Judging by the look on your face," Roman growled, "I don't think you understand. Let me put it to you straight. *I want my baby, Theodosia!*"

She stared at him so hard that everything else in the room disappeared from her vision. He said he wanted the *baby*.

He had not said that he wanted *her*.

She'd never known such heartache could exist. No longer could she resist her tears; they streamed down her cheeks and quickly dampened the front of her dress.

"Your tears don't move me," Roman snapped. "If giving a baby to your precious sister means that much to you, then you can get with child again after you've given me my baby. Hell, you can have a dozen kids for Lillian, but the one you carry now is *mine!*"

He spun on his heel and strode to the door. "We're staying right here in Willow Patch until my baby is born," he continued vehemently. "After the birth, you can go to Brazil and study beetle spit for the rest of your life for all I care, but you are leaving my baby with me!"

Yanking the door open, he continued to glare at her. "I'm going to find a place where we can live for the next eight or nine months, or however long it is before the baby comes. I'm also going to see the town doctor and find out when he can see you. Nothing's going to happen to my child, got that? I'm going to watch you every second until I have my baby in my arms. After that, you're free to do whatever the hell it is you want to do."

He stepped into the corridor, then turned to face her again. "If you leave this room, I'll hunt you down, Theodosia," he warned. "No matter where you go, I'll find you."

He slammed the door.

Theodosia's knees buckled. She fell to the bed behind her. For a moment she sat frozen, then began to shiver uncontrollably. As if someone were stabbing at her skin with sharp icicles.

Her hands felt so cold as she cupped them over her face. Not even her hot tears warmed them.

Why do you not love me, Roman?

She didn't know what to do.

Yes, she did know what to do.

She wanted to stay with Roman. In the house he found for them in Willow Patch. And during the coming months, she realized, her love for him would deepen and fill her with the greatest of joy.

No, she would leave Willow Patch, now, while he was gone, before her love for him deepened and filled her with the deepest of sorrow.

He didn't want her.

Where would she go?

Anywhere, and when she got there, she would decide where to go. What to do.

On trembling legs, she stood and shuffled to the window. There in the street below she saw Roman lead Secret out of the livery stable. Even from where she stood at the window, she could see his terrible frown. He mounted, urged his stallion forward, and galloped out of town.

Dust and speed and rage swirled all down the street.

He'd be back.

"I love you," she whispered.

The breath of her farewell left a large foggy circle on the windowpane. With the tip of her finger, she wrote Roman's name in the mist. Sunlight burst through the humid letters, then dried them.

And right before Theodosia's eyes, Roman's name disappeared.

Roman stalked into the Willow Patch mercantile and ordered provisions for traveling.

"Goin' on a trip?" the shop owner asked while gathering the articles of his customer's order.

Roman didn't feel like being friendly. He gave a stiff nod, then turned his back on the man.

Dammit! he raged. After three hours of searching, he hadn't found a single house for rent in or anywhere around Willow Patch. The boarding house had rooms available, but the lady who ran the establishment sheltered a cluster of whores beneath its roof. The thought of Theodosia living in such a squalid place sickened him.

They'd have to move on to another town, one in

which he might be able to find a house to rent during the coming months.

"Here you are," the shopkeeper said when he'd finished piling the supplies on the counter.

Roman turned back around, withdrew a wad of money from his pocket, and peeled off several bills. While waiting for the mercantile owner to count out his change, he stared absently at the merchandise on display inside the glass-topped counter.

He saw a highly polished violin, a crystal wineglass, and a pair of sterling silver candlestick holders. A gold calling-card case with the name ALFRED CHIPPERS engraved upon it twinkled up at him, as well as a small emerald ring and a brooch.

Roman frowned. Then narrowed his eyes. Then clenched his fists.

The brooch. A heart-shaped ruby, and from its bottom dangled fragile gold chains.

Theodosia was gone. She'd sold the pin and left town.

Fury tightened around him like a thorny vine.

"Purty, ain't it?" the shopkeeper said. Tapping his fingers on the top of the glass case, he too peered down at the brooch. "Jest bought it about three hours ago. A girl come in here askin' a hunnerd and fifty dollars fer it. Her eyes was real red and swollen, and I could tell she'd been cryin'. I figgered she'd run into a spell o' bad luck, but her woes was my gain. I give her thirty-five dollars, and she tuk it. I reckon I can sell that pin fer two hunnerd and make me a hunnerd-and-sixty-five-dollar profit. Ain't bad, huh?"

Roman grabbed the man's shirt collar and pulled him up and across the counter. "You bastard! How could you have cheated her like that?" he shouted.

The man's eyes bulged; his face reddened.

"Where did she go?" Roman demanded.

"Don't—don't know! She did—didn't say!"

His eyes glittering, Roman released the sniveling man. "Give me the brooch."

The man rubbed his throat for a moment and then reached for the gun he kept behind the counter.

But he stilled instantly when he felt cold metal at his temple and the clicking sound of a gun hammer in his ears.

"Give me the brooch, you damned son-of-a-bitch," Roman ordered again, pressing the barrel of his Colt further into the man's fleshy temple.

The man practically tore the doors off the back of the counter in his haste to retrieve the ruby brooch.

Roman snatched it out of the shopkeeper's hand and stormed out of the mercantile. Recalling that he'd just seen Theodosia's horse and wagon in the livery when he'd stabled Secret, he realized she'd left Willow Patch by other means. He went back to the hotel but learned nothing from the hotel manager.

Most of her belongings remained in the room, which meant she'd packed only what she could carry.

If you leave this room, I'll hunt you down, he had warned her. *No matter where you go, I'll find you.*

His vow a chant that beat through him in cadence with his heart, Roman left the hotel again and soon found out that no stages had left Willow Patch. Several travelers had come and gone during the course of the day, but no one in town knew who the travelers were or where they'd gone.

For hours, Roman described Theodosia to everyone he met. Many townspeople remembered seeing her, but not a one could recall her leaving.

Only the arrival of nighttime, when everyone had gone home to sleep or into the saloon to drink, did Roman finally cease his frenzied inquisition and admit to himself that Theodosia had really escaped him.

He was filled with rage. Worry. Guilt.

And emptiness.

Secret and moonbeams showed him the way out of Willow Patch. He didn't know where to go and so he headed nowhere. Just straight ahead, into the darkness. Night creatures talked to him with hisses, chirps, buzzes, and snarls, but he heard no wagon wheels behind him.

"*Can* I ask you a question?" he shouted into the darkness.

No one corrected his grammar.

"Fifteen plus three equals twenty!"

No one corrected his arithmetic.

Starlight shimmered over the grassy field to his left. The grass remained green.

But the wild flowers were gone.

He lost all awareness of time as his stallion ambled through the black night.

Thoughts of his baby pulled at his mind.

Memories of its mother tugged at his heart.

He stopped Secret and dismounted. Mulberry branches swayed above him. Glancing up at them, he wondered what their scientific name was. "*Mullinas berrisinium*," he guessed.

His head bowed low, he kicked at pebbles as he walked circles around Secret.

When dawn whispered through the sky, he was

still walking around his horse, but there were no more pebbles for him to kick.

Bewilderment sat in his mind like a rock, too heavy to move, too large to see past.

He stopped in front of Secret's face. "What would I do with a baby, anyway?" he asked the stallion. "I'll be so busy raising horses, I won't have time to raise a child. What the hell is the matter with me? I don't need some dumb kid tagging along after me!"

He kicked at dirt and watched it fly over Secret's leg. "And it'll probably be a girl," he muttered. "I've taken care of women for forever and a day, and I'll be damned if I need another one to take care of."

He shoved his fingers through his hair. "I bet she'll go back to Boston," he muttered, staring into his steed's huge black eyes. "She won't stay in Texas because she'll be afraid I'll find her. She'll wire her rich sister and brother-in-law, they'll send her another trunk full of gold, and she'll head east. And where she goes, my baby goes."

He turned in the dirt and glanced at the pink and yellow horizon. Threads of blue wove through the pink and yellow, and he decided the sky resembled a pastel baby blanket.

He tried to visualize his child. First, he saw a little person with black hair and big brown eyes. Then he saw one with golden hair and blue eyes. He saw dark skin, and pale skin. He saw the child riding a horse; the child peering into a microscope.

He couldn't understand his own child. Couldn't imagine him or her, no matter how hard he tried.

But he could see its mother as if she stood right before him.

Melted butter. Her hair. Flowing, soft, warm, and fragrant. "And your eyes," he whispered into the early morning breeze. "The color of tree bark. A well-worn saddle. Of whiskey."

He saw her lips. Parted. Shining because she'd licked them. "Pink as Secret's tongue. As boiled gulf shrimp. Pink as dawn," he murmured.

Secret's soft nickers floated around him. *Secret.* Soon he'd have thousands of Secrets. Horses that could reach a full gallop within seconds and stop on a dime. He'd live in his huge ranch house, look out over his twenty-five thousand acres of land, and know he was one of the wealthiest men in all of Texas.

Quite a feat for a young man who had dared to reach for a dream. In only a short time he would turn the fantasy into reality.

Nodding to himself, he took a deep breath of air and satisfaction, stuffed his hands into his pockets, and winced.

Something sharp pricked his right thumb. He pinched the object between his fingers and withdrew it from his pocket.

The pink and yellow glimmers of dawn struck the bloodred depths of ruby and fragile chains of gold.

He stared at the heart-shaped ruby, the dainty gold strings, and he remembered the pale slender throat against which it had once gleamed.

Something pulled at his heart again. Tenderly but insistently.

He closed his eyes. In the darkness he heard her.

Back in the fifteenth century, the heartstring was believed to be a nerve that sustained the heart. Presently the expression is used to describe deep emotion and affection, and one is said to feel a tug at the heart when so touched.

He stared down at the pin again, seeing a diamond in the middle of the ruby. Strange, he'd never noticed the diamond before.

He looked closer. The diamond wasn't a diamond.

A tear pooled on the ruby. His tear, and then he watched another fall. And another, and soon the ruby was wet with the spill of his emotions.

Deep emotion. Affection.

. . . one is supposed to feel a tug at the heart when so touched.

Roman closed his fingers over the wet ruby. The pin stuck his palm, and as his tears seeped into the wound, he realized with startling clarity the name of the feeling he harbored for Theodosia.

He stood transfixed, gazing into the softly lit heavens. His ranch materialized within the early morning clouds. He saw his horses running through fields. He'd carried the image in his mind for ten long years, and he knew it by heart.

It faded right before his eyes, and in its place a woman's face floated into the mellow sky. Her lips moved as she whispered to him.

When you truly love someone, Roman, no sacrifice is too great to make.

The heart-shaped ruby clutched in his hand, Roman mounted.

He followed the pull in his heart.

The tug on his heartstrings.

He headed west, toward Templeton. He needed money. All the money he had.

Señor Madrigal would have to find another buyer

for the twenty-five thousand acres of Rio Grande grassland.

Roman was going to Boston.

From there, he reckoned he'd set sail for Brazil.

The man and woman chattered endlessly. Luby and Pinky Scrully were their names, and Theodosia sat between them as Luby directed the ox-driven wagon down the mulberry-tree-edged road.

She had just sold her ruby brooch to the owner of the Willow Patch mercantile when Luby Scrully entered the store, announced that he was passing through town, and ordered supplies for his trip. She hadn't cared where the man was headed; when she heard him say he was passing through Willow Patch, the only thing she cared about was leaving with him.

The Scrullys had been more than willing to have her along on their journey to Gull Sky and had refused to accept the money she'd tried to offer them.

They'd been traveling for two days now, and Roman had not found them. He wouldn't. No one in Willow Patch knew she'd left with the Scrullys, so no one in Willow Patch could tell Roman where she'd gone.

She hugged John the Baptist's cage to her breasts, and as the wagon rumbled along, she watched red, yellow, and orange leaves fall from the trees and flutter to the ground.

"Yeah, Theodosia, honey," Pinky said, patting Theodosia's arm, "me and Luby's on our way fer a visit with our son, Gilly. Don't 'spect we'll enjoy the visit much, though, what with his wife there."

Luby threw his wife a sidelong frown. "You're jealous, Pinky, and that's the truth of it. It pains you somethin' awful to know Gilly loves another woman 'sides you.''

Pinky laughed. "I reckon you're right, Luby. I'll git along with that wife o' his as best as I can, but Lord how I long fer them days when Gilly was jest a young'un. 'Member how happy we was then, Luby?''

Luby nodded. "Time goes on, though, Pinky. Least we still got each other. Be worser if one of us was dead.''

"Speakin' o' the dead," Pinky said, "I heared tell that four men in the Blanco y Negro Gang's done meeted up with the only knowed cure fer birth. Yeah, dead's what they are, and I heared it said right in the street back in Willer Patch. Don't nobody know who killed 'em, but they was shore killed and dead. Where you headin', anyway, Theodosia, honey? Y'ain't said more'n a handful o' words in two days' time. Me? Well, I've been curious as all git out about you, but I been mindin' my manners and keepin' quiet. Cain't keep quiet no more, though. Where you headin'?''

Lost in the memory of the day Roman had saved her from the notorious gang, it was a moment before Theodosia could answer. "Boston," she murmured.

Pinky nodded. "That's a place on the Missersipper River, ain't it? Yeah, me and Luby was there 'bout two years past. S'where Luby buyed me a new kitchen knife. I busted the ole one when I throwed it at a rattler that slithered itsef into the house. Didn't hit the rattler. Hit the stove. Knife broke, and the rattler bit my leg.''

A fresh wave of nostalgia sucked Theodosia into deeper grief as she recalled the day Roman had caught a rattlesnake with his bare hands. That had been the day he'd made her eat baby hotcakes. "And play in the mud," she whispered.

"What was that, honey?" Pinky asked.

"Nothing," Theodosia replied. "Nothing." Feeling tears fill her eyes, she pretended to sneeze into her hands. Her action squeezed the tears onto her fingers. They slid down her palm and disappeared beneath her sleeves.

"Bless you," Pinky said. She hiked her patched skirts up to her knees, pushed down her sock, and pointed to two fang marks on her plump calf. "Look here at where the rattler bit me, Theodosia. I didn't die, though. What I done to save my own life, y'see, was I drank a whole bottle o' whiskey jest as soon as that snake let go o' me. Don't rightly know what it is about bein' likkered up, but somehow a body full o' likker ain't bothered none a'tall by a little bit o' snake poison. Luby says he can drink more likker'n I can, but he ain't nothin' but a liar."

Country chatter, Theodosia thought, remembering the morning Roman had taught her to imitate Oble Smott's chatter. That had been the day after they'd made love for the first time. And when Oble had gone, they'd made love again.

She closed her eyes and felt sunrays beam onto her eyelids. A swirl of colors floated through the darkness, and in the midst of the colors Roman appeared. She saw his brilliant blue eyes, crooked grin, and long charcoal hair. His scent came to her; sunshine, wind, leather, and the musky smell of hard-worked muscles.

"See the marks, Theodosia?" Pinky pressed.

Opening her eyes, Theodosia looked at the marks. "Yes, I see them, Mrs. Scrully."

Luby glanced at his wife's snake fang scars, too, and scratched the gray grizzle on his chin. "Pinky, what in the world? Theodosia don't wanna see your fat leg. And you're thinkin' o' the time we was in *Tosten*, not Boston. Boston ain't on the Missersipper River, and neither's Tosten, fer that matter. Boston's in Massertuchetts, and Tosten's up in the Oklerhomer Terr'tory." He looked at Theodosia. "You're a long way from Boston, darlin'. How you gonna git there?"

Theodosia felt one swift tear escape down her cheek and reached up to wipe it away before the Scrullys saw it. How *was* she going to get all the way to Boston? She only had thirty-five dollars. The mercantile owner in Willow Patch had refused to pay a penny more for the ruby brooch. She knew the fine piece of jewelry was worth much more, but as terrified as she'd been of the possibility that Roman would find her before she left Willow Patch, she'd accepted the measly amount of money and given the store proprietor her most treasured possession.

"Theodosia, honey, you all right?" Pinky asked, spotting the wet sparkle in Theodosia's eyes.

"There now, darlin', don't you go to frettin', hear?" Luby said. "We'll be in Gull Sky tomorrer. From there, you can git you a seat on a stage that'll take you to Oates' Junction. Trains run through Oates' Junction, and I 'spect one of 'em might head toward Boston."

Theodosia turned her head sharply toward him and peered intensely into his bleary gray eyes. "Oates' Junction," she whispered. "How far away is Templeton from where we are right now?"

Luby rubbed his chin grizzle again. "Templeton, y'say? Well, it's just a holler away, darlin'."

"A holler? How much distance is a holler?"

Luby pointed ahead. "See the other road that turns off the one we're on now?"

Theodosia saw the small dirt road that veered to the right.

"Down that road a piece is Templeton."

"A piece?" Theodosia asked, thoroughly bewildered. "Mr. Scrully, I'm afraid I do not know the distance of *a piece*, either."

"Well, darlin', in the case o' Templeton, both a holler and a piece'd mean about ten miles. You know somebody in Templeton?"

"Dr. Wallaby," she murmured. Was it possible that the scientist was still in Templeton?

She doubted it. Months had passed since she'd last seen him. His research funds had more than likely arrived from New England, and at this very moment he was probably deep within the Brazilian jungles.

Still, the slim chance that he might yet remain in Templeton was a chance she was going to take. If he was there, she'd stay with him until Lillian and Upton sent her enough money to get back to Boston. "Mr. Scrully, would you mind—"

"Takin' you to Templeton?" he finished for her. "Be my pleasure, darlin'." He turned the wagon onto the side road.

Dusk fell quietly. Soon a crisp evening breeze swayed through the air, carrying the faint sound of lively music. Before long, Luby drove past a small country fair. Watching the goings-on, Theodosia thought of children bobbing for apples. She pon-

dered displays of country crafts, squealing livestock, the Father of Pie, and game booths.

She remembered Roman and wondered if there
was anything in the world that wouldn't somehow
remind her of him.

"Well, here we are, darlin'," Luby said as he
urged his ox down the main street of Templeton.
"Where to now?"

Theodosia directed him to the house that Dr.
Wallaby had rented at the end of the street and
bade him stop before the small cottage. Her parrot's cage in one hand, her bag of belongings in the
other, she stepped over Pinky's legs and climbed
out of the wagon. "Thank you ever so much, Mr.
and Mrs. Scrully," she said, managing a smile.

"Don't you want us to wait and see if you git
inside all right, Theodosia?" Pinky asked.

Unwilling to bother the kindly couple any further, Theodosia shook her head. "I'll be fine."

"Well, you take care, then, darlin'," Luby said.

She waved to them until their wagon reached the
end of the street, then turned toward the house.
Hoping with all her heart that she would find Dr.
Wallaby inside, she walked to the door, set her pos-
sessions on the ground, and knocked.

The door opened slowly.

Theodosia felt as though she were peering into a
mirror.

"Lillian?" she whispered.

In the next moment she found herself in her sister's loving arms.

Chapter 19

"Theodosia," Lillian murmured, holding Theodosia tightly. "Oh, my sweet little sister, you've no notion how happy I am at this moment."

The familiar scent of lemon verbena and love flowing around her, Theodosia took great comfort in her older sister's embrace. She sighed with exhaustion and with relief, then blew a kiss to Upton, who stood behind Lillian.

"Lillian, if you do not mind," Upton said, tapping Lillian's arm. When she moved away, he too embraced Theodosia. "We have missed you, my dear. Missed you terribly."

"As I have you," Theodosia whispered, deeply soothed by Upton's loving hug.

He released her, smiled into her big brown eyes, and cupped her cheeks. "I suppose you are wondering why we are here?"

"We came to wait for you," Lillian explained. She took Theodosia's hand and led her into the house.

The same sparse furnishings remained in the front room, Theodosia noted, but gone were the books, microscopes, and other scientific equipment.

"He's gone," Lillian announced when she saw Theodosia looking around the room. "That's why we're here. We received a letter from Dr. Wallaby a little over two months ago. His research funding had arrived, and he was about to set sail for Brazil. He said you would be returning to Templeton as soon as you had concluded your studies of southern speech and that he regretted not being here when you arrived. His letter ended with his assurance that he would eagerly await you in Brazil."

Upton brought Theodosia's things into the house and shut the door. "The thought of you returning to Templeton and finding this house empty disturbed us, especially since we had no way of knowing if your escort, Roman Montana, would remain with you. Your letters and wires arrived regularly for a period of time but then became few and far between. Out of worry, we decided to come and wait for you here."

Guilt seized Theodosia. "I'm sorry," she squeaked. "But Roman and I—we—there were long stretches of time when we were not near any towns. I could not write—"

"Don't trouble yourself a moment longer," Lillian scolded gently. "The important thing is that you are safe and with us again." Impulsively, she gave Theodosia another hug. "Besides, we only arrived two weeks ago and have not been waiting for you so very long, darling."

John the Baptist squawked loudly. "If it weren't for nightgowns gittin' pulled up and seed gittin' spilt, there wouldn't be no people in the world," he said.

Theodosia stifled a gasp.

"Why's a Yankee bird singing the Confederate

anthem, anyway?'' the parrot continued. "Tark, y'see, is Krat spelled back'ards.''

Lillian and Upton stared at the parrot.

The bird pecked at the door of his cage. "How do. I'm Oble Smott. You don't put that kind of doll behind a glass case and stare at her.''

Upton nodded in sudden comprehension. "I take it John the Baptist has heard a great deal of the digressive discourse common to the people here.''

"What?'' Theodosia whispered. "Oh. Yes. Yes, Upton, he has been in the company of many people given to oral meandering.''

"And did you enjoy your research concerning the patterns of southern speech, my dear?'' Upton asked. "I assume you made a great many notes concerning the subject, and I must say that I am extraordinarily interested in seeing them. How I have missed our discussions, Theodosia.''

"I—''

"How did you come to possess such interest in the speech patterns of the people here?'' Upton pressed. "You failed to mention your reasons in your letters. Lillian and I decided that perhaps your escort, Roman Montana, spoke in such a manner. Where is Mr. Montana, by the way?''

"Oh, for goodness' sake, Upton,'' Lillian chided. "You are barely giving our poor Theodosia time to think about one question before asking her another. Later you will have plenty of time to study her notes concerning digressive discourse. As for you, Theodosia, you look very tired. Your eyes are red as well.''

Theodosia was as yet unprepared to relate her story to Lillian and Upton. Her pain remained too raw, and she knew her tears would deeply upset them.

Soon, she thought. Very soon she would tell them about the child she'd conceived for them.

Bowing her head, she pretended to brush dust from the front of her gown. In actuality, however, she only wanted to feel the special place where the child dwelled. As her hand brushed past her lower abdomen, she swore she could feel Roman's presence.

"Then don't do anything, Theodosia," John the Baptist said, splashing water. "Just be with me for a while."

The parrot's reminder of what Roman had once said to her forced Theodosia to blink back tears.

"Theodosia?" Lillian said. "Is something the matter?"

Quickly, Theodosia feigned a smile and reached out to caress Lillian's cheek. "I may not look my best, Lillian, but you certainly do. You have finally put on some weight and look better than I have ever seen you."

Lillian looked at her husband. "Shall we tell her, Upton?"

"Yes." Upton put his arm around Lillian's shoulder. "Theodosia, we have exciting tidings to share with you."

Lillian laid Theodosia's hand over her lower belly. "I am with child, darling, and am well past the first trimester. Indeed, I have almost reached my fifth month. All four physicians who have examined me believe that I will give birth to a healthy baby."

The moment Lillian's announcement registered in her mind, Theodosia felt as though the world had

been turned upside down. Off balance both physically and mentally, she felt her legs weaken.

"Upton!" Lillian shouted.

He caught Theodosia just as she began to slip to
the floor and helped her to the small wooden bench
near the window. "Bring some water, Lillian," he
said, patting Theodosia's alabaster cheek.

Lillian rushed to get the water. "Theodosia, forgive me," she gushed. "But I had no idea that our
news would give you such a shock. I'm profoundly
sorry to have given it to you so suddenly."

Theodosia watched Lillian's lips move, but her
sister's voice sounded as if it were coming from a
hundred miles away.

*Lillian and Upton did not need the child she car-
ried.*

The realization tightened around her like a thick
rope, at first choking her with disbelief, then suffo-
cating her with overwhelming despair.

Escape, she thought desperately. She had to escape Lillian and Upton. The house. Her own
stunned emotions.

She had to think. Alone. Outside. Yes, outside.

Oh, God, what was she going to do?

"Theodosia?" Upton murmured, holding the
glass of water to her mouth. "Drink a bit, my dear."

She did as bade and, with much effort, forced
herself to appear in perfect control. "Your news has
astonished me. I am thrilled for you. Truly thrilled.
But I fear that my excitement has taken a toll on
me, and I feel the need for—"

"Of course, Theodosia, darling," Lillian blurted.
"You must lie down and rest. After a nap, you will
feel—"

"I would rather walk outside first, Lillian," Theodosia protested. "After a bit of fresh air, I will rest."

Lillian nodded. "I shall accompany you," she said, then turned to cross the room and fetch her outerwear.

"Oh, no, you will not," Upton said, catching his wife's hand. "You will nap while Theodosia walks. Then when she returns to rest, you will have sufficient energy to fuss over her, which I know full well you will do. You must think of the baby, Lillian. Go along, Theodosia, but don't venture far, and don't tarry. It will soon be dark."

Grateful for his intervention, she left quickly and, once outside, hurried away from the house. Following the road that led out of town, she passed the area where the country fair had been held. Only a few people remained there, disassembling booths and loading livestock back into wooden crates.

Paying little attention to her surroundings or where she was going, she continued down the soft dirt road, rounded a sharp curve, and soon came to an empty pasture. Masses of dead brush, clusters of large jagged rocks, and scraggly cedars scattered the deserted field. Near an old and dilapidated shed, a flock of sea gulls screamed and fought over a small dead animal.

Theodosia welcomed the ugliness of the landscape. Bending, she slipped between two fence rails and ran into the pasture.

She stopped beside a group of the craggy rocks and leaned into them. They pressed into her, and they hurt.

But not as much as her heart.

She thought of the child Lillian carried. The babe

would be blessed with both parents and a warm and loving home.

She thought of Roman and the child they'd created together.

I want my baby, Theodosia!

His words screamed through her.

"How can I do this to you, Roman?" she asked his memory. "You do not love me, but you want to love your child. How can I possibly take that chance away from you?"

But how could she give up the child? The precious babe was all she had left of Roman, and she loved the tiny being every bit as much as she loved its father.

She shivered suddenly as the cool evening breeze strengthened into a strong wind. Dusk became darker as black clouds gathered in the rolling sky above. The wind picked up her hair and sent it lashing at her face.

Fear of the impending storm told her to flee. Misery forced her to her knees.

"Roman," she whispered. She closed her eyes. Raindrops mingled with her tears. Soundless sobs shook her frame.

But she stilled instantly when she felt a large hand curl around her shoulder and strong fingers dig into her flesh.

She opened her eyes. Two men stared down at her, both smiling grins she'd seen before.

They wore rat hats.

Fear licked at her like a serpent's tongue.

"It's a small, small world, ain't it Gordie?" Burris Jister said.

Gordie chuckled. "Yeah, Burris, real small." He reached down and fingered a damp gold curl.

"Nice to see you again, purty lady. Saw you walkin' down the road a while ago and thought we'd foller you."

The country fair outside town, Theodosia thought hysterically. She'd walked straight past it!

"Why didn't you come to the fair, purty lady?" Gordie asked, still holding a lock of gold hair. "It's over now."

Burris nodded. "Too bad y'didn't come. We made us a bundle. Thought y'ruined us forever that day in Kidder Pass, huh? Yeah, well, it took us a long time, but we got our games runnin' again."

Theodosia screamed when Gordie yanked her to her feet.

He slapped her full across the face. "The day the sheriff and deputy of Kidder Pass took us away, we told you we wouldn't forget what you done, lady."

Burris jerked her away from his brother and leered into her eyes. "We told you that somewhere, someday we'd meet up again, and that day's here. And since that long-haired bodyguard o' yours ain't with you no more, there ain't nobody to stop us from makin' you pay for what you done to us."

Revenge. The Jisters wanted revenge. Comprehension exploded into Theodosia's mind, just as lightning and thunder crashed through the black sky.

With a strength she never realized she had, she tore free of Burris's hold and, blinded by rain and tears, raced toward a rickety lean-to she'd seen earlier. As she ran, she heard the Jisters' heavy footsteps behind her, swore she felt their hot breaths on her neck, and remembered the day she'd tried to flee from the Blanco y Negro Gang.

Today was the same. Rain battered down on her.

Thunder shook through her. Evil chased her, and lightning flamed above her.

The only difference was that there was no enchanted hill upon which to wish for Roman.

In the next moment a scream rent the air. Seething with fear, grief, and defeat, the cry had no end but tore from her throat on an unbroken stream of misery.

And then without warning, gunfire silenced her.

The heavy footsteps behind her faded and finally disappeared. She no longer felt hot breath on her neck.

The evil chased her no more.

She stopped, thoroughly bewildered, when she saw the Jisters running out of the rain-swept field as if haunted by a thousand demons.

She caught sight of him then. Sheets of rain tried to veil him from her view, but she knew who he was.

He was mounted, and his gray stallion stood pawing the mud. His long raven hair blew all around him, like a black halo.

He was far away, across the pasture, but she felt his startling blue gaze slice across the field and pierce her very soul.

Roman.

She tried to speak his name, but the sinister fire of lightning felt so near. Inches from her head. She could feel its heat, its powerful danger, and she felt sure that it was daring her to move so it could strike.

Terror plunged into her. She felt it slash through her like so many daggers plummeting from the malevolent sky.

The shelter of the shed was behind her, only a few feet away.

Roman was on the other side of the sodden field.

Her mind pulled her toward the safety of the shed.

But her heart tugged her forward.

Defying the lightning, she flew across the pasture.

Roman met her halfway, and as his stallion bore down upon her, he leaned down from the saddle and lifted her into his arms. Holding her securely to his chest, he stopped Secret in the middle of the field.

Theodosia raised her face to the man she loved more with each beat of her pulse. For a long while she could only stare at him, blending the real sight of him with the indelible image she had of him in her mind. The lightning behind him flashed, but the glitter in his eyes flamed far more brightly. "I believe," she began softly, watching rain course down his face, "that I have overcome my fear of lightning."

He slid his hand over her belly, over his child.

His action reminded her of what he wanted from her. Her joy came apart and fell away, like a broken string of pearls. "You came to Templeton," she murmured, rain splashing her lips, "to tell me again that you want the child."

He gave a long, slow nod, and continued staring into her eyes. "And to see Señor Madrigal."

"Señor Madrigal." She tried to nod, but felt paralyzed. "To buy your ranch. You—you'll raise the child on your ranch. With all your horses."

He frowned, then raised his wet brow. "Then

you've changed your mind about giving my baby to your sister?"

She wanted him to release her so she could run again. Being so close to him while knowing he cared only for their child tormented her.

But if she ran, she would take the child with her. She realized now she could not do such a thing to Roman. She loved him, and no sacrifice she could think of was too great to make for him.

"I am not giving the baby to my sister," she answered, her chest tight with pain. "I am giving the child to you. And then . . ." She paused and turned her face into his shoulder. "Then I will sail for Brazil."

Roman raised her higher, so her eyes were level with his. "And I'll go with you."

She stiffened. With shock and confusion. "You'll go with—"

"I won't raise my child on a ranch. I'll raise him or her in Brazil. With monkeys instead of horses."

Her confusion deepened. "But I just said I would give you—"

"I came to Templeton to tell Señor Madrigal that I no longer want to buy the land. I'll get all my money back from him."

She struggled in vain for a shred of understanding. "You're—you're giving up your ranch?" she asked incredulously. "But you've been working for it for ten years! Why would you give it up?"

He glided his long tanned fingers into her wet gold hair. "Once, not so very long ago, a genius told me something that made no sense to me at the time. Now, though, I understand what she meant. She said that when you love someone, no sacrifice is too great to make."

Theodosia felt her entire body begin to shake. She couldn't read the expression in his eyes, didn't dare guess what he would say next.

Roman smiled into her wide rain-dappled eyes. "How could I be content on a horse ranch when the woman I love is in Brazil?"

Her mind spun crazily. She couldn't think.

But her heart beat steadily. She could feel.

And she felt the warmth of his next words before he even said them.

"I love you, Theodosia."

A bolt of joy burst through her, more powerful than the sizzle of lightning in the sky.

Roman held her more tightly and spoke a promise into her eyes. "I know I'm not the kind of man you—I didn't go to school long—you can't love a man like me because—well, because I don't have a diploma of any kind. But Theodosia," he murmured tenderly, "I swear I'll get one. I'll learn everything you know. I'll practice using good word choices. I'll study the stars, the sun, and plant roots. I'll learn Latin and Swedish, and I'll never be roinous, facinorous, or tonitruous again. I'll try to be everything you want me to be, Theodosia, if that will help you to love me the way I love you."

His poignant vow made her weep. She reached up and lost sight of her hands as she buried them within the mass of his raven hair. "You already are, Roman, and I already do," she declared through her tears. "I have loved you since the day I first saw you."

He crushed her to him, then kissed tears and rain from her face. "Marry me, Theodosia."

She touched her lips to his and tasted not only

her tears, but his as well. "On one condition," she whispered.

"Anything. God, anything at all."

She smiled into eyes almost too blue to be true. "I desire to possess the same wisdom you do, Roman," she murmured with all the love she felt for him. "Therefore I will marry you only if you'll teach me common sense."

Remembering all the hundreds of illogical things he'd seen her do and heard her say, he decided it would take an entire lifetime to teach common sense to her.

An entire lifetime. Spent with a woman so beautiful, so wonderful, that he could not understand what good thing he'd done to deserve such a precious gift.

"Agreed, Miss Worth," he whispered tenderly.

"Then I will marry you, Mr. Montana."

Smiling a lopsided grin, he leaned down to her. And as his lips met hers, he made a wondrous discovery.

Sacrificing in the name of love was not sacrificing at all.

For in giving one received more than one ever dreamed of having.

Epilogue

Her arms full of freshly picked bluebonnets, Theodosia gazed out over twenty-five thousand acres of the richest grassland the Rio Grande Plains had to offer. In separate fields raced Thoroughbred stallions, the very best from her father's farm in New York. In other meadows fine Spanish mares grazed along with their beautiful foals.

And riding toward her astride a gray stallion, his long ebony hair spilling about his broad shoulders, was the man who had pulled a castle from the air and planted it on solid ground.

The sight of him never failed to mesmerize her. "Roman," she whispered into the warm spring breeze.

He stopped Secret before her. "If you don't quit picking so many bluebonnets, there won't be a one left in the entire state of Texas, sweetheart."

She glanced down at the mass of blue-flowered stalks in her arms. "Roman, I will have you know that I have collected thousands of seeds to plant. I would never pick so many flowers without thought to their survival."

He realized she hadn't understood that he'd only

been teasing her and smiled over her endearing lack of common sense. "Oh, well in that case Texas has nothing to fear. The name Theodosia Montana will go down in history as the woman who saved the bluebonnet from extinction."

A small head with a mop of black curls upon it poked out from behind him. "How is your research, Mommy? Will Dr. Wallaby be pleased with your findings when he comes to visit us from Brazil?"

She gazed lovingly at her precocious five-year-old daughter, the child she'd once thought would belong to Lillian and Upton. "I suspect Dr. Wallaby will be highly pleased, Genevieve. I have not as yet made the startling discovery he hopes for, but I feel I am at the brink."

She glanced at the assortment of microscopes, racks of vials and test tubes, and piles of notebooks she'd placed on sturdy wooden tables beneath the towering oak tree. Dr. Wallaby had been ecstatic over her offer to remain in Texas and continue his search for the cure for impotence.

She'd never seen the green jungles of Brazil, and she never would.

But every morning when she opened her eyes, she saw the heaven-blue of Roman's eyes.

"When will you tell me what discovery you are trying to make, Mommy?" Genevieve asked. She lifted her leg over the saddle and, with her father's help, slid to the ground.

Theodosia smiled. Although she had tutored her daughter in a wide variety of areas, the subject of impotence was not among them.

"Mommy will tell you when you're older, Genevieve," Roman answered for Theodosia. "Much older."

"Mommy will tell you when you're older, Genevieve," John the Baptist echoed, waddling amidst the tall grass and patches of bluebonnets. "How is your research, Mommy?"

Genevieve patted the parrot's soft head. "How long can African grays live, Mommy?"

"About seventy years," Theodosia replied. "We'll have John the Baptist for a long while."

"He really is an astonishing *Psittacus erithacus*, isn't he, Papa?" Genevieve asked, turning her startling blue gaze to her father.

Roman grinned. "Maybe so, but he can still be a mimicking, maddening, meddlesome, molting moron when he feels like it," he said. But his insult was laced with genuine affection for the bird he felt sure would outlive him and go on to aggravate the hell out of future generations of Montanas.

The parrot flapped his right wing. "I suspect Dr. Wallaby will be highly pleased, Genevieve. He really is an astonishing *Psittacus erithacus*."

"Genevieve," Theodosia said, "do you know who is coming to help you celebrate your birthday next month?"

"Who?"

"Aunt Lillian, Uncle Upton, and Cousin Chancellor."

Genevieve squealed and clapped. "And I'll teach Chancellor how to track!" she exclaimed. "Poor Chancellor. Living in that big city, he doesn't have the chance to learn much. I'm becoming as skilled as Papa at tracking now. He hid from me this afternoon, but I remembered everything he taught me and it took me only ten minutes to find him. He was in one of the barns, the one where that mother cat had her kittens. I wish I could take one of the kittens into the house, Mommy. They're so soft. Soft as my hair ribbons. The satin ones Papa got for me.

"Do you remember when he gave me those ribbons, Mommy?" she continued merrily. "It was when he took me to town. He bought me peppermints that day, too, but they burned my nose when I ate them. I've tried to like peppermints, Mommy, but I cannot like them any more than I like green beans. Green beans give me nightmares, just like ghosts do. Do you believe in ghosts, Mommy? Some days come when I believe in them, and some days come when I know they aren't real. Could I have one of the kittens in the barn? I would like to save one of them just in case there are ghosts in the barn."

Theodosia laughed. Her daughter was a master at country chatting and could meander orally right along with the best of them.

"When may I learn to track you like Genevieve, Papa?" another small voice asked.

Roman watched his four-year-old son, Bo, come out from behind Theodosia's skirts. With his golden hair and huge brown eyes, the child looked just like his beautiful mother.

Bo stuck his thumb in his mouth, sucked it for a moment, then pulled it out. "Mommy told me about the time you tracked John the Baptist, Papa. She said you looked for sand on the grass."

Roman dismounted and scooped his son into his arms. "I thought you were too interested in Mommy's bluebonnet studies to take time to learn the art of tracking."

"I can do both things," Bo declared firmly, running his small, plump fingers through his father's long, thick hair. "Yesterday Genevieve taught me to whistle through cracker crumbs."

"It took him a long time to learn, though," Genevieve clarified. "He was in a roinous mood, Papa."

Roman laughed, then kissed Bo's forehead. "Don't worry about it, son. I've been trying to teach your mother how to whistle through cracker crumbs for years, and she still hasn't learned. As for teaching you to track, I'll give you your first lesson just as soon as I talk to Mommy." Gently, he set his son back down on the ground and watched as he and Genevieve scampered toward the pastures to play with the horses.

John the Baptist scooted along behind the children. "He was in a roinous mood, Papa," he squawked as he scurried through the grass. "Yesterday Genevieve taught me to whistle through cracker crumbs."

Grinning crookedly, Roman took Theodosia's arm and led her into the shade of the majestic oak tree.

There she looked up and saw her name carved on the largest branch. Indeed, over the years Roman had chiseled her name into every tree he'd found on his ranch. And every time he performed the tradition, he carried her into the tree and fed her raisin sandwiches.

"If you want, I could test some of that impotence potion you've been making," Roman offered, sliding his hands over the sides of her lush breasts. With a nod of his head, he gestured toward the vials of liquid on the wooden tables. "In a few hours, after it's had a chance to do what it's supposed to do, we could sneak up to our room and see just how well it works."

Theodosia thought of the hours-long lovemaking session they'd enjoyed at dawn. Such early morning pleasures were quite often the start of their days. Roman had sired Genevieve and Bo on two such mornings . . .

. . . and in all likelihood, during a beautiful sunrise two months ago, he'd fathered the baby she carried now.

She smiled up at him. "Roman, believe me when I tell you that you've no need for even a drop of the remedy for impotence."

He saw a secret in her smile and two in her gorgeous whiskey eyes. Instantly, he cupped his hand over her lower belly.

Theodosia laid her hand over his. "We'll have another child in January."

He held her gaze for a long tender moment. "I love you, Theodosia."

"And I love you, Roman."

Pulling her into his arms, he held her close for a long moment and pondered how much she meant to him. And when at last he ended the loving embrace, he touched his lips to hers, then drew his gaze down to the pin at her throat.

He caressed the heart-shaped ruby.

And watched the blaze of sunlight dance over the shimmering heartstrings.

Be sure to look for Rebecca Paisley's next enchanting romance, A BASKET OF WISHES, coming from Dell in the fall of 1995. Turn the page for an exciting glimpse of the novel's prologue and opening chapter.

A BASKET OF WISHES

The power of Faerie glittered most brightly on All Hallows Eve, for it was a time of the year when mortal rules were suspended. The tiny inhabitants of the enchanted world were always capricious with their moods, but never more so than on this date. With a twinkle of their eyes they could grant a bounty of good fortune.

Or a lifetime of doom.

Out of fear and uncertainty, most people remained close to home on this magical night.

Virgil Trinity was not one of them . . .

PROLOGUE

English countryside
October 31st

Panting with the exertion of running, Virgil stopped and glanced over his shoulder. Across the moonlit meadow glowed the lights of his cottage. Within the small dwelling his wife lay dying, and Virgil would have sworn he could hear her cries of agony.

Deeper fear fired his determination anew. He fled into the black woods ahead, instantly blinded by the darkness. Shivering with apprehension and cold, he eased his pace and forced his mind to summon every notion he'd ever heard about the Wee Folk.

"Fairy ring," he whispered. "I must find a ring."

Eyes cast to the shadowed forest floor, he searched for evidence of the circle. A long while passed; his brow began to bead with the sweat of desperation, and a tinge of hopelessness slowed the frantic beat of his heart.

"Little People," he called, his voice barely louder than the drifting of a cloud. "I beg your help."

He saw nothing. Heard nothing.

Covering his face with his hands, he fell to his knees at the foot of an ancient oak. Stones and gnarled twigs cut into his legs, but he could only feel the painful knowledge that his sweet Pegeen was going to die.

And with her would die their unborn child.

He wept, his tears seeping through his fingers and splashing to the ground. Many moments passed before he perceived eerie changes occurring all around him. The cool night breeze warmed as if heated by sunbeams of high noon. The rustling of the oak, birch, and alder branches became almost musical, a soft, stirring melody that sounded like hundreds of flutes playing in harmony. Through the narrow spaces of his fingers, Virgil saw lights. Among the mist dampened leaves, the sparkles swirled in a small, perfect circle.

They were here. They'd come.

The fairies.

"Virgil," a small male voice sang out.

Virgil took great care to stay outside the edge of the circle, for he knew full well that if he stepped inside the dazzling ring he would be pulled into the world of Faerie with little chance of escaping. Crouching lower to the ground, he strained to see the fairies. He saw nothing but the leaping shimmers of light, but remembered suddenly that the Wee Folk could swiftly turn themselves into human form.

He edged away.

"Speak now, Virgil," the voice demanded, "or the aid you seek will be swiftly denied you."

Although the voice was tiny, Virgil couldn't fail to hear the authority that laced every word it spoke. "My wife," he blurted out, more tears slipping to the ground. "Pegeen. The babe—the babe won't come. It's been near two days. Please . . ."

"What would you be willing to sacrifice to save the child and its mother?" the voice asked.

"Anything," Virgil answered impulsively, clasping his hands together as if in prayer. "Anything you ask."

He saw the sparkles come together on the dark ground to form one large ball of gleam, and he realized the little people were discussing the bargain. Silence ensued, and then the lights separated once more.

"In return for the lives of your wife and child," the voice finally said, "I demand a betrothal. One of your descendants must wed one of mine."

Virgil could not dwell on his descendants, kin who had not even been conceived. His only concern at the moment was for his wife and child. "Yes!" he exclaimed. "Oh, yes!"

The lights glowing among the leaves grew brighter, so bright that Virgil could not bear to look at them any longer. He shut his eyes.

A BASKET OF WISHES

"Your plea is granted," the small voice announced. "Pegeen is delivered of a fine healthy girl."

Virgil shook with joy, but he didn't respond. To thank a fairy was to invite disaster, for the Wee Folk shunned gratitude.

"Go now, Virgil Trinity, and raise your daughter, but speak of our bargain to no one," the fairy voice instructed. "Although you will have naught to do with its fulfillment, you may be sure that the promise you have made on this night will come to pass."

His eyes still shut, Virgil rose from the ground. Without a backward glance at the shining fairy troop, he raced out of the woods, bolted across the wide, grassy field, and finally burst into his cottage.

The proof of fairy magic met his eyes. Pegeen sat upright in the sagging cot, her dimpled cheeks aglow with candlelight and happiness.

And suckling at her breast was a plump, black-haired infant girl, her tiny hands clutching at her mother's long, ebony tresses, her small bare feet kicking at the tattered blankets.

"It happened so quickly, husband," Pegeen said, smiling. "One moment the pain fairly split me in two, it did, and I knew in the heart of my soul that I would die with my next breath. And then, fast as the twinkle of a star, she came. Our darling Isabel was born."

Running his fingers through his thick hair, Virgil moved slowly toward the bed, every shred of his being captivated by the enchanting sight of his lovely wife and beautiful baby daughter.

" 'Twas like magic," Pegeen whispered. "Sweet magic."

"Magic," Virgil repeated. Slowly, he slid his gaze toward the window.

There, in the distant woods, the fairy lights continued to shimmer faintly.

In return for the lives of your wife and child, I demand a betrothal. One of your descendants must wed one of mine.

The fairy's decree flamed through Virgil's mind like a lethal bolt of lightning. Now that he was assured of Pegeen and Isabel's wellbeing, the true significance of his agreement with the fairies came to him at last.

He grappled for the windowsill and looked at his infant daughter. Was it Isabel who would one day marry into the enchanted world? Would it be one of his grandchildren? Great-grandchildren? He could not begin to guess, for the fairy voice had given no hint whatsoever.

All he knew for certain was that the rash and desperate promise he'd given only a short while ago had irrevocably doomed *someone* of Trinity descent to the powerful clutches of Faerie.

ONE

Jourdian Amberville, the twelfth Duke of Heathcourte, had reached the point of doubting there was a single female in the world who met the requirements he'd set for the woman who would be his duchess.

"Bloody hell," he muttered and swallowed his second glass of brandy.

"I beg your pardon?" his cousin, Lord Elliot Challen, asked, confused by Jourdian's sudden curse. They'd been discussing Jourdian's recent purchase of a diamond mine in Africa, but it was obvious now that Jourdian had dismissed the subject and was now deliberating upon something else.

Elliot thought about the diamond mine for a moment longer, then recalled the time when as young boys he and Jourdian had run through a mass of wildflowers. Seconds later Jourdian had found a handful of tiny diamonds within the mass of trodden blossoms. Only Jourdian Amberville could have discovered diamonds scattered amidst a lot of broken weeds, and his discovery had been the first indication that everything he touched would turn to wealth.

Yes, Jourdian led a charmed life and he always had.

Sipping his own brandy, Elliot leaned forward in the satin settee by the fire. "You were never even stung by a wasp, Jourdian, do you remember? Whenever we came upon the vicious creatures . . . It was almost as if they were blown away from you. Why, even the snake we found that day near the pavilion slithered out of your way."

Jourdian turned a sideways glance toward his cousin. "What the devil are you talking about, Elliot?"

"I might ask the same of you. In fact, I think I did."

Jourdian dismissed Elliot's rambling and poured more brandy. Liquor wouldn't get him a wife, but it for damn sure would help him forget he didn't have one.

He finished the brandy and stared into the empty snifter. Nothing had ever been difficult for him to obtain and, accustomed as he was to having everything he desired the moment it occurred to him to want it, he could not understand why the trivial task of choosing a bride had proved so infuriating.

"Bloody hell," he growled again, pouring yet another glass of the fine brandy.

Elliot rose from the settee and joined his cousin in front of the huge, satin draped window. "For pity's sake, Jourdian, what is the matter with you?"

In answer, Jourdian shrugged his broad shoulders. No one in society, including Elliot, knew of his quest for a bride. On the contrary, the general consensus was that he would never marry, would fail to sire an heir, and would therefore be the reason why the fine, centuries-old name of Amberville would soon cease to exist. Jourdian had done nothing to dispel such conjecture. To do so would be to cause a furor among every title-hungry, money-wanting woman in the blasted country, and he had little patience for batting eyelashes, coy smiles, insipid small talk, and, least of all, the fluttering of those damned little fans.

Ever since he'd been a boy he'd done things by himself, and he would find his duchess the same way. He'd been covertly watching society's marital offerings for over a year, when he'd first decided that the time had come to marry and produce an heir. But for reasons he couldn't quite define not a single woman he'd observed suited him, and each time he rejected one his anger and frustration grew.

It should have been so simple, Jourdian mused irritably, finishing his brandy and setting his glass upon a silver tray. As effortless to accomplish as any and all undertakings had ever been for him. And yet finding the perfect wife . . .

He shook his head. "Finding a basket of wishes would be far easier."

"A basket of wishes?" Elliot repeated. "Uh—Yes. Yes, of course. A basket of wishes."

Ignoring his cousin's bewilderment, Jourdian strode toward the fireplace and picked up a solid gold frame from the mantel. From within the gleaming oval his parents' likenesses peered up at him.

He'd been a boy of eleven when his mother died, and a young man of seventeen when his father passed away.

And yet he'd never really known either of them; had never had the chance to know them. A painful emptiness seized him, a void he knew would never be filled.

He returned the frame to its place on the mantel. Running his fingers through his wavy hair, he glanced at his surroundings.

The green salon was a lofty room, its elaborately sculpted ceiling supported by pink marble columns. Four exquisite crystal chandeliers dripped from the ceiling, their sparkles of light dancing upon the silk draperies and magnificent gilt chairs, all of which were a warm shade of moss green.

This room had been his parents' favorite. "A pity they were rarely home long enough to truly enjoy it," he mumbled. "Always off on some exotic journey to see and do bizarre things, they spent little time in their home."

Or with their son, he added silently.

He dragged his fingers through his hair again.

"Jourdian, you've a penchant for mumbling tonight, old boy," Elliot said. "What was that you said?"

"Nothing," came Jourdian's swift and irate reply. He pulled back his shoulders, angry at himself for unconsciously speaking his thoughts.

Elliot placed his glass on the tray beside Jourdian's. "Why can't you discuss what is on your mind? That's your problem—"

"Exactly. It's *my* problem, and no one else's."

Elliot bowed his head and stared at the raspberry-colored carpet. He knew more about Jourdian Amberville than did anyone else, and yet his knowledge amounted to practically nothing. Trying to get Jourdian to talk about himself was about as useless as attempting to converse with a stone.

"Jourdian," he began again, "you—"

"I will hear no more, Elliot."

Trepidation quieted Elliot instantly, a distinct fear that Jourdian's very bearing commanded. He turned away for a moment, pondering his cousin.

The slightest hint of anger in Jourdian's cool gray eyes could clear a room faster than a raging fire. And when that firmly chiseled Amberville jaw tightened, men tensed with apprehension and women either paled or quickly turned away. Even the matrons of society, elderly women well-known for and highly deserving of their forbidding authority, flinched when faced with the displeasure of the powerful and fabulously wealthy Duke of Heathcourte.

It was quite strange, really, Elliot thought, for Jourdian never lost his composure. But His Grace's arrogant, yet coldly detached demeanor served as a veil behind which lurked a dangerous temper. No one had to witness its existence. It was like an aura, or perhaps a scent, Elliot amended to himself. Yes, a menacing scent, invisible but perceived immediately.

And Elliot knew of no one in the entire country of England who would dare to rouse Jourdian's barely leashed volatility. To do so was akin to freeing a fire-breathing dragon.

But the dragon would be slain.

Tugging at his coat sleeve, Elliot turned back around and saw cynical gray eyes staring straight at him. That sharp gaze sliced across the room like the precise thrust of a silver sword, and Elliot could have sworn that Jourdian had sought, found, and deciphered his every feeling and thought.

Deeply disturbed by the possibility, he pulled at his coat sleeve again. "Yes, well, I believe I shall be on my way now, cousin." He quit the room in the most dignified manner his haste would allow.

When his cousin was gone, Jourdian sent orders for his stallion, Magnus, to be saddled. He then changed into riding attire and was ready to ride before the stable hands brought Magnus around to the manor house.

Impatient, he stalked out of his palatial home and headed toward the barn. A cold October wind blasted into him, ruffling his hair and the colorful mass of pansies that bloomed along the edges of the pebbled path that led to the stables. His boots scraped through the glittering white stones, which crunched beneath his heels.

He didn't like the grating sound, nor did he care for the way the red and yellow leaves blew into his face and settled on his broad shoulders. The chill in the air irritated him, as did the crisp scent of the autumn sunshine and the vivid orange of the pumpkins that filled a small wooden cart a short distance away.

His Grace found no pleasure, no beauty in anything, and if indeed there had ever been a time in his life when he had, he couldn't remember it.

His mood darkened further when he arrived at the barn and saw that the groom still had not finished the task of readying Magnus.

"S-sorry, Yer Gr-grace," Hopkins stuttered. "He's a b-bit skittish today. It's the sn-snap in the air, I vow." Quickly Hopkins finished tightening the saddle girth, then handed the reins to the duke.

Jourdian mounted, and as he slowly worked Magnus into a pounding gallop through the countryside, his long-ago oath seared through him, hot with intensity, burning to be fulfilled.

His duchess would never surprise him, he'd sworn. Indeed, she would be utterly predictable, and he would know her thoughts before she spoke them. He would expect orthodox behavior from her at all times, and he would receive exactly that.

Yes, his elusive duchess would be quite ordinary. Oh, she could and *would* be beautiful, for Jourdian was very particular where looks were concerned, but her character would be the epitome of conventionality, for he wouldn't tolerate anything that remotely reminded him of the reasons for his lonely childhood.

Oh, and there was one other little vow he'd made concerning his bride.

He wouldn't love her.

Sparkles swirling in her wake, Splendor moved away from the small mound of earth beneath which her father's glittering kingdom lay hidden. As she stepped soundlessly through the brittle fall leaves that blanketed the forest floor, her vibrant red curls shimmered down the full length of her bare body, and each of her graceful movements sent the sweet scent of spring wildflowers into the autumn air.

She'd escaped the assembly her father had called. As the eldest princess, she knew she was supposed to pay strict attention to the affairs that affected Pillywiggin, the province of Faerie her father ruled. But such issues very nearly put her to sleep. Besides, she mused, her sister would be present at the court gathering, and Harmony could tell her everything later.

At that thought, Splendor frowned over her lapse of sense. Harmony would consent to nothing if it would not in some way benefit her. Although it was simply not in Splendor not to love Harmony, she sometimes wondered why her vain and often cruel sister had been given a name that implied peace and benevolence. Why, only days ago Harmony had taken great delight in tying a donkey's tail into a hopeless mass of knots. The beast hadn't seemed to care, but its poor owner had had a terrible time combing out the tangles. Harmony enjoyed tormenting humans.

Splendor could not understand why. To her, humans were the most intriguing creatures in existence.

She stopped beside a massive oak, leaned against the tree trunk, and peered down at the blades of grass that barely reached her slim ankles. Little gave her more pleasure than her powers of shape-shifting. It wasn't that she minded her original size—which was about the same as the span of a large butterfly's wings—but she adored being statuesque.

She smiled a secret smile, knowing full well that her pleasure in being tall stemmed from her fascination with humans—most especially the human man who lived nearby.

She breathed deeply of the cool, woodsy air, and couldn't suppress a shiver of excitement. "He's going to be near today, Delicious," she murmured to her pet swan, who stood near her feet preening his snowy feathers. "That handsome human."

Another smile touched her delicate lips and illuminated her lavender eyes. She had no earthly idea who the human man was, but she always knew when he would be near enough to watch. A lovely feeling passed through her, whispering that he was coming. She'd felt it from the very first time she'd ever seen the man, when he was a small boy and she a fairy child.

Joy spinning inside her, she floated to the edge of the forest, looked out across the fields, and pondered the man she waited to see. With hair as dark as the inky-black ravens that soared through the heavens and eyes the color of the sky right before a silvery rain shower, he was the most beautiful living thing she'd ever seen. And his vigor amazed her. He never seemed to lose strength the way fairies did, but could ride his huge ebony horse for hours without tiring.

"Oh, Delicious," she murmured, "he is simply—"

"Splendor!" King Einor's voice boomed through the forest.

Her alabaster skin paling further, Splendor whirled around and saw her father, Harmony, and a host of Pillywiggin's peers standing before her, some of whom were her other relatives. They, too, had used their powers of shape-shifting and stood as tall as she.

A vague feeling of foreboding curled through her. She looked into her beloved Aunt Maloochy's eyes for reassurance, but saw a disturbing combination of sorrow and pity within the elderly fairy's gaze.

Something was amiss, she realized, wringing her hands within the thick tumble of her fiery curls. "Father?"

His knee-length white hair and beard falling over his round body like a swath of frost, the king strode forward. Stars fell all around him, and the very ground upon which he walked began to shine like silver. "Splendor, you did not attend the assembly I called."

"Splendor never does what is expected of her," Harmony stated. Her tone of voice was as bitter as the expression in her dark brown eyes as she contemplated the fact that Splendor was heiress to the throne of Pillywiggin. It was grossly unfair. Just because Splendor was the eldest did not mean she would make the best ruler. On the contrary, always laughing, dancing, and flitting about like some intoxicated butterfly, Splendor was too much of a ninny to fulfill the important responsibilities of queen.

And Harmony had vowed long ago that her father's kingdom of Pillywiggin deserved the most competent queen possible.

Biting back a secret smile, she gave an imperious toss of her head, her action causing her golden hair to sway across her body. "I cannot imagine how you find the patience to resign yourself to Splendor's wayward ways, Father."

The king gave a great sigh. The beings of Faerie were capable of performing striking acts of kindness as well as shocking feats of evil. His daughters had inherited aptitudes for both, but not in combination. Harmony found her happiness in rendering gloom. Indeed, she'd done much in the way of encouraging the human fear of Faerie.

But Splendor was goodness itself. The king worried about her, for the world could be a very sinister place. Harmony could protect herself from iniquity. Indeed, she would probably thrive on it.

But not Splendor. Her heart was surely made of sunshine and moonbeams. Velvety flower petals, the music of songbirds, and every other soft and gentle thing nature had to offer.

It was for that reason that he had come to his all-important decision, a verdict that he had announced to his kingdom shortly ago. "The time has come to fulfill the betrothal made by my father, Splendor," he said, his anger at her tempered by his tender thoughts of her.

Splendor's huge eyes widened. She knew about the betrothal, as did everyone in the realm, and she also understood its extreme importance.

Faerie was of fragile and ancient ancestry, and over the centuries the delicate race had continued to weaken. The seed of Faerie's men was very nearly ineffectual, and many of the women were barren. Those women who did manage to conceive often gave birth to sickly infants who quickly perished.

By contrast, humans were strong and fruitful in offspring, and it had been Splendor's grandfather who had devised a concrete way to obtain such strength and fecundity for Faerie. He'd realized that a union between a human and a fairy would result in children who would fortify the enchanted race with human vitality.

Everyone knew the union was the only way to save the world of Faerie, but no one had ever been aware of which Pillywiggin monarch would put into play the long-ago bargain made between Faerie and the human called Trinity. All that was understood was that by way of a dream the chosen king would know of his mission and the details concerning it.

"A dream," Splendor whispered. "*You* had the dream, Father?"

He gave a slow nod.

So many questions darted through Splendor's mind, she didn't know which to ask first. "Is the Trinity male or female? Which fairy will wed—"

"If you had attended the assembly I called earlier, your every query would be answered." Turning, King Einor took Harmony's hand. "The Trinity is a male, Splendor, and it is Harmony who will marry him. She will conceive his child, and then she will leave the Trinity and return to our world. My grandchild will be born, will mature, wed, and procreate in Faerie. Why, just having the half-human child within our midst will strengthen our race."

"Harmony?" Splendor asked, confusion stinging her. "But—but Father, Harmony *detests* humans!"

"That is precisely why she will wed the Trinity," the king answered sternly. "There can be no emotional ties to bond her to him when the time comes for her to return to Faerie, for I'll not have a Pillywiggin living in the mortal world for longer than is necessary. Therefore, it is my opinion that Harmony's dislike for humans will facilitate her task.''

He didn't add that it was Harmony's rather unpleasant character that had helped him decide who would marry the Trinity. Although he was often irritated by her excessive fondness for nasty mischief, he knew she could and would withstand whatever form of vileness she might encounter in the human world. ''And now,'' he said to his subjects, ''we must bid farewell to Harmony and wish her well.''

As everyone gathered around her, Harmony thought about the ultimate outcome of her marriage to the Trinity. All of Faerie would pay her homage for consenting to be the instrument necessary for the race's salvation, and she would glory in the adulation.

But most delightful of all was the fact that her union with the Trinity was going to deliver so stunning and painful a blow to Splendor that the frail and spineless little fool might very well expire from sheer shock. At the very least Splendor would most likely weaken to the point of becoming completely unable to ever manage the royal duties necessary to rule Pillywiggin.

Harmony started to laugh, but the pounding of hoofbeats sounding in the distance quickly sobered her.

''The time has come, Harmony,'' King Einor said. ''The Trinity is near. Now, when he appears you must swiftly show yourself to him and perform the enchanting. He will succumb to fairy thrall and become instantly captivated by you. Make haste, child.''

When Harmony, the king, and the other fairies glided to the edge of the woods to await the appearance of the Trinity, Splendor looked for the mysterious human as well.

What she saw in the meadow so upset her, she almost shrank to her original size.

Her human man rode through the field, his big black horse bringing him closer and closer to the forest. Indeed, he was near enough now that she could see the lights in his beautiful silver-gray eyes.

''Harmony, now!'' the king shouted. ''Go now!''

Instantly Harmony swept out of the forest and skimmed over the meadow, heading straight toward the Trinity.

Splendor could only watch in silent horror, as if seeing a nightmare unfold before her very eyes. Her delicate frame began to tremble, her strength began to fail her, and she felt herself begin to disappear.

A firm hand on her arm jolted her back to full awareness.

"Splendor!" her Aunt Maloochy said quietly but forcefully in her ear, "will you merely stand here and allow Harmony to enchant the man so dear to your heart? Don't be a noodle, child! Go and claim him for your own!"

In that second, Splendor knew that no matter what she had to do to save the Trinity from Harmony's spite, she would do it. Summoning strength, she rose into the air, cast her father a swift look of apology, and then began to fly with all the might her dainty form held.

But Harmony had had a head start, and Splendor soon realized that catching up was an impossible feat.

Sorrow further slowed her flight until she felt a strong breeze behind her. She glanced over her shoulder and saw Delicious sailing at her feet, the swan's powerful white wings stirring up a wind that thrust her fragile body forward.

She caught up with Harmony. Side by side the sisters strained toward the Trinity, and Splendor wondered if they would reach him at the same time.

She needed more speed, more strength to save him.

Memories of him came to her then. She remembered when he'd been a child crying in the rose garden and hiding from a grim woman who'd tried to strike him with a cane. She recalled all the times when she'd seen him wave good-bye to two people she believed to be his parents, and the countless occasions she'd observed him staring into the distance with a look of longing on his face—as if waiting for something or someone to return to him.

And she remembered all the nights she'd seen his silent wishes soar into the dark sky to be cuddled by the wishing stars.

Each memory that drifted through her mind bolstered her with momentum and force. With one final burst of energy, she shot past Harmony . . .

. . . and crashed directly into Jourdian Trinity Amberville.